LONDON GIRLS

A TWO BOOK SET

JANET ELIZABETH HENDERSON

ISBN: 9780473461287

Cover design by Janet Elizabeth Henderson

Editing by Liz Dempsey

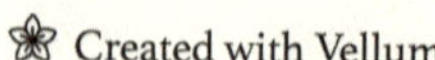 Created with Vellum

ALSO BY JANET ELIZABETH HENDERSON

Lingerie Wars

Goody Two Shoes

Magenta Mine

Calamity Jena

Bad Boy

Here Comes The Rainne Again

Caught

Reckless

Relentless

Rage

Ransom

Can't Tie Me Down

Can't Stop The Feeling

Can't Buy Me Love

A NOTE FROM THE AUTHOR

Hello!

Thank you for reading *London Girls*. These two books are the first romance novels I ever wrote and they're very dear to my heart. *Laura's Big Break* was the first book I won an award for—the Romance Writers of America's Silken Sands Award —and that was a huge encouragement at the time. It's also a book that brings back some great memories for me. It's set in Holland, where I lived for some time after I met my Dutch husband. A lot of the experiences I had during that time, especially the ones where I screwed up learning to cycle, are shared by Laura in this story. At the end of the book—don't worry, no spoilers—she also visits Bolivia, another country I've worked and lived in and love dearly. So yeah, *Laura's Big Break* has a lot of personal experience woven into the tale.

As for *Mad Love*, Dean has always been one of my favourite heroes. He's so dedicated to Maddie, so in love with her, that it blows me away to think about it. The way he encourages her and delights in her craziness are attributes I think all men should have—that and his abdominal six pack! And yeah, London is another place I've lived. What can I say? I get around!

So there you have it. My first two books in one handy volume. I really hope you enjoy reading them!

janet

MAD LOVE

LONDON GIRLS, BOOK 1

Janet Elizabeth Henderson

PROLOGUE

Icarus was an idiot. Everybody knew that. If you are going to fly to the sun you don't use wax to stick your wings together. With this insight nine year old Maddie had used extra strength sticking tape. As she stood on the roof ready to jump her only concern was that she didn't want to fly too high. She'd run out of sunscreen and didn't want another red nose.

"I don't think this is a good idea," Laura said.

Her best friend sat perched in Maddie's bedroom window. With her knees pulled up to her chest and thick round glasses she looked a lot like an owl.

"I used good magazines. Look." Maddie held out a wing clad arm for inspection. "Nice thick paper."

Laura bit her lower lip.

"Your mum says if you break something else she's not taking you to the hospital this time."

Maddie's deep chocolate eyes narrowed with determination.

"Mum isn't here."

She inched closer to the edge. It didn't bother her that it was a long way down, she planned to go up.

"Okay, I'm going," she announced as Laura went pale.

She pulled her swimming goggles over her eyes. Now, she looked like Amelia Earhart – only with wings. Without another word she spread her arms, held her chin high and launched herself off the roof.

She didn't go up.

As the ground rushed towards her she felt annoyed. Obviously she should have used real feathers rather than the ones she'd made from magazine pages.

Thankfully Dean was there to break her fall; with his head. Her older brother's best friend was often in the wrong place, at least this time it was handy.

"Madeline!" her fifteen year old brother shouted as she hit Dean, and the ground, with a thud.

"I'm okay."

She stood and dusted herself off. Dean groaned beside her.

"Thanks Dean," Maddie said before stomping back towards the house.

"You alright?" she heard her brother say.

"I think so. I feel like a nine-year-old fell on my head."

Maddie glanced over her shoulder to see Dean rubbing his neck. She felt a momentary pang of guilt which slowed her pace slightly. Charlie shook his head as he glared at Maddie. She stuck out her tongue at him before pushing the front door open. She knew that his loud disgusted sigh was aimed at her. Before the door closed, Maddie watched as her brother helped Dean to his feet.

"What happened?" Dean asked; he looked a little dazed.

"You just saved Maddie's backside. That's what happened."

1

———

PRESENT DAY

Dean Montgomery had been saving Madeline Lewis for the past twenty years. He was done playing Sir Galahad. This time he was going to let her fall. He leaned back in his scientifically designed office chair and raised a sceptical eyebrow in her direction.

"I don't think so." He sounded firm because he felt firm.

"Come on Dean. I need your help. This is a great idea; even you can see that."

Maddie's brown velvet bob made her look a lot like Velma Kelly from the movie Chicago. The comparison was right on the money. He'd often imagined that under her carefully maintained exterior beat the heart of a man eater. Although she was batting her cow length lashes at him in a picture of innocence, he knew better. Dean tented his fingers in front of him, a look that intimidated boards of directors.

"It's time you got a real job, or better yet finish any one of the degrees you've started."

The look in her eye told him she was regrouping, working on a new tactic to suck him into her latest misadventure. He gave a mental eye roll; if only Charlie was here to deal with her, but he was in Afghanistan for at least another month. Dean couldn't help wonder if Charlie had chosen the easier option.

"Just listen to my pitch okay?"

Although he'd seen her enthusiasm before it still weakened his resolve.

"Fine, I'll listen. But that doesn't mean I'm going to support you."

A wide Julia Roberts grin lit up her face. He felt a tightening in his stomach. Man, she was breath-taking. Her pencil skirt was the colour of mulled wine, slit to mid thigh. She'd teamed it with the cashmere sweater of the same colour that he'd given her last Christmas. Get a grip, he ordered himself as he tried to focus on her words.

"So, it's like this. The hours people work in the city are long then there is the commute on top of that. There often isn't time to do domestic chores, like shopping, or paying bills, or taking clothes to the dry cleaner. I thought I could offer a service that took care of all that. Kind of like a personal assistant for your life. What do you think?'

"Or a butler?"

Her hair caught the light as she shook her head, bringing out the golden hues.

"Nope. A butler works with one person at a time and most people can't afford to keep a member of staff on full time. I'm talking about something else. You register and pay a fee to be part of the service then you pay as you use it. So a client would only have to pay me for the time I spent picking up her dry cleaning, not for the whole week."

She didn't bounce around in her seat the way she did when she was a kid, but the same intense energy was still there.

"What do you think?'

"It might work," he said sceptically.

He couldn't stop his mathematician's brain from going over the possibilities. He had a lot of colleagues who could probably use a service like the one she described. And she was right; the commute from the centre of London to the suburbs did eat up a lot of time. His eyes narrowed. She was hooking him. He was a bloody fish. Again.

"I don't want to be involved."

As he sat forward in his chair he could feel his shoulder muscles strain against his suit jacket. He really had to make the time to get it altered. Maybe he could get his secretary to run it over to his tailor later. No, that definitely wasn't her job. He reluctantly admitted to himself that the service Maddie was offering might actually come in handy. He shook his head. The fact the idea had merit wasn't the point. This time he was taking a stand. Maddie's wide eyes pleaded with him. She'd definitely learnt to work the charm over the years. When she was a kid she barrelled over everyone to get what she wanted; now she tried gentle cajoling first.

"Come on Dean, it's a great idea. I'm sure it's going to pick up momentum quickly. I can see a proper office in my future. I've got a website all planned, a friend of Laura's is building it for me, and I'm having a leaflet designed by a professional. But right now I lack credibility. It won't be easy for people to trust a stranger with their personal lives. That's where you come in. I need someone to vouch for me. All you have to do," she said as she leaned across his wide Scandinavian style desk, "is recommend my service to some of your colleagues. Get me started."

"That isn't going to happen."

There was a flicker of a frown. Any minute now she

would decide she'd had enough and order him to comply. He had to actively stop himself from grinning.

"Only a couple of people, then once the word is out I'll get customers through my website."

She drummed her red nails on his desk as her patience began to slip. That didn't take long.

"I'm not letting you try out any more business ideas on the people I know. My reputation is getting screwed by association."

"That's not true."

She crossed her long legs and folded her arms over her breasts. They squeezed together and Dean felt his mouth go dry. He'd been in a perpetual state of semi arousal around her for years. Not that she would ever notice. He concentrated on the matter at hand.

"There was the adventure therapy idea. Deal with your stress by doing something daring for a day. Dave MacIlvoy broke his hip hang gliding."

"He was very old and no one held a gun to his head."

As she huffed, he counted her efforts off on his fingers.

"There was the aromatherapy at work idea. Ten minutes to get away from it all with the smells and sounds of the rain forest. The candles set off smoke alarms. The fire brigade came."

"Again, not my fault. The smoke detectors were too sensitive."

"And then there is my personal favourite," he drawled. "Alpaca walking in St James's Park as a lunchtime diversion."

She leaned forward, cheeks flushed in earnest.

"That man swore they were alpaca. How was I to know that llamas weren't as friendly, or as trainable, as their family members? Alpaca and llama do look very similar."

"It took my lawyer and a lot of money to make that fiasco go away."

She got up from her seat and came around to his side of the desk. As she perched her perfectly round behind on the corner, Dean momentarily lost track of the conversation.

"Look, this one is different. No animals. No dangerous sports. No fire hazards."

She was seriously kissable. How did women get lipstick to match the colour of their clothes anyway? Was it like buying paint? Did they take in a sample of the colour and an assistant mixed the shade to match?

There was clicking. She was snapping her fingers in front of his face. Now she was tired of playing nice.

"Am I boring you?"

"No, but it doesn't change my answer."

Her eyes narrowed.

"Dean Montgomery, you are being annoying."

The last time she said that he ended up with a head full of peanut butter, but she was only ten at the time. He suspected that now the punishment wouldn't involve a jar of food. He cleared his throat.

"I'm being sensible."

"You're always being sensible," she said with exasperation. "What do I have to do to convince you? I have a business plan. I have projected figures. I have a marketing campaign ready. This is a good idea. You run your own business, why can't you see that I could do that too?'

As she stomped over to his large picture window he could practically see her brain work. One thing was for sure, she made his panorama of central London pale in comparison.

"I've got it." Her grin was feral.

"Oh no."

She ignored him.

"You will be my first client. I'll prove to you how brilliant I can be then you'll fall over yourself to vouch for me."

Suddenly his tie felt too tight.

"I don't think so."

He swivelled in his chair to get away from her. Maddie put a hand on each of his shoulders and spun him around to look her in the eye. The passion in her expression took his breath away. Be still my heart.

"One week, Dean. I'll be at your beck and call. I'm going to make life so much easier for you. You'll wonder how you ever managed without me."

He gulped.

"We start this afternoon. Prepare a list and I'll meet you at Mimosa at noon."

With that order she stood, straightened her skirt and marched to the door. She held her head high as a satisfied smile played about her lips. He was a goner.

"What's the business called?" To his disgust his voice croaked.

With a Rita Hayworth glance over her shoulder she smiled.

"Wife for Hire."

As she shut the door Dean leaned forward and banged his head repeatedly on his pristine desk. What was it about that woman that turned him into an idiot? To the rest of London he had a reputation for being tough, frightening even. But to Maddie he was the equivalent of the neighbour-hood moggie.

When the door opened again he wasn't surprised to see his business associate Ted grinning at him.

"Well, what's the big idea this time?'

Ted threw himself into the corner of a large red sofa that

took up almost a whole wall of Dean's office. It was the only spark of colour in an otherwise neutral environment. Maddie had insisted that he needed somewhere comfortable for his clients to sit. She also insisted that it was red. Dean had explained patiently that his business was a financial advisory not a brothel. The couch stayed. He groaned as he looked at the sofa and at Ted's grinning face.

"Apparently she's going to be my personal assistant in charge of non work related matters for one whole week. I'm supposed to write up a list of jobs for her to do."

Ted's grin widened, making him look more like an Australian surfer than a financial whizz kid.

"What, no animals this time?'

Dean gave him the look he reserved for testy bank managers.

"The girl has no direction." Ted ignored the look. "I don't see why you don't marry her and give her some babies to worry about. That should keep her occupied."

If he didn't actually see the women Ted dated he'd find it hard to believe it was possible.

"There are reasons," was all he said.

"Yeah, yeah, yeah. Heard it all before. You're practically her brother. If the relationship went belly up you'd lose the girl and your best friend. You're worried how Charlie will react. Oh, and she doesn't think of you like that. It's getting old, mate. You turn into an idiot around her and the drool is messing up the carpet."

"Thanks for the insight."

"Look, this latest idea of hers might be just what you need. One whole week with you in charge. If I was you, I'd use that time to change how she sees you. Turn on the charm. Seduce her."

Ted shrugged like it was that simple. And maybe it was.

Dean could feel the adrenalin surge through him. He couldn't go on like this forever. His fear of hurting Maddie was stopping him from showing her how much he loved her. Something had to be done. And if she insisted on inflicting her latest idea on him, even though he'd made it clear that he had no intention of supporting it, he may as well get some mileage out of it. This was his time. He was done waiting. He'd take the risk of losing her and deal with Charlie later.

"You're right," he said. "Don't let it go to your head."

"You're going to need a plan. You do know how to seduce a woman, don't you? We've been working together for what? Ten years now and I've only seen you with a handful of women. I wasn't too impressed. For a while there I thought you were paying librarians to accompany you to work functions."

"You're a funny guy."

"Seriously, Maddie thinks you're another brother. I've seen how she behaves around you. She either babies you, treats you like an idiot, or uses you to further her latest business venture. How do you plan to turn that around?'

Dean looked blank. He felt blank. He'd managed fine with women in the past. There just hadn't been a lot of time to devote to his love life. The fact he was the go-to guy for financial advice in London was testament to how neglected it had been. Then there was Maddie: for the past few years she had eclipsed everyone else. The problem was, he was so used to treating her like a little sister that he didn't quite know how to change the balance in the relationship. The last thing he wanted was to come on too strong and scare her off.

"You're stuffed, mate." Ted read his mind.

They sat in silence. Dean imagined if he could see his face that he'd look much like a Basset Hound.

"There's only one thing for it," Ted said with a worrying gleam in his eye. "You need me. I'll be your coach. Follow my advice and you'll have her in bed in no time."

"I don't think so."

"Here's what to do." Ted pulled his chair in closer to the desk. "Don't you have a list of duties to write? Well all you need to do is think of things that will put the two of you together in a romantic way."

All Dean could come up with were trips to the tailor and stocking the pantry.

"Mate, you're sad. Your head is full of the things you actually need doing, isn't it?'

Dean growled at him again. It had no effect.

"The point is," Ted continued, "you make stuff up. Things that will keep her close to you, things that will force her to see you in a new way."

"Like box tickets at the theatre?'

"Yeah, that kind of thing. You ask her to get tickets for you and a client, then the client can't make it and you take her instead. Only don't get tickets for Mamma Mia! Trust me, women only go there to sing the songs. There is nothing romantic about that. Get a pen. I'm going to help you sort this out once and for all."

That was what was worrying him. As Dean dutifully made a list, Ted hummed a tune - Crazy Little Thing Called Love by Queen. When Dean growled at him, he spread his hands wide with amusement. Ted was right about one thing. He was stuffed.

· · ·

MADDIE SPOTTED Dean sitting at one of the round tables by the window. The sight of him always brought a smile to her face while instantly calming her naturally restless personality. She wasn't sure why, but being around Dean was like coming home.

"I'm sorry I'm late," Maddie said breathlessly as she threw her things into the chic silver coloured chair beside him. "Traffic was abominable."

He'd obviously left space opposite him at the table, but she wanted to sit beside him to share the best view of the street outside. Mimosa Café, on the Strand, was the chic place of the moment and consequently packed full of yuppies, tourists and the odd local hoping to get fed before the lunch service ended. There was paperwork strewn all over the table in front of Dean. Honestly, all the guy did was work.

"Deadline," he said by way of an excuse as he cleared the papers away.

"Dean." She patted his hand in a sisterly sort of way. "You really have to get some sort of life. I can't remember the last time I saw you with anyone outside of Charlie, Ted and me. You can afford to take time off, hell, you could even retire if you wanted to."

"I like what I do."

"I can't even remember the last time I saw you with a girlfriend," she said.

Dean slowly relaxed back into his chair with a knowing smile on his face. Maddie felt like she was missing something. What did he have to smile about? His black tie had been loosened and the top button of his shirt was undone. His wavy dark hair was styled to perfection as usual.

"You look like an undertaker in all that black," she told him. "Where's that tie I got you?'

"The purple one?'

As he toyed with the water glass in front of him, Maddie began to feel slightly flustered. There was something different about him, but she couldn't put her finger on what exactly.

"The lavender one. It goes with your eyes."

"My eyes are grey, Maddie."

"No, they're violet. How are you ever going to get a woman if you don't take my advice?'

A rather humiliating thought tripped through her mind and came straight out of her mouth, as these things often did.

"You still like women, don't you?" She lowered her voice so that the diners close to them wouldn't hear.

To her immense surprise Dean tipped back his head and rumbled with laughter, drawing inquisitive but amused glances from the neighbouring tables. One woman in particular tried to catch his eye.

"I'll take that as a yes," Maddie said dryly.

Honestly, at twenty nine you'd think she'd have learnt the ability to self-censor.

Dean leaned over the table and captured her hand. He wound his fingers through hers watching as he did so. The gesture had romantic connotations. The woman who had been trying to catch his eye shrugged, assuming he was taken. Maddie tried to relax; Dean never held her hand. Never. She shook off the notion that something other than friendship was going on.

"I have plenty of women in my life. If you're curious about my sex life I can go into detail for you. But let's say that I like women." He gave her a long dark look from beneath lashes any woman would kill for. "Some, more than others."

His thumb stoked the fleshy part of her hand. Butterflies

assaulted her stomach. She couldn't concentrate on his words as she watched his fingers caress hers. She could feel a flush assault her cheeks. Flustered, she used reaching for a glass of water as an excuse to pull her hand free from his.

"Glad to hear it," she said with forced lightness. "I worry about you, being as you're practically family."

He cocked an eyebrow in her direction. It stopped her in her tracks. Smoldering. That was the word she was looking for, smoldering. She was too hasty in reaching for her glass. The water spilled, the glass flew off the table and landed at the feet of a diner sitting beside them.

"I'm so sorry," Maddie told her.

Dean grinned like a lunatic.

"Where's that list?" she said as she mopped up the mess.

Dean rubbed between her shoulders in a gesture meant to calm her. It did nothing to make her feel relaxed. Her whole body tingled with each circle he traced on her sweater. Concentrate.

"List?" she said with exasperation.

He fished around in his breast pocket and came out with a piece of paper.

"Here it is, as ordered."

She felt like patting his head in a well done gesture. This was more like it. This was the relationship she knew – she told him what to do and he did it. Or she got into trouble and he got her out of it. Either way it was working fine.

"House-warming party? You've been in the flat six months and now you want a party?'

He shrugged and Maddie wondered when his shoulders had become so broad. He looked good in suits. She often told him that. He had a rat pack swagger to him that demanded a Dean Martin look, but that didn't mean they all had to be black. Maybe a soft grey? Or a navy with a fine pinstripe?

"I've been meaning to do it." His words brought her back to the issue at hand. "But I can never find the time to organise it. That's why a personal assistant for all things personal might come in handy after all."

"Okay," she said slowly.

She'd envisioned shopping, or waiting at home for repairmen, not planning a party. Fine. She was a Girl Friday. A Wife for Hire. Although, technically she was more like a personal assistant for hire than a wife, but the name was a catchy one and she liked it. She was getting distracted. The point was, she could do anything and would do anything to make her business a success. She honestly couldn't take another failure. Apart from the fact it was hard to look everyone she knew in the eye when they obviously thought she was barmy, it was getting harder to pick herself up and start again every time. Her self-esteem had taken a severe bashing over the years and she was beginning to think that she should settle for any old job and put her dreams in a drawer marked "over". And for reasons she couldn't quite explain it meant a lot to her for Dean to see her succeed.

"Theatre tickets?'

"I have a client that I need to entertain. I want box seats for one of the big shows. Not Mamma Mia."

"Doesn't your secretary usually handle this?'

"I thought you might like to."

She picked at her salad wishing she'd ordered the burger along with Dean. Even though she watched what she ate with meticulous care, she still struggled with keeping her hips from being described as "good for child bearing". She turned her attention back to the list.

"A bed?" She stared into his laser coloured eyes. "You want me to buy you a bed?'

"I want you to help me buy a bed. It's always better if there are two of you. And I don't plan to be alone in it all of the time."

She felt like she was caught in headlights. It was difficult to look away.

"Good, good." She eventually realised that she was staring and blinked repeatedly. "We talked about this. You should definitely have balance in your life. A bed is good. I mean, you should be prepared. No, that's not what I mean. If you find a woman, then you might need a bed. Oh my, help me out here?'

"Oh I don't know, I kind of like where you're going with this."

Maddie took a deep breath. She was going insane. For a minute she'd actually thought that Dean was flirting with her. She resisted the urge to shake her head in an attempt to dislodge all unwanted thoughts.

"You've got some food on your cheek," he said with a predatory smile. "Allow me."

Before she could stop him, he took up his white linen napkin and brushed the corner of her mouth. With lazy grace he ran a fingertip along her bottom lip. It felt like a caress. She stopped breathing.

"There," he said softly, "all better."

He traced his knuckles over her cheek before leaning back into his seat.

Alarm bells went off in Maddie's head. It had finally happened, she was going insane. Charlie had always teased her that one day the family would talk about her in the same hushed tones they used for crazy Aunt Ida. That day had come. Why else would she be imagining that one of her best friends was coming on to her? There was no explanation. None.

"Are you okay?" Dean smiled and his eyes crinkled. "You look flushed."

She stared at him unable to talk as thoughts ran through her mind. And then it hit her. She wasn't going nuts. She was picking up on Dean's desperate need for a girlfriend. With a deep smile she sighed with relief.

"Yes, I'm fine. I was a bit worried about something for a minute there, but now I know what to do."

"Oh?"

"Yep, I'll sort it," she said gaily.

Dean obviously needed her help. He was far too busy to sort out his own love life. The poor man was seriously deprived of female company and the sooner she found him a nice woman the better.

"It'll be okay," she reassured him as she patted his hand.

His eyes narrowed with suspicion. With what she hoped was an innocent smile Maddie resolved to add match-making to her list of tasks.

2

"Laura? I think Dean needs a girlfriend, do you know anybody we could set him up with?" Maddie said by way of hello.

Laura had a mouth full of panini, but her face said that she thought her friend was crazy. Maddie plonked herself down in the only free chair in Laura's tiny office.

"Why would you want to do that?" Laura said after she swallowed her food.

"He's obviously lonely and has no idea how to get a woman on his own. He'd too busy working to socialise."

Laura's eyes got wider.

"I don't think Dean needs our help getting a woman."

"Of course he does, otherwise he wouldn't be alone."

Laura balanced her plate on one of the stacks of paperwork that covered her desk and reached for a full sugar Coke.

"You know, it isn't fair that you eat the way you do and can still fit into your old school uniform. That drink alone would add half a stone to my hips."

"I was born lucky." Laura grinned. "Now go away, I have

an article to write. Share your crazy theories with someone else."

"It isn't crazy."

Maddie flicked through one of the teen magazines that were piled on the filing cabinet beside her. How did Laura write this rubbish? Did teens really want to read it? Was she ever that obsessed with make up and boys? Probably. She threw the magazine back on top of the nearest pile.

"Maddie," Laura said gently, "Dean doesn't need you interfering in his love life."

"Well obviously he does. If he was able to sort it himself he wouldn't be single."

"He chooses to be single. Trust me - he's what our readers would call a hottie."

"Dean?" Hot?

Laura swung her chair around to face her friend and made no attempt to hide her exasperation.

"Have you ever actually looked at him? He obviously works out; he has a backside that makes women drool, and killer eyes. Plus he wears a suit the same way George Clooney wears a suit – like it's a sex toy."

"Dean?"

"Haven't you noticed how sexy his smile is? He has this way of looking at you that makes you think he knows things about women that even we don't know."

"Dean? Sexy?" She sounded like an old 12inch stuck in a groove.

"Honestly, how could you not notice? I've even thought of him a time or two, but he doesn't look at me that way."

Maddie thought about it for a minute. The concept of her Dean being sexy was a new one. She knew he was attractive, she wasn't blind. With his build, broad jaw and perfectly straight nose he was obviously handsome, but

Laura made him sound dangerously sexy. That didn't equate with the guy she knew.

And the concept of him knowing what to do with a woman was plainly bizarre. She had no recollection of him pursuing women at all. Growing up all she remembered was Dean studying, Dean working, Dean poring over endless streams of paper, or staring at a computer screen for days on end. And the girlfriends he'd brought home from Uni were exactly like him – grey, dull and brainy.

"This doesn't make sense," she told her friend. "I've never seen Dean chase women and the ones he did show an interest in were pretty dull. I think you're imagining things."

"Did it ever occur to you that Dean didn't want you to see what he was up to? I mean, think about it for a minute, you're his best friend's little sister. And you had a big mouth growing up; goodness knows what you would have told your parents. Do you know what your brother was up to in college?'

"Not really, I wasn't interested."

"Well I can tell you for a fact that Charlie and Dean spent most of their youth chasing and catching pretty much any woman that took their fancy. Right through school, and college, there were girls queueing up to get their hands on both of them."

"Why didn't you tell me this before?'

"I didn't think you were interested."

With a huff Maddie propped her feet on a pile of Sparkle magazines.

"Well, it doesn't change things. The poor boy needs a woman in his life and obviously his work schedule is getting in the way of him finding the right one. He needs to settle down, have someone to come home to. He might be a hottie," she tripped over the word, the concept was alien to her, "but he's so desperate for company that he has to buy a bed with me. Seriously is that not sad?'

"Okay, as usual, I have no idea what you're talking about and I'm actually on a deadline here. So wrap it up or tell me all about it later."

Laura ripped open a bar of chocolate and Maddie's mouth began to water. With a roll of her eyes Laura threw her half.

"Seriously, you need to stop trying to diet. It doesn't suit you."

Maddie waved her comment away as the chocolate melted in her mouth. Wasn't there a diet that consisted of only chocolate and wine? She was sure she'd read about it somewhere.

Her friend ignored her as her fingers flew over her keyboard.

"So," Maddie persisted, "do you know anyone nice that we can set him up with?'

With a deep sigh her friend got on board with the plan at last.

"Well there is Janine from the fashion department, she's between men."

"The blonde who looks like Barbie?'

"That's the one."

"Wasn't she dating the Italian guy from Coronation Street?'

"Yep."

"I don't think she's Dean's type."

"Sweetie," Laura said as she pushed away from her desk to retrieve a file from the table behind her, "she's every guy's type."

"Fine. I'll invite her to Dean's housewarming party."

"How is the new business going anyway?'

"Great. I think. Dean wrote a list full of tasks and I'm working my way through them. Tomorrow I'll start unpacking the boxes in his spare room while he's at work."

"It sounds thrilling. Are you sure this is what you want to do?"

"I'm sure," Maddie said with conviction. "I just need to convince Dean that it's a good idea too. Without him vouching for me I don't think I'd get past the receptionist in most of the buildings."

She licked her lips as she fished for one last taste of chocolate. Laura opened her desk drawer, took out a packet of Minstrels and threw them at her. With a grin Maddie dug into the tiny bag of chocolate treats, but vowed that as soon as she was home she'd look up that new diet on the Internet.

"I wish I didn't have to ask him to help me," she said as her friend typed again. "He already thinks that I have no focus. Honestly, he only sees me as Charlie's kid sister. It's catch 22. I need him so I can be a success, but he won't take me seriously unless I am a success. That's why this week is so important. I need him on board."

Laura raised an eyebrow in amusement.

"Oh, he's on board, honey. But it might be a different train from the one you want him on."

"Is that the kind of thing you write for your teen readers? Because it makes no sense at all."

"Okay." Laura pointed at the door. "Out. I'm sure you have work to do. I know I have. I might work late tonight so I'll see you in the morning. What time are you starting?'

"I told Dean I'd be there bright and early."

"I'm sure that cleared things up for him."

When they parted company her friend gave her a hug that smacked of "I love you anyway" and as the office door closed Maddie could see Laura shaking her head. With a sigh she wondered what she'd done this time.

It was 6.30 the following morning when Maddie rang Dean's doorbell. Although she'd been to his Chelsea flat loads of times she felt strangely nervous. First proper day on the job she assumed. She was dressed for the chilly spring weather in black boot cut trousers, sensible heels, white blouse and long black woollen coat. She thought of it as her butler outfit – sensible, no nonsense, reliable.

There was no answer, so she juggled her handbag along with the tray of coffee and bran muffins she was carrying and banged on the door instead. Where was he? She knew he liked to get into work early to prepare for the day, but this was the middle of the night. She'd had to set three alarm clocks to make it in time. Laura had broken the last one with her shoe. In their tiny Clapham flat a ringing alarm clock sounded like Big Ben.

She was about to dig out her cell phone and call him when the door flew open. Dean was dripping on the hall rug. He had a white towel wrapped around his waist and was rubbing his wet head with another one. The rest of him was a bare, wet flesh.

"I'm sorry." She stammered over her words. "I didn't realise you were in the shower. I'll come back later."

Her face flushed a little at the sudden intimacy of a barely covered Dean.

"It's 6.30, Maddie," he said without expression.

"I did say bright and early. You agreed."

"I thought you meant work day bright and early. As in nine o'clock."

"I can come back."

He threw the door open wide.

"Get in here," he growled.

She slid past him, careful not to touch any of the seemingly vast expanse of glistening skin.

"You told me that you go to work early," she said. "I wanted to make sure I got you before you left."

She thought she heard muttering as he walked up the hall behind her.

As Maddie put her breakfast takeout on the kitchen counter Dean opened the drawer under the sink.

"Here." He handed her a key. "Now you can come and go as you please."

The annoyance she'd seen when he'd first opened the door was gone, replaced by something that she couldn't quite identify. He looked pleased with himself, although it could also have been that he was laughing at her - it was hard to tell. His state of undress was getting in the way of her thought process.

Sure she had seen him in swimming trunks once or twice, but that had been when they were teenagers. And to be honest, mainly she'd thought that he looked malnourished. The man dripping all over the kitchen floor definitely didn't need to put on any weight. A six pack stomach, a smattering of dark hair and shoulders that almost begged to be bitten made up the new Dean. She felt embarrassed that she even noticed.

"I have coffee," she said gaily in an attempt to act normally.

"I gave it up."

"Since when?'

"About a week now."

She rolled her eyes. Another one of his health kicks. She loved Dean's kitchen, mainly because she'd helped decorate it. It was a tasteful array of stainless steel appliances, eggshell blue cupboards and lavender walls. It was a peaceful room and the only spot of colour in an otherwise cream existence. She sighed, why didn't he listen to her when she told him what furniture to buy? Couldn't the man see that he needed colour in his life?

"You never told me that you gave up coffee."

"I don't tell you everything," he said as he reached for a bran muffin.

She wished he would go put some clothes on. As he leaned against the counter scoffing his food her eyes kept being drawn back to his chest.

"Can I have the other muffin?" he asked.

She sighed.

"Fine," she said. "I wanted cinnamon buns anyway."

He gave her a killer grin before he bit into her muffin.

"Is it hot in here?" she asked as she opened a window. "It is stuffy, isn't it?'

"I hadn't noticed."

The man didn't seem to care that he was practically naked. What if the towel slipped? Oh my. This was awkward. It was Dean, it shouldn't have made any difference what he wore – or didn't wear. But it was having a rather strange effect. The harder she tried not to look at him, the more she managed to look at him. It was like dealing with someone who had a huge pimple on their nose, you know it isn't a big deal, you know you shouldn't stare and all that happens is you end up acting awkwardly and staring anyway.

"Will you please go put some clothes on?" she demanded at last.

A strange smile played along his lips.

"Am I bothering you?" He pushed away from the

counter. As he drew level with her he stopped. "After all, I am practically your brother. Isn't that right?'

Maddie froze. The look in his eyes was anything but brotherly. A second later he disappeared through his bedroom door. She couldn't think. She'd obviously misread him. After all this was one of her best friends she was talking about. It was too early, she hadn't had any coffee yet and she was obviously hallucinating. As Dean got dressed she gulped down first her coffee then his.

When he emerged from his bedroom he was dressed in a black Valentino suit. The cut fit him like a glove. His shirt was pristine white. His short black hair was parted on the left and his violet eyes sparkled as he walked towards her. My, was he in a good mood this morning. She felt a surge of pride. This was the reaction she wanted to her new business enterprise. People should feel happier knowing that the load was lightened. She had a good feeling about this idea. This one was going to be a success.

Dean handed a pale blue tie to her.

"Do you mind? I seem to be all thumbs this morning. And you are at my beck and call."

She grinned as she wrapped the tie around his neck and tucked it under the collar of his crisp white shirt.

"I'm pleased to see that you took my advice about your ties, this one suits you much better."

With an indulgent smile he stood awfully close to her as she tied the knot. He smelled spicy, like cardamom cake.

"There you go."

She patted his chest and instantly regretted the gesture. In her mind she saw the muscles he'd been flaunting not two minutes ago.

"I think the weather is turning," she told him. "It's definitely stuffy in here."

She rushed to pour some orange juice leaving Dean to grin like an imbecile.

"Okay," she said with forced cheer. "Now that you're off to work, I'll get right onto emptying out those boxes."

He leaned against the door frame and folded his arms in front of him. His suit jacket strained at the seams. For what seemed like an eternity he studied her. Maddie could feel her skin begin to burn.

"I can take the day off and we can work on those boxes together." His tone was deep and intense. "If you like?"

"No!"

He gave her a quirky little half smile.

"I mean," she said more calmly, "that defeats the point of this venture. The idea is that I do chores for you to free you up to concentrate on work."

"I can concentrate on work from here."

There was that look again. Predatory. Sexual. There was definitely something wrong with her. She was losing her mind.

"Go," she ordered, then pointed at the door in case there was any doubt what she meant.

"Fine," he drawled as he pushed away from the doorway.

Maddie let out a deep breath that she wasn't aware she'd been holding as Dean set about gathering his things for work. She was obviously still picking up on his desperation vibes. This wouldn't do. She needed to step up her efforts to find him a woman. As she started to clear away the breakfast dishes he came up behind her.

"Well I guess I'll see you tonight," he said.

To her surprise he leaned towards her and kissed her on the cheek. His lips lingered and it seemed that he was breathing her in. As he stepped away from her he tucked a stray strand of hair behind her ear.

"I'll be home around six," he told her as he picked up his laptop case.

She didn't trust herself to speak so she nodded. As she heard the click of the front door closing she sagged against the counter. Her cheek vibrated from his touch. He'd never kissed her before. She sometimes gave him a peck on the cheek. Sure, friends did it all the time, cheek kiss hello, cheek kiss goodbye. Hell, most Europeans kissed at every opportunity. But not Dean. And then there were the looks. She wasn't sure what they meant but they freaked the life out of her. To hell with unpacking the boxes. Finding Dean a woman had just jumped to the number one position on her list.

When Dean let himself into his flat the smell of coq au vin made him instantly salivate. *Now we're talking. Warm home, good food, beautiful woman.* Only the beautiful woman was nowhere in sight.

"Maddie?'

No answer. He dumped his bag on the hall table, hung his suit jacket in the closet and went in search of the smell, and he hoped, Maddie. There was a large pot bubbling on the stove top, potatoes in the oven and a bottle of wine airing on the counter, but no Maddie. Dean shrugged; he didn't think he'd scared her off yet so she had to be nearby. He went to change into a pair of jeans. As he pulled on worn blue jeans that he'd had for years and an old grey t-shirt that Maddie had given him, he could feel the tension of the day begin to fade. Now he could enjoy an evening of slowly seducing the woman he loved.

As he prowled the apartment, with a cold beer in his hand, he went over his progress so far. He was definitely getting to her, he knew that. He'd seen her blush more in the past couple of days than he had in five years, but it was also clear that she didn't recognise the feelings he was stirring. Or to be more accurate, she knew what the feelings were, but she didn't know how to attribute them to him. He'd have to help her with that. As he surfed news channels on the large flat screen, which was fixed to the wall above his living room fireplace, the door opened. He was about to amble out and give her a very unnecessary welcome home hug, when he heard voices.

Damn, she's up to something. With a resigned shrug of his shoulders, he went to see who Maddie had invited over.

"Dean!"

Maddie sounded far too enthusiastic. And she wasn't alone. His eyes narrowed. Turning to the petite redheaded woman beside her Maddie smiled a little too brightly. He was instantly suspicious.

"This is Sarah. She moved into the building this week. Poor girl doesn't know anyone in London, so I thought she might like to join us for dinner. I'm sure you don't mind."

"Not at all," he said as he played along waiting for the penny to drop. "Nice to meet you Sarah, where did you move from?'

"Edinburgh."

She shook his hand with hardly any grip at all. It was a slightly disconcerting.

"Please have a seat." Maddie pointed to the couch and then threw herself into the only other chair in the room.

Dean was forced to sit beside Sarah.

"Sarah has a new job with Lloyds, you're in similar fields," Maddie said helpfully. "You must introduce her to some of your colleagues."

The penny was dropping.

"And," she gave Sarah a sympathetic look, "the poor dear broke up with her boyfriend a month ago. We really should help her take her mind off of that. Don't you think?'

Her look was all wide eyed innocence. Plop. The penny hit his belly with a thud. He was in the middle of another one of her schemes. Here he was trying to seduce her, and she was busy setting him up with the first woman she came across. Obviously he should have taken her comments about finding him a woman a little more seriously. If he'd knocked it on the head straight away he wouldn't be sitting next to some strange redhead who was barely out of her teens wondering what the hell he was going to do to get rid of her.

"Drink?" Dean asked Sarah.

Before she could answer Maddie was on her feet.

"I'll get it. You two stay and chat. I'm sure Sarah has lots of questions about the city and the building.'

Maddie disappeared humming a tune from Hello Dolly as she went. Dean wondered if she even knew what she was singing a song from a musical about a matchmaker? He smiled politely at the tiny woman in front of him as she droned on about the study she'd taken in Edinburgh and how excited she was about her new job. And he listened with interest as she told him that she wasn't new to London, but was actually staying in an apartment her parents owned and kept for when they visited the city. Maddie was about to pay, big time. He just wasn't sure what form that payment was going to take.

Dinner was a dull affair. Dean let the women talk while he planned. Obviously he had to turn his seduction up a notch. It was going right over her head and now he had Sarah interested in him. There was only one thing for it, and it was a brilliant plan: he had to convince Sarah that Maddie was his girlfriend. That way her matchmaking would be seen as a misconstrued attempt at being friendly. It was perfect.

"You must come to Dean's housewarming party," Maddie was saying, "you'll meet all of the neighbours there."

"Yeah," he kept his eyes on Maddie as he spoke. "I'll introduce you to my colleague Ted. He knows everyone in London. Isn't that right, darling?'

It took all his self-control not to laugh - he didn't know who was more confused, Maddie or the woman she was trying to set him up with. Tough. This was his house. His rules.

He rose to retrieve the wine bottle from the counter. First he topped up Sarah's glass, then as he topped up Maddie's he stroked her shoulder in what he hoped looked like a loving caress.

Her back straightened as Sarah's eyes widened.

"It's a pity we couldn't get the four of us together this weekend," he said casually, "but Maddie and I are going bed shopping tomorrow. Isn't that right, darling?'

As she looked up at him he allowed himself to let all of the emotion he normally kept hidden from her show in his eyes. Man, she was beautiful. It made him feel like he'd been sucker punched. Her eyebrows arched into her fringe, her eyes went dark and a slight flush appeared on her cheeks. He gently tucked a stray strand of hair behind her ear. For a minute he forgot that Sarah was still sitting there.

"Oh," Sarah said with a more than a little embarrassment. "You two are..."

It was clear she stopped herself from saying that she'd only just realised they were a couple.

"You two are bed shopping? Well that will be fun. This

weekend wouldn't work for me anyway, I have to get settled. But the party sounds lovely."

"It's all sorted then." Dean put the wine back on the counter. "Who would like coffee? Tea? I'll clear the table while you two chat."

Both ladies put in their order. As Maddie stood from the table Dean stepped in front of her.

"Wonderful meal as usual, darling," he said without trying to contain the glint of evil delight in his eye.

And before she could say anything, or stop him, he threaded a hand into her hair and pulled her towards him. Her lips felt like overripe peaches. He only allowed himself a small kiss. How he managed to pull himself away he honestly couldn't say, because kissing Maddie was like ripping open a bag of crisps and only having one. Her eyes fluttered shut and although she didn't kiss him back, she didn't stop him. He took that as a good sign. He held her lips for a second, before releasing her. She stood there stunned. Her lips were full, pouting and ready for more.

"Maybe I should go," Sarah said beside them.

Maddie seemed flustered. Her cheeks went a deep shade of red which made her hair glow almost auburn. Delightful.

"Not at all." Dean aimed Maddie towards the living room. "I'm sure Maddie would love to talk about Edinburgh. She started one of her degrees up there, archaeology I think?'

"You have more than one degree?" Sarah was impressed.

"Not quite."

Maddie glanced over her shoulder at Dean as she led Sarah into the living room. The best thing he could say about her expression was that it wasn't disgust. He grinned while he gave a mock salute. Let her think about that for a while, he thought as he turned on the kettle.

Half an hour later Sarah left and Maddie let rip.

"Just what did you think you were doing?'

Dean stretched out on the large leather sofa in his living room and plopped his feet on the blond wooden coffee table. As he watched Maddie glare down at him he felt inordinately pleased with himself.

"Well?'

It occurred to Dean that, apart from a framed Matisse print that Maddie had given him as a house warming present, she was the only spot of colour in the room. He couldn't ignore her any longer.

"I wanted to let her know that I'm not available."

"But you are available!'

She threw up her hands in disgust.

"Not for her."

"Honestly! What must she think?'

"That we're an item?'

With a frustrated grunt Maddie pushed his feet from the table as though his house belonged to her. Dean grinned.

"This isn't funny." She stood over him and wagged her finger like an old fashioned school teacher. "I was trying to set you up with her. I thought she would be a nice woman for you."

"I know. I don't want her."

"Well what do you want?'

You! He wanted to shout. I want you. If it wasn't for the fear that his revelation would drive her away from him instead of to him, he would have shouted the words from the rooftop. It was killing him, but he had to give her time. With great effort, he worked to appear unaffected by the conversation.

"I don't see why you're getting so upset."

Something flashed in her eyes. It looked suspiciously like confusion. Good.

"You lied to her. What is she going to think when she finds out that we aren't a couple?'

"We don't let her find out."

"Great. And how do you propose we do that?" She threw herself onto the sofa beside him. "We put on an act every time we see her? I visit you often. Should I fall all over you every time she's around? And what about the party? Am I supposed to pretend that you and I are together then too? Because our other friends will be there as well and they'll know it isn't true. What a mess. Honestly Dean, for someone with such a big brain you really didn't think this through."

She looked genuinely upset. Dean pulled her to him in a friendly hug, one he'd given her many times before.

"I'm sorry, okay? I'll sort this out."

She angled her head to look up at him. Those deep chocolate coloured eyes made her look like a pleading kitten. Every inch of him wanted her.

"Thanks, Dean," she said before snuggling closer into him.

Man, she was killing him.

"Would it be so bad?" he couldn't stop himself from saying. "You and me? Would I be such a terrible catch?'

"What?" She squirmed to sit up before taking what he said completely the wrong way. "There is nothing wrong with you, Dean. Any woman would be proud to be seen with you. Why just this afternoon Laura was saying what a hottie you are. I overreacted, because of the lies and the confusion it will cause. That's all. You'll make a great catch for someone."

She patted his hand sincerely. Dean was beginning to hate all that hand patting. Great, now she pitied him. With all of his efforts he'd taken a step backwards in seducing her. He needed to rethink his approach.

"Thanks," was all he said.

"Right." Maddie stood. "We've got a busy day tomorrow, so I better get going."

"Why don't you stay here?" Dean said, trying to keep his voice as casual as possible.

He watched as she tripped slightly over the edge of the rug; maybe he was getting to her after all.

"No, that's okay. I have to go home. I don't have any clothes here and I can't wear this again tomorrow."

"You do have clothes here," he said with a gleeful grin. "Remember last January when you and Laura hit the sales? You forced me to watch a fashion show all evening while you two downed a bottle of my favourite wine. Well you left some of your clothes."

"I don't remember that." She was curious now. "What did I leave?'

She traipsed after Dean into the bedroom. He rummaged around in the back of his closet and came out with a Tesco supermarket carrier bag. Maddie emptied the contents onto the bed. A pair of chocolate coloured trousers and a baby pink cashmere sweater toppled out of the bag.

"I wondered where these had gone."

She acted as though she'd found treasure. It made him chuckle.

"So now you have clothes."

Obviously the problem was solved.

"But I don't have anything else."

Obviously the problem wasn't solved. Why did women make these things so damn hard?

"There is a new toothbrush in the bathroom. You can wash and dry whatever you need. And I'm assuming that you have make up in that suitcase you call a handbag. So what's the problem, Maddie? Are you scared to be alone with me for the night?'

"Of course not," her mouth said, but her expression told him that she was looking for an exit strategy.

This was fun. It wasn't often he had her backed into a corner. It was usually the other way around. To the world he was a hard headed businessman, but to Maddie he was a pussycat. He let her boss him around because he honestly would do anything for her. She was Maddie. The exception to the rule. Still it was good to see her confidence shaken for a change and he couldn't resist pushing the issue.

"Are you worried about the kiss?'

He took a step towards her invading her space.

"After all we are friends, practically family. So what's an innocent kiss among such close friends?'

He watched her brown eyes pool darker.

"Now a girlfriend I would kiss differently. I would start slowly, much the way we started, then I would run my tongue along her bottom lip, to get an idea how she tasted. As soon as she opened her mouth for me I'd tease her until her breath caught in her throat and her knees went weak." He leaned towards her and whispered in her ear. "Or until she begged me to make love to her."

When Dean stepped back to look at her, he found her lips parted as she stared at him. Her chest rose and fell rapidly, but it was the heat coming off of her that really mesmerised him. She was on fire.

"Now that would be a kiss," he said.

His voice was deep and low. More like a rumble than actual words. Gently, he stroked a finger down her cheek. He stood there, his fingers resting against her skin, wondering at how soft she was. Should he show her? Was it too soon? He saw a flicker of doubt in her eyes. Yes, too soon.

With a lazy smile that cost him dearly, he stepped away from her.

"Why don't you call Laura while I change the bedding? You can sleep here, I'll take the couch."

He watched as she clutched her new found clothing to her chest and stumbled into the living room.

3

I'm going insane, Maddie thought. That was the only explanation. As she listened to her home phone ring, she kept a wary eye on Dean's bedroom door. Something was going on but for the life of her she couldn't figure it out. It was almost, and she felt embarrassed to think about it, but it was almost as though Dean was coming on to her. But that couldn't be the case. Could it? They'd known each other practically their whole lives, they were almost family. Surely he couldn't be coming on to her? But a sneaky little part of her brain was wondering if that would be so bad. To touch him? To kiss him? To be kissed by him?

When he'd been describing what he considered to be a real kiss she'd almost melted. It was as though she was suspended in the moment, like nothing else had existed. Part of her had wanted him to stop talking and show her. What was wrong with her?! This was her friend. Her brother's friend. Obviously it had been too long since she'd had a serious relationship. Hell, too long since she'd had any relationship. Things were always so busy, what with the new business ideas and all the help she'd been giving Dean.

Without her his office, and his new home, would be a mess. She'd been the one to organise him, to make things comfortable for him. After all, that was what friends did, wasn't it?

No, she must be imagining things. Ergo, insane. She ran a finger along her lips. They felt like they had been burning ever since he'd kissed her. He must have had something spicy to eat, but then she hadn't put anything spicy in the food. And why oh why couldn't she get that image of him in a towel out of her head. She wanted to scream.

"Hello," Laura said breathlessly into her ear.

"Thank goodness. I wondered where you were."

"Maddie," her long suffering friend sighed. "It's only ten o'clock. I just got in from work. More to the point where are you?'

"I'm at Dean's. I'm going to spend the night here, so that we can get an early start on the bed shopping tomorrow morning."

There was a pause. Maddie watched as Dean passed her, arms full of bedding ready for the laundry. He grinned. She gulped.

"What's wrong, Maddie? You sound strange."

She opened her mouth, but nothing came out. What would she say? Dean looked at me funny, he held my hand, he rubbed my back and he gave me a chaste kiss to fool a neighbour? Even to her own ears she sounded stupid. It hardly added up to a great seduction. It was definitely all in her imagination.

"Nothing, nothing is wrong."

There was silence. She took a deep breath.

"Honestly Laura, nothing is wrong. I guess I'm tired. Anyway, I won't be home tonight, so don't worry. We'll catch up tomorrow. Okay?'

"Okay," Laura sounded worried. "But remember, I won't

be here tomorrow. I'm off on that work bonding weekend I told you about. I'll make sure to keep my phone with me, you can call if you need me, all right?'

"You go and enjoy yourself," Maddie said with a forced smile.

There was a pause. They had been friends so long that they could almost read each other's minds. It was hard to put anything past Laura.

"I will," Laura said, "but I'm still here if you want to talk. Take care of yourself. Okay?'

"I will."

They said their goodbyes and hung up. Maybe when Laura got home she'd explain everything to her and see what she thought. Yep, that seemed like a good idea. Right now, all she needed was a decent night's sleep. With all the worry of trying to start a new business, and get it right this time, she couldn't remember when she last slept soundly. Sleep deprivation would definitely explain the craziness in her head.

"Right." Dean dumped some blankets on the sofa beside her. "The bed is all yours."

"I can't take your bed from you," Maddie said. "I'm much smaller than you, it makes more sense for me to take the couch."

"No. This is fine."

She started to argue but he put a hand up to stop her.

"Look once you deal with your list and unpack my guest room then I'll have space to put a bed in it. In the meantime this is all I've got. You're my guest. You get the bed. No arguments."

"Fine." She gave a huge yawn.

Dean dragged her to her feet and pointed her in the direction of the bedroom door.

"Try not to dream about me while you're in there," he said behind her. She could hear the smile in his voice.

She scowled as she closed the door behind her. Now why did he have to go and plant that idea in her head?

Maddie didn't sleep well and she was sure that fact was written all over her face. When she staggered into the kitchen the following morning the last thing she wanted to see was a half naked Dean smiling politely at her. No such luck.

"Coffee," she ordered before throwing herself onto a stool at the breakfast bar.

Dean pushed himself away from the counter where he'd been leaning as he ate a bowl of bran flakes. Yet again he was baring his chest to the world while wearing only a pair of faded jeans. What was it with him? Why was he always flashing himself at her?

"Don't you wear clothes anymore?" she grumped at him.

He smiled far too innocently.

"It may surprise you to know Madeline, but this is my house and I've actually been known to go naked here."

"Bloody comedian."

He poured her a large mug of coffee and pushed a plate of toast under her nose.

"Too much wine last night?"

He seemed to be enjoying this and she wasn't sure why.

"No."

What she wanted to say was: back off, buster.

"Trouble sleeping?"

There was definitely a glint in his eye almost as though he knew what she'd been thinking all night long.

"Strange bed," was all she said.

As he turned his back on her to fix himself some toast, Madddie watched the muscles in his shoulders ripple gently. A well rounded, yet firm looking behind was hugged by butter soft denim. Her mouth began to water. Well hell, she thought, Laura was right. His rear did make women drool.

Maddie gulped down her coffee hoping the caffeine would help give clarity to her situation. She'd literally spent all night tossing and turning, thinking about Dean. She'd wondered what a kiss like the one he'd described would feel like. She couldn't imagine begging any man to make love to her and definitely not based on one kiss. It must be a helluva kiss.

She'd forced that thought out of her mind by making a list of women that she could invite over for Dean to meet. It was woefully short. None of them seemed to meet her criteria for him. Round about 2 a.m. she decided that she should post his requirements with an online dating agency. He didn't have to know about it. At least that way she could vet applicants and make sure that he got someone good.

She'd been pleased about her plan until she started to drift off to sleep and a whole new wave of inappropriate thoughts assaulted her. The image of a half naked Dean wouldn't leave and to make matters worse she was in his bed. All she could think about was him naked in his bed. Him making love in his bed. Him. Full stop. After beating up his pillows for the hundredth time she'd eventually drifted off to sleep. Only to dream about the damn man. It was impossible.

She knew her thoughts were wrong. People did not think these things about their friends. Not the ones they wanted to keep, anyway. The only conclusion she could come to was that she was so starved for male company that anyone near her was becoming a fantasy object. She was an abominable friend. She'd tried to stop the thoughts, really she had, but they wouldn't go away and short of frying her brain in the microwave she wasn't sure how to get rid of them. Worst of all she was reading meaning into Dean's behaviour that couldn't possibly be there. There was no way her friend would come on to her. Which took her right back to where she started - she was obviously going insane.

There was only one course of action. Denial. She closed her eyes and when she opened them she found Dean back leaning against the counter staring at her.

"What?" she demanded.

This was his bloody fault. Somebody make the man wear clothes!

"Do you want to go back to bed?" he said casually and Maddie spat her coffee all over the counter.

With a wry glance he threw a cloth at her.

"Excuse me?"

Did she really hear what he said or was it her imagination? Was that an offer?

"I said, do you want to go back to bed?'

She stared at him for a moment. Her mouth was open and she was sure she was doing a great fish impersonation.

"Alone?" she asked with uncertainty.

Dean grinned widely at her and Maddie could feel her face burn. Of course alone. What an idiot. And seriously if he had said no, then what would she have done?

"Right." She changed the subject. Time to focus on something else. "You." She pointed at him and barked an order. "Put some clothes on, then we can get out of here and buy that damn bed."

"Yes ma'am," he saluted as he sauntered past her, a stupid grin still plastered to his impossibly handsome face.

Maddie cupped her cheeks with her hands. What was she going to do now? The only thing for it was to do her job.

This business meant a lot to her. Not because the business itself was something special, but because she wanted something to be a success. Her whole life she'd been full of ideas, great schemes as Dean called them, but none of them ever turned out the way she had expected. They started off great, she was fantastic at starting things, full of enthusiasm and brilliant at planning. Not so good at the follow through. The problem was that she got bored easily. Nothing ever lived up to her expectation and there was always another brilliant idea waiting in the wings calling to her to try that instead.

She sighed. She was tired of failing. Okay, it was mainly her fault that she failed, but she was tired of it nonetheless. So enough of the inappropriate drooling and more of the focused hard work, she ordered herself.

While she waited for Dean to put on the rest of his clothes she got out a notebook and wrote a list for Friday's party. Less than a week to organise a party - it wasn't a very long time. The only consolation was that he wanted a low key affair, some nibbles and drinks. She could manage that. And instead of sending invites she would get a list from him and phone the people he wanted to be there. Yep, she could sort that out. Now all she had to do was get through the whole bed buying thing.

Ten minutes into bed shopping Maddie wished she'd taken Dean up on his offer to go back to sleep. The sales clerk had chatted to Dean about what he was looking for while her mind wandered. He was wearing those old faded jeans again. This time he'd thrown on a navy sweater made of the softest merino wool. The jumper was a plain crew neck but the colour and the cut made him seem even more muscular. Plus she knew how soft and cuddly that jumper was; she'd told him on several occasions that it made her want to bury her face in it and hold him tight. As she watched him his lips curled up into a hint of a smile and then his eyes did that thing again. He was looking at her like he was hungry and she was steak. Maddie busied herself with a display of cotton bedding.

"Maybe we should get some new sheets while we're at it?" Dean's low rumbling voice gave her a start.

She plastered her new professional business smile to her face.

"Whatever you want. I'm here to help."

"Good. Come with me. We've got beds to try."

He swallowed her hand with his and led her through the maze of beds to a row at the back of the cavernous store.

"We'll start here."

Her hand felt cold when he released it. Maddie stood rooted to the spot as she watched him lie down on the white mattress. The bed was so huge it seemed to swallow him.

"Come on, Maddie. I don't have time for this. Lie down."

He crossed his ankles and rested his hands behind his head, the picture of a man at ease. Maddie wasn't fooled, she knew that he was getting a kick out of this. There was a hint of a smile in the corner of his mouth and his eyes had an I-dare-you glint to them.

"I was studying the bed. It's important to make an informed opinion of these things and, after all, I am here to help."

Even to her own ears she sounded pompous and uncomfortable.

"Whatever you say," Dean said in a tone that made Maddie want to reach for the nearest pillow and thump him with it.

"If your research has ended it's time to try the bed," he said.

She slipped off her shoes in what she hoped with a

detached professional manner, but a slight hesitation gave her away.

Dean patted the bed beside him.

"Just lie down and think of England," he said with obvious delight.

"Funny," Maddie grumbled as she lay down beside him. "There is something completely unnatural about lying down on a bed in the middle of a store," she told him.

"How else are we supposed to find the right one?'

"That's not the point." She wiggled to get comfortable. "We're in bed, fully dressed, with people watching. Don't you feel odd?'

"Would it feel more natural if we were naked?'

He was laughing at her again. Maddie decided to ignore him.

"Could you get any further away?" he said.

"This is an awfully big bed. Are you sure you want one this big?"

Dean rolled onto his side, angling himself up on an elbow to look at her.

"You think it's too big?'

"That's up to you."

"Do you think a woman sleeping beside me would want to be closer to me, or have her own space?'

Unbidden, an image of her arm draped over Dean's naked chest as she snuggled up to him, popped into her mind. She bit her lower lip. *I will not think these thoughts about my brother's best friend. I will not.*

"I don't know Dean," she said without thinking. "Do you plan to use the bed to sleep or to...'

She could feel her face going a deep shade of red. All she had intended to do was to help him decide what he wanted to do with the bed, not ask about his sex life. The bed began to shudder slightly and she glanced over to find Dean laughing at her. Again.

"I'm one great big source of entertainment for you, aren't I?"

"You have no idea, Velma, you have no idea."

Great, now he was back to calling her a man killing sex bomb. What was that supposed to mean? The man was impossible.

"Look," she said in her crabbiest tone, "perhaps you'd be better off focusing on whether you want a firm mattress or a soft one. That would be sensible. After all no matter what you'll do in your new bed, you'll still spend far more time sleeping on it."

"Oh, I don't know about that."

He trailed a finger down the top of her arm, sending shudders through her body. It took all of her self-control not to jump off the bed and run away from him. She scrunched her eyes shut. The last thing she wanted was to speculate about how much time he spent love making.

"Do you like a firm mattress or a soft one?" she said through gritted teeth.

"What do you like?'

"This isn't my bed."

Was he being deliberately annoying? And why did it seem that he was getting closer to her? Maybe there was a dip in the middle of the mattress?

"I know it isn't but you're a woman. What kind of mattress would you like on your half of the bed?'

She could feel his breath on her cheek. She tried hard to focus. All he wanted was her female opinion. Okay, she could do that.

"I think soft to medium."

"I like firm."

"Well get firm then."

Honestly, she was about five minutes away from sacking her first client.

"Can I help you with anything?"

A crisp female voice cut through Maddie's thoughts. Dean growled beside her, obviously unhappy with the interruption. Maddie propped herself up on her elbows and eyed the sales assistant. She was dressed in a pristine blue uniform, with her hair pulled tight into a bun high on her head. Her back was ramrod straight. She didn't look like she knew anything about comfy beds. She looked like she slept on a bed of nails.

"Maybe you could help my boss pick out a bed. I seem to be having problems keeping his mind focused on the task," she told the woman.

It was only when the woman's eyes widened and Dean started to chuckle beside her that she realised how that sounded.

"I mean," she said as she swung her legs over the side of the bed, "he's my friend and he needs help."

"Uh, huh," the woman said before pursing her lips.

Maddie swallowed the urge to tell her that she was going to get some seriously ugly lines pursing her lips like that.

"Dean, tell this woman what you want," she ordered.

Her attempts at trying to appear professional would have been a lot more convincing if he hadn't been draped across the bed like some model in a TV commercial.

"Of course," he said as he got out of the bed. "It's like this," he told the woman, "thing get complicated when you have a personal relationship with your staff. My girlfriend here doesn't want to give her honest opinion of the bed in case I fire her for being difficult."

Maddie's jaw dropped to her chest. Dean turned to her as he thrust his hands into his pockets.

"It's that right, honey?" he said with a wink.

"Get your own bloody bed," she told him and stalked off.

"Women," she heard him say to the assistant, "they want to be liberated but they can't seem to mix work and play the way we guys can."

Maddie shook her head violently to clear it and watched while Dean worked his way around the store trying beds, dragging the poor bewildered assistant behind him. Every now and then he'd give her a wave or blow her a kiss. He was definitely keeping himself amused. What was it about Dean lately that made her develop foot in mouth disease every time she was around him? What must that poor woman think?

As she watched him stroll around the store she felt a wave of calm surge through her. There was so much confidence showing in everything he did that it was mesmerising. Each task he set for himself got his absolute concentration and attention. For a second Maddie wondered what it would be like to be the focus of that kind of attention to detail. It made her feel dizzy. Turning her back on them, she perched herself on the edge of a divan, got out her phone and notebook and set about working her way through other items on Dean's list.

DEAN KEPT an eye on Maddie as he prowled through the beds. This was intolerable. He didn't do subtle. Not in business. Not in life. He thought that gently leading Maddie to an awareness of him would be easy. It wasn't. It was driving him crazy. Being so close and not touching her. Having to control all of his feelings, all of his needs. And most of all he needed her. If the situation didn't change soon he was going to have to throw Ted's plan out of the window and go for it. Friendship be damned. The woman was his and he wanted her now.

Stomping around the store his mood became grumpier and grumpier. At last he picked out a bed. A split mattress, half firm and half medium soft for Maddie, because one way or another it was going to be her bed too. She was sitting perched on the edge of a large divan when he went to find her. Notebook open on the bed beside her, she was clearly making a huge effort for the party he didn't want. His good humour had run dry.

"Let's go," he ordered.

Her head snapped up and she smiled at him. The kind of smile that made a man want to get down on one knee. He held his breath.

"Oh, you're done." She gathered her things together.

Dean marvelled at how wonderful she looked in her old pink sweater. The pale shade made her skin glow and her hair sparkle. He rolled his eyes. Listen to him, he'd be writing poetry next.

"Okay." She smiled again. "I'll go home and work on your party. I have theatre tickets booked for Monday evening."

"Great, what did you get?'

He held the door open for her as they went out into the bright Spring sunshine.

"The Lion King," she said.

He stopped dead.

"The Lion King?'

Maddie turned towards him and looked at him with the same patient look she would give a four year old.

"Yes. You said you were entertaining a client."

"And you thought The Lion King was the best option for that?'

"Well you wouldn't want something too romantic, or too heavy, or something that everyone sang along to, would you?'

Dean shook his head in complete bewilderment.

"I guess not." He hoped that was the right answer.

"Exactly," Maddie said and then turned on her heels.

She strode towards the underground station.

"So," she said over her shoulder. "That leaves The Lion King. And I couldn't get box seats, but I did get good ones, front row of the Royal Circle."

Dean put his hand on her arm to stop her quick march. He pulled her against a shop window to get out of the flow of Saturday shoppers.

"So let me get this right. I'm taking a client to see a Disney cartoon and I'm sitting with a bunch of other people while we watch it?'

For a minute he forgot that the client was a figment of his imagination.

"This is good family friendly fun. Ideal for entertaining someone you don't know."

"But..."

Dean stopped himself short of telling her that the tickets were for them. He had envisioned a Pretty Woman scenario – a romantic performance, a darkly lit and private space. It would have been perfect. Instead he got a cartoon and a balcony full of tourists.

"But what?" She tapped her toe as she demanded the answer.

With a deep sigh, and the start of a headache, he shrugged.

"I guess you're right. The Lion King it is."

"Good," she spun around and resumed her march.

He felt like she'd given him a pat on the head. Now what? Did he let her wander off until he found something else to occupy her? He didn't like playing games. It wasn't him. As he followed her swaying hips along the crowded pavement his heart squeezed. If he wasn't so crazy about her he'd be able to think straight.

At the entrance to the underground she turned and patted his chest. It was the first time she'd touched him all day and it burned a hole through his body.

"This is my stop. Don't worry I'll sort out the party in plenty of time."

As she turned away Dean felt like he might burst. Things were not going well.

"Don't go, Maddie."

She gave him a curious glance. He stuffed his fists into his pockets to stop from grabbing her.

"Let's do something together, just for fun. The party can wait."

One eyebrow rose as she looked at him.

"Dean, I haven't even been home yet. I have a lot to do."

He rocked on his heels. Damn, he'd beg if he had to, but now that he'd started wooing her he couldn't bear for her to be out of his sight.

"Come on Mad, let's go on the London Eye. I've never done that and it's a beautiful day."

He could see she was considering it.

"We can have lunch at the Tate Modern."

It was one of her favourite places to eat, a hangover from her art student phase.

"I don't know, there's such a lot to do."

He reached for her. He couldn't stop himself. Her hand felt soft and tender, making his seem unwieldy and huge.

"Come play with me, Maddie," he teased. "You know you want to."

He grinned at her as he imagined all sorts of fun they could have together. A tiny bubble of laughter escaped from her plump pink lips.

"Fine, but if my boss hears about me slacking...'

"I'll make sure that never happens." He threw an arm round her shoulders. "Anyway, you have such a cool boss at the moment I'm sure he'll understand."

"You're cool, huh?" She grinned up at him, her eyes sparkling with amusement.

"You better believe it."

He pulled her to him in another friendly gesture as they walked down the steps into the underground station. Before he let her go he took a deep breath. She smelled of lavender. An agonising surge of pain swept through him. He had to make her love him. He had to.

4

____

Maddie sat back on the old wooden bench and gazed out over the river. It would soon be sunset and the air had taken on a deeper chill. She shivered slightly wishing she'd bothered to bring her coat with her, but she hadn't intended to stay out this long. The Tate Modern had a way of sucking up your time with room after room of fabulous art.

After a lovely lunch in the café, they'd wandered through the rest of the galleries. The old power station was crammed full of wonderful art. She felt that there would never be enough time to look at all of it properly. She'd pointed out her favourite Lucien Freud painting, a nude standing against a huge pile of white rags, and the new sculptures by Rachael Whiteread that used old discarded dolls houses made up to look like a tiny town. She thought they were wonderful, although Dean wasn't as impressed. He'd been much more knowledgeable about art than she had realised. She'd even been surprised to discover that his firm had held some of their functions in the top floor dining area that over looked Shakespeare's Globe theatre.

It occurred to her, as they wandered through the gallery shop, that over the years she had treated Dean much like a child treated an adult. She'd told him all about her life, but had shown very little interest in his, assuming that the large things that took up his time made up the sum of him. It was a strange thing to realise. They'd socialised together on millions of occasions, but usually in a group or with her brother and the only times she hung out alone with him were on the occasional lunch or when she wanted something. Now that was an embarrassing realisation. She wondered how much of Dean she had missed over the years and how much more of him there was to discover.

She loved the South Bank. Loved the view over the river towards the Savoy Hotel, that wonderful building with its white brickwork and large art deco clock. She vaguely remembered reading that Monet had once roomed there and painted his views of a smog covered parliament from his room window. She loved the Saturday market nestled beside the train bridges with its supposedly handmade jewellery and tie-dye skirts. She even loved the abomination that was the National Theatre and Hayward Gallery. The huge chunk of concrete that had passed for architecture during the 60's and had been the bane of London ever since. No matter what anyone did to brighten it up, it was still the concrete equivalent of a kid's building block effort. At least the skateboarders got good use out of it. Yep, she loved the South Bank.

"Want some fish and chips?'

Dean was sprawled beside her. His proportions weren't quite suited to a public bench and his legs stretched in front of him awkwardly.

"I thought you were going to buy me dinner?" she teased.

"Did I say anything about you paying?"

His smile was slow and intimate. As she watched him amble away from her, digging into his pocket for change, she felt unreasonably proud. Almost as though he belonged to her. She shook the notion off.

Bliss. This was how she was supposed to spend every afternoon. She watched him wait in line outside the van selling food. Against the concrete structure, which looked a lot like a badly built parking lot, standing beside boys in baggy trousers with skateboards under their arms, he seemed incredibly out of place. Maddie felt herself smile.

A river taxi zigzagged up the dark water. Two Japanese tourists stopped in front of her to take photos of themselves beside a busker dressed as Bob Marley. A two year old whooped as he chased pigeons from the black iron handrail. She felt deliciously content. It was a lovely day and Dean was definitely easy to be around.

"Here you go." He interrupted her musings.

She noticed wryly that he had a double portion for himself. Men.

"I can't remember the last time I had fish and chips," she said as she tucked into the hot battered fish.

"Yep." He paused. "We should do this more often."

She twisted in the seat to face him.

"This is fun isn't it?'

"I'm having a good day," Dean said.

His eyes were dark and unreadable.

"I was thinking." She paused to allow him to roll his eyes at her as he usually did, instead he watched her calmly. "I owe you an apology. Over the years I've been pretty selfish in our friendship, I haven't actually spent a lot of time letting you tell me what you were up to, or what you were interested in. I'm sorry." She gave him what she hoped was an angelic, yet determined look. "So go ahead, what's on your mind? What interests you? I'm all ears."

With an odd lopsided grin, he shook his head.

"You are a funny girl," he said softly.

"I'm serious; I think I've done you a disservice."

"Okay, you can make it up to be by letting me finish your chips."

He scooted closer to her on the bench to help himself.

"You're a pig," she informed him, but moved the paper bag over towards him.

"I'm a big guy. I need energy."

As the sun set and the air chilled considerably Maddie felt like she was sitting next to a radiator. It was tempting to lean against him and absorb the heat. She wondered if he would mind holding her and letting her snuggle for a little while. Just to get warm. Before she could ask he gathered up their rubbish and threw it in the bin beside them.

"Come on," he stood in front of her and held out his hand. "Let's go see London at night."

With a grin she let him pull her to her feet. She tucked her hand into his elbow and leaned against him. Two friends out for a walk, that was all, yet she couldn't resist brushing her cheek against his warm woollen arm and allowing herself to feel ever so slightly cared for.

Dark night came quickly as though someone had turned out all the lights. London began to flicker like one large set of Christmas decorations. As they waited in line, surrounded by tourists who were appropriately dressed for a chilly spring day, Maddie began to feel her nose go cold. Any minute now her teeth would start chattering. She wasn't good with the cold. Dean on the other hand seemed to come equipped with his own central heating system. She stood as close to him as she dared without wrapping herself around him.

At last the line moved and they climbed into one of the glass capsules on the large wheel. Maddie held onto the rail on the river side of the pod and Dean stood behind her. A strange sense of anticipation coursed through her, almost like a kid visiting the fair. Only this was the biggest and flashiest Ferris wheel she had ever seen. The wheel started to move with a jolt and then they shifted ever so slowly up into the air.

The river became black beneath them, the surface sparkling as though strewn with glitter. Parliament was lit up a vast glow of orange. As they rose higher, St Paul's dome came into view. The lights around Trafalgar Square glimmered as traffic zoomed around it. And off in the distance the vast suburbs of London became one mass of golden light. The London skyline was mesmerising beautiful.

"You're shivering." Dean's voice, like liquid chocolate whispered in her ear. "Let me help."

A strong arm threaded around her stomach and pulled her tight up against him. Instantly the back of her body became warm and fluid as it absorbed his heat. She let herself sink into him. His other arm reached over her shoulders as he anchored her to him. Maddie sighed deeply as she rested her chin on his arm. She felt his cheek rub against her hair and thought that he kissed her.

Never in her life had she felt so completely secure. His strength engulfed her. For the first time, as an adult, she felt like she didn't have to stand alone. There was a depth to him that she hadn't been aware of before. A deep reservoir of strength that she could tap into any time she liked. It made her giddy knowing that she had a friend like that.

"Look," he whispered huskily.

She didn't know what he was pointing to and honestly didn't care. Her every sense was focused on him. The smell of him was like warm cinnamon buns straight from the oven. The feel of him, solid muscle yet overlaid with soft seductive wool and cotton. The sound of him, his breath on her cheek, his heartbeat thumping steadily against her back. As they reached the top of the circle she realised that she wanted to taste him too. To know the kiss he'd described to her.

She bit her bottom lip as she tried to focus on the view. What would he do if she turned and offered herself up to him? Would he reject her? Would it ruin their friendship? If he didn't want her, if it all went wrong, they would probably never get over the embarrassment of it all. And the awkwardness would damage his friendship with Charlie. She couldn't do that, they had been friends their whole life and she would be incredibly selfish to let her feelings get in the way of that. As he held her tight to him she felt like crying. No, she couldn't take the risk and ruin their friendship, it meant too much to her. These feelings would go away just as fast as they had come. She was sure they would. They had to.

But for the moment she would just enjoy being in his arms.

Maddie didn't see anything else. Her eyes were closed through the second half of the wheel's circle. Her focus was entirely on Dean and the warmth he gave her. As he whispered a commentary in her ear, she heard only the tone of his voice as she snuggled deeper in to him. It was a delightful agony.

As the ride gently shuddered to a stop, Dean turned her around to face him, still keeping her close.

"You're cold, Maddie," he said softly, then brushed her

hair back from her face as he had been doing a lot lately. She looked at him adoringly. She felt like the veil that had covered her view of him had been removed. He was a new creature.

"Come on," he said, "let's go back to my place and I'll make you some hot chocolate."

They rushed up the steps to Westminster Bridge. Big Ben ticked away on the other side of the water. As he hailed a black taxi, Maddie realised that at that moment in time, she would have followed Dean anywhere he asked.

He held her close to him in the darkness of the taxi, wrapping her under his arm like she belonged there. Maddie wrapped her arm across his body and rested her cheek on his chest. With her eyes closed they rode in silence through the city to Chelsea. Occasionally she felt Dean caress her hair. They were in their own cocoon. She didn't want to think about anything else, or analyse how she was feeling, all she wanted was to be close to him.

He held her hand tightly as he led her out of the taxi and up the stairs to his door. Maddie felt a strange mixture of anticipation and acceptance. It was as though she was hypnotised by him. Dean was silent, his eyes dark as he looked at her. They didn't speak.

Holding her with his left hand, Dean turned his key with his right. And Maddie followed him into his home, holding him tightly.

"I don't suppose you brought pizza with you," a voice said.

Maddie threw off Dean's hand as though it had burnt her. She turned towards the voice and when she saw her brother standing in the living room doorway she flushed as though she was a teenager caught out after bedtime.

"Charlie." She sounded breathless.

To cover her embarrassment she threw herself at her brother and enveloped him in a much too enthusiastic hug.

"You're back early. I wasn't expecting you home for another three weeks at least. Are you okay? You're not injured are you?'

Her brother grinned at her.

"I'm fine."

"Welcome home," Dean said as they did the man hug thing.

"I'm starving and there's nothing in the fridge but rabbit food," Charlie complained.

Now that she'd gotten over the shock of finding her brother in Dean's living room, she was pleased to see him.

"Isn't it great to have Charlie home?" she asked Dean enthusiastically.

"Absolutely," he said in monotone.

His jaw seemed tight and Maddie got the distinct impression that he was grinding his teeth.

"How about that pizza?" she said to Charlie. "I can ring out for one."

"Sounds good to me."

While she called out for food, Dean and Charlie took up positions on the couch. It felt good to have everyone together again. Relief surged through her. She'd almost thrown herself at Dean and what if he hadn't caught her? It was too humiliating to contemplate. Thank goodness Charlie was home. Maybe having him around would clear her head.

"So where are you staying?" she asked her brother when she got off the phone. "There are tenants in your place until the end of May."

He shook his short sandy brown hair and gave her the

grin that had charmed him out of trouble throughout their childhood.

"I thought I'd crash here."

There was a long silence.

"Dean," Maddie prompted, "did you hear him?'

Dean stared at Charlie like he was financial problem that needed resolving.

"I'm thinking," he said. "The spare room is full of boxes."

A look passed between the men that she couldn't quite read. She wondered if they had unresolved issues from before Charlie left for Afghanistan.

"The couch is fine," Charlie said evenly. "It's still a step up from a tent in the desert."

Dean grunted.

"I'll take that as a yes then."

"Good," Maddie declared. "I'm going home."

As she stood, Dean got up with her.

"You'll be back tomorrow to unpack the boxes, right?'

She could feel her eyebrows shoot up her forehead.

"You want me to work on a Sunday?'

"I didn't realise that you're business was working-hours only."

The meaning was clear; he didn't think that she was being professional enough. Maddie stared at the ceiling while she counted to ten. What did she have to do to get through to this man that she was serious about her business?

"Fine. I'll be here at ten." She turned her back on his approving smile.

"Make sure you've got clothes on," she ordered as she gathered her things.

As the front door closed behind her she rested her back against the cool wood and took a deep shaky breath. What had she been thinking? The only explanation was that she'd been caught up in the mood of the day and had mistaken Dean's friendly behaviour as something more romantic. Her cheeks burned as she cringed at the thought of what she might have done. Her stupid hormones could have led her to ruin a friendship. She bit her lip as she worried. It had to be hormones, right?

There was no denying that something had shifted in her awareness of Dean. She was plagued with inappropriate thoughts. In the meantime, she'd try to forget how close she came to disaster. It was time to concentrate on business. Time to make Dean realise how wonderful her new idea was, and when he did he would have no option but to support her.

With a shaky smile Maddie headed out into the cool spring air and made her way to the underground station. Tomorrow she would be friendly and professional. She would not let herself be distracted by how sexy Dean looked. She would not think about how strong Dean felt when he held her. And she would definitely erase all thoughts of kissing him from her head. Yep, that was the plan.

5

———————

"Is there something going on between you and my sister?'

Charlie sipped his beer casually as he sat at the breakfast bar, but his eyes never left Dean's face.

Dean leaned against the kitchen counter, his ankles crossed, a cold drink in his hand - the picture of a man at ease, when all he really wanted to do was punch something. Preferably Charlie.

"Would it bother you if there was?" he asked back.

Charlie seemed to give the question some serious thought.

"Only if you break her heart," he said. His tone was deceptively casual. "Then I would have to break your legs."

"I'd say that was fair," Dean said as he reached for another slice of pizza.

"I'm glad we cleared that up," Charlie said and grinned. "Now show me to the sofa. I'm knackered and I need my sleep."

Dean threw a crumpled up paper napkin at his friend's head as he went into his bedroom. The evening hadn't turned out as planned. He thought he would be spending the night with a Lewis, he got that part right, problem was he had the wrong Lewis.

For a while he really thought that Maddie was seeing him in a different light. He'd done everything he could to make sure that she was aware of him. Gently. Maybe he'd been too gentle. Damn it, he should have kissed her after the ride in the London Eye. It was the least he wanted to do.

As Dean climbed between his white cotton sheets he realised that they hadn't been changed since Maddie had slept there. There was an agonising aroma of lavender that smelled exactly like her. Nothing was right. The bed seemed too big. The duvet was too restrictive. The pillow too hard. He wanted to howl that he'd had enough. Obviously subtle wasn't cutting it. Fine. He wasn't very good at subtle anyway. Tomorrow he'd make things clearer. Damn, he hated all this finessing. Bring back the days when you threw a woman over your shoulder and declared she was yours. If there ever were days like that. One thing was for sure, this situation was intolerable. Things had to change.

"I hope you're not in there dreaming of my sister," Charlie shouted through the darkness.

There was the unmistakable sound of a smile in his voice. Argh! Dean pulled a pillow over his face. Kill me now, he thought as he tried to fall asleep.

The morning wasn't any better. After a sleepless night Dean staggered into the kitchen, hell bent on breaking his vow of no coffee, only to find Charlie sitting at the breakfast bar fully dressed in a khaki t-shirt and cargo pants, whereas Dean was wearing only boxers and his hair stood on end.

"Isn't that a little under dressed?" his best friend said with a grin.

Dean ignored him as he poured coffee into the biggest mug he could find.

"Maddie did say to wear clothes today, which made me wonder exactly what you've been doing around my sister."

Charlie was getting far too much amusement out of Dean's predicament.

"Are you going to stick around all day?" he asked pointedly.

"What and miss you trying to woo my sister?" he said. "Woo, such a lovely old fashioned word. A sex free word. And who better to help keep it sex free than her brother."

Dean looked around for something hard to throw at Charlie's head, but there was nothing within reach.

"This isn't funny," he said.

"Oh, I don't know. I think it's hysterical. All those years of women falling over themselves to get to you and you decide you want Maddie."

"What's that supposed to mean?'

"I think she rates you on the same level as a Border Collie."

Dean frowned; unfortunately he'd been thinking the same thing.

"I'm working at changing that."

"Stop." Charlie's humour disappeared. "I said I was okay with this. I'm not okay with hearing a play by play of your seduction plan. That's disgusting."

"I wasn't planning on keeping you in the loop anyway."

Dean looked into his already empty mug in disgust. There wasn't enough coffee in the world to get him through the day.

"But," Charlie said with another wide grin, "I don't mind hanging around to watch you crash and burn. That's entertainment."

"Well it's only fair," said Dean, "after all I was a witness to your disastrous love life right through college."

He stuck his head in the fridge only to find that his latest health kick meant there was nothing to eat. As Charlie had put it, no man food. Maybe he could add shopping to Maddie's list. Women liked to shop.

"I'm going to get dressed," he said. "Don't say anything to your sister when she arrives. The last thing I need is you interfering."

His best friend threw his hands up in an act of surrender.

"I'm staying out of this. If she thumps you for this lovesick routine you've got going then it's your own fault."

"Great," Dean mumbled as he shut his bedroom door behind him.

Now he was entertainment for Charlie as well as Ted. What happened to being in control? To being feared? Maddie was turning him into a wimp. And there was nothing he could do, or would do, to stop it. He'd turn himself into the laughing stock of London if that's what it took to win Maddie's heart. He was pathetic. A desperate man. But somehow he had to find the right balance between being forceful enough in his intentions to make them clear, without coming on so strong that he scared the living daylights out of her. When did his life get so complicated? About twenty years ago when a fairy landed on his head. With a grunt, Dean got dressed in grey jeans and an old black t-shirt that had faded to charcoal.

By the time the doorbell rang he'd worked out a plan of action. He would gently, but firmly, talk to Maddie about their day spent together and explain that he was in love with her. Easy. With calm determination he threw the door wide. And his heart sank.

"Good morning," Maddie said brightly. "Point me in the direction of those boxes."

He groaned inwardly. He'd seen this mood before. This was supposed to be efficient Maddie. More like in-denial Maddie. Although he knew there wouldn't be a lot of point in trying to talk to her, he persisted anyway.

"About yesterday," he started but she cut him off.

"Where's Charlie?'

"He's gone to get food and coffee. As I was saying...'

"No time for talking, there's work to be done."

Although her tone was light and airy she had yet to look him in the eye. This was no good. She was determined to pretend that there hadn't been any intimacy between them the day before. It was like talking to a brick wall. Dean decided to retreat and regroup. He would make her feel at ease then he would bring the topic up.

"Do you want a drink, or do you want to get started?" he said politely.

"I'll get started. There's a lot to do this week, no time to waste."

She rolled up her sleeves on the oversize denim shirt she wore. It was so worn it was almost threadbare and its proportions seemed to swamp her. Underneath she wore what looked like a black sports vest and a pair of black leggings. The message was clear. She was here to work. She may as well have been wearing armour.

"Okay," she declared. "Time to get on with it."

Dean couldn't take it anymore. He stepped in front of her effectively blocking her path to his spare room. Maddie took a step back in the narrow hallway, making sure that there was plenty of space between them. She smiled politely. He gritted his teeth.

"About yesterday," he said as he took a step towards her.

The hallway seemed to close in on him. The surroundings were all wrong for a heart to heart. Too clinical. Yet again he found himself wondering why he'd painted the whole house white. He was beginning to feel like he lived in an institution.

"We have some things to talk about," he used the same tone he used to command the room at board meetings.

It didn't work.

Her back straightened and her eyes glazed over.

"Yesterday was lovely wasn't it?" she said in an obviously forced light hearted tone. "We really must do it again sometime."

Dean tried to resist the urge to shout "enough!" He stepped even closer to her.

"There are a couple of things I'd like to clear up," he said.

"Great." She sounded a little hysterical. "We'll do that as soon as I get this room organised. After all that's why I'm here isn't it?'

Sidestepping him she practically ran into the spare room and closed the door behind her. There was the tell-tale click of a lock turning. Dean stood rooted to the spot in disbelief. She'd locked him out. He rattled the handle.

"Maddie," he said through gritted teeth, "let me in. I can help you."

"Fooey!" She shouted gaily. "You'll only get in the way. Now go do something else with your time and let me get on with the job."

Very slowly, Dean rested his forehead on the closed door. It took all of his self-control not to kick the damn thing down. Why did he have to fall in love with the world's most infuriating woman? There was nothing logical in anything she did. In fact she was borderline insane. Resisting the urge to kick the door he stomped back into the living room and over to the sofa. He threw himself onto it. Fine. She couldn't stay in there forever. He'd wait.

When Charlie let himself into the flat, Dean was sitting on the sofa, feet on the coffee table.

"Where's Maddie?" Charlie said.

Dean grunted.

"Is she here?'

"She's in the spare room. She's locked me out."

His friend doubled over with laughter. When he'd finished wiping the tears from his eyes he started unpacking the shopping onto the coffee table.

"Pringles?" he said as he threw a tube to Dean.

Dean popped the top and gulped them down. He was too damn tense for healthy eating. Now he knew why so many men went to seed and had heart attacks by the time they were forty. Women drove them to it.

"I guess she doesn't want to be next on your play list," Charlie said.

"I thought you were going to mind your own business."

"Only until it all goes belly up," his friend said cheerfully, "then I'm going to break your legs, remember?'

"I don't plan on it going belly up."

Maddie had been alone in that room for long enough, it was time he went in to help her. Even if he had to climb in the window to do it.

"She's been in there long enough." He declared his thoughts aloud.

"I have Diet Coke," Charlie said, actually making the effort to be helpful for once.

"Hand me a can. I'm going in.'"

Charlie threw him a soft drink as Dean strode past to the spare room. He didn't look at his friend, he didn't want to see his thoughts written all over his face. He didn't need confirmation that he'd lost the plot entirely.

He rapped the door with his knuckles, when what he really wanted to do was thump it with his fist and roar.

"Open up," he said.

"It's okay," Maddie called back through the wood.

What the hell was that supposed to mean?

He could hear Charlie trying to stifle a chuckle behind him. He looked over his shoulder to find his friend leaning against the kitchen doorway and obviously enjoying the show. He growled and thumped the door harder.

"This is my house and I want to help empty my boxes. So open the bloody door."

Never in his life had he felt so angry and so impotent at the same time. There was silence. He imagined she was chewing her lip while she tried to decide what she could get away with.

"I have Diet Coke," he said.

The door opened. It was as though he'd found the password. Charlie howled with laughter.

"Why didn't you say so?" Maddie said as she took the can from him clenched fist. "I could use a drink."

"We need to talk," he said firmly as he strode through the door.

Once inside, he shut it behind him and leaned against it. It took extreme effort on his part to look like he was relaxed and happy to be in the room.

"Talk?"

Maddie held the drink in front of her as though it was a shield. Her eyebrows disappeared into her fringe and a faint pink tinge appeared on her porcelain skin.

But it was the eyes that undid him. She looked like a kitten pleading for asylum and he felt like a brute for trying to make her deal with their situation. Anger and determination seeped from him. He'd waited years. He could wait a little longer.

"Yes, talk," he said firmly as she gulped her drink. "I would like to have a say in where my possessions are being placed."

Her shoulders sagged with relief and she gave him the brightest smile yet. Dean's heart clenched tightly.

"Well great, we can start with all of this technical stuff."

She pointed to a pile of old computer equipment.

"Do you want it in here or in the office?'

"Actually, we can recycle that lot. I've upgraded."

"Fine," she said as she packed it back into the box.

The baggy shirt did nothing to hide her curves. Instead it clung to them as she bent and moved. Dean wanted to groan with need; instead he busied himself putting text books on the bookcases.

"Do you realise that you only own two novels?" Maddie asked.

"I don't have much time to read for pleasure," he said.

She bent over to pick up a small box and his knees went weak. Tight black leggings showed off every inch of her calf and thigh. An image of him sliding his hand up the outside curve of her leg to her hip popped into his mind. His hand actually itched to touch her.

"That's the problem," she was saying. "You don't have much time for anything. You really need to do something about that."

Her words hardly registered as he concentrated on how her lips moved as she talked. He wanted to lick them. Bite them. Watch them as they kissed their way up his body.

Something moved in front of his face. Maddie stood, hand on hip, waving a dust cloth at him.

She rolled her eyes as he focused on her again.

"As I was saying this is a boring guest room. There's nothing welcoming in here at all."

"I don't see that as a bad thing. Charlie will be staying and I don't want him to get too comfortable."

She ignored him.

"You need a nice comfy couch, as well as a decent bed, and some paintings on the walls. I saw some lovely ones in Cork Street the other day; they would make a good investment for you."

As Maddie waxed lyrical about her plans for his home Dean wondered if there was ever going to be a good time to tell her how he felt. He was probably doomed to go around horny and frustrated for the rest of his life. Even dressed in that old shirt of his, she was stunning. And the sheer delight she took in every little thing she did was contagious. It was like a breath of fresh air in his otherwise dusty and dull life. With Maddie around nothing was boring, she always had a new way of looking at things or a new idea to make everything that little bit more interesting.

"You look good in that shirt," he told her.

Flustered, she looked up from the box she was opening.

"Thanks, I've had it for ages. I think it must be Charlie's."

"It's mine."

Knowing who the shirt belonged to was important, as though the knowledge cemented a connection between them, somehow.

"Oh," she said, "I didn't realise. I can't even remember where I got it."

"I do."

He unpacked some keepsakes from university while he spoke.

"It was about five years ago. We were at that concert in

Hyde Park when it got a bit chilly and you ordered me to give you my shirt."

"I remember." Her face lit up with a smile; it made his stomach squeeze tight. "I told you that you were a walking radiator and didn't need the extra layer. I'm sorry I kept it - do you want it back."

"No, I like seeing you in it. I like knowing that you're wearing something of mine."

Wearing his shirt wasn't enough. He wanted to see her wearing his ring. To be his. Forever. Really he'd loved her ever since she landed on his head twenty years ago. And if she would let him, he'd love her till the day he died.

"Dean," she said softly, "you're looking at me a little oddly. Should I be worried?'

He gave a dry chuckle. Maybe she should be worried, because he would move heaven and earth to make her his wife.

"No, I was thinking about how cold you get. It's kind of cute."

She breathed an audible sigh of relief that hurt him more than any word could have.

"And you are so hot it's unbelievable."

"I'm hot, eh?'

He raised an eyebrow as he watched her realise what she'd said. There was never a dull moment with Maddie.

"No, I mean, yes, I mean, oh dear. Of course you're attractive. You know you're attractive. I meant that you give off a lot of heat." She rolled her eyes towards heaven. "I'm digging a deeper hole. Like last night, you were great to cuddle up to, you kept me warm."

It took all of Dean's self-control not to turn the conversation towards something deeper. At least she was talking about yesterday. That was a step forward.

"And a good thing too, I thought you were going to turn blue."

Her delighted smile said it all. She felt like she was on safe ground again, comfortable with him.

"I'm going to go get us some coffee," he said.

"I thought you'd given it up?'

"Turns out I need it more now than ever."

With that he headed to the kitchen.

Maddie shook her head as she unpacked the last box. Dean was getting stranger and stranger. At least things were back to normal between them with friendly banter that she enjoyed. She snuggled down into her old denim shirt. She was glad it had belonged to Dean. It somehow added a new dimension to it and made her feel a tinge of security wearing it. She wasn't stupid; she understood what Dean said about liking her in something he owned. It was as though the shirt created a kind of intimacy between them. That was fine, she could live with that. After all they were very close friends weren't they?

The last box contained some personal items. She felt relieved to see them, for a minute she'd thought Dean didn't even own a photograph. She pulled out a graduation picture of him and his parents. They looked happy. She set it aside for pride of place on his desk. His parents had had him later in life and both had passed away a few years ago. For the first time she was aware that the Lewis's were the only real family he had left.

There were framed certificates that could be hung on the wall, snap shots of him and Charlie when they went backpacking round Europe during college - and a silver framed photograph of her. She stopped dead with the photo in her hand. The frame was obviously expensive and beautiful with a delicately engraved flower design. It showed a picture of her in what looked like sunlight; she was smiling softly, almost intimately into the camera. Even to Maddie's critical eye it was a good photo of her, but it was the look she was giving the camera that startled her. It was the kind of look that passed between lovers. A knowing and intimate look, a look filled with love and awareness. She'd seen it before, mainly passing between her parents, but she'd never knowingly given the look to anyone and yet here it was framed in silver sitting in Dean's spare room. She couldn't remember when the photo was taken, let alone who took it and how Dean got it.

Dean opened the door with his foot, two mugs of coffee in his hand. As he noticed what she was holding he stopped still, waiting for her to speak.

"I don't remember this picture," she said. Her voice sounded shaky even to her own ears.

He put the cups on the window ledge and crouched down to where she knelt on the floor.

"It was a couple of years ago. We were at Charlie's leaving party. Well, one of them."

She looked up at him.

"You took the picture?"

"Yep."

She stared at him for a moment before turning back to the photo.

"I keep it on my desk."

A thousand thoughts raced through her mind. She felt like pieces were falling into place, but she still couldn't make out the larger picture. Nothing made sense.

He reached out and stroked her hair, not even pretending to brush it from her face. Maddie was stunned. What did it all mean? She needed time to think.

"Here," she thrust the photo into his hand and hastily stood.

It occurred to her that all she had to do was ask Dean what was going on. But what would she say? Do you fancy me? That reeked of teenagers at a disco! Overwhelmed by the thoughts and sensations that were assaulting her, she needed time to regroup and figure things out.

"I'm going home, we're finished here anyway," she said.

"Why don't you stay for dinner?"

Although there was nothing in Dean's voice to suggest it she got the distinct impression that he was a bit cheesed off by her retreat. Fine, she could handle that.

"No thanks, got plans," she said.

And before Dean could stop her she ran. She wasn't proud that she ran, but the hysteria she felt was driving her, not her brain.

"Bye Charlie," she called as she let herself out of the flat.

Gasping for air Maddie felt like she was drowning and desperate to breath. In a panic, she ran for the subway. She desperately wished that Laura hadn't gone away for the weekend because she needed someone to talk things through with. And as Laura was on a work bonding weekend, she couldn't even call her and moan over the phone. No, she had to figure things out by herself. Logically. She needed to get the hormone surges and inappropriate feelings out of the way and concentrate on logic.

Then she would know what to do.

"Not going well then?'

Ted was already in Dean's office when he arrived.

"I have no idea," Dean grumbled. When had his life become so complicated? "I spent all day yesterday dealing with Charlie. And the last I saw of Maddie she was running faster than a racehorse in the other direction."

"Big brother is back. Interesting."

Dean threw himself heavily into his desk chair and felt something snap beneath him. So much for the superior design.

"Is he alright with you and Maddie? Are you still mates?'

"Oh we're still mates," Dean drawled sarcastically. "Charlie has set up camp in my spare room until his place is empty. He's eating my food. Drinking my beer and doing everything he can think of to wind me up. Apparently I'm a great source of amusement for him."

Ted's blond head bobbed as he silently chuckled.

"So what's the plan with Maddie, are you calling the whole seduction thing off?'

"Hell no. It's the only reason I agreed to be a guinea pig for her latest crazy idea."

Ted pulled his chair closer.

"Good. Let's plan the next stage then," he said gleefully.

"And then I suppose we'll paint each other's nails and braid hair?'

Dean felt he was, at most, two conversations away from booking into a beauty salon and gossiping like a girl. How could chasing a woman make you feel like less of a man? It was the damn strategy and planning. Enough.

"No more planning. I'm going to do it my way. I'm going to corner her and tell her how I feel. Get everything out in the open."

Ted shook his head slowly, making it clear he thought Dean was a prize idiot.

"It's amazing you ever get laid," he said with disgust. "You won't get into her pants with that attitude. Women want romance, they want heart and flowers and all that crap. You have to plan it out, mate, manipulate them a little and then before they know what's hit them, bam, it's bed time."

With complete bewilderment Dean watched the gleam in Ted's eye.

"I am not manipulating Maddie."

He leaned forward over his desk giving Ted his full attention to emphasise his point.

"I'm not trying to get into her pants. This is something else."

Ted raised an eloquent eyebrow.

"Okay, getting her into bed is part of it. But I'm fed up playing games. It's the theatre tonight. We're going to have a good time and then I'm going to tell her how I feel."

"You're making a mistake." Ted pushed himself up out of the chair.

"What mistake are you making?'

They turned to find Maddie smiling at them from the open door.

Dean felt a surge of panic. His mouth went dry. How much had she heard?

"Business stuff, darling," Ted said as he gave her a peck on the cheek.

"And speaking of businesses -" He changed the subject. "How's your new one going? Have to say it broke my heart to hear that there weren't any animals involved."

Maddie gave Ted a playful shove.

"It's going great." She turned to Dean. "Isn't it?'

"Absolutely," he said without conviction.

"And the sooner we get on with things the sooner I'll be out of your hair," she said.

From behind Maddie, Ted rolled his eyes and mouthed "I told you so'.

"Don't you have something to do?" Dean said pointedly.

"Yeah." Ted kissed Maddie's cheek. "Bye bye, darling. As for you, I'll help you plan that strategy later. You definitely need my help."

Before Dean could say anything else Ted was gone, leaving Maddie sitting much too far away on the huge red sofa. He came round his desk to sit beside her. That was better. She smelled of orange blossom today.

"I really need a list of guests for your party so that I can ring round, or email. It's far too late to send invitations."

"I'll write one up."

"And we need to talk about food. I know you want informal, but there is a great little caterer in Fulham who would do a lovely job. What do you think? Shall I book her?'

"Whatever you want is fine with me."

"Good. It will be a fantastic party."

"I'm sure it will." He took a deep breath and lied. "Listen, my client has cancelled on me tonight and I now have two tickets for The Lion King."

"Do you want me to get a refund?'

"No, I was thinking that we could go together. No point in wasting them and you did say they were your favourite seats."

She hesitated. Guilt surged through him. So much for his moral high ground. In one split second he'd done exactly what he told Ted he wouldn't do, manipulate Maddie.

"Look," he said, on the verge of begging. "Come out with me. It's only a show and I don't want to waste the tickets."

Her eyes skirted around the room as she thought of an answer.

"It's not really part of the job, Dean. I'm a personal assistant type person, not an escort."

"Thanks for clearing that up," Dean said drolly.

"You know what I mean. Isn't there someone else you want to take?'

"I want to take you."

His tone was final. He leaned in towards her lessening the gap, forcing her to look at him instead of everything else in the room.

"Okay, Dean, that would be lovely," she said at last.

"Good."

Dressed in a chocolate brown shift dress Maddie looked good enough to eat. Dean wanted to press her back into the red couch and kiss her till he drove her crazy. Something flickered in her eye. She stood up from the sofa and away from him.

"Dean?" She perched on the edge of his desk. "I hope you don't mind but I invited a date for you to your party."

That was honestly the last thing he thought he would hear come out of her mouth.

"What?'

"She's a lovely girl." Her words tumbled out one on top of the other. "Looks like a Barbie doll, very talented, works the fashion section of Sparkle magazine. I hope you don't mind."

"You're setting me up with Barbie?" He sank back into a sofa that was far too soft to be in an office.

"You're going to love her...'

With clear exasperation he ran a hand through his hair making the normal pristine cut stand on end.

"Maddie, I told you this before. I can find my own women."

"But you're not doing a very good job at it are you? And you're obviously lonely, otherwise...'

He leaned forward. He felt like a cat about to pounce.

"Otherwise what?'

Her arms folded over her chest.

"It's embarrassing."

She wouldn't look at him as she spoke. Dean walked over to stand in front of her.

"What's embarrassing?" he said softly.

"Nothing, I, oh my...'

He put a finger under her chin and tipped her face up to look at him.

"What is it? You can tell me."

With a deep resigned sigh, she batted cow lashes at him and made the bottom fall out of his world.

"I keep thinking that you're flirting with me." She rushed the words out. "I thought I was going insane, imagining all of it. But last night I had a chance to think things through logically and it makes sense now. You don't have time to meet new women. You're lonely and you're flirting with me because I'm around so much. And I am, you know, a woman."

"Seriously?" he said with utter astonishment. "That's the conclusion your logic led you to?'

He moved towards Maddie making her press against the desk as she leaned away from him. Something inside of him snapped. He'd had enough messing around.

"Let's clear a couple of things up," he said evenly. "I'm not desperate for a woman and hitting on the most convenient one, regardless of who she happens to be."

It made the mind boggle that she could even think that. Desperate?

She was holding her breath. Her eyes were dark and there was a hint of wary expectation in them.

"On top of that, I don't flirt accidentally."

He leaned in towards her, close enough to feel the heat coming off of her.

"If you thought I was flirting with you..." His voice was soft and low, he was close enough for it to be almost a whisper. "Then I was flirting with you."

Her eyes flashed wide as her lips made a little circle "Oh" of realisation. Without another moment's hesitation he did what he'd been dreaming of doing for years. He leaned in and kissed Maddie. Properly.

Dean was kissing her. Dean! Dean said he had been flirting with her. Dean! A million confused thoughts assaulted her. A million feelings fought for attention. And then all she could think of was Dean.

His touch was soft. It felt like he was breathing her in as he brushed his lips over hers. His hand snaked around her waist and pulled her to him. Maddie gasped and he took full advantage of her open mouth as his tongue slid across her lips. He teased, he caressed, he tasted all of her and she tasted all of him. And her mind left her completely. The kiss wouldn't end. She wrapped her arms around him and held on for dear life, curling her fingers into the fabric of his suit. When he gently bit her bottom lip a tiny groan of need escaped her. He pulled her even tighter to him in response. He filled up all of her senses. She felt light headed, weak at the knees and desperate for more.

Then he pulled away.

"I hope we're clear," he said.

Her lips felt swollen and tender. She didn't trust herself to speak so she nodded.

Another kiss like that and she would be begging for more – just like he'd predicted.

"I have a meeting."

She felt his fingers on her cheek. They burned through her and made her eyelids flutter shut.

"I'll pick you up tonight."

His eyes held promises that she couldn't put into words, but they made her mouth water.

As Dean moved away from her she let the desk take her weight because her legs wouldn't. She watched as he gathered some paperwork together. When he'd finished he came to stand in front of her again. It took all of her self-control not to pull him to her and demand that he stay. He tucked her wayward hair behind her ear.

"I want you, Maddie." His deep lingering tone made the words vibrate through her whole body. "I've wanted you for a long time."

She heard another sentence. One he didn't say. He meant to have her.

Maddie found her voice.

"Well hell," she croaked.

With a lopsided grin Dean leaned in and brushed his lips gently over her swollen mouth.

"We'll deal with this later."

With that he strode from the room, every inch the man in control, leaving Maddie in a puddle by his desk.

Time passed. She wasn't sure how much of it. But it went. And in that time she sat looking at central London and felt blissfully and utterly stunned.

What was going on?

Her world had shifted on its axis. It was a whole new place. The Dean she had been used to was someone else entirely. It wasn't even as though she was really seeing him for the first time. She actually had no idea who he was at all. Some elements of him were still there; his sense of humour, his reliability and his sharp brain - but there were new characteristics too. There was now a sexuality that oozed from him and assaulted her at every turn. It was like looking into a fire, being entranced by the flames and desperately wanting to be a part of it but at the same time knowing that it would probably destroy you. Maddie rolled her eyes at the thought; here she was waxing lyrical about one of her best friends. But truth be told, Dean was suddenly hot. With a capital H. She couldn't believe that she hadn't seen it before. The broad shoulders that screamed to have nails dug into them. The piercing violet eyes that seemed to see right into her. And on top of all that, a backside that Brad Pitt would envy. She felt like a switch had been flicked inside of her. She was definitely tuned into Dean.

Maddie needed to talk to someone, so she bundled herself into a taxi and made the short journey to the Sparkle offices.

Laura was on the phone. Laura was always on the phone. She signalled Maddie to sit while she wound up her call. Instead Maddie paced the tiny office; the trip over had done nothing to slow her heartbeat. As soon as her friend hung up Maddie spoke.

"Dean kissed me."

"Wow, was it good?'

Maddie smacked her hands on a stack of periodicals.

"That's all you have to say? I tell you one of my best friends kissed me and you ask, how was it?'

"It was only a kiss."

"Oh no, it wasn't," Maddie groaned as she covered her face with her hands. "I know kisses. I've had plenty of kisses. And this wasn't a kiss. This was...'

"...an invitation?'

"More like a demand."

"Wow again." Laura fanned herself. "So are you going to meet his demands?'

"He's my friend. Sure, I admit I've been having thoughts and feelings about him. You didn't help telling me that his backside was to drool over. But he's my friend. Worse still, he's Charlie's friend. I don't want to come between them."

"And how would you do that?'

"When it all goes wrong of course. Then I would lose my friend and Charlie would, at best, have a strained relation-ship with Dean."

Laura took off her owl-like glasses, the same style she'd worn her whole life. Maddie had been trying to talk her out of wearing them for years, saying that something more deli-cate would suit her fine features, but the glasses stayed. Laura pulled a hair band out of her desk drawer and tied back her sandy coloured hair as she spoke.

"That's better, it was driving me mad." She gave Maddie a gentle smile. "Honey, what makes you think it will go badly?'

Maddie sat up with a jolt giving Laura her full attention.

"I didn't think it could go any other way."

"What if this is it?" Laura's voice had a note of awe to it. "What if he's the one for you? What if you don't try and you never know if he was your soul mate?'

There was a dramatic pause while each of them considered Laura's words. Maddie took a deep breath before sitting down on the guest chair with a thud.

"Have you been writing those teen love articles again? You really need to get a proper job, with a magazine that's interested in more than make up and how to get a boyfriend."

"Look who's talking. You never hold down any job longer than it takes you to save up money for your next business plan. I'm not taking career advice from you."

Maddie rolled her eyes.

"We're getting off track here. What am I going to do about Dean?'

"Well, what do you want to do with him?'

Images flashed through Maddie's mind that she definitely couldn't put into words; she felt her face burn up.

"It's like that huh? Well I say go for it. Don't ask yourself what if it goes wrong, ask what if it goes right? Can you imagine waking up to that body every day for the rest of your life?'

"This isn't about sex."

Laura pulled her rickety office chair round to sit beside her friend. When she got there she held Maddie's hands in hers.

"Maddie honey, Dean's been crazy about you for years. Everybody can see it. Even your half wit brother. To be honest, we all thought it would happen before now, but you seemed to think that Dean was invisible. I don't know what's going on now, I don't know why he's suddenly on your radar, but I recommend going for the ride and see where it takes you. That's what I would do given half a chance."

"With Dean?" Laura had lost Maddie round about Dean being crazy about her.

"No, you fool, with any man who'll have me!'

"I need to think about this," Maddie declared as she stood to go.

"Of course you do."

"This is happening at totally the wrong time. I'm working with Dean. I'm showing him how professional I can be so that I'll get some decent recommendations. I need him to see that I can run a business professionally."

Laura didn't say anything, but she wore her best sympathetic face.

"Look," Maddie said, "you know what this means to me. It's not just the business being a success, it's showing people that one of my ideas actually works. I understand what people think, for years all I've been hearing is that I should get a real job, or finish a degree. But it isn't me. I get bored so easily and at the same time all of these plans are chugging through my head. If I was a guy I'd be Richard Branson."

"Only he's a billionaire, honey."

"See what I mean?" Maddie threw up her hands in despair. "All I need is for one of my ideas to take off then I won't be flighty Maddie with the crazy schemes, I'll be a business woman, an entrepreneur. I'll be a success. This is important to me, Laura, and I can't help but think that letting things get romantic with Dean is going to screw everything up for me."

"I don't understand why you can't have both - a successful business with Dean's help, and a great time with a hunky guy who is crazy about you. Why is it one or the other? Maybe you're worrying too much."

"I don't want him to think that I'm not taking this seriously."

"Honestly Maddie, I don't think you can do anything wrong in his eyes right now. You should take a chance, see what happens. He's rich, he's gorgeous and he makes your knees turn to jelly. That's three things your last boyfriend didn't have going for him."

"You're right." Maddie gave her friend a hug. "Anyway, I need to go. We're going to see The Lion King tonight."

"You're first date is a Disney show?" Laura looked disgusted.

"It's not really a date, it's just some tickets that are going asking."

"Let me see. You are drooling at the thought of seeing him again and he is probably itching to get his hands on you. There will be darkness, music and shared food." She raised an eyebrow at Maddie's stupidity. "It's a date."

Maddie said goodbye and wrapped herself into her camel coloured woollen coat, wishing that the April weather was a little warmer. Her stomach was doing flips. She wasn't sure, but she thought she might be about to go on a date with Dean. If she had been a comic book character there would have been a bubble above her head with the word "gulp!" in it.

7

Only ten minutes had elapsed since Maddie last looked at the clock. Dean would be arriving to pick her up soon. She'd already eaten more antacids than the packet recommended. Again she wished that Laura wasn't working late so that her friend could take her mind off things. It was silly, getting into a state about going out with Dean, it wasn't like she hadn't done it before. But it felt like the first time.

Her new dress was a throwback to the fifties. It was fitting until the waist and then flared out into a full skirt that skimmed her knees. The material was the colour of hazelnuts, which matched her eyes. It also shimmered slightly when it caught the light. At her waist she wore a slim hot pink belt, which she matched with peep toes shoes. The dress came with a pashmina which would keep her warm, although she was hoping that her date would help with that. Her date. The phrase sent shivers down her spine.

As the minutes crawled past she checked her make up again. Smoky eyes, pale pink lips, not too much blush as she tended to go red at the drop of a hat anyway. She didn't wear perfume because she had used her favourite shower gel and the smell still lingered. She checked the clock again, wondering if it was broken. Maybe time had slowed because the batteries had to be changed? As she was about to take it apart to check it, the doorbell rang. A sudden urge to lock herself in the bathroom assaulted her. Breathe. Three deep breaths and she felt less hysterical. Grabbing her tiny pink shoulder bag she went to answer the door.

Dean's eyes darkened with appreciation when he saw her.

"You are beautiful," he murmured as he looked the length of her.

Dressed in a form fitting black suit with crisp white shirt, he was pretty stunning too. She suspected that he didn't wear a tie to avoid her teasing him about his undertaker look. The top button of his shirt was open, revealing a hint of his toned chest, an image that had been burned into her retinas. Naturally wavy dark hair was styled slightly less severely than usual and his scent reminded her of mulled wine. It was heady.

"Ready to go?"

He offered her his hand. Maddie looked at it, so huge, so strong and then with the slightest hesitation she looked up into his eyes. They were heavy with an unspoken question. It was up to her to decide which way the evening would go. With a shaky breath she put her hand in his.

I'm doing this, she thought, I'm actually doing this.

He held her hand tightly as he hailed a taxi. In the back of the cab he sat close to her so that his leg and arm touched hers but he didn't hold her, didn't invade her space. Maddie wasn't sure what she'd expected but a restrained Dean hadn't been on her list. She half wondered if she had imagined the passionate kiss of the morning.

The cab let them out in front of the Lyceum theatre. The lights of Covent Garden filled the sky. Maddie drank in the atmosphere - smiling people dressed up for a night on the town and the air filled with delighted chatter. They passed the posters showing scenes from the show and moved slowly with the crowd into the dark wood clad foyer. After their tickets were checked they wove their way up the russet carpeted stairs to the Royal Circle. Dean stayed close by her so that they wouldn't be separated in the throng. Although his hand rested gently against the small of her back he may as well have been a million miles away. This behaviour she had seen before and it smacked of friendly politeness. Where was the passion? The romance? Did he still want her? Maddie couldn't contain herself any longer. She spun around to make him stop dead behind her.

"Is this an actual date?" she asked him.

He paused on the step beneath her, making her almost eye level with him. Those mesmerising violet eyes were laughing at her again.

"Do you want it to be?'

They stood against the wall so that they wouldn't stop the flow of people.

"That isn't an answer," she reprimanded him. "Is this a date?'

"I intend for it to be."

He held her gaze and her insides melted into one big sloshy mess. Although there were reasons she should resist him – her fear of what would happen, what she would lose if it all went belly up and the fact she needed him to make her business work – her excuses didn't seem all that important any more. Instead she felt like her emotions were the equivalent of a snowball rolling down a hill. They got bigger and bigger, gaining momentum all of their own until an avalanche happened. Just standing facing Dean, holding his hand, made her giddy. The whole evening smacked of promise and she found herself acting like a teenager, wondering if he would kiss her.

"You're thinking something," he said with unconcealed amusement.

Her eyes narrowed. Why should she be the one waiting? This was the twenty first century. If it was a date then it was a date. She bit her lower lip as she thought about the situation.

"Maddie," Dean said softly, "what are you thinking?'

She couldn't look at his lips without reliving that kiss. Couldn't stand this close to him without feeling the heat come off him and knowing how good it felt to be wrapped in his strength.

"Oh hell," she said, "I'm thinking that this is definitely a date."

And with that she wrapped her fingers in his lapels and pulled his mouth to hers.

As soon as their lips touched the world faded. He tasted so good. His lips were so soft. His touch so firm. Maddie opened her mouth to him as she wrapped one arm around his shoulders pulling him to her. Delicious. Like the best French pastry with rich hot chocolate.

"Get a room," someone teased as they passed.

Maddie slowly pulled back as if coming out of a daze. She was glad that she hadn't worn a brighter lipstick. The look on Dean's face was dark and dangerous, like he was planning on taking charge to make sure the kiss didn't end next time. She smiled with a sense of achievement. She did that.

"Now it's a date," she declared with heady delight. "Come on, let's go see the show."

She suspected that Dean allowed himself to be led to their seats, she didn't care, she held his hand firmly and pulled him along. She was on new territory. And she loved it.

THE LAST THING Dean wanted to do was watch a Disney musical about a bunch of talking animals. He'd never been so uncomfortable in his life. The seat was too small, he felt like he had been wedged in with a shoe horn. The woman on his left laughed loudly at every little thing and every time she moved she dug her elbow into his ribs. And even though Maddie was right next to him it was nowhere near as close as he wanted her to be.

Her kiss on the stairs had blown his mind. Just when he thought he had her figured out, she turned the tables on him. All day he'd been planning how he would seduce her. He was sure that her brain would have gotten in the way again and he'd be back to square one trying to convince her that they were meant to be together. How wrong he'd been.

And now, when he was getting the response from her that he wanted, they were stuck in a theatre. Maddie sat perched on the edge of her seat watching the show over the handrail. He wasn't interested on what was happening on stage, he was only interested in what was happening with her. As some dancers in vast animal costumes pranced around she turned to him and smiled. His breath quickened. He wanted her now, this minute, and waiting was nothing short of cruel.

As she laughed at the action she slid her hand onto his knee. It was a friendly gesture, comfortable even - he doubted that she was aware of what she was doing - but he felt her touch like a branding iron, marking him as hers. He reached up and rubbed her back watching her shiver as he did so. Good. His hand slid up to her neck. As he massaged and caressed he saw her eyes close and her mouth open slightly. He was definitely getting to her. With a gentle shudder she shook off his hand, sitting back in her seat to stop him from touching her any further. He put his arm around her and stoked the bare skin of her shoulder. She scowled at him, which almost made him laugh out loud.

"Am I distracting you?" he whispered in her ear.

"Yes," she hissed. "Stop it."

"No."

Her hair smelled like some exotic flower that he couldn't identify. He brushed it away from her neck and leaned in as if he was going to whisper again, instead he nuzzled her earlobe. He felt her breath catch in her throat.

"Two can play," she whispered to him, her eyes heavy with meaning.

Dean didn't have time to smile as Maddie's hand caressed the inside of his thigh. He narrowed his eyes - she was playing dirty. He lowered his head to gently bite her neck. Her hand stopped moving. When he looked at her face her eyes were fixed firmly in the distance. She turned her head with a wicked smile before shifting in her seat so that her cheek rested on his chest and her arm curled around his waist. Damn, now he didn't have any access to her neck.

He stilled as her hand moved on his chest, her delicate fingers tracing patterns. His traitor heart pounded louder than the music and he felt Maddie grin against him, aware of the mischief she was causing. Dean shifted in his seat. Now his trousers were uncomfortably tight. She would pay for that.

As he caressed down her body to the curve of her hip

her stoking hand stilled. It felt like she was holding her breath as she waited to see what he would do. Dean ran his hand over the curve of her hip and traced along the top of her behind. She pressed deeper into him.

And then Maddie took it a step further. Slowly, but confidently, she undid a button on his shirt. Dean thought the top of his head might blow off. Her slender hand slipped through the gap she'd made and covered the flesh beneath it. Years of wanting her rushed at him in one ferocious wave of need. Her fingers traced his muscles and made circles in his chest hair. He grasped the curve of her hip with his right hand and wove his fingers through her hair with his left, holding her head to his heart, hoping that she would hear the truth beating out in rhythm to her touch.

It took every tiny drop of his self-control not to pull her up to him and kiss her into oblivion. As the curtain on the first act fell and the lights came up Dean could honestly say he had absolutely no idea what The Lion King was about. Maddie pushed away from him. Her eyes were wide, her face was flushed. It gave him immense pleasure to know that he wasn't the only one feeling uncomfortable. He wanted to groan out loud as she pulled her bottom lip between her teeth. He couldn't stand anymore.

"Let's get out of here," he growled.

He didn't try to hide the meaning behind his words or his intense desire for her. A slight flicker of doubt crossed her eyes before she nodded. He didn't wait for any more encouragement than that, in a second he was on his feet and dragging her after him out of the theatre.

MADDIE HAD BEEN PLAYING with fire during the show and she knew it. There was something about Dean that made her want to see how far she could push things and how much she could get away with. It had a lot to do with feeling secure with him. At the end of the day, he was her friend and he knew her. She couldn't scare him off with her overwhelming personality, or make him feel insecure with her confidence. He was Dean, he knew her practically inside out and that was liberating.

She hadn't meant to take their physical tit for tat so far, but the more she touched him, the more she wanted to touch him. It was intoxicating. And boy did he feel good. When she put her hand inside his shirt and touched the chest she'd been dreaming about since she'd seen him in the kitchen, she honestly thought that she wouldn't be able to stop. She wanted to pull at that pristine white shirt until the buttons popped and she could brush her cheek against his chest. She wanted to run her tongue across those perfect muscles and leave tiny bite marks in her wake. When she heard Dean's heart racing faster than hers she felt powerful and thrilled that she had caused such a reaction, especially since he was the epitome of self-control.

Dean strode down the stairs into the foyer and out of the doors dragging Maddie behind him. It felt like her feet didn't quite touch the ground as she was subject to his stark determination. Outside the chill night air was a balm to her burning skin. She clutched her bag and wrap to her chest as she tottered after him. She wasn't sure where he was going, but they were making good time.

Suddenly Dean ducked around the corner of the theatre into one of the dark lanes. He swung her in front of him and pressed her back up against the cold hard wall. In an instant the distance between them disappeared. She looked up into his face and saw such raw desire it made her gasp.

"I can't wait," he said simply before winding his fingers into the back of her hair and angling her face up to him.

He kissed her with the force and desperate need of unrestrained passion. Maddie didn't have time to think, her instincts kicked in as she responded instantly. She pulled him to her, frustrated that no matter how close he got, it wasn't close enough. His lips were soft yet firm as he teased and coaxed and tasted her. Her fingers grabbed the hair at the back of his head and a frustrated gasp escaped her lips. His hair was too short to get a decent hold.

One strong hand pressed on the small of her back anchoring her to him. The other cupped her cheek. Maddie was on fire. Her leg snaked up Dean's outer thigh. At once the hand caressing her face dropped to hook under her thigh. His thumb traced circles on her skin making her feel dizzy. Suddenly his lips were gone. She almost screamed out demanding that he continue, and then he nuzzled into the soft spot under her earlobe. She groaned, turning her head so that he could get a better angle. Gentle kisses traced down to her shoulder where he softly bit her muscle. Any resolve she had to slow things down evaporated. She wanted Dean, and she wanted him now.

As if reading her mind he positioned himself so that he could look in her eyes. His hands still anchored on her body.

Maddie could imagine what she looked like, her face was burning, her lips were red and swollen and her eyes heavy lidded with desire. Dean gave her a half smile. His normally violet eyes were completely black with the intensity of his reaction to her.

"I think we better slow down or there will be another sort of show going on here tonight," he said.

With his words the world came slowly into focus. The

hard cold brick of the building bit into her shoulders, the chill night air made her skin tingle and the volume of Covent Garden went from mute to high in one second flat. Never in her life had she been kissed to the point of losing control in a public place. Her eyes widened. He had done that. To her.

"Maddie," he almost groaned her name, "I realise this may be too soon for you, but I have been waiting forever to touch you. I don't want it to stop. Please say you'll come back to my house with me."

He'd been waiting forever to touch her? Forever? She hadn't guessed. How was it possible to be so close to someone and not see how they felt about you? The things he said were almost too much to comprehend. She didn't know what had overwhelmed her most, the intense physical reaction she had to his touch, or the bare emotion that he let her see. He stood there, caressing her as she clung to him, waiting for her answer. He didn't push or persuade, he simply waited. And she adored him for that.

But he was right, wasn't he? It was too soon for her. She'd only really been aware of him for a matter of days, not the forever he talked about. Surely she couldn't go to bed with him based on that? On the other hand, he was Dean. There wasn't another man in the world that she trusted as much or felt as secure around. A pulse beat low in his neck betraying his patience, showing her how desperate he was for her to say yes. As she saw that tiny sign of his insecurity, her heart melted. The reasons for not touching him became far less powerful than the reasons for touching him. And she really wanted to touch him.

"Well?" he whispered, his eyes locked on hers. "Do you want me to make love to you?'

The thought of it sent her heartbeat into overdrive.

Without thinking she wanted to scream loud and clear – hell yes! Instead she bit her lower lip, making him groan faintly, feeling the power she had over him.

"I would like that very much," she said and felt the tension flow out of him only to be replaced by a sense of urgency.

With lightning speed he stepped away from her taking her hand firmly in his. In two long strides he was out of the shadows and hailing a cab. As they climbed into the back of the taxi, Dean barked directions. Maddie felt light headed, as though she was in some sort of trance. She was really going to do this. With Dean. And she could barely wait to get her hands on him.

The cab raced through central London towards Chelsea. The lights blurred into one great big orange glow. Every inch of her body was aware of his. He'd seeped into her being, setting up camp in her mind, bringing the full force of him to bear on her emotions. It felt wonderful.

And then she remembered Charlie. He was still living in Dean's spare room. Obviously Dean had forgotten. She turned to him in the darkness.

"What about Charlie?" she said.

He squeezed her hand in a gesture of reassurance.

"Don't worry about him. Charlie and I had a talk and he gave us his blessing."

Time stopped. Desire fled. Everything within Maddie went cold. Clearly he'd missed her meaning. She stared at him in astonishment as he gave her a reassuring smile. They had a chat? She had her brother's blessing?

"Stop the car," she ordered the driver.

With skill he dodged through heavy traffic to deposit her at the side of the road in Piccadilly Circus. Before Dean could vocalise the look of confusion on his face she was out of the cab and standing on the pavement. Traffic zoomed up and down the road beside her. The pavement was crammed with people, and the huge flashing billboard above Boots the chemist told her to go buy Pepsi right now. Maddie tuned it all out. Her focus was on Dean.

If Maddie was water she'd have gone from fluid warmth to ice in ten seconds flat. Suddenly, the last thing she wanted to do was go to bed with Dean. She thought he knew her, but he didn't. He may be attracted to the woman, but in his head she was still his best friend's kid sister and apparently that meant getting permission to touch her before even she knew how he felt. She fought the desire to vent her anger by kicking him in the shin. As she stood glaring at him people swerved to pass her.

"What's wrong, honey?" he said after he'd thrown some money at the taxi driver.

She shook her finger at him.

"Don't you honey me," she warned.

The fact that he was standing there completely oblivious to what he had done made her even more furious.

"You." She pointed at him. "Asked my brother's permission to sleep with me."

A young woman gasped at Maddie's words and pulled her boyfriend to a stop to listen. Dean frowned, she could see he was thinking, and then his eyebrows arched as he realised what he'd done. He stepped towards her hands wide in a gesture of supplication.

"It's not what you think," he said in a tone most people reserved for small children.

Now that didn't help.

She took a step back folding her arms across her chest.

"You arranged my life with my brother. Talked about

seducing me. With my brother. What other way is there to look at this?'

"You're kidding," said the young man watching. Dean gave him a look that made the couple duck their heads and keep on walking. He turned his attention back to Maddie.

"I only wanted to make sure that he was okay with it and that it wasn't going to damage our friendship."

"Let me get this right, you were more worried about the damage sleeping with me would do to your best friend than the impact it would have on our friendship. Is that right?'

He shook his head as he took another step towards her. She held up her hand at arm's length to stop him. Her eyes turned mean as she thought: come any closer, buster, and I'm thumping you. He stopped.

"No, you're getting this all wrong. I knew you would be worried about how this would affect Charlie so I wanted to clear the air first." He smiled. "See? You don't have to worry."

Maddie thought the top of her head might blow off with the pressure building from her need to hit some sense into him.

"So, you were really doing me a favour?"

He sighed, visibly relieved that she got it at last.

"Making sure that there were no hurdles in the way of me going to bed with you. Making sure that I wouldn't worry how my brother felt about my love life. Even though it is my love life and none of his business. You were saving me from the embarrassment of telling him what? That I was overcome by lust and fell into your arms?'

She stomped towards him, making him back up this time.

"You tell him, girl!" an American woman called out.

"Let me clear some things up for you, as you put it earlier today. Firstly, I am in charge of my life, not my brother, not my parents and I will see and sleep with whomever I choose regardless of what my family may think or might feel about it. Secondly." She glared at him. "That person is not going to be you."

There was a smattering of applause. Without another glance at Dean she threw her arm in the air and brought a taxi screeching to a halt beside her. With pure fury she wrenched the door open and threw herself into the back seat. Bloody stupid men, she fumed as the car drove away, leaving Dean to deal with the judgmental stares of the people who had stopped to listen to their fight.

Honestly. What had she been thinking? She had almost climbed into bed with him. She'd convinced herself that no one knew her like Dean knew her, that she could feel safe because he was her close friend. She'd been entranced by him saying that he wanted her since forever. But really when it came right down to it she wasn't sure who he wanted, because it seemed that he didn't know the real her at all or he would never have taken something so personal to Charlie first.

And he definitely wouldn't have thought that she would need anyone's permission to live her life.

Men. She was done with them.

8

———

Charlie was lying on the sofa when Dean got home. There were Chinese takeaway cartons all over the coffee table and the TV was tuned to the sports channel.

"You're early," he said as he swung his legs around to sitting position.

"It didn't go well."

Even with the foul mood he had going he couldn't bring himself to throw his suit jacket any old place. After he hung it in his closet, he grabbed a couple of beers from the fridge and went into the living room.

"Here."

He thrust a beer at Charlie then sat down in the armchair with a thud.

"If this was a chick flick I'd be breaking out ice cream round about now," Charlie said.

Dean's eyes narrowed at him. This whole fiasco was partly his fault.

"I told Maddie that I talked to you about the two of us going out," he said grimly.

"Well that was a bloody stupid thing to do."

Charlie gave him much the same look that Maddie had given him in the taxi.

"I get that now."

They sat in silence for a minute.

"Is she upset?" Charlie said.

Dean raised an eyebrow at him, resisting the urge to sneer.

"What do you think?'

Charlie gulped down the last of his beer and plonked the bottle in amongst the rest of the mess on the table.

"I think you're on your own with this one." He stood up. "I'm going to stay at Mum and Dad's till my place is clear."

"Seriously?" Dean said. "Now you leave?'

His best friend shrugged and gave him the boyish grin women fell over.

"Remember," he said, "Dad taught Maddie how to box too. I've been on the receiving end of a few right hooks and that's enough for me. Plus, let's face it, she's much more likely to hit me than you."

"Great," Dean grumbled as Charlie went off to pack.

About ten minutes later Charlie found Dean in exactly the same position as he'd left him. He gave him a pat on the shoulder.

"Cheer up," he said, "it can only get better from here."

Dean growled at him as he left the flat, whistling Queen's Crazy Little Thing Called Love as he went. Dean stared at the blank wall as he thought things through. Two thoughts occurred to him. One, that he really needed to get some art on his walls, the place looked like a mausoleum. And two, that the Lewises were right, it was a stupid thing to do. He took a long drink from his cold beer. Now what was it going to take to get him out of this mess?

. . .

MADDIE SPENT Tuesday fuelled by anger. The man was an idiot, and as for Charlie, the sooner she got her hands on him the better. She'd waited till she knew Dean was at work to phone his flat only to get the answer machine. Her brother was obviously hiding. Coward.

It was another grey day outside. At least it was cosy inside and she had no intentions of leaving. Thank goodness that Laura had insisted that central heating be a priority in the flat they rented. The last place had been like an icebox. Absentmindedly Maddie picked up the odd item of discarded clothing to lob into the laundry basket. Neither she nor Laura were much good at housekeeping, there was always a more interesting way to spend their time. After making hot chocolate in her cupboard sized kitchen she decided that she'd wasted enough time being annoyed. She cleared a pile of magazines from the second-hand couch and settled in to work.

Even though Dean had screwed things up it didn't mean that she wasn't going to be professional, so she spent her time on the phone. She organised the caterer for the party, called around as many of the people invited as possible and then went online to hire a CD collection from a guy who rented it out for parties. That way they wouldn't have to listen to Dean's sorry taste in music all night. Who ever heard of people partying to Mozart? She shook her head.

The caterer was bringing glasses, plates and cutlery. Apart from getting the flat ready for a party and shopping for little bits and pieces there was nothing more to do. She sat down on her old ratty sofa wondering how to spend the rest of her day. It wasn't even three o'clock, Laura wouldn't be home from work for hours and Maddie was feeling miserable.

Just when she had decided to take a chance on ruining her friendship and get her hands on Dean, he had to go and blow it all. She'd never before gone from completely turned on to feeling nothing but cold fury in such a short space of time. And what a waste of the beautiful dress she'd bought especially for the evening. When you go to that much effort you at least like to think that the date will end romantically.

To stop herself from becoming completely self-absorbed, she switched on her laptop and spent some time working on the website content for her business. At least this mess was good for something; even he would be able to see that she could stay professional in difficult circumstances. The thought cheered her.

She was completely engrossed in writing a description of her service, when the doorbell rang. Dressed in leggings and Dean's old shirt, she padded barefoot to the door. When she opened it, she wished that they had gotten around to installing a spy hole.

"I'm sorry," Dean said before she could slam the door in his face.

He was in his regulation black suit which made her unreasonably annoyed. It was his buttoned up and proper attitude that got them in this mess in the first place. She folded her arms across her chest and glared at him.

"For what?'

It was the classic female test. Make sure the man knew why he was being sorry; otherwise the experience was wasted on him.

"I'm sorry that I spoke to Charlie," he said contritely. "I'm sorry that I thought it was a good idea to get his blessing. And I'm sorry that I told you."

She narrowed her eyes at the last one, which sent the instant message that he had said something wrong. She watched as he backtracked.

"I mean, I'm sorry that I had to tell you, which I shouldn't have had to, if I hadn't done it in the first place."

Even she had difficulty following that one. He looked so cute, standing there holding a carrier bag with such a woeful expression on his face. But she wasn't finished with him yet.

"I tried to call Charlie," she said in her sternest tone.

"He's gone to your parents."

"Did you talk to him?"

"That's why he's gone to your parents."

She frowned. Charlie knew she was less likely to thump him in front of Dad. Her father had drummed it into them that a boxer never hits unless cornered. She'd deal with her brother later.

"Can I come in, Maddie?"

It was tempting to slam the door and leave him standing in the stairwell, but he did seem genuinely sorry.

"Fine," she said grumpily, "but don't try anything. I'm not finished being mad at you yet."

He gave her a sheepish smile as he slipped past her into her tiny apartment.

"This is for you," he said as he handed her the plastic bag. "I thought it was better than flowers."

Genuinely curious she opened the bag. Inside was a large bakery bag. And inside that were half a dozen cinnamon buns. Her heart melted.

"You said the other day that you wanted them, so here they are."

He shoved his hands into his pockets and rocked back

on his heels looking at her through his impossibly thick lashes.

Well hell. The man found cinnamon buns for her. She had to remind herself that she was still mad at him, but honestly she wasn't, not anymore. And he was irresistible standing there nervously waiting for her reaction. It was the best guilt gift she'd ever received.

Without thinking too much about it, she stepped towards him, grabbed a handful of his shirt and pulled his mouth down to hers. She kissed him deeply, registering a look of shock just before she did so that made her feel wonderful. When she let go, he hadn't even had a chance to get his hands out of his pockets and he looked slightly dazed. At last the power dynamics were in her favour. As they should have been all along.

She smiled knowingly at him.

"You're forgiven," she said primly. "Let's have a cup of tea and a bun."

And with that she went to put the kettle on.

Even if he was married to Maddie for a hundred years he would never be able to figure her out. But right now, he was grateful that everything was okay between them. All day long he'd been worried about her reaction. His concentration had been shattered and his participation in meetings had been pointless. He felt relief flood through him and wondered if cinnamon buns would do the trick every time.

As Maddie made tea in the cubby hole of a kitchen Dean tried to figure out where to sit. He felt like a fish out of water in her flat. To his orderly eye it was nothing but chaos. There were scarves over lamps, piles of books on every surface, shoes lying beside the couch and the walls were full of pictures. Carefully he cleared a space for himself on the sofa, noting that the paperwork he shifted was essentially the business plan for her new idea. While she made tea he read - at least this was something he was familiar with.

"What do you think?"

Maddie nodded towards his reading material as she put a tray on the table. She looked so eager and enthusiastic that he couldn't say what he really thought. On top of that, he'd only managed to get back into her good books and didn't want to ruin it with a dose of reality. From what he'd read so far, her business didn't have a hope in hell of making a go of it. It was obvious, even to him, that he couldn't say that so instead he smiled at her.

"I haven't read all of it yet, but it's definitely interesting."

He figured that answer could cover a number of bases.

She was delighted and curled up beside him on the couch, cradling a cup of steaming tea in her hands. He wanted to take the cup from her and carry on from where they'd left off the night before. He settled for a sticky bun and resigned himself to another evening of coaxing Maddie to love him. He wished she'd get on with it so that he could get on with her.

"I really think this business is going to be a great success," she was saying.

He had to concentrate on the words and not on how sexy she looked in his old shirt. She batted her eyelids at him. "Especially once you get word out to all of those contacts of yours."

Inwardly Dean cringed. He had no intention of letting Maddie's latest idea loose on his colleagues and, by default, his reputation. As he looked into her hopeful face he decided that shattering her latest dream could wait.

"Speaking of work," he said, "how's it going with that party of mine?'

His shoulders fell with relief as she launched into an enthusiastic description of everything she'd done so far.

"You know I don't want to go overboard right? Something low key and tasteful, that's all I want."

She patted his hand.

"Don't worry. I've got it all under control."

That was the part that made him worry.

"Would you like to stay for dinner? Laura will be home soon and I'm making ravioli."

He shook his head with genuine regret.

"I have to get some work done to email to Tokyo."

"Oh, okay. I understand."

He was pleased to see that she was disappointed. He wound his fingers through hers, making his heart race excitedly.

"I don't have to be in the office tomorrow. How about you and I do something together? Whatever you like."

"Great." Her face lit up. "Let's go to the beach."

"In April?'

"It will be fun," she coaxed. "When was the last time you went to the beach?'

He had to give it some serious thought.

"College, I think."

Maddie was clearly horrified.

"You go on holiday right? I don't honestly remember if you do or not. What do you do then?'

"I've been too busy building up the business to take a holiday. I haven't had one in years."

She leaned towards him, concern written all over her face.

"Dean, honey, your business is well established now. Ted

can take care of anything that comes up and you have good staff to back him up. Isn't it time you relaxed a little? If I had your money, I'd blow off work all together and go round the world for a year."

Her grin was contagious.

"Imagine spring in Paris, followed by a trip to Cairo and the pyramids, then on to Nepal. If you kept going you could spend Christmas on Christmas Island. Although I'm not sure that there is actually anything on Christmas Island. Maybe Hawaii would be a better idea."

It sounded wonderful, but only if she was with him. Through her eyes he'd see the excitement in every destination. And he was certain that his mind wouldn't turn to work even once. Maybe one day he'd take her, when he was sure that what she felt for him was way beyond the attraction stage. Nothing less than undying love would satisfy him – especially now that he had taken the risk and changed the dynamics of their relationship. Now he knew that she was attracted to him, surely it was only a matter of time before she loved him. Although he was a patient man, he wasn't certain that he could wait that long.

"The beach it is," he said.

"I'll meet you at Victoria Station at eight, we'll get the train to Brighton."

As he stood he pulled Maddie to her feet alongside him.

"It's a date," his voice was husky with longing.

Then with the slow and meticulous attention to detail that he was famous for, he kissed the smile right off of her face.

"Wow," she said as she pressed her finger tips to her lips.

"And don't you forget it," he said as he opened the door.

Before he could close it behind him she called out.

"Don't even think about wearing a suit tomorrow."

Dean floated down the street with a silly grin plastered to his face. It was going to be all right. Maddie wanted him. He knew that. One touch was enough to make her eyes close and her heart pound. Now he only had to make her love him before he told her that her latest business idea was doomed to failure.

9

Maddie danced from one foot to another as she waited for Dean to arrive. She wore dark blue jeans, a purple t-shirt and a long cream cable knit cardigan. But it was what she wore underneath that made her the most anxious - she'd broken out her Victoria Secret pink lingerie that had hardly seen the light of day. The knowledge that she had picked underwear with Dean in mind almost made her crazy. She'd stood in front of the mirror for what seemed like hours trying to decide between her run of the mill underwear and the Victoria Secret set. She'd bitten her lip almost raw worrying what it meant to wear the sexy lingerie. Was she planning to go to bed with him? Had she already decided? In the end she figured that although she had no idea what she was going to do with him, she was definitely going to be prepared for all possible outcomes.

From her position at the W.H. Smith corner she could see most of Victoria Station as well as the entrance to the underground. If he didn't turn up soon, they'd miss the train. She'd already taken the liberty of getting tickets, now all she needed was her man.

Her man. The thought astounded her. Barely a week ago she hadn't noticed how gorgeous Dean was, now she couldn't get him out of her head. Every time he was around her she became lightheaded with lust. There was no other way to describe it. She knew that they should do the dating thing, like they were doing that morning, go to places, eat meals out, all the usual stuff. But truth be told, all she really wanted to do was jump his bones. She felt that the getting to know each other part of dating was really pretty pointless. After all she'd known him practically her whole life so the stupid first date questions were a waste of time. She knew what food he liked, what his favourite colour was. She knew what his house looked like, and she definitely approved of his friends. No, she shook her head as she thought about it, dating was definitely pointless.

So what were they doing? Friends with benefits? She'd read all about the concept in American magazines. Is that what this was about, having a friend that you could sleep with whenever you wanted to? She thought of Dean and his conservative ways, there was absolutely no way that he would risk their friendship for the "benefits'. In fact she was pretty sure that he could get "benefits" with any woman he liked. Her mind kept popping back to her conversation with Laura. Could it be that what they were doing was trying to find out if they had found "the one'? Now that was a terrifying thought.

"You are definitely thinking too much." Dean's voice startled her. "You have no idea how much that scares me."

His smile was contagious and intimate. Maddie knew that no one else got a smile from him like she did. It was a wondrous thought.

"Good morning, gorgeous," he whispered as he wrapped her in his arms and kissed her hello.

The kind of hello kiss that made her toes curl up into her boots.

"I'm glad to see you aren't wearing a suit," she said as she surveyed his clothing.

He was dressed pretty much the way he'd been the Saturday before when they'd gone on the London Eye. The same wool jumper clung to him defining his muscles and gently coaxing her to snuggle up. As well as faded jeans he had a rain jacket in one hand and a McDonald's bag in the other.

"Breakfast." He shook the bag.

As she dragged him off in the direction of the platform, she looked skyward.

"I had breakfast already," she said.

"So did I. This is a train breakfast. That's completely different."

They pushed through the ticket barrier and ran for the train. It was an old style train with several doors on each carriage and little booth-like seating areas along its length. They sat side by side with an empty seat facing them. Dean promptly tucked into his second breakfast while she sipped a hot chocolate.

He obviously hadn't shaved as there was a slight shadow on his jaw. His hair was ruffled as though he'd recently gotten out of bed, but he smelled of fresh shower gel. When he finished his food and wrapped an arm around her pulling her tight against him, Maddie decided that she didn't care how to define this new relationship, she was happy to go along for the ride and see where it ended.

While she cuddled up to the blue jumper that she loved and felt the soft wool on her cheek, she felt Dean stroke her hair. There was no need to talk. With the rhythm of the train she found herself lulled to sleep.

The sun was shining in Brighton making it pleasantly warm. They trawled round The Lanes where Dean bought her a pair of Mexican silver earrings that she adored. She put them on instantly and delighted in the way the little silver feathers jingled down to her shoulders.

"There's a platinum pair, are you sure you wouldn't rather have those?" Dean said.

"It's not about money, I like these."

"Well fine then." His voice was husky. "You look good in them."

"How good?" she teased.

He shrugged as he stuffed his hands into his pockets.

"About as good as you normally look," he said.

Maddie rolled her eyes at him. She backed him into the jeweller's window as people bustled past them. The smell of the bakery squashed in between the jewellers and the funky clothes shops made her mouth water. But not as much as Dean did.

"What does a girl have to do to get a compliment around here?'

With his back against the wall she felt free to lean into him. It was frustrating. There were way too many layers between them. Suddenly his expression turned serious.

"Maddie, no woman looks better to me than you do, and a pair of earrings can't make you more beautiful. It isn't possible."

"I don't know what to say." She stumbled over her words.

"Don't say anything."

He gave her the sweetest, gentlest kiss before taking her hand in his.

They meandered down to the seafront where she

insisted that they get ice cream cones then teased Dean for choosing plain vanilla. They leaned on the old mint green handrails as they looked out over the calm water. Even though they were barely out of winter there was life on the pier - she could see some of the rides moving at the end of it. The white Georgian houses overlooking the water gleamed as they caught the afternoon sun. It made no difference that the surf was too far out to hear above the traffic that zoomed behind them - she still felt soothed by what she saw.

"So tell me," Dean said lazily, "why is it so important for you to have your own business?'

Maddie stopped eating and pointed her cone at him.

"Well, why don't you go work for some other firm? Why did you start a business of your own?'

He shook his head.

"It's not the same thing. I trained for this. It isn't some idea I cooked up one afternoon when I was bored."

If it wasn't for the teasing twinkle in his eye she would have taken offence.

"I don't come by these ideas easily," she said, affecting an offended air. "I'll have you know they're carefully researched. I'm trying to find a gap in the market."

"You carefully researched alpaca walking?" He raised an eyebrow.

With a slump of her shoulders she conceded that one.

"No, I read about that in an American adventure magazine and thought it would be a great idea for the city. I should have thought it through a little bit more."

"Yeah, getting permits might have been an idea too."

Maddie playfully punched his arm.

"That was a long time ago, I've learnt from my mistakes. There's nothing hinky about this new venture. Come on, admit it, it's a good idea isn't it?'

Something that looked suspiciously like guilt flitted across his face. It was gone so quickly that she wasn't sure if she had actually seen it or not. She threw the rest of her cone at a seagull, which was the size of a small car. He swooped at it catching it before it hit the ground.

"Well, I agree," Dean said stiffly, "the fundamental idea has merit."

"Oo, high praise." She grinned.

"But there are some things you really need to think through. I don't think you've looked far enough ahead. I mean what happens if…'

She cut him off with a dismissive wave of her hand. Now was not the time to discuss her business plan.

"It can wait," she said as she tucked her arm in his.

"Maddie, if you're serious about this you need to think it through some more. There are gaps in your planning."

"You worry too much."

With a frustrated sigh he let the subject drop.

Maddie took a deep breath of the salt air and rested her gaze on the pale blue sky. Beneath her, on the walkway beside the beach, people wandered around lazily looking at the large sculptures or stopping for a coffee in one of the many cafes. She felt more relaxed than she had in weeks.

"Do you know why I want this so badly?" she said as she snuggled in closer to him.

Dean wrapped her tightly in his arms.

"Tell me." His deep voice rumbled through her body.

"I want something that's mine. I know that sounds silly. But right through school I was always compared to Charlie and let's face it he is brilliant at everything he does. And that's fine. But I always feel like I'm stepping where someone else has gone before. I'd like to achieve something that is all me. My idea, my hard work. I want to be the one making the decisions. And at the end of the day I want to feel pleased that my success was my making. Plus," she confessed to herself more than Dean, "I want the excitement of it too. When I work for someone else I get bored. There's no danger of failure, no hope of success, no unexpected turn of events. It's just not me. I like the challenge of trying to make something work. I realise I get carried away without thinking, but it's fun. And Dean, seriously, shouldn't life be fun?'

She could feel Dean sigh.

"What are you thinking?" she said.

"I'm thinking that I can't argue with that, but it's also good that you have Laura and me to back you up. You need someone around you to pick up the pieces."

"I'm not sure how to take that."

"Well think about it like this. You leap and we look. Teamwork."

She gave him a tight squeeze.

"Teamwork. I like that."

"Come on," Dean said.

He led her down one of the ramps to the pathway beneath it and out onto the pebbled beach towards the water. When they reached the water's edge he stood behind her and wrapped his arms around her. Maddie felt the same sensations of strength and security that she had felt the last time he held her like that, only this time there was something deeper that she couldn't quite put her finger on.

"I always wanted to live by the sea," Dean murmured against her hair.

"I would never have pictured you by the sea. I guess I always thought that you were central London through and through."

"I have layers," he mocked.

"I know, and they're getting in the way of me touching you."

The words were out of her mouth before she could stop them. He stilled behind her, she could feel the tension in him.

"I can remove them."

His voice sounded tight.

"I know."

She sighed as she pressed into his embrace.

"You're killing me," he whispered before kissing her cheek.

They walked along the beach towards Hove holding hands and talking about everything and nothing. Every now and then they would stop to throw stones into the water, or to kiss. Mainly to kiss. She found that she couldn't stop touching him, whether it was holding his hand, or hugging him tight, or stroking his back. Dean in turn never let her get out of arms reach and every touch he gave her was like stoking a fire.

"There's a great Italian restaurant in George Street," she said.

"Food good," Dean grunted in his best caveman impersonation.

They wove their way up from the seafront, through the Victorian semis and into Hove's shopping area. Maddie pulled her cardigan tight around her to fend off the early evening chill. They didn't say a word until they were in George Street, each lost in their own thoughts.

Although she had eaten in the restaurant almost every time she came to Brighton she honestly couldn't remember what she ate while she was there with Dean. The food wasn't important. They sat as close as they could at a tiny table in the window and watched as night fell and the street lights came on. People wandered in and out of the cafes and pubs. Mothers marched past pushing prams. Now and then a student would wander down from the supermarket, arms heavy with grocery bags. It was the most ordinary view in the world and yet the most divine.

As Dean poured her a glass of rich red wine she reached under the table to stroke his thigh. The muscle was firm yet warm enough to make her fingers tingle. His eyes became heavy with desire, which made her giggle.

"I'm funny?"

His eyebrows arched at her reaction.

"Kind of." She grinned. "Sometimes you look like you would jump me without a second thought."

He took a deep breath and let it out slowly.

"Just say the word," he said.

Her heart missed a beat. She couldn't rip her eyes from his. It was all there, blatant, raw and exhilarating - his desire for her. She gulped her wine as though it was blackcurrant juice. A nervous tingling made its way up from her stomach to her throat. Anticipation met passion head on as she confronted the fact that she wanted to unleash Dean's desire for her.

"I want to go home," she said and watched him struggle with disappointment.

She grasped his arm as she leaned into him.

"No Dean, not that. I want to go to your home. Now."

She saw relief flit across his face. His lips brushed softly against hers.

"Are you sure?'

"It's either that or under the table."

A loud chesty laugh erupted from him.

"I'm tempted, but maybe we should get to the train."

Paying for the meal and running for the train was a blur.

In the carriage she wrapped her arms around Dean, shut her eyes and blocked out the rest of the world. She wanted only to feel him, to know him, everything else was an intrusion. Something had shifted inside of her. She felt a deep comfort being with him, but also a desperate need for him to touch her.

He ran his fingers up and down her arm. He played with her hair. Every now and then he made her sit up so that he could kiss her. She wished they had the carriage to themselves so that she could touch Dean the way she wanted to. Unfortunately the train was packed and the two business suits facing them would have been disturbed by the show.

"This is the longest journey of my life," she told Dean, making him laugh again.

"I can't do anything about that, Brighton was your idea."

"It was a sucky one."

"I would have suggested a day of scrabble at my place," he said innocently.

"You know what's sad? I actually believe you."

She slid her hand under his jumper and t-shirt to splay her fingers across his belly. He stilled beside her.

"I'm fed up being on this train," she declared.

"It's only an hour."

She traced lines back and forth across the muscles on his stomach. It was fascinating, as far as she was aware only Hugh Jackman had a stomach like that.

"How often do you work out?'

He gave her an odd look.

"Not as often as I should."

"You're fitter than I am."

"Uh huh."

She worked her hand up to his chest feeling the rough hair between her fingertips. She didn't have the same toned body that he did. She looked more like white blancmange. What if it put him off? Sure she looked good in clothes, but that was easy. Naked was another thing entirely. She frowned into space.

"I have fat thighs," she told him.

One of the guys facing them choked on his coffee. Dean gave him a steady look as Maddie wondered what was going on. He wasn't listening to her, so she sat up and looked him in the eye.

"I said, I have fat thighs. My hips are too wide and I'm pretty sure that one boob is bigger than the other."

Dean looked up towards heaven and shook his head slowly. She poked him in the ribs.

"Are you listening to me?'

With a sigh that could only be described as long suffering, he gave her his full attention.

"Maddie," he said carefully, "everyone is listening to you."

Slowly, she took her eyes off Dean to look at the two men sitting facing her. One of them was beetroot red and staring into space, the other winked at her.

"You look all right to me darling," he said.

Gathering what dignity she could, she turned to Dean.

"I'm going to the toilet. I'll be there for the rest of the trip. Come get me when we arrive."

And before he could stop her she ran for the sanctuary of the public loo.

She stared at her red flushed face in the mirror and groaned. Honestly, if she had a gun she'd put it to her head. Pulling down the tiny flip up stool attached to the wall she resolved never to show her face in public again.

"Maddie?" Dean's voice boomed through the door. "We're pulling in to Victoria. You can come out now."

She opened the toilet door and gave him a sheepish look.

"I need to learn to self-censor," she said.

He wrapped his arm around her.

"You wouldn't be you if you did."

She was still reeling from her humiliation all the way back to Chelsea. As Dean stroked the palm of her hand she felt anxious. She followed him up to his apartment aware that her mood had changed.

Dean led her in to the living room and turned to face her.

"Do you want a drink?'

"No," she said. "Look, I know this was my idea, but I've kind of lost the mood."

A slow smile, heavy with meaning, lit up his face as he closed the distance between them.

"I can help with that," he said.

He placed one hand on each side of her face and leaned into kiss her. All Maddie could think was that she had fat thighs and not only did he know it, but the world knew it. And then he touched her lips and she didn't think at all. It was like a match to kindling. Whoosh. She was gone.

She grabbed fistfuls of his jumper in a desperate attempt to get closer to him and felt him grin against her mouth. He pulled away from her.

"See," he said, "you were worried about nothing."

"When my brain is working again," she told him, "I'm going to think of something scathing to say."

"I'll look forward to it."

He took her hand and led her to his bedroom, which was perfectly neat as usual.

"Last chance to back out," he said.

For a second she thought she'd play with him a little and

make him think that was actually an option, but he was so endearing that she couldn't.

"You're mine now," she told him.

Dean's eyes went from violet to black as he wrapped his arms around her. His kisses were like waves pounding on the sand. Soft teasing bites, deep exploring tastes, gentle feather kisses, hungry desperate kisses. It seemed to go on forever making her react in rhythm to his touch. At last he released her bruised mouth and nibbled his way down her neck, removing her cardigan as he did so and allowing it to puddle at her feet.

Maddie pulled at his jumper trying to get it over his head, but he was in the way. She stepped back from him in frustration.

"This isn't working." She frowned. "Take off your clothes. Now."

"Yes ma'am."

He saluted before doing exactly what she told him.

The jumper was thrown in a heap on the chair in the corner of the room, the t-shirt followed allowing Maddie to feast her eyes on a bare-chested Dean. With mischief in his eyes he slowly unbuttoned his jeans. She pulled her bottom lip between her teeth and thought she might faint. His blue jeans slid slowly down his legs. He kicked them off. He hooked his thumbs in the waist band of his grey jockey briefs, but kept his eyes on her. There was no mistaking what lay underneath.

"Oh my," she said breathlessly.

Slowly the pants were discarded. Maddie felt her face burn and her breath quicken as he stood before her in all his glory. For a minute she feasted her eyes on him. And he let her, obviously pleased at her reaction. Every inch of the man was toned perfection. Her legs wouldn't keep her up any longer and she landed with a dull thud on the edge of the bed.

"Your turn." His voice was husky.

She gulped. Hesitating. She didn't have his confidence or his perfect physique. He almost read her mind.

"You're beautiful. There is absolutely nothing about you that I would change."

With shaky confidence she stood before him. Quickly, before she changed her mind and demanded that the lights be turned off, she ripped off her t-shirt. He gasped, which made her feel stronger, sexier.

She unzipped her jeans and stepped out of them, standing before him in pink satin underwear. He looked like he was about to start drooling. Maddie smiled. He'd said she was beautiful and she felt beautiful. She reached behind her back to unclasp her bra.

"No."

He reached for her and grasped her wrist in his huge hand. A flicker of insecurity rushed through her.

"Underwear like that should be enjoyed first," he said as he pulled her into his arms.

Relief and desire overwhelmed her in equal measures. And then the sensation of being skin to skin with Dean replaced any thought she might have had. At last she was able to get her hands on his body.

Maddie didn't know what to touch first - it was driving her crazy. She ran her hands over his shoulders, down his back and over his backside. Dean walked her back to his bed as he kissed her; she fell into the thick soft duvet, the soft cotton felt delicious on her skin. Dean lay the length of her, one arm under her shoulders, the other caressed her breast through the satin material. She gasped as she arched up to him. Her eyes closed without her telling them to.

He bent his head low to kiss her breast through the fabric. Maddie groaned. This was Dean. Her friend. And now her lover. It made perfect sense. His body fit hers as though they had been designed as one unit. Weaving her fingers through his hair, she let him love her. Each touch set off a chain reaction of need throughout her body. When he hooked his fingers into the waistband of her pants and tugged them over her hips, she was gone. All she could feel was Dean. All she could think was Dean. All she wanted was Dean. Forever. And as she took all of him, she knew then that she was in love. Heady, over the top, love with her friend. And she hoped it would never end.

MORNING CAME FAST after a short and active night. Maddie stretched out in Dean's bed languorously enjoying the thrill of the plump bedding against her naked body. She could hear banging around in the kitchen and indulged herself with a wide satisfied smile. Perfect. Everything was perfect. Dean had been everything she imagined and more. He was a considerate and talented lover who made her crazy with the slightest touch. And she loved him. Her chest burst with it.

She loved the way he made her feel. She loved the way he made her laugh. She loved his dark hair and those light penetrating eyes. She loved his body and the way his movements were a symphony of precision and power. She loved the way his voice sent vibrations right through her. She loved his kindness and his strength. She even loved the way he'd taken time to fold their discarded clothes and pile them neatly on the chair. She loved him. And it felt wonderful.

The door opened. Dean sauntered in looking delightfully ruffled in blue jeans and nothing else. He carried a tray, which he placed on the bed beside her. It had a carafe of coffee and a plate of her favourite cinnamon buns.

"Did you buy these in because you were counting on me having breakfast here?" she asked.

"No, I keep a stock on hand in case I need them to fix anything else I screw up."

She patted his arm.

"Poor delusional boy, what works once won't necessarily work the next time."

"Well, I guess we better not fight because after the buns I'm all out of ideas."

"You know," she told him, "this room looks like a hospital waiting room. It needs colour. I'll buy you some nice bright linen that should help."

"Does the linen come with you attached?'

"Maybe," she teased.

He reached over the tray to kiss her good morning. A nice thorough kiss that made her forget all about breakfast.

"Let's eat later," she whispered into his shoulder.

He made a strangled sound.

"I have a meeting with Ted at nine. I need to brief him on a new client."

She did her best Marilyn Monroe impersonation as she pouted and batted her eyelashes at the same time.

"And that's more important than me?'

"You're a wicked woman," he said as he pretended to hit her with the pillow. "I'll come back as soon as I can."

"No can do," she said with regret, "I'm meeting with the caterer this morning. I'll come into work with you and get the contact details for the colleagues that you want to invite then I have to go over to Fulham."

Dean looked at the clock; she could almost hear his mind tick over as he tried to calculate just what he could fit in to the time they had and still make it to work for nine. Taking the bun out of her hand he put it, and the tray, on the floor.

"I think there may be time to give you something to remember me by," he said as he climbed into bed beside her.

"You still have your jeans on, idiot."

"This isn't about me," he drawled with promise as his head disappeared under the duvet.

"Oh my," Maddie said as she closed her eyes and concentrated on his delicious caress.

It was definitely a step up from a cinnamon bun.

10

———

She felt like a giddy teenager stunned by her first love. She couldn't bear being in the same room with Dean without touching him. As she sat on the red sofa in the office, while he worked behind his desk, she groaned out loud. His look was a question.

"I want to go home and get naked," she answered.

The look he gave her turned her knees to jelly.

"Do you have any self-control?" he asked.

"Apparently not where you're concerned," she said. "Come on, Dean, blow this off and come with me. I'm sure the caterer can cope on her own and Ted may be immature but he is fine with the business."

"Why thank you, Maddie," Ted said with a grin as he entered the office. "That's the best compliment I've had all week."

She rolled her eyes at Dean who had gone into professional mode. The look on his face was as sombre as his suit. But Laura had been right about one thing. He did look irresistible in a suit.

"Well it's true," Maddie told Ted, "I don't know how you get away with half the things you do."

"Because I'm charming," he said as he sat beside her.

She felt her eyes sparkle as Dean bristled, upset that someone was crowding his territory.

"Unfortunately," Dean said, all business, "I do need to talk to Ted this morning, but I'll call you when I'm done."

Maddie knew a dismissal when she heard one. Mischief bubbled inside of her desperate to get out. He was so buttoned up sitting there acting all king of his domain. The Dean she had spent the night with, the one that laughed and played and teased her into a frenzy, that Dean was safely hidden under his crisp white shirt. That wouldn't do at all.

"Okay," she said breezily, pleased that his eyes narrowed with suspicion. "I guess it's time to get out of here."

She stood, taking time to smooth down yesterday's clothes. If she was going to make a habit of staying at his place she really needed to leave some fresh clothes there.

"I'll just get that list from you," she said as she walked towards him.

"I emailed it to you," he said, but she was already round his side of the desk.

"Well thank you for that."

She smiled innocently. Before he could stop her she bent down grasped the back of his head and kissed him till her toes curled. When she finished she licked her lips and was pleased to see that Dean's polished persona was more than a little flustered.

"I'll see you later," she said as she practically danced from the room.

"Bye, Ted," she called to the grinning fool.

Maddie was on cloud nine as she waited for the lift.

This was it, she could feel it. This was the way her life was meant to be. She felt energised and tingly with anticipation knowing that later she would be alone with Dean. The only fly in her honey was the fact that she didn't know if he loved her or not, because she was sure that she loved him. In fact she suspected that some part of her had always loved him.

As the lift doors opened she reached for her shoulder bag before realising she'd left it on the office couch. She turned on her heels and made her way back to Dean's office, smiling at his staff as she went.

The door was slightly ajar, the way she'd left it. As Maddie reached for the knob she stopped suddenly at the sound of Ted's Aussie accent.

"So the seduction plan worked, I see."

His lascivious tone cut right through her joy, knocking it stone dead.

"That's none of your business," Dean growled.

"Ah, but it's a bit obvious isn't it. She's all over you like white on rice. See, I told you this latest idea of hers was good for something. You got her into bed at last. Now maybe you can concentrate on work instead of mooning over her all the time."

"How about you keep out of my love life? Let's focus on solely on the agenda for this meeting." Dean sounded irritated.

Maddie's cheeks burned as she listened. Her hand shook so she took it away from the door knob, folding it across her chest instead.

"So was it worth it?" Ted said. "All the effort you put in, going along with this business of hers, setting up the theatre trip, having a party that you don't want. Was it worth it?'

"I'm done talking about this," Dean said with a tone that

shook her. He hadn't denied any of it to Ted. "What goes on with Maddie and I is none of your business."

"Anymore," Ted clarified, "although you can thank me for my advice later. A nice bottle of decent Aussie wine should do it."

Dean grunted. Nausea assaulted Maddie. She'd heard enough, but her feet wouldn't move and just when she thought it couldn't get worse... It did.

"Have you told her that her business is doomed to failure?" Ted said.

"The conversation hasn't come up," Dean said.

"You mean you didn't want to ruin your chances with her over a healthy dose of reality," Ted mocked. "You know she might catch on when all those recommendations she's expecting don't materialise."

"I'll deal with that when it comes up," Dean said.

Tears stung her eyes. Nothing was making any sense. Her friend wouldn't use her like that. Wouldn't manipulate her like that. He was an honourable man. At least she always thought he was. Nothing made sense.

"If I was you, mate," Ted said, "I'd tell her before the week's trial is over otherwise what are you going to say – your business didn't impress me but you were great in bed, love?'

"I've had enough of this," Dean ordered.

"So have I," Maddie said as she pushed open the door.

The look of horror on Dean's face made her cringe. She felt ashamed to be around him. Ted on the other hand wasn't even embarrassed.

"I'll make things easy for you," she told Dean and was inordinately pleased to hear that her voice didn't shake. "I don't want you to vouch for me anymore. I'll manage without you. I will finish the party for you because, unlike you, I started this week honestly and in good faith. But after that we're through. I don't want you touching me and I definitely don't want to be your friend."

"Maddie, it's not like that." Dean stood, but she put out a hand to stop him.

"I better go," Ted said.

"No," she told him coldly, "you planned this together - you can hear the outcome together."

She turned to Dean.

"I thought you were an honourable man, I guess I was wrong. The friend I thought I had, wouldn't have played games with me or manipulated me. He wouldn't have led me to believe that he supported me, and would help me, while all along laughing at my efforts with his colleague. My friend definitely wouldn't have made love to me just because he wanted a woman and I was the nearest, and apparently easiest, option."

"You've got it all wrong," Dean said.

"I don't see how. I heard that you plotted to get me into bed. I heard that the theatre was a ruse, along with the party that you really don't want. I heard him ask how I was. And I heard that you never intended to support me."

She took a shaky step towards him, her heart shattering, sending shrapnel throughout her body and making all of her bleed.

"Did Ted help you figure out a way to seduce me?'

He said nothing. She felt a tear run down her cheek.

"Did you ever intend to help me get clients?'

His silence was deafening.

She walked over to the sofa and calmly picked up her bag. She tried to walk in a straight line to the door as her vision blurred.

"Now I know what it's like to feel cheap," she told them as she closed the door gently behind her.

Maddie didn't see or hear anything else during her long walk to the elevator. A pain she never knew was possible exploded inside of her. It took all of her self-control not to succumb to the agony and curl up in a ball on the floor. Instead she held her head high as she stumbled out into Central London. Her only plan was to get as far away from Dean as she could. Before she broke entirely.

DEAN DIDN'T KNOW what had hit him.

"This meeting is over," he told Ted.

"What about the clients?'

"Make it up."

He grabbed his jacket and ran from the building.

Maddie was nowhere in sight. He wasn't sure if that was a good thing or a bad thing as he really didn't know what he would say to her. He couldn't deny any of it. He had spent a week lying to her, inventing work so that he could get her into bed. He did think her business was a disaster and didn't want to be associated with it. It was all true. And it wasn't. He had only done these things because he was crazy in love with her and desperate to make her love him too. And now it seemed like he had blown his chances. The pain made him double over and gasp for air. Passers-by gawped at him. He didn't care. He had to sort this. He had to find Maddie and make it right. Somehow.

He hailed a taxi and ordered the driver to take him to her Clapham flat. She wasn't there, or if she was she was hiding out and refusing to answer the door. He sat on the stairs outside her door and tried to calm down, to think logically. If only he'd told her that he loved her. That he'd always loved her. Now if he said it she wouldn't believe him. But he had to try. He had to find her. Think, he ordered himself. Approach this logically. She said she was going to the caterer in Fulham. He ran down the stairs and straight into another cab.

The caterer told him that Maddie had cancelled her appointment. He assured her that the party was still on, excused himself from a tasting session and went to the Sparkle offices to see if Laura had seen her.

"I expected better from you," Laura told him with a scowl as soon as he entered her office.

Even though her words cut, he was relieved to discover that Maddie had at least talked to her best friend.

"Where is she, Laura?"

"I'm not telling you." She glared at him with her huge owl-like eyes. "You really screwed this up."

"I know."

He ran his hand over his face. If only the panic would go away.

"She doesn't want to talk to you."

"Yeah, I get that, but I need to explain things to her."

"What is there to explain? She says you manipulated her into bed and that you had no intention of supporting her business."

"But I love her," he croaked.

It was the first time he'd said the words out loud and instead of causing joy they stung him.

She frowned at him.

"Well you have a funny way of showing it."

He threw himself into the only other chair in Laura's tiny office. He was far too big for it and heard it creak beneath him.

"How can I fix this?'

"I have no idea. But you sure put a lot of effort into screwing it up, so maybe you could deploy that huge brain of yours into sorting it out."

He deserved that.

"Tell me where she is - I need to explain why this happened."

She raised a sceptical eyebrow.

"Are you sure you know?'

He shrugged.

"I love her. I want to marry her. I have to fix this."

His stark honesty softened her tone.

"You put your reputation before hers. You weren't honest or open with her. And to make everything worse you involved Ted. He's the sleaziest man alive."

"I know, I know."

"That's the tip of the iceberg. Maddie thinks that your aim was only to bed her. Even you know that she thought you were coming on to her because you don't have time to find another woman. You just confirmed that for her."

"That's ridiculous," he scoffed.

"That's Maddie," she said earnestly. "You proved her fears. She feels convenient rather than wanted. Honestly, Dean, there are teenagers who read this magazine who know more about relationships than you do."

He held up his hands in a plea for understanding.

"It's Maddie, I can't think straight when I'm around her."

"Well you better start now, or you can kiss goodbye to any sort of forgiveness."

Laura walked around her cluttered desk to pat him on the shoulder.

"Fix this. No matter what it costs," she ordered him. "She's at her parents'."

Relief flooded through him.

"Thanks," he said as he ran for the door.

"Don't screw it up," she called after him.

He caught a train to Surrey and got off at Wallington. While he waited for a ride to the Lewis house he went over what he would say. Mainly he wanted to tell her that it wasn't cheap. That she wasn't cheap. Somehow he had to convince her that he loved her. The cab let him out in front of the Victorian semi and he took a deep breath.

"Can you wait?" he said.

He wasn't sure what his reception would be.

"It's your money," the driver said.

With grim determination he walked up the rose-bordered path to ring the bell. The lace curtains, in the bay window belonging to the living room, twitched. A few seconds later the door swung open.

"Well hell," Charlie said, then punched Dean in the face.

Dean didn't see it coming. One minute he was looking at his friend, the next he was staring into a blue spring sky. A hand materialised above his face. He grasped it and let Charlie pull him to his feet.

"Just so we're clear," Charlie said.

Dean would have done nothing less.

"I need to talk to Maddie," he said as he rubbed his eye.

"You've done enough." Charlie shook his head in disgust.

"It's not what you think."

"Knowing you, it probably isn't, but I told you right from the start what side I came down on in this. She's my sister. You don't screw with my sister. In any sense of the word."

"I need to fix this."

"It's too late. She doesn't want to see you."

Dean stood with his hands on his hips glaring at Charlie. They'd had stand offs before. There was no getting past either of them when the stubborn streak kicked in.

"Can you ask her if she wants to see me?'

"I did. She said no."

He let out a deep frustrated sigh.

"Look," he tried again, "I only want a minute."

"Find another way to get your message across. As far as Maddie is concerned your friendship is over." Charlie moved to close the door. "I'm still undecided. I told you not to hurt her, now you need to fix it."

Dean spoke through clenched teeth.

"Everyone keeps telling me that like I don't already know. And how, exactly, am I supposed to do that when no one will let me near her?'

"You're a smart guy. Figure it out. Fast."

The door shut in his face.

He wanted to roar at the top of his lungs. Instead he marched back to the waiting taxi.

"Are you okay?" his shocked driver asked.

"Fine," Dean growled. "Take me to Chelsea."

"You want to go all the way to Central London?" The taxi driver asked incredulously.

"Yes," Dean said in a clipped tone.

The driver manoeuvred the car out into traffic.

"As I said before mister. It's your money."

As the car wound its way through the Surrey streets up into South London, Dean sat in the back and planned. His eye throbbed, but it was the least he deserved for being such an idiot. An idea began to formulate. If he couldn't tell Maddie how much he loved her, he would have to show her.

Reaching into his inside jacket pocket he pulled out his Blackberry and went through his address list. As he dialled the first number he hoped his idea would work. All he needed was to soften her defences enough to make her want to talk to him. He needed a chance to apologise. The alternative was too painful to contemplate. He had only just managed to get her in his life the way he wanted. He couldn't lose her forever.

11

"Maddie, it's the phone for you, darling," he mother said sweetly.

She hadn't told her family the whole story of what was going on between her and Dean. The last thing her parents needed was the sorry details of her love life, but they knew enough to tread lightly around her and to be angry with him on her behalf.

"I don't want to talk to anyone," she told her mother.

"You might want to take this. It's the CEO's secretary from Dunbar Finance."

With confusion Maddie took the phone from her mother's hand.

"Madeline Lewis," she said.

"Hello, my name is Patrick Smart, I work for Patricia Dunbar. We heard that you were starting a service for overworked executives and we'd like to know more."

Maddie's heart beat faster. She didn't need Dean after all. At last something was going right in the day from hell.

"That's right," she told the caller. "I'm just getting it off the ground. Our website goes live a week from now and then we'll start booking in work."

"Do you have something you could send us in the meantime?'

Maddie's mind raced. She had leaflets already designed. If she called as soon as she hung up and paid for a rush job she would be able to post it out over the weekend.

"Let me take your details," she said in her best professional voice, "and I'll have my brochure sent out to you for Monday."

"That sounds great." The man rattled off the company address for her.

"Do you mind me asking how you heard about Wife For Hire? I haven't even started advertising yet."

"Oh word gets around," Patrick said vaguely. "Central London is like small town. Everybody talks to everybody else. Well thank you for your help. I'll look forward to receiving that information."

Maddie hung up to face her mother's curious look.

"Someone is interested in my business," she told her with bewilderment.

"That's fantastic, dear." her mother kissed her on the head. "I knew this one was a winner."

Maddie beamed at her, aware that her red tear-stained eyes made her look rather pathetic. Before she could say anything else the phone rang.

"It's for you," her mother said, her eyes wide with astonishment. "TSB investment division."

Maddie took the call with a sense of excitement. As soon as she was finished she called her designer and asked her to send the leaflet to the printer for a rushed run, then she pressurised her into working up some headed paper and business cards for her as well. She'd pay a premium for weekend work but she was certain that she had to make a good impression. She couldn't screw this opportunity up.

Round about the fifth call of the afternoon she began to wonder how all of these corporate assistants had managed to track her to her parent's house. All of the callers mysteriously knew where to find her. All gave the same vague answer when she asked how they had found out about her business. And all of them were dealing in the financial sector in one way or another. After the twelfth call it was clear that Dean was behind the sudden interest in her new venture. If her brain hadn't been so clogged up with Dean's garbage the thought might have occurred to her a little earlier. Unfortunately she wasn't in her right mind. Last night pretty much proved that.

She sat in the middle of the living room floor surrounded by paperwork, the phone at her side, wondering what to do.

"Sandwich," her brother said as he came into the room.

He plonked a tuna creation big enough to feed a family of four beside her. Maddie recognised her mother's loving touch when she saw it. To her mother there was nothing that couldn't be fixed with a good meal and a hug. She smiled as she bit into the thing.

Charlie sat on the Lazy-boy, threw one leg over the arm and munched a matching sandwich.

"Dean," she told him. "He's sending me new clients. Calling all over London apparently."

"That's good isn't it?"

"I don't know," she said. "I really should throw the whole thing back in his face. He made it clear that he thought the business was doomed to failure. So this is his new version of a cinnamon bun."

"Now you've lost me, sis," Charlie said as he eyed up her

half-eaten sandwich. She handed it to him without thinking.

"Guilt present. His version of an apology. Or a bribe. I'm not sure which."

"Ah," Charlie said through a full mouth. "Must be an apology. Dean's not sneaky enough to think bribe."

A week ago she would have agreed with him.

"So are you going to give the gift back?'

"It's tempting, but this is a huge chance for me. I think I'll take it and consider it payment for services rendered," she said with disgust.

"I really don't want to hear that." Charlie frowned at her.

"It's how I feel. I put out. Now he's buying me off."

"You know Dean as well as I do. That would never occur to him."

She looked up at her brother as she felt a new batch of tears sting her eyes.

"I don't know what he would think anymore."

He ruffled her hair before leaving the room, shaking his head as he went.

The phone calls stopped when the business day ended. Maddie had fourteen companies interested in using her service. She should have been elated. She'd known it was a good business venture and the interest it had generated proved her right. Instead she felt broken. It hurt to think and her eyes were scratchy from crying through pretty much the whole day. After struggling to eat another lovely meal for her mother's sake, Maddie climbed into her old bed, relieved to be away from the concerned faces of her family.

The posters on the walls hadn't been taken down from her teen years. The dresser held photos of her and Laura doing everything teenage girls were expected to do, and always with grins on their faces. In amongst the pictures younger versions of Charlie and Dean beamed out at her. The tears started again. She closed her eyes as she hugged herself to sleep. Things would be better tomorrow. They had to be.

FRIDAY DIDN'T START WELL. She dragged herself down to breakfast without even stopping to brush her hair. As her mother poured her a cup of tea, her father gently kissed her cheek.

"Say the word, poppet, and he's fish food," he told her.

She gave him a big hug, revelling in how much she loved her parents.

As her mother put a full cooked breakfast in front of her, and Maddie wondered how she was going to eat it, the phone rang.

"It's probably for you," her mother said as she answered it.

There was a long silence while her mother listened to the caller. Her face was grim.

"I'll tell her," was all her mother said before hanging up.

Maddie waited for the inevitable bad news.

"That was Dean. He said you two have a deal and he expects you to be at the party tonight to make sure things go as planned."

Any appetite she had disappeared.

"You don't need to go just because he tells you to," her father said gruffly.

"I know."

She also knew that Dean was pulling the strings. A lot of the executives who were interested in her business would be at his party. If she didn't show up and make it go smoothly they would think she couldn't do the job. He was smart, she gave him that. Well fine. She could be as professional and uptight as him any day. She'd run his bloody party, but it wouldn't do him any good.

"It's okay, Dad," she said. "I want to do a good job. Plus Charlie will be there to run interference."

At least she hoped so. As soon as he dragged his lazy backside out of bed she'd order him to go.

It was while she was brushing her teeth that panic set in. If she took on all of the business that had been promised there was absolutely no way that she could cope. Organising Dean's work had taken up most of her time in the past week - how was she supposed to juggle the demands of fourteen, maybe many more, clients? She sat down on the toilet seat with a thud. She needed staff and fast. The sad thing was that she hadn't even considered this before it hit her. A slow realisation nudged her brain. She remembered Dean trying to talk to her about planning ahead the day they went to Brighton. He had read her business plan, she bet he'd seen the problem. She felt like a fool, she'd gotten the recommendations she'd craved but now she needed help and there was nothing she could do about it. How was she supposed to support staff when her whole start up fund barely covered her marketing plan?

It was exactly the type of problem she would have taken to Dean, hoping he would come to her rescue. For years she had taken it for granted that he would always be there to catch her when she fell. This time she had to figure it out for herself.

By the time she was dressed and seated at the dining room table ready to brainstorm, she'd worked herself into a state. The phone rang. Charlie picked it up and handed it to Maddie without even saying hello.

"Madeline Lewis," she said.

"This is Tanya Gibbs at Recruitment Solutions. I'm sorry to disturb you at home, but your assistant said that this needed your approval. He was quite adamant about that. We've emailed the contracts over for you to read and sign, but if you're happy with the arrangement then we are too."

"Okay," Maddie said slowly, her mind buzzing.

"Great," Tanya said. "Have a good weekend, Ms Lewis, we look forward to working for you."

As soon as she hung up she logged on to her parents" computer. Her brother sat on the dining table swinging his legs and eating as usual.

"What is it?" he said.

"I'm not sure."

She opened the email from the recruitment people and read the attachment, her eyes widening as she did so.

"Well?" Charlie nudged her with his foot.

"It's Dean's version of flowers," she said.

"English, little sister, English."

She spun around in the chair to look at him.

"Dean was a step ahead of me. He knew I needed staff for this idea to work, otherwise I would be overwhelmed very quickly by the workload. He also figured out that I couldn't afford staff."

She took a deep breath.

"And?" He made a wind up motion with his hand like they did on TV.

"He's used his muscle to negotiate a deal with a leading temp agency. I agree to use their staff for a year at a very decent rate and on a pay as you go basis, in return I put their name on everything and recommend them to all of my powerful clients. They get free advertising where they need it most, and I get the staff I need."

"That is pretty cool."

"Yeah," she said feeling more than a little stunned.

"What are you going to do now?'

"We," she said pointedly, "are going to give Dean the best party he could hope for and then I am going to say goodbye and get on with my life."

He looked pained.

"Isn't that a bit harsh? I mean the man saved your business."

"Not because he wanted to."

"No, but he did do it. It makes you wonder what else he would do for you."

"No," her eyes narrowed, "it makes me wonder what he wants in return."

Maddie called Dean's office to make sure that he was still at work before she went to his house to prepare for the party. She let herself in and wished her brother was there with her. His other commitments meant that he wouldn"t be turning up until the later in the evening. In the meantime she was on her own until the caterer arrived.

The place was as cold and pristine as usual. Even the paintings on his walls were black and white. She shook her head sadly. Maybe deep down Dean was closer to his stark environment than to the passionate guy she'd known during their night together. She wondered what had been real and what hadn't. Thinking about it made her head hurt.

She arranged the CDs that she'd collected on her way over, making sure they were in the order that she wanted them to be played. After that she made sure the lighting was perfect. The bathrooms were checked for towels, soap and plenty of paper. Furniture was rearranged so that nobody would fall over anything and there was plenty of space to mingle. She didn't bother clearing space to dance - none of Dean's friends would dare let loose in his home. She sighed.

It was easier to think mean things about him than to concentrate on the memories that assaulted her from being in his home.

When she got the living areas sorted to her liking she took a deep breath and pushed open his bedroom door. She let out a long shaky sigh of relief when she saw the silver frame of the new bed Dean had ordered. At least that bed didn't have any memories attached to it. She caught sight of herself in the full length mirror in the corner of the room and it made her heart sink. Although she'd worn her classic little black dress and plain black heels to appear business-like, they actually gave the impression that she was in mourning. And she supposed she was. In her haste to get the evening over with, she hadn't even put on any jewellery. It was as though all colour had been drained from her. For the first time in her life, that she was aware of, she fit perfectly into her surroundings.

The room was spotless. Between Dean and his cleaning staff, there wasn't an item out of place. Slowly, she ran her fingertips over the pale cotton duvet cover. She had intended to buy Dean some colourful sets to brighten up the place, which would never happen now.

"I'm sorry, Maddie."

His deep voice startled her and she spun around to find him standing in the doorway. He had the look of a penitent man. Remorse wasn't the problem. The problem was that she didn't know what to believe anymore. Did he have an agenda? Did he want something else from her? Was he playing her again? She couldn't look at him, it hurt too much.

Dean took a step into the room, making her back up towards the bathroom. She thought she heard him curse under his breath.

"I never meant to hurt you," he said.

"Well you did."

Thankfully her voice sounded strong.

"Can we sit and talk?'

"I don't think so, Dean. I have nothing to say."

"But I do," he said with determination. "I need you to listen to me and then you can keep on hating me if you want to."

"I don't hate you. I feel nothing," she lied.

"Let's get out of here. We'll go find a café and talk. The party can run itself."

She felt the tug of temptation, but shook her head instead. There was nothing to say and nothing that she wanted to hear. She'd been hurt enough.

"No," she said.

She looked up at him and gave a small gasp at the black eye he sported. He saw her reaction and smiled slightly.

"Charlie," he said by way of an explanation.

"Well," she said with bravado, "it saves me the trouble."

Dean gave her a timid grin and she felt herself weaken towards him. No. She wasn't that easy. Not again. She straightened her back, held her head high and pushed past him into the living room.

"Thanks for the flowers," she said coldly.

He knew exactly what she meant and nodded. Maddie ignored the tug at her heart. There wasn't an explanation in the world for how he'd behaved towards her.

The caterer arrived a minute later, allowing Maddie to breathe a sigh of relief that there was a buffer between them. Dean's bedroom door closed with him on the other side, no doubt getting ready for the party.

When the guests started to arrive there was no sign of Dean. Maddie did her best to be a gracious host, directing people to food and drink, putting jackets in the spare room and answering curious questions about her business from those who knew who she was. Charlie turned up wearing jeans and a t-shirt that said "party hearty" across it. The women in the room began to swoon and Maddie rolled her eyes as he flirted his way across to greet her.

"You are a tart," she told him.

"Apparently so are you," he said and watched her face fall.

He gave her a hug.

"Sorry sis, forgot that we weren't doing humour. Where is he anyway?'

"Probably trying to cover the shiner you gave him."

Charlie grinned.

"He got off lightly. I was planning on breaking his legs."

She didn't know whether to thank him or tell him off. She didn't need to decide; Charlie caught the eye of a cute blonde in the corner and went to keep her company leaving Maddie standing alone by the kitchen counter. Laura arrived not long afterwards. She marched directly over to Maddie and gave her a big hug.

"Are you okay?"

"Holding up," Maddie said.

It was hard not to start crying again now that her friend was there with her.

"Maybe you should talk to him," Laura said gently.

"And say what?" She was genuinely at a loss.

"Well, perhaps you could just listen. He might have a good explanation."

She shook her head.

"I can't."

Her friend squeezed her hand before Charlie's loud laugh caught her attention.

"I see the Neanderthal is here," Laura said grimly.

"Play nice," Maddie told her, "please."

"Fine," Laura grumped and wandered off to get a drink.

Dean materialised a minute later. To her surprise he wore black jeans and a grey t-shirt. She had been expecting another suit, like most of the men in the room. He smiled his way through the throng of people shaking hands and exchanging small talk. Although Maddie didn't make it obvious, she kept a close eye on where he was at all times and did her best to keep at least five people between them.

The stereo played soft easy-listening in the background as the crowd chatted and mingled. The nibbles were going down a treat. She'd been right about how good the caterer was; she'd definitely use her again. She'd been momentarily distracted by her assessment of the party and she didn't notice when Dean came up behind her. It was only when she heard him speak softly beside her ear that she realised where he was. Her traitorous body tingled at the sound of his voice.

"Are you ever going to talk to me?" he said.

She instantly felt tense and teary. Damn him.

"I don't plan to," she said without turning around.

"Well then, you leave me no choice," he said.

She didn't have time to ask him what he meant. When she turned he was climbing up onto a dining room chair.

"Can I have everyone's attention?" he boomed.

Slowly the room went silent as people turned towards him with smiling faces and glasses full of champagne or wine.

Somebody turned the music off. Maddie didn't know why, but she had a sudden desire to run.

"Thank you for coming tonight. I appreciate it," said his deep voice. "Now I have to ask you to leave."

A shocked gasp swept around the room.

Maddie felt her cheeks burn. Was this her punishment for not talking to him? Was he going to ruin the same business opportunities that he'd set up for her?

"We'll do this again some other time," he was telling the stunned group, "but right now I need to talk to Maddie and you people are getting in my way."

Maddie's eyes widened in complete horror, but her feet were rooted to the spot. She saw Charlie push away from the wall on the other side of the room and amble towards them, shaking his head as he did so. Nobody else moved. She felt Laura's hand on her arm in a gesture of solidarity. Dean's behaviour was not only rude but completely out of character. Everyone stood staring at him, waiting for the punch line.

"Ted will help you get your coats," Dean said, "won't you?'

It wasn't a request. Ted threw open the door to the spare room.

"What's going on Montgomery?" one of the business suits shouted.

Dean frowned then looked at Maddie. She thought she saw indecision in his eyes, which was quickly replaced by a steely determination.

"It's like this Bob," he told the man. "I screwed up my relationship and I need to fix it."

The men in the room nodded with grim identification while the women melted. Maddie couldn't believe that stiff upper lipped Dean was broadcasting his personal life. Their personal lives. She got the impression that he sensed the room was working for him rather than against him, but she was still stunned to see him carry on.

"The truth is," he told his friends and colleagues, "I love

Madeline Lewis but I haven't told her yet. So she thinks that I've been manipulating her to get her into bed."

She wished the ground would open up and swallow her as the men in the room grinned. A couple of women made a big deal out of fanning themselves. Maddie felt the urge to punch Dean's other eye.

He turned to her and she got the full force of the single-minded and intimidating persona that he used to good effect in business.

"And I do love you, Maddie," he said without a hint of ulterior motive. "I've always loved you. I always will."

A few people started to clap and Maddie felt like she was trapped in some American reality television show. She half expected someone to thrust a mic in her face and demand to know her response. With everyone's eyes on her it was tempting to behave the way they wanted her to, to declare undying love and fall into his arms. She bet Dean was counting on that too. It was a double whammy for him. Instant forgiveness along with the fact most of the people present wouldn't even care that he'd chucked them out. Well to hell with that. She put her hands on her hips and glared up at him.

"It's going to take a lot more than you making a fool of yourself to earn my forgiveness," she told him.

She promptly turned on her heels and marched towards the door.

Charlie grinned at her as she stormed past him.

Suddenly a strong arm snaked around her waist. She was thrown into the air and dumped unceremoniously over Dean's shoulder. Maddie fumed at the thought of her huge backside in the air for everyone to see. And the worst thing was that everybody watching seemed much more amused than disgusted by his behaviour.

"Let me down," she shouted as she pounded Dean's back.

He held her tightly around her legs rendering her unable to kick. Maddie reviewed her options. There weren't many. She wasn't even hanging at the right angle to bite him. It made her even more furious.

"Charlie," she shouted.

Dean stopped abruptly in front of her brother.

"I let you get away with the right hook. You interfere now and I'm taking you down," he told his friend.

Maddie saw an upside down Charlie shrug.

"You're on your own, sis," he said.

Oh, he'd pay for that later.

"Isn't anyone going to help me?" she shouted to the room. Laura smiled weakly at her and she felt betrayed.

There was a rippling of laughter.

"Honey," a female voice shouted back, "I'd sit back and enjoy the ride if I was you. I know I would."

Dean threw open his bedroom door and manoeuvred her in.

"Thank you for coming," he told everyone, "either stay and enjoy the food or go. I don't care. I'm going to be busy."

He then shut the door to whoops of delight and raucous laughter. Maddie heard the door click and felt Dean pocket the key.

"This is kidnapping, you idiot," she told him.

"If that's what it takes."

He plopped her down in the middle of his bed. Maddie couldn't decide where to hit him first.

He narrowed his eyes.

"I can take you in a fight," he told her calmly.

"I might take my chances anyway," she snarled at him.

"We're talking," he told her, "and I'm not letting you out until I'm finished. Maybe not even then."

Maddie was so furious she couldn't see straight. He stood at the edge of the bed, arms folded across his chest, giving her a look that told her clearly he wasn't playing games.

"Fine. Talk," she snapped.

"I'm sorry," he started.

"Ha!'

"If you aren't going to listen properly I'm going to gag you," he told her.

She wasn't sure if he was serious, but a thrill coursed through her body. She stamped the feeling dead. He was being a bully and an idiot if he thought this approach was going to work.

"I'm sorry," he said again. "I'm an idiot."

"You get no arguments there."

He ran a frustrated hand through his hair, making it stand on end.

"I can't seem to see straight or think clearly where you're concerned."

"That's your excuse? You were blinded by lust?" she mocked.

"No." He leaned over the bed placing a hand on each side of her hips and stared directly into her eyes. "Not lust - love."

Her traitorous heart beat itself silly with happiness. Her brain wasn't so easily charmed.

"I'm supposed to believe that? You never mentioned love the whole time we were together. Not once. And now suddenly I'm the love of your life. It's a bit hard to swallow."

Dean ground his teeth.

"Maddie, think for a minute," he said. "What do I have to gain by lying to you about this?'

Her brain ticked over, hampered by his handsome face.

"Maybe this whole love thing is to buy you some time to make sure that your friendship with Charlie will be okay when you dump me?'

He shook his head in astonishment.

"I should never, ever, ask you to think something through. There is no telling where it will lead."

He pushed himself off of the bed and paced in front of her. Adrenalin coursed through Maddie. What was he thinking, what should she do? She wanted to believe him.

With purpose, he unlocked the door and threw it wide.

"Charlie," he shouted, "you still here?'

A minute later Charlie appeared in the doorway.

"What is it?" he said.

"I'm letting you know that this friendship is over. I choose your sister." He turned to Maddie. "Happy now? That shoots a hole through your theory. I'm not doing this to make sure I stay friends with your brother."

Charlie looked between the two of them. His expression was blank.

"Do you know what I think?" her brother said. "I think that you're both crazy and deserve each other. I'm out of here."

Dean shut the door again, taking the time to re-lock it and pocket the key.

"Happy now?" he demanded.

More bewildered, Maddie thought. As she started to calm down she took more notice of her surroundings. The light in the room was purple because there was a scarf draped over the beside lamp. The two framed black and white photos on the wall had been replaced by colourful abstract paintings. The cream cotton duvet was now an embroidered shock of colours on a purple satin background. She looked at Dean in astonishment.

"I need colour in my life," he said softly. "I need to wake up every day wondering what it will bring because you are in it and I have no idea where that will lead me. I need to trip over clutter that drives me crazy and spend my free time saving your latest idea from certain failure. I need to be able to wrap my arms around you and feel your excitement for life. I need all of you." He paused and then gave her a slow mischievous grin. "I even need those uneven boobs of yours."

It was the humour that knocked down Maddie's last defence against him. The Dean the world knew would never joke at a time like this, especially not in such an inappropriate way, but her Dean would.

"Did you really get Ted to plan a seduction for you?" she asked and watched as some of the tension went out of his shoulders. He knew he was forgiven.

"What can I say? I was a desperate man."

"Don't you know how to seduce a woman?" She pretended to mock him.

"I'm still not sure how to seduce you," he said with a brutal honesty that undid her. "I'm so damned scared of screwing it up and losing you forever." His eyes seemed to see right through her. "That's why I'm not letting you out of this room until you agree to marry me. That way I know I'll have to screw up big time to make you leave me."

She gasped. Marry him?

Dean reached out and pulled her up to sit on the edge of the bed. Maddie was in shock as she watched him root around in his pocket for something. Slowly, he knelt in front of her between her legs, getting as close to her as possible.

"Marry me?" he said as he showed her a ring. "Please."

She sat stunned as he lifted her left hand and slipped a pink plastic ring, with a red enamel heart stuck to it, over her ring finger.

He rested his hands on her thighs as he waited for her answer. There was a raw vulnerability in his face that melted her heart.

Marry him?

She looked at the ring on her finger. It was perfect.

"I still haven't forgiven you," she told him.

"Marry me and you can take your time making me pay."

"And I haven't said that I love you."

If she didn't know better she would think that he held her legs so tightly to stop his hands from trembling.

"Do you?" he said.

Maddie stared into those impossibly violet eyes and forgot why she was angry. Every inch of her body screamed yes.

"I tell you what," she told him, "why don't you make me."

A slow smile lit up his face.

"So you do love me." He grinned widely.

"I didn't say that. You have to put in more effort than one week and two dates to get love out of this girl. Not to mention the whole lying to me and planning to sabotage my business."

"I never intended to sabotage your business. But I knew that there were holes in the planning."

"But you thought it was going to be a failure and you were determined not to support me even though I needed you."

He looked skyward.

"Okay. Name your price. What is it going to take to make this go away?'

She smiled gleefully.

"I want it in the vows. I want you to promise to support whatever idea I may come up with no matter how stupid you think it is."

Dean slid his hands under the hem of her dress, making her breath catch in her throat.

"Stop trying to distract me. I want a promise here."

As he slid his hands up and down her thighs, making her mouth go dry, his voice became dangerously low.

"Okay, I will vow to support all of your crazy ideas on the condition that you at least take my advice about how to make them work."

She pretended to think about that for a minute even though she was actually focusing on the wonderful sensation of his touch on her thighs.

"But you can't mock me or put me down, no matter how insane you think it is."

"I promise," he said solemnly.

He leaned in towards her neck.

"I'm not finished," she told him.

"I'm listening," he said as he kissed along her collar bone.

She swallowed hard.

"I want you to send Ted to one of those workshops that treat sexism in the workplace. Something run by a big old scary woman."

A guffaw of laughter escaped him before he continued kissing up her neck to her ear.

"That I will happily do."

As he nibbled on her earlobe she briefly lost her train of thought. What was it now? Oh yeah, she was still mad.

"I also want you to vow that I am solely in charge of all future house decoration."

"Done."

"With no complaints."

"Fine," he whispered in her ear sending a surge of adrenalin straight to her head and all the other important bits of her.

"Anything else?" he asked, as kissed his way around to her lips.

"I want to be called Madeline from now on," she said. "I think being called Maddie is detracting from my business persona."

She felt him grin against her cheek before he found her lips.

"Well," he spoke against her lips, making her eager for him to kiss them, "if that's all Madeline. I would like to get on with seducing you. We both know I need the practice."

"Quite right," she whispered as his lips covered hers.

She clung onto him for dear life as he kissed her until she wanted to beg for more. When he released her lips she was dizzy and weak. If she hadn't been sitting she would have fallen down.

Gently he brushed her hair back from her face.

"I love you, Madeline Lewis," he said softly.

Maddie was so overwhelmed by him that she couldn't speak. Instead she pulled him to her and tried to show him what she felt.

Dean made love to her tenderly, as though she was something precious. Afterwards, she lay wrapped in his arms and marvelled at how much had changed in her life in only a week. She traced her fingers in circles through the hair above his heart and listened to its steady beat.

"I do love you," she said and heard his heart pick up

speed. "I love you so much that it blows my mind to think about it. I think part of me has always loved you, and now all of me does."

Dean's strong arm wrapped her in tightly to him.

"I want to get married in Kenya," she said.

"Kenya?" She imagined he was rolling her eyes and she smiled. "You've never shown any interest in Africa. I've never heard you mention it before."

"Okay, how about Las Vegas then?'

"Is this some sort of test?" he said. "I only promised to support crazy business ideas. I didn't say I would any support other ones."

That was an oversight; she'd have to rethink their vows.

"Well I want to do something exciting," she told him.

"You will be, honey." She could hear the grin in his voice, "you'll be marrying me."

When she started to laugh Dean flipped her over onto her back and kissed her again.

EPILOGUE

They got married in London. At least he'd won that battle. It had been important to him that everyone he knew was able to see him marry the most amazing woman in the world. He wanted it out there that she was off the market for good. It took a little effort but he eventually found a minister who would perform a service in the London Eye. Each pod was equipped with a wide screen so that everyone could be part of the ceremony as they made their way to the top of the wheel.

Maddie wore pink, which made her skin glow and her hair shimmer. Laura was forced to wear a darker shade of the same colour and he overheard her complain that they looked like walking, talking candy floss. He wore a pale grey morning suit because Maddie had forbidden any black formal wear. Charlie insisted on being best man, even though Dean had made himself clear about dumping him as his friend. As far as he was concerned Maddie was the only Lewis who earned a say in his life. He figured that if Charlie insisted that he hadn't been sacked then he might as well let him hang around. His friend was rarely in the country long enough to cause trouble anyway.

Maddie had been adamant about keeping the toy he'd bought as an engagement ring, so he made sure that they got designer platinum wedding bands. He engraved hers with "love forever" and she engraved his with "Maddie is the boss'.

They had their reception at the Lyceum Theatre bar. Dean had tried to get some of the cast of The Lion King to make an appearance, in their costumes of course, but they thought he was nuts. Being in love with Maddie had that effect on a man. Their wedding dinner took place at the Savoy and was peppered with completely inappropriate speeches. One of which was made by Maddie, who insisted it was her wedding and she could make a speech if she wanted to.

"This is to my husband," she had said. "Without me he would be a dull old fart obsessed with money and black three piece suits. I bring colour and excitement to his life."

The crowd had laughed and joined in her toast.

"He is also the love of my life," she continued, "the man who keeps my feet on the ground, who gives me direction and encourages all of my dreams. He holds me when I hurt, he kisses me when I'm down and he supports me when I'm clearly wrong. To Dean."

He had never wanted her more than when she'd given her speech. And the sparkle in her eye told him that she knew exactly what was on his mind.

Of course he'd vowed to support all of her crazy ideas no questions asked. After all he was one of them. And she had vowed to at least run them past him first before she acted on them. And their guests cracked up laughing when he promised she'd be in charge of interior design. It was safe to say his reputation wouldn't survive his wedding.

During the wedding reception he slow danced with his wife across the barroom floor. She still wore her puffy pink dress although her matching make up appeared to be long gone.

"You know," she said. "I'm tired of the Wife For Hire business. I think I'll get someone else to run it for me. It's time I branched out."

He rolled his eyes in exasperation. He hadn't vowed not to do that.

"I realised that I like starting things more than continuing them," she said ignoring his expression.

"Except for me."

"Of course."

She gave him a silly grin that made him feel like he'd been sucker punched.

"This time I thought I'd start a business that helped people start their own business. That way I'll only ever be involved in ideas for the exciting part. What do you think?'

He was genuinely, and pleasantly, surprised.

"I think it's a great idea."

"Good." She snuggled into him. "I'll need your help with it."

As usual, he thought as he hugged her close.

"Where are we going on honeymoon?" she asked, her voice muffled against his chest.

"Everywhere," he told her, as he thought of the round the world tickets he'd bought and the deal he'd made with Ted to take a year off work.

"I'm giving you the world Maddie."

"It's the least you can do," she told him.

LAURA'S BIG BREAK

LONDON GIRLS, BOOK 2

Janet Elizabeth Henderson

PROLOGUE

Laura Prentice gave away her cherry to her best friend's brother in the shed they called a summer house, at the bottom of his parent's garden. In fact, she gave away the whole sundae. He licked it up without so much as a thank you. Sure, he'd whispered sweet nothings as he'd peeled her pants down her legs and he'd gushed over her beauty as he reached for a condom, but as soon as the deed was done, he was gone. He ran faster than a fake hare on a rail at the race track. Meanwhile, Laura had adjusted her summer dress, hunted for her underwear and wondered what on earth she'd done.

She was a good girl, a sensible girl, sometimes the only sensible one in a life full of lunatics and yet there she was worshipping at the feet of Charlie Lewis, or as she had called him her whole life – the Neanderthal. It wasn't losing her virginity to Charlie that bothered her, it was the fact he'd run afterwards. Sure, she hadn't expected a lovefest, but she had hoped for a little civility, some polite conversation, maybe. Anything but a look that telegraphed –– oh no, what have I done? Now, that was one way to destroy a girl's self-esteem. Fortunately Laura Prentice's self-esteem was just fine. Why else would she have followed him to the shed and asked for sex? Well, apart from the fact she'd been crushing on him since forever and wasn't sure if she'd ever see him again when she went off to college. In the back of her mind she knew this wasn't her best decision, but she could take responsibility for her actions. What she couldn't stomach was the look on Charlie's face when he ran.

Her eyes narrowed as she tried to stalk up the path to his house. She had no idea sex would hurt so much. It felt pretty much the same as the time she'd landed astride on a fence, after her best friend Maddie had dared her to climb into a locked garden. Fine, she reminded herself, she was fine. She picked up the garden hose, which was fitted with Mr Lewis's new power blaster attachment, and aimed at the back of the house.

"Charlie," she called sweetly.

Silence.

Her eyes narrowed. Now she was getting annoyed.

"Charlie, come out here. I need to talk to you."

A window opened high in the house; Maddie stuck her head out.

"What?" she began, but the look on Laura's face silenced her. Instead she made a little oh shape with her mouth.

"Charlie," Laura shouted. "Get your backside out here NOW!"

The kitchen door slammed open and a red faced Charlie stepped out onto the back patio.

"What do you want?"

A powerful blast of water hit him square in the chest.

Laura smiled with some satisfaction as he fought the stream of water. He slipped. He slid. He fell on his backside. He choked and coughed and held up his hand to shield his face. Once she knew he was well and truly soaked she threw the hose on the ground and stomped over to him. His parents stood in the doorway, open mouthed.

"That," she pointed at the sorry excuse for a man, "is for not saying thank you Charlie Lewis."

She stormed past him.

"It's not going to be the same around here when she's at Uni," Mr Lewis said behind her as she strode through their home and out across the road to her own house.

Well, she'd learnt a lesson. Obviously the other girls he'd slept with had been soft in the head, because as far as she could see, sex with Charlie Lewis was nothing to write home about. In fact, she was pretty sure all sex wasn't worth the effort. As she slammed her bedroom door behind her she came to the conclusion that the male race as a whole were seriously overrated.

She was better off buying one of those rabbit things they were always talking about in Sex in the City.

1

———

"He's the star of the most watched clip on YouTube and you know him personally?" Claire Douglas almost had a stroke at the thought. "I've watched it myself about a million times. The way he carries that injured child out through gunfire, then tends to her wounds while his commander is calling for him to run. It makes the heart pound. He is the complete package – doctor, soldier, hero and absolutely gorgeous. The whole world wants to interview him and you have a way in. Why didn't you mention this?"

Because he's a Neanderthal. Because he's an idiot. Because I'd rather pickle my own eyeballs than talk to him.

Unfortunately she couldn't tell any of these reasons to her new boss, so Laura went with all she had left.

"Because he doesn't want to be interviewed."

"Piffle!" Claire threw her hands in the air.

Laura resisted the urge to grind her teeth. Her old boss had told her that everyone knew when she was doing it and it was a sure sign she was cheesed off.

"Of course he wants to be interviewed," Claire said. "He just hasn't been given the right opportunity."

She leaned over a desk the size of a football pitch.

"He needs to bare his soul to someone he trusts."

She pointed a well-manicured finger at Laura in case she was slow to catch up.

"You are the opportunity he's been looking for."

Laura took a long, slow, deep breath and went through a mental list of things you shouldn't do to your boss. 1 – Don't insult their intelligence. 2 – Don't throw staplers at their head.

"Charlie doesn't like me." She tried to sound reasonable and professional. "We hardly know each other and we never, ever talk. Ever."

"Pooh. I heard you tell one of the other staffers that you were his neighbour as a child. You said he's your best friend's brother. Why, he's practically family."

"Yes," Laura seized on that, "dysfunctional family. Family that hates each other."

Her boss folded her arms over her skeletal frame and pouted. Laura briefly wondered if there should be an age limit for pouting, because at fifty two Claire was definitely past it. Claire angled her chair so that she could cross her legs and point one red stiletto toe at Laura.

"You've been here what? Two weeks?"

Laura nodded, hence the stupid comments during lunch hour in an attempt to make friends with her new colleagues. She should have known better than to admit a relationship with the Neanderthal; it never went well.

"And after several, long years plodding away in teen magazines, you've decided to move up to publications for real women."

Laura couldn't help it, she gritted her teeth.

"Let's face it, although your work is good enough to get you a position here, it may not be good enough to keep you here. Am I making myself clear?"

Unfortunately, she was crystal.

"This isn't the same environment as you're used to; we care little about which vampire is biting which and whether Justin Bieber is a girl or a boy."

Laura was grinding her teeth so hard she would have to visit her dentist straight after the meeting.

"We deal with real stories, adult stories, and this is hot right now. To get this story is to get the coup. So stop making excuses, be the journalist we hired and get me the story. This is your only assignment for the time being. You have two weeks. Consider yourself on probation until then."

Claire waved a hand in dismissal. Laura stood stiffly, squelching the urge to throw something at her boss as she did so. She made it sound as though Laura was working for The Times not Francine, a woman's monthly magazine. They wrote stories about wrinkle cream and how to declutter your life. Why Claire wanted a story about an ex-solider she had no idea.

"And what if he won't talk to me?"

A cold blank stare was her answer.

Laura spun in her Converse and let herself out of the office. It took all of her self-control not to slam the door.

Maggie, Claire's assistant, smiled sympathetically as Laura passed her. No doubt she'd heard the whole thing. Laura stopped at the ladies room on her way to her desk. She splashed cold water on her face, soaking her striped t-shirt as she did so. Her reflection did nothing to lighten her mood; she looked haggard and homicidal - a great combination.

Three years she'd been chasing vacancies in the

women's magazines. Three long years of writing about Glee and Twilight. Three years of articles on how to create a great Facebook page, or how to tell if a boy likes you or – worse yet – why you haven't gotten your period when all your friends have theirs. She couldn't go back to that. She leaned her forehead on the cold glass of the mirror. How hard could this be? She'd seen Charlie at Maddie's wedding and he'd hardly annoyed her at all. Maybe being in Afghanistan had mellowed him. Maybe he wouldn't mind telling his story to a friend. She choked on the word.

Maybe a house would fall on Claire and leave nothing but her red shoes behind.

"Hey Doctor Hottie, I need some special medical attention."

Charlie kept his eyes on the chart in front of him while he took a deep breath. There was nothing quite as sexy as being hit on by a seriously drunk patient. Her mascara was halfway down her face, her boobs were halfway out her top and she had half a pizza in her hair. She still managed to wink at him when he eventually looked her in the eye.

"You need to go to x-ray," he said evenly. "The nurses will sort it out."

"No, I need to run my fingers through that thick hair of yours, blue eyes." She batted eyelashes that looked like spider legs.

She leaned towards him, reeking of stale alcohol and vomit.

"How about you and me draw the curtains and go a round first?"

Another wink.

"Tempting, but no."

He stepped back into the traffic of the busy Emergency Department, pulling the curtain shut behind him. Two nurses who'd witnessed the exchange burst out laughing.

"You can go "a round" with us if you like?"

One pretended to bat her eyelashes, while the other twirled her hair and licked her lips seductively.

"Yeah, Doctor Hottie, we're good to go."

They both winked before collapsing into another fit of hysterics. Charlie smiled indulgently. This had been going on all week. If he could get his hands on the moron who'd posted that video on YouTube, he'd cause him some serious damage. Between the incessant teasing of the other staff, fending off the amorous advances of drunken women and dodging phone calls from the press, he was seriously in need of a break. He looked at the clock high on the wall above the nurse's station. Three hours to go. Three long hours and then two glorious weeks" holiday.

He slipped the chart back into place with the others and picked up the next one on his list. Abdomen pains. Female. Great, a gynaecological problem. His day was just getting better.

"Don't let them get to you," Frank said. "It'll pass soon enough."

Charlie cocked an eyebrow at his friend, the senior nurse in ED; he wished he was that certain.

His rubber soled shoes made no noise as he wandered down to the last cubicle in the row. With a deep sigh he pulled back the curtain. His shoulders slumped even further.

"Please tell me this is a fake illness," he told his sister's best friend. "The last thing I want to do is give you a gyny exam."

"The feeling is mutual," Laura told him.

The ever present look of disgust, and disappointment, was firmly in place. Her hair was longer than the last time he'd seen her; apart from that she looked exactly the same – like an evil fairy. With her freckles, wide eyes and honey coloured hair she was innocence personified. He knew better. She sat on the edge of the bed, even though there was a chair in the cubicle. No doubt to give her a height advantage. At five two Laura was always thinking about height.

"What do you want?"

He crossed his arms over his worn blue scrubs and leaned against the wall. She pushed her oversized glasses up the bridge of her nose and straightened her shoulders.

"I want an interview."

That was one thing he liked about Laura. You always knew where you stood with her.

"No."

You could also be as blunt as you wanted and she never played the poor-delicate-girl card. Her eyes narrowed slightly.

"I need an interview."

"I need sleep. Looks like we're both disappointed."

He watched her jaw for the tell-tale sign she was grinding her teeth. Sure enough there it was. Any minute now there would be violence - that was something she'd learnt from his sister. Hit first, ask questions later.

"I'll get fired from my new job if you don't give me an interview."

"And I care, why?"

"You owe me."

He reeled back as though she'd hit him.

"You've got to be kidding? After a dozen years you're going to pull that one. I don't owe you anything. You came to me." He cocked an eyebrow and gave her his most lecherous leer. "You came for me."

No blush. That was Laura. Proper girls blushed. Not the Iron Maiden.

"I didn't come for you. You couldn't make me come if you tried. You have to have actual skill to achieve that and believe me, you don't have anywhere near the skill level. You owe me, moron, because you were an ass about the whole thing. I gave you my virginity and you never even said thanks. In fact you ran like the devil was on your heels." She jumped off the bed and pulled herself up to her full miniature height. "Now I'm collecting."

He was almost amused. Almost.

"So I'm supposed to lay my life at your feet for you to write about in some teen magazine because I didn't thank you for opening your legs for me a dozen years ago?"

He stepped towards her, crowding her space. She didn't back off, instead she put her hands on her denim clad hips and glared up at him.

"I don't work for a teen mag."

He had to shake his head to follow the conversation.

"Yeah, that was the most important part." He pointed at her tiny button nose. "I'm not giving you an interview. And I don't care if you're holding a grudge about my lack of manners. You begged me for sex."

"I didn't beg."

She poked him in the chest, making him growl.

"I remember exactly what happened," he said. "You followed me to the summer house. I told you to go away. You wouldn't. I said what the hell do you want? You said – sex. I gave you what you wanted. It's you who should have said thank you. Instead you had a hissy fit. So no, I don't owe you."

For a second he thought her green eyes flashed Satan red.

"We'll see about that," she warned. "This isn't over. I want an interview. I need an interview and I'm going to get an interview. Got it, Neanderthal?"

She poked him in the chest again before storming out of the cubicle. Charlie resisted the urge to shout something childish behind her, something like – yeah, right, you and whose army? Mature. She always did bring out the mature in him.

"Thanks for the show, Charlie boy," Frank said beside him.

Charlie looked around him as the emergency room came back into focus. He had a rapt audience. Just what he needed - more gossip fodder. People were staring at him open mouthed. The women were frowning. Laura brought out the worst in him; he said things to her, deliberately crude things, that he would never say to another woman. And now they had all heard. His last three hours were going to feel like three hundred. There wasn't a woman in the place who didn't look like she would eat him alive.

"Find a paddle, it's creek time," Frank said, confirming his thoughts. "You can't be a woman's first time then bolt for the exit. They don't like that."

He said it as though it was sage advice.

"I was twenty three." Charlie felt the need to explain before the women grouped together and attacked. "I was having a bad day. She took me by surprise."

The room actually grew colder.

"Not helping," Frank told him out the corner of his mouth.

"You've seen her." Charlie motioned to the exit. "She's like a praying mantis. I was scared for my life."

"You're on your own." Frank made a hasty exit.

Charlie ran his hand over his longer than fashionable hair. If he was going to make it through the rest of the shift without getting his balls handed to him on a plate there was only one thing that could save him – heartfelt honesty. Women loved that.

"I was young," he told the women in the room. "She was my sister's best friend and she took me by surprise. I didn't know she felt like that about me. I should have said no, but I was a young guy with raging hormones and no self-control. Afterwards I didn't know what to think or what to feel. I freaked out and ran away. I'm sorry."

He tried to look contrite while keeping an eye on the room to see if the women were softening.

"Don't you think you should tell her that, instead of us?" one of the older women said.

"Absolutely." He nodded in what he hoped was a shame faced manner. "As soon as I finish this shift." If I get out alive. "I will tell her exactly that."

They didn't look like they were about to kill him, but they sure didn't look friendly either.

"Maybe you should apologise for tonight as well," another woman said. "You were downright rude."

"Yeah," another agreed. "You're not my Doctor Hottie anymore."

"Doctor Moron," someone mumbled and heads nodded in agreement.

Charlie clenched his jaw.

"Okay people," Frank shouted. "The man is sorry. Let's get back to work. There are sick people to deal with."

Slowly, people wandered back to their jobs.

"Thanks man," Charlie said when he was no longer the focus of attention.

"Don't thank me," Frank said solemnly. "I agree with them."

With a growl Charlie grabbed the offered chart and threw back the curtain for his next patient. An old woman and her husband glared at him.

"Look dear," the woman said. "I thought I was getting Doctor Hottie, but it seems we have Mr Misogynist instead."

Charlie's shoulders slumped as he pulled the curtain behind him.

FOR THE FIRST time in months Charlie didn't have a nightmare. There were no bullets whizzing in his head. No children he couldn't save. No comrades in arms that he had to watch die. He didn't wake in a sweat gasping for air and he didn't shake just thinking about trying to sleep again. For the first time in months Charlie got almost a full night's sleep. And he had Laura to thank for it.

He padded into the kitchen in his boxer shorts, scratching his belly and wondering what the time was. He felt rested. All because of the Iron Maiden. Who would have thought? Instead of his usual nightmares, he'd dreamed about arguing with Laura. He'd actually laughed in his dream. It boggled his mind just thinking about it. The stress of dealing with Laura outweighed his experience in Afghanistan. Now wasn't that something she could put on her C.V.? Under the heading of "other abilities" she could write "scarier than armed conflict'.

He filled an extra-large mug with black coffee and pottered into the living room. He was halfway through a BBC news bulletin when the doorbell rang. With one eye on the large screen TV, he went to answer it.

"Oh no," he said when he saw who was on the other side.

"Oh yes," Laura said as she barged her way past him.

With a look of disgust she took in his surroundings.

"You better clean this place before Maddie and Dean get back."

He looked at the surfaces covered with empty takeaway wrappers and old newspapers. There was even some discarded underwear behind the couch, although he had no idea how it got there. Yep, he was a pig and proud of it.

"They're gone for another six months."

"It might take you that long to clean up."

He frowned at her.

"I'm not giving you an interview."

He folded his arms over his chest, belatedly remembering that he was almost naked. Laura didn't seem to notice, or to care. That rankled. Sure he hadn't been as physical since he left the army, but he still had muscle. He looked down at himself. Yep, still looking good.

"Go put something on," she ordered. "It's too early in the morning to look at you. I need coffee."

"Well get it in your own flat."

She ignored him as she headed for the kitchen.

"Get a wiggle on," she said over her shoulder. "We need to talk and I'm on a schedule."

Charlie stared after her. In her tiny shorts and halter top she looked like a school kid. He narrowed his eyes as he thought about it. He bet she dressed like that deliberately, thinking that if she looked like butter wouldn't melt in her mouth then he would give into her more easily. Not likely. As it didn't look like she was going anywhere fast, he decided to pull on some clothes. One semi clean t-shirt and a pair of jeans later, he found her sitting at the breakfast bar eating his last bagel.

"Bye bye," he said as he refilled his mug. "Be sure to let the door hit you on the way out."

"What's it going to take to get an interview?"

Her wavy hair was tied back in a ponytail and it swung as she turned towards him.

"More than you have to offer," he told her.

Something like a blush nipped at the base of her neck. Had he said something that embarrassed the Iron Maiden? And here he was thinking it wasn't possible. Slowly her eyes met his and he stilled. For some reason it was hard to swallow.

"I'll do anything," she said without emotion.

His stomach clenched. Was she offering sex? No. That wasn't it. This was Laura. If she was offering sex she'd say – how about I sleep with you? So, no she didn't mean that.

"I don't need anything."

"Nothing? Everybody needs something."

A flash from the night before entered his mind. Maybe Laura could chase away his dreams for him? He shook his head to clear it.

"You know I'll just bug you until you give in. And if that doesn't work I'll get Maddie and your Mum and Dad to bug you too."

"I'm not ten, that won't work."

He could see her regrouping and it occurred to him that he was having fun.

"Fine, I'll hound your every waking moment until you say something worthwhile that I can write down."

He grinned.

"I'm on holiday, sweet cakes. Two weeks cycling holiday to be exact."

She cringed. Charlie remembered vividly how anti sport she'd been as a kid. Maddie had been the dare devil, Laura was always the side kick. At one point she was forging a note a week to get out of gym class. A wicked thought occurred to him.

"I tell you what," he said casually. "If you come with me, I'll give you an interview."

She balked, making him grin even wider.

"Two weeks on a bike?"

"With a tent."

"Sleeping in a tent, on an airbed?"

She said it in a tone that implied it may as well have been a bed of nails.

"Roll mattress," he clarified helpfully and watched her pale.

She drummed her pale pink nails on the counter top as she cast her eyes around the room, desperately looking for some solution to the problem.

"Where are you cycling?"

"Haven't decided yet."

There was no way she would go for this. Laura's idea of a holiday stretched to taxi rides and room service. She pursed her lips, which were the exact same colour as her nails, as she thought it through. The orange halter she wore made her hair look golden. It caught the light from the kitchen window and glowed. Charlie sipped his coffee as he waited for her answer.

"I'll go if you let me choose the destination."

He spat coffee all over the kitchen floor. With a roll of her eyes Laura threw a towel at him so he could wipe it up.

"You did hear me right?" He crouched on the white tiles and looked up at her. "Two weeks. Bike. Tent. And you need to keep up because I'm not waiting for you."

"Fine."

Her expression said it was anything but fine. Her expression said it was a visit to the dentist for a root canal.

"You'll have to carry your own stuff and put up your own tent."

He threw the dirty dishtowel into the sink, belatedly thinking he should have used a cloth to wipe the floor.

"I get it," she said through gritted teeth.

"Well, okay." Charlie was stumped. Had she developed a love of the outdoors when he wasn't looking? "Where do you want to go then?"

With a look of triumph, she folded her arms over her cute little breasts.

"Holland," she said.

Charlie stared at her for a moment before he threw back his head and roared with laughter. She thought picking somewhere flat would make it easy. Rubbing the tears from his eyes, he laughed until he ached. Laura was not amused. She scowled at him while she waited.

"Holland it is, short stuff," he said at last. "We leave in the morning. Better get your gear ready. I'll pick you up at eight."

Her eyebrows arched.

"We're driving there?"

He could feel laughter bubbling up within him all over again.

"How else will we get the bikes over the Channel?"

The look on her face was priceless. One thing was clear; she wanted this interview pretty badly. He honestly couldn't remember the last time he'd laughed so hard. Charlie rubbed his palms together in anticipation. This could turn out to be the best holiday of his life.

2

———

Charlie hadn't felt even a pang of guilt about abandoning Laura for the first day of their trip. At least not until he'd arrived back at the campsite after an evening with a pretty, but vapid, blond girl. With a sinking feeling, he elbowed his way through the crowd that had gathered around the spot where he'd pitched his tent. He stopped beside two young British guys who handed him a bottle of beer without comment.

"How long has she been like this?" Charlie asked as he screwed the cap off.

"She conked out about half an hour ago."

Charlie nodded.

"Anybody help her?"

"Naw man, it was too entertaining to watch."

He could believe that. Facing him was the sorriest excuse for a tent that he'd ever seen. It was a brand new two layer dome and Laura obviously had no idea how to put the thing up. She'd managed to join the rods together and get most of them into the slots in the corners, but nothing was fastened to the ground and at some point her bike had fallen onto the tent making the whole thing squish to the left. Outside the tent was a tiny camping stove with a pot on top of it, the flame still burning beneath it.

"Anybody tell her there's a camp kitchen?" Charlie asked, although he knew the answer already.

One of the young guys grinned at him.

"That's the second gas canister. The first one blew up in her face and made her hair go funny."

He motioned that it went straight in the air with his hands.

"We think she's cooking beans," the other said helpfully.

Charlie pointed to the tent and the current fascination for the crowd.

"And how did that happen?"

"Well," the guy with the floppy hair said. "We think that blowing up her air bed was too much for her. She disappeared inside the tent without a pump. We could see her struggle to get the thing in the right position."

"Yeah, it was obvious she was blowing it up, you could hear her sucking in air," the other one said helpfully.

"Then she just sort of keeled forward," the first one pointed to the tent.

Charlie studied the view. Gaping through the tent door was Laura's backside, looking fine in denim shorts. It looked as though she had been kneeling and then slumped forward onto her face.

"She's alive man," the floppy guy said. "Madge checked."

He signalled to an older woman, who waved back when she heard her name.

"We're waiting to see what happens next," the other kid said. "I think the whole tent is going to come down, but Mark here thinks she's going to wake up and freak out."

"Or the food will go on fire," Mark nodded solemnly.

Charlie let out a deep sigh. It was his own fault. He shouldn't have left her alone. He told her their agreement was for her to come on the trip, not for him to spend time with her, and then he'd cycled off leaving her to breathe a dust cloud in his wake. He sighed heavily. As tempting as it was to leave her as entertainment for the crowd, he couldn't do it. Knowing Laura she'd find some way to blame him for this fiasco and make him suffer. A scheming Laura was a dangerous Laura. He drained his beer and handed the bottle back to the boys.

"Show's over folks," he said to the small group. "Unfortunately, that sorry excuse for a camper belongs to me."

There were groans of disappointment along with one "way to go man, great ass," which came from an American guy.

The little group wandered back to their tents while Charlie went to sort the mess - but not before taking a picture on his phone. With a shake of his head, he turned off the stove before the base of the pot burned through. What was she thinking? There was a McDonald's ten minutes down the road.

Then he looked at the rest of the mess and didn't know where to start. As he bent to pull back the tent flap he kicked something. A book. The complete idiot's guide to camping. Well - he looked at the bum sticking out of the floppy tent - they obviously never had Laura in mind when they wrote it. He tossed it in the direction of the rubbish, along with most of the other kit he could find. The woman had brought gas lanterns. To Holland. There were no words for it. He stuck his head into the tent. Sure enough, she'd managed to get the mattress blown up before blacking out on top of it. One look at the tube of cream for muscle pain, which lay beside her, explained the fact her backside was in the air. He bet it hurt too much to lay any other way.

With the cliché about disturbing sleeping dogs - or was it bears? - in his head he was careful not to wake her as he moved her. He needn't have worried, she was out cold. He picked her up, placed her on her belly on the air bed and covered her with her opened sleeping bag. He rolled his eyes at the weight of it. It was the kind they sold to serious adventure types who were going to Antarctica. The guys in the camping store must have loved dealing with her. One hour with her and they would have made enough on commission for the year. There was nothing else to do except move the bike away from the side of her tent, stick a couple of pegs in the ground so she wouldn't blow away and leave her to it.

As he backed out of the tent a tiny little groan escaped from her lips, making him stop dead in his tracks. Her cheeks were burned from the sun, which made the freckles on her nose darken. Her golden hair had come loose from its tie and brushed across her cheek. His breath hitched. Her pink tongue flicked out to lick her lips and in her sleep she reached for a drink. When her hand settled on something, she pulled it to her. It was the tube of muscle cream. Her breathing slowed as she sank back into a deep sleep.

Charlie started to breathe again as he hastily retreated from the tent. After he'd secured it, he picked up the cooking equipment and headed for the bin. Obviously he needed to keep a closer eye on her. If there was going to be another campsite show, he didn't want to miss it.

LAURA WOKE IN PAIN. Her first thought was that she had to engineer things so that Charlie didn't dump her again and cycle off into the sun. At this rate she'd never get her interview. Her second thought involved the words bike and never again. She had no recollection of getting into her sleeping bag, well under it at least, but she was grateful that she'd managed to blow up her bed. Her belly rumbled reminding her that she never made it to dinner. Even if it was just a plate of beans.

"Oh no!" She threw herself off the mattress and out of the tent.

The stove was missing.

"Good morning, sunshine."

She spun around in the direction of the voice, immediately regretting that she'd moved so quickly. Charlie's face peered at her through the slit of a tiny triangular tent that looked suspiciously like a black Toblerone box. It was only tall enough to sit up in, with barely enough space for one person to lie down.

"That's your tent?" She pointed at it as though there was something suspicious about it.

"It's a one man tent." He pointed at his bare chest. "One man. One tent."

Laura bent over to peer inside. He was wedged into a sleeping bag as thin as a sheet and lying on the kind of mat people took to yoga class. And he appeared to be naked. He unzipped the flap and leered at her.

"Want to climb in and get a better look?"

"Where's your camp light, stove, your cooking gear?" she asked before a thought hit her. "Now that I think about it, where are mine?"

He leaned up onto an elbow, making his shoulder muscle bulge.

"Now that you bring it up, I had a little clear out while

you were sleeping. Got rid of the stuff you don't need. You should ride a lot lighter today."

Laura spun towards her tent. She stalked as best she could towards her gear. Although the bags were still there, most of her stuff was gone.

"I spent money on that gear. I needed it."

"You needed a state of the art first aid kit? You were planning to do your own dental work, or stitch up your leg?" He waved around. "We're in Holland. The country is the size of a postage stamp with the population of South England. If you need a dentist, we can find one. And if you need something stitched, you have me."

"But I don't have you, do I? We're not exactly cycling side by side."

She raked through her bag.

"I threw your book out too." He told her.

Laura gritted her teeth. How was she supposed to put up her tent now?

"As for food," the Neanderthal continued, blithely unaware of how close he was to death, "you'll never be more than an hour from a fast food place on this trip. And seriously Laura, you brought water?"

Her eye began to twitch. She put a finger on it to stop it.

"Don't touch my stuff again." She infused the words with every unsaid threat she could think of.

He held up his hands in a gesture of innocence.

"Thank you would have been enough."

Laura grabbed her towel and toilet bag, something he'd thankfully left untouched, and headed towards the showers, painfully aware that she was walking bowlegged from the tenderness in her rear end.

"Don't forget your magic cream," Charlie called behind

her and something new happened: both eyes began to twitch at the same time.

LAURA HAD HALF EXPECTED to find Charlie gone when she got out of the shower. After all that was his M.O. – dump her and run. Instead she found him sitting on the fold-up chair she'd brought with her, scoffing a McDonald's breakfast. There was an unopened bag beside him which drew her attention and made her mouth water. He jerked his head in its direction and Laura took that as an invitation to eat.

"Up," she ordered when she had her hands on the bag.

"Come on, I bought you breakfast."

"Up."

He rolled out of the chair to sit on the grass. Laura gently lowered herself into the soft fabric seat. Bliss. Coffee and sausage muffin. She bit into it with the kind of groan she usually reserved for pure pleasure.

"We need to set some ground rules." Charlie's words cut through her joy and ruined the moment.

"You're embarrassing me," he said.

"You've always embarrassed me," she told him through a mouthful of food. "First there's your obsession with empty headed bimbos, then there's your refusal to take anything seriously. Don't even get me started on your juvenile sense of humour or the fact you still technically live with your parents."

He shook her chair making her wobble precariously.

"Focus, short stuff, we're talking about you."

Laura wasn't surprised that he didn't take issue with anything she said. Who could argue with the evidence? It made it all the more maddening that she was supposed to get a serious article out of the imbecile.

"Ground rules," he reminded her.

"Fine, rules, got it. Carry on."

Honestly. She tuned him out as she polished off her food. At least he was talking to her, which was a step up already.

"One," he counted off on his fingers. "I will stay near you for the rest of the trip, mainly to stop you injuring yourself, but you've got to stop cycling like an old person and speed up."

Laura searched the bag for more food. Nothing. Charlie rolled his eyes, reached into his pannier and threw a chocolate bar at her.

"Two, no endless questions as we ride or I'll leave you for good."

"Wait a minute," Laura protested. "We had a deal, I come with you on your stupid excuse for a holiday and you give me an interview."

"That doesn't mean you get to ruin my trip by badgering me all the time."

"So when do I get my interview?"

"At the end." He smirked at her. "If you make it."

"And what are we supposed to talk about until then?"

"I'm kind of hoping that there will just be silence."

"Well, what was the point of me coming with you if I don't get to interview you until the end? I could have waited until you came back home."

Or not, since her deadline expired before his holiday ended. Charlie shrugged.

"Not my problem. This was your plan."

"So why did you agree to it?"

"You're the entertainment, short stuff," he told her as he jumped to his feet. "And just so you know, I updated my Facebook page while you were sleeping."

He flicked his phone in her direction. The caption above the photo said: having a great time with Laura. And there was her huge backside poking out of her tent for the world to see.

"Well," Laura said as she stood in front of him, hands on hips, "just so you know. I'm keeping score."

"I wouldn't expect anything less. Now saddle up. We leave in ten minutes."

Charlie sauntered off in the direction of the office leaving Laura wondering what she would do to get even. Her thoughts didn't linger long. One look at her tent reminded her she had bigger problems. How was she supposed to get it all back into the tiny little bag it came out of?

With a sigh she reached to pull up the peg nearest her.

THE NEXT TWO days were spent enduring an uneasy truce. Charlie was true to his word and stayed within hailing distance. He helped her to put her tent up at the campsites and then he slapped on a clean t-shirt, saluted her and disappeared into the nearest bar. That was the last she saw of him until the following day, although she heard him come back in the small hours of the morning. Thankfully, alone. The last thing she needed was to listen to Charlie and his latest bimbo getting hot and heavy in his tiny tent. She gritted her teeth. This had to stop. It was a mind numbing endurance test and she'd reached her limit. All day long her attempts at conversation were met with grunts, which did nothing to take her mind off her backside. Then she spent her evenings alone. It sucked. It had to change. She was going to make it change.

While Charlie was in the shower, Laura scanned the

campsite for help. Her eyes found the two English boys she'd seen at the first camping ground. She put on her most trustworthy smile, tried not to look mental and went to say hello.

"Hi there," she called as she approached.

"Hey, it's you. Airbed girl."

They seemed pleased to see her. They also seemed not to have showered since they last met. She took a step backwards.

"How's the holiday going?" one of them asked.

Laura cast a glance towards the shower block. There was no time for chit chat.

"I need a favour, boys," she said.

They actually leered at each other. Yeah, like that was going to happen.

"Which one of you can sabotage a bike?"

Blank looks.

"I need help to break a bike."

"Your bike?" They pointed towards it in case she was confused.

Laura gritted her teeth and reminded herself to be patient.

"No, not my bike. My friend's bike. I need it to be out of action." She let out a heavy breath. "I need a day where I don't cycle."

"Got ya." One of them winked at the other.

"Sore lady parts huh?" the other one said.

Laura's jaw dropped open.

"Listen, dumb and dumber, I need help. Now who's up for it?"

"I'll do it," said the floppy one.

"Good, now get a move on, he'll be out of the shower any minute."

The floppy guy picked up a small bag and followed her back to the tent. The bag contained a tiny tool kit.

"I'm going to mess with the gears and the chain. It won't be an easy fix. He'll need a shop. It should buy you a day."

Laura's heart fluttered. A day. No bike. Yay. Less than a minute later, the young guy was ready to leave, taking some spare bike parts with him.

"So," he sidled up to her, "I helped you. Now what's in it for me?"

Laura almost decked him. Instead she looked around, grabbed her folding chair and thrust it at him.

"Cool," he grinned and waved it in the air towards his friend, who gave two thumbs up. "See you later, airbed girl."

With that he was gone. Laura rolled her eyes then did a happy dance. She had to get it out of her system before Charlie appeared, otherwise it would be impossible to keep a straight face when he told her his bike was broken. When she stopped her happy dance her eyes rested on the two English guys. She got a double thumbs up from each of them.

"Damn it," Charlie knelt beside his bike. "Someone's been messing around with my bike. I can't cycle this. I need to find a repair place."

"Shame," Laura said beside him.

He stood slowly. If he wasn't mistaken the Iron Maiden was struggling to contain a grin. His eyes narrowed.

"Did you do something to my bike?"

He folded his arms across his chest and glared at her.

"Yes, absolutely," she said. "Because I know so much about bikes. Think about it Neanderthal. I need a book to put up my tent and I still can't work the gears on my bike. Do you really think I could have messed with yours?"

"Let me see your phone."

"What?"

She tried to look indignant; she was hiding something.

"Hand it over sweet cakes." He took a step towards her, invading her space. "Don't make me come and get it."

"Fine," she huffed and made a big deal about handing it over.

Charlie flicked through her Internet history. Nope, she hadn't Googled how to do it either. Reluctantly, he returned the phone. She looked far too smug about the whole thing, which set off alarm bells. Unfortunately there was nothing he could do about it.

"Well," he said at last. "We can't cycle today."

"Oh. Shame."

Her eyes got wider.

"Yeah, shame," he said sarcastically.

She just blinked at him.

"I need to find a repair shop."

He put the bike right way up.

"And then we can do something?" She sounded breathless. "Together?"

It was on the tip of his tongue to tell her that she was on her own, but she looked so eager. Like a little puppy with those huge eyes of hers.

"Fine, we can do something together." Laura squealed, making him regret the decision as soon as it was out of his mouth. "But no talking," he told her. "None."

She zipped her mouth before digging around in her backpack. She produced a thick tourist guide to Holland and flicked to the region they were in.

"Oh, there's a lot we could do," she said excitedly.

"There's a flower market nearby, or we can make cheese, or there is a museum with a miniature town, or we can go shopping. What do you think?"

Charlie was thinking, mainly, why hadn't he found that book at the same time as the other one and dumped them both in the bin.

"Charlie?"

"I'm not making cheese," he growled. "And I'm not going shopping."

"Miniature town and flower market it is then. This will be great."

"Yeah, great."

Laura punched him on the arm, it was like getting pummelled by a flea.

"Get a grip, Neanderthal, all I'm proposing is one day's sightseeing. I'm not asking you to marry me."

To his disgust he honestly couldn't think of a comeback. Marriage was no laughing matter. In fact, he'd always figured that guys who joked about it jinxed their carefree lifestyles. And he liked his carefree lifestyle, thank you very much.

"Get ready, we leave in ten minutes," he said.

Laura gave him an odd look before heading for the camp toilets. When she thought he wasn't looking she grinned and punched the air. Oh, yeah, she had nothing to do with his broken bike. And he was the Queen of Holland.

"Why don't you tell me about Afghanistan and then you can enjoy the rest of your holiday alone?"

They'd been about five minutes into their day when Charlie realised that there was no way she was going to keep her mouth shut. Thankfully the odd comment and grunt had been enough to get him through the flower market and round the model town. Laura had ooed and ahed over each miniature building and fake canal as though it was amazing. He couldn't see it himself. Tiny buildings? So what? The real thing was all around him. What was the point in being awe struck by a doll's house while behind you there were seventeenth century crooked houses and winding canals? He figured Laura related to the little version because, well, she was little.

"Charlie, wake up. Let's get this over with. You can't possibly be enjoying this holiday. Let's cut our losses. Give me the interview and you can have fun for the rest of it."

She wasn't going to let him have any peace. It was heart breaking. A complete waste of a lazy afternoon in the sun. They sat at an outdoor table belonging to one of the many cafes that had spilt onto the town square. He should have been sipping thick Dutch coffee and watching tall blond girls walk by; instead he was listening to Laura nag.

"Well?" She prodded his leg with her toe. "Why don't you give me the interview now?"

Charlie stretched out in one of the cafe's rattan chairs, his long legs crossed at the ankles. He lazily reached up to pull his shades down his nose, so he could look at her over the top of them.

"We made a deal."

"Who cares about the deal?" She waved her hands around for emphasis, then clutched her belly. She looked a little green. Well, he did tell her that two huge portions of fries with mayonnaise was a bad idea.

"I care about the deal." He pushed the shades back into place. Man it was warm. He should have been swinging in a hammock somewhere instead of listening to Laura.

"Come on Charlie, you don't want me here anymore

than I want to be here. Give me the story and then we can both get on with our lives."

Silence.

"Seriously, you enjoy having me here that much?"

Now that was funny. There was nothing enjoyable about this. Although the first night with the tent was pretty funny. Still, it was worth all the suffering. With Laura around he could sleep. That alone was worth any amount of trouble she caused. But he definitely wasn't going to tell her that. In his experience if you gave a woman any insight at all, it always came back to bite you in the bum.

"You have your moments," he said.

Even over the noise of the busy street he imagined he could hear her grit her teeth. He smiled.

"Okay," she said at last. "Tell me something else. Anything else. This whole silence thing is driving me insane and trust me; you don't want me to snap."

That made him grin.

"You don't snap, you plan. You schedule. You reason things through. You might get round to writing an angry email - well worded of course - but you definitely don't snap."

"I can snap."

She sounded affronted. As long as he lived he would never figure women out. He tells her that she's not unbalanced and she's upset. Go figure. He looked around at the crowded terrace crammed with people enjoying nice relaxed lunches and envied them.

"I can snap," Laura said again.

"Sure you can," he said and patted her hand.

He could practically see steam coming out of her ears.

"I've snapped." She sounded indignant. Fine. He would play along.

"Name one time."

She bit her lip as she thought about it, making him grin.

"You." She said with an air of triumph. "I snapped with you. The day we had our," she cast around for a word but couldn't come up with one. "The day we had sex," she said at last.

She looked really pleased with herself.

"And that was what? Twelve years ago. And let's face it, it was only a little snap."

Her eyes narrowed.

"Is that it? Is that what you think of me? That I plan every tiny detail of my life? That I never take any risks or do anything irresponsible?"

Yeah, like he was going to answer that question.

"Come on," she pulled her chair towards him. "Tell me what you think of me."

"No way."

Laura's hand slid onto his thigh. Everything within him stilled. She slid her fingers towards the sensitive part of his inner thigh. Charlie's mouth went dry. And then she pinched him. Hard.

"Hey," he shot upright. "That was out of order."

"Come on Charlie. You think I'm uptight?"

"Fine." He removed his sunglasses, put them on the table in front of them and ran his fingers through his overgrown hair making it stand on end. He had no idea why she wanted to know what he thought of her, but he could see that he wasn't getting out of it anytime soon.

"You were born responsible. You never cut loose. Never take a chance. Ever. You live like a coward. You're so scared of losing control you're constantly puckered. Watch out for those lines Laura. They're going to scream uptight old spinster."

Laura sucked in a breath. She looked like she'd been slapped. Charlie instantly regretted that his words had been so harsh.

"Well, at least I won't die sad and alone after a life trying to emulate Hugh Heffner."

Now that was a low blow. Before he could think it through he was talking.

"I suppose you have it all figured out. Two point four kids, a people carrier for a car and a house in the burbs. Don't forget the boring grey husband who never does anything out of the ordinary."

"You just described the perfectly happy life that millions of people lead, moron."

Charlie placed a hand on each arm of her chair and leaned in towards her.

"You're a coward, Laura Prentice. You think you're doing the sensible thing, but you never take any chances at all. You live half a life and then get mad at the rest of us who live a full life. Think on that while you're bored out of you mind for the next fifty years."

"I do take chances. I'm here, right?"

"You're here because I blackmailed you into coming. Let's face it. You would never do anything you term irresponsible. Ever."

"And I suppose that you'll just continue to sleep your way around the world, terrified of ever doing anything real, of ever getting close to anyone or of making a difference to someone."

"Exactly. Live free. Live easy. And when women start to ask stupid questions, say goodbye."

He wasn't exactly sure how they'd managed to go from enjoying lunch to being mad with each other, but they had.

Laura pursed her lips. He could see she was regrouping.

He could also tell he'd hurt her. Although he couldn't figure out why the truth would bother her so much. Women.

Her phone rang. She looked at the caller ID and her shoulders slumped.

"My boss," she said as she stood. "Don't even think about dumping me and running off."

She pointed at him before walking off to take the call. Charlie shook his head. Seriously, the woman was midget sized, with huge puppy dog eyes, and yet she still felt she could threaten him and he would listen. It must be great to be in Laura's head. He bet that in her head she was a giant who ruled the world.

He rested his head on the back of the chair, closed his eyes against the sun and dozed. He had never been able to figure Laura out; he wasn't going to today. It would take a lifetime and he wasn't that invested. Nope, a nice little nap was a better use of his time.

3

———

Laura was so angry with Charlie that she couldn't see straight. She tripped over two German tourists and one dog on her way out of the cafe's terrace. If her boss, the evil witch, was going to chew her out then she didn't want to be within hearing distance of the Neanderthal when it happened. Responsible? Uptight? Cowardly? Huh! She took chances all the time. Okay, so right now she couldn't think of one, but that didn't matter. She was sure she would when she calmed down. And as for being responsible, well that was a good thing. He could use being more responsible. She glared at him through the crowded street but he appeared to be asleep. If she could have made his head explode just by looking at him, she would have. With a frustrated groan she answered her phone.

"Hi Claire." She knew her tone said exactly how she felt about the call.

"Where is my interview?"

Laura pinched the bridge of her nose and tried to

remember the Dutch word for pharmacy, because she was about to need migraine medication.

"You gave me two weeks."

"Well I didn't think you'd fall off the planet for the whole time. I need photos, I need blurb, I need something that we can use on the website as a teaser. There's no point in chasing this interview if I can't advertise the fact that it's coming. It's called business, Laura. I am running a business here. Try to remember."

Laura gritted her teeth with relish. There was no one around to witness it.

"This isn't easy." She tried not to sound whiny. "I haven't had a minute to talk to him. He cycles off and leaves me."

It didn't matter how hard she tried, she sounded whiny and pathetic even to her own ears.

"Boo hoo," said Claire. "This isn't the teen scene. When you're writing for adults you have to make the extra effort. What exactly are you doing? Having a holiday?"

"No, I'm trying to get the story. But I told you at the start of this that we don't exactly get along. We have a history. A very bad history."

"Save it for the story. I want photos of your trip and some copy we can use to sell the piece. And I want it tonight. Do you understand? I want to find it waiting for me as soon as I log in in the morning."

"Yes. I understand." That you are evil and must be obeyed.

"Good. I'll look forward to it." Her voice was like ice. "And Laura, make sure you send me something sexy. I don't want a travel log and pictures of you two on bikes."

With that the phone went dead.

Black dots appeared in Laura's vision. Her left temple was throbbing. In all her reading about migraines she'd never once seen Claire's name in the list of things that could trigger one. Laura rooted around in her bag and came up with her last strip of medication. As she popped the pills she wondered how on earth she was going to get the material Claire wanted. There was no way that Charlie would agree to it. There was only one thing for it. She would have to do it without his permission. Her stomach clenched. A niggle at the back of her mind told her this was a bad decision.

She wove through the tables, over the cobble stone square, towards Charlie. He looked exactly like he was on holiday in his worn jeans and faded Iron Maiden t-shirt. She swallowed hard. How the heck was she supposed to get sexy pictures of him by the end of the day? What exactly was a sexy picture anyway? There was a serious pounding in her left temple and she was sure worry was burning a hole in her stomach lining. On the whole she would be lucky to get out of this trip alive.

LAURA WAS SUSPICIOUSLY SILENT. Charlie was even beginning to think that he may have upset her by saying she was boring. But surely comments like that bounced off Laura. She was the Iron Maiden. Teflon coated. Still, he looked at her out of the corner of his eye; the quiet was a worry.

It was early evening as they walked along the river towards the campsite. There were one or two large boats on the water and a few guys fishing along the edge of the river. They walked beside the cycle path which was busy with people making their way home from the town centre. Bikes were laden with everything from shopping, to kids and their toys. One guys held on to a canoe which was strapped into his pannier and poked up tall behind him. The sight made him smile. Charlie had to admit that a day off cycling to sightsee was kind of relaxing. It was even strangely nice to have some company. Even if she was scarily quiet.

"It's cool the way we look down on the houses, yet the water is right beside us, isn't it?"

Damn, he was making small talk. Now he knew he felt guilty. Laura looked up at him with those green owl eyes; there was something going on inside her head for sure. He just didn't know what. She looked upset. No, she looked worried. He had the overwhelming urge to make it better. Now that was insane.

"Look, we can see right into this guy's bedroom and it's on the third floor." He just could not shut up. "Must be weird to sit in the living room and know the water level is up near the roof. Wonder if they worry the dam will break?"

Yak, yak, yak, he was a man possessed.

"So, have you been here before?"

He wanted to walk into a pit. Have you been here before? Seriously?

Laura stopped walking and looked up at him. Charlie felt oddly cornered, as though she could read his mind.

"I'm okay about our talk," she said at last. "You're right. I am sensible, and responsible and probably boring. I don't travel round the world like you do. Save lives or anything. But I'm okay with it. I worked hard at being boring and sensible. It's who I am. It's what I want."

Now he really felt like a heel. He ran his hand through his hair, wondering again if it was time for a haircut.

"Look, you're not boring, I was winding you up." Why was he trying to make this better? Why was he making excuses? Because she looked like Bambi in the scene where he lost his mother.

Laura reached out and put her hand on his arm. She

blinked her huge eyes and smiled. Her ponytail swayed in the breeze.

"You're off the hook. I'm fine. I don't care what you said. Better boring than a drama queen or a basket case like my parents."

He couldn't argue with that.

"Tell you what." She fluttered her eyelashes and he was instantly suspicious. Was she flirting? No, she'd tell him if she was.

"What?"

He'd play along. At least now she was talking, which was a relief. And he knew how insane that was considering he'd spent days wishing she would shut up.

"How about we go for a swim?"

What? "Swim?"

"There's a little beach along here, I saw it when we were cycling yesterday. How about we have a swim?"

He could tell by the way her eye began to twitch that she was losing patience with him.

"Okay," he said. "Let me get this right. You want to skinny dip."

Now she was grinding her teeth.

"No, you can wear your underwear and I'll wear my top and my pants."

Her face flushed. He was missing something. He looked down at Laura in her cute cut-off jeans and yellow halter top. Sure, he could go swimming.

"Why not?" He said with a shrug.

With a slow calculating smile that made his guts twist tight, Laura turned in the direction of the beach.

There were a couple of kids playing in the sand but other than that there was no one in the water. Laura was beginning to regret this idea. But since it was the only one she had, she decided to go with it.

"Perfect," she said with forced cheer. "Do you think its cold?"

"Only one way to find out."

Charlie pulled his t-shirt over his head and Laura felt her cheeks flush.

"See anything you like?" he said with a cocky grin.

"I've seen it all before." She forced a yawn. He smiled knowingly.

A second later he was stripped to pale grey cotton briefs that left little to the imagination. Laura cast a worrying glance towards the kids playing, but they were gone. She hadn't even noticed them leave. Now it was just her, Charlie and the river.

"Your turn, shorty," he challenged.

Laura stuck her chin in the air. This was her idea. She could do it. Without looking at him she kicked off her flip flops, put her bag on the sand and reached for the button on her shorts.

"Need any help with that?"

She ignored him. It's no big deal, she told herself. It's not like he hasn't seen it all before. Still, her heart beat fast.

"Come on, it's going to be dark soon," he said. "Unless you want to go with my idea and skinny dip. In that case, dark is better."

She frowned at him before slipping her shorts down her legs.

"Barbie?"

Her head snapped up to see him smother a smile.

"Great underwear," he said instead.

Laura looked down at her bubble gum pink Barbie pants.

"I'm petite," she said with irritation, "sometimes I can shop in the kids section."

"I'm impressed, short stuff, that's the first time you've ever acknowledged that you're vertically challenged."

She growled, making him laugh.

"Now the top. You don't seriously want to swim in that. Better to keep it dry and swim in your bra. Is that Barbie too? No, let me guess, Sponge Bob."

He folded his arms over his impossibly muscled chest. Oh to be so simple minded that anything amused you.

"I have to wear this. I'm not wearing a bra."

That stopped the laughter. His eyes zoomed in on her breasts.

"Now," he said in a hoarse voice, "if I'd known that earlier, this day would have been a whole lot more interesting."

Laura crossed her arms, blocking his view.

"Get in the water," she ordered.

"Ladies before gentlemen."

"I want to take some pictures before I forget; I haven't taken any so far this trip. You go ahead and I'll be there in a minute."

"Is this some sort of ploy? Are you going to run away with my clothes?"

She rolled her eyes.

"Yes that's exactly what I'm going to do; because there is no way that you are fast enough to catch me."

"Good point," he said and turned towards the water.

Laura's stomach tensed as she dug out her camera. What she was doing felt so wrong. It was sneaky, underhanded and wrong. Wrong. Wrong. She bit her lip as she watched Charlie dive under the water. It was also necessary. No pictures. No interview. No Job. Her boss had her over a barrel and they both knew it.

She turned the camera towards Charlie and began to snap. In the warm light of the sunset he looked amazing. Muscled, tanned and delicious. He stirred up desire within her. Even knowing that he had the personality of a skunk, she was still drooling over his water covered pecs. Pathetic. Still if he had that effect on her, surely other women would like the pictures too? She hushed her complaining conscience and took all the photos she needed.

"ARE YOU COMING IN HERE?"

Charlie brushed his hair from his face and decided that he definitely needed a haircut. He was all for relaxed, but this was borderline hippy and that was too far.

Laura took some pictures of the river, and then spun around to take some of the people cycling behind them on the dike. She walked to the edge of the water.

"Smile," she told him.

Little warning bells went off in his head.

"Why?"

She gave him her teacher look.

"I want one nice picture. Something I can send to your sister to prove we aren't killing each other."

It sounded innocent. It looked innocent. So why did he get the feeling something else was going on?

"Smile, moron," she ordered.

Ah, that was more like it. He grinned and she snapped the picture.

"Right, enough of this, get your boring backside in the water sweet cakes. This was your idea, your sad attempt at doing something spontaneous, so get on with it. Or I'm coming to get you."

Oh, he liked that idea. She looked alarmed, which made it even more appealing.

"Stuff it," he said with a wide grin. "I'm coming to get you anyway."

She yelped which made him laugh. Laura ran like a girl to her bag and stuffed her camera into it. Then she actually stopped her escape to put her shorts back on. It was laughable. Charlie was on her before she got one leg in.

"I don't think so," he told her as he scooped her up. "This was your idea. So you go in too."

"I don't want to." She wriggled and kicked, but he held her tight. "I've changed my mind. Put me down."

Not for the first time in his life, Charlie was grateful that she was small. It was pretty much the only advantage he had over her.

"You're making me wet," she told him.

He cocked an eyebrow.

"Good to know I still rock your world."

"You're disgusting."

"So you've told me."

"Let me go this instant. I do not want to go in the water. I want to go back to the tent. This was a bad idea."

"I think this was a great idea. In fact the best you've had the whole trip."

He walked into the river until he was knee deep.

"Charlie," her voice softened, she was changing tactic. He smiled knowingly. "Come on, you're not a bully, I know you respect women, even when they change their minds." She batted those long lashes and pursed those pretty pink lips. She patted his chest with her long fingers, making his blood pump faster. "You don't want to do this," she said sweetly.

For a second, a split second, he almost kissed those full lips. He shook his head. She was using magic on him. Brainwashing.

"Oh, but I do want to do this."

And with that, he let her go. There was a big splash, a scream and a stream of curse words he'd never heard her utter before. He was laughing when something hit him hard on the back of his knees and he crumpled. Laura was on his head like lice at a kids party and the next thing he knew, he was breathing water. Which made him laugh harder. She actually thought she could take him. Unfortunately laughing under water isn't a great idea and he started to choke. Time to take charge. He grabbed her round the waist and flipped her so that her back was to his front, then he wrapped his arms around her and held her tight. In all of the commotion they had drifted out into deeper water; he could stand with his feet on the ground and his head out of the water, but there was no way she could.

"Charlie Lewis, let me go."

"Sure." He let go. She sank.

Just as she started to kick and swim he grabbed her again.

"Looks like you're out of your depth, shorty," he said into her hair.

He waited while she struggled, knowing full well it was pointless. It was entertaining to watch her try to kick him through the water. At last she calmed down. He kept his arms wrapped around her, her back to his front.

"Okay, what now?" she said at last.

"I think we need to clear the air between us," he said and was pleased at how reasonable he sounded.

She growled. He felt it vibrate through his body.

"About what?" she said.

"You have been harbouring bad feeling about our interaction years ago, and I think it's time we dealt with your anger."

Another bout of struggling. He waited for her to exhaust herself, it didn't take long.

"I think it's time to admit that you had a part to play in that fiasco too," he said. "I'm sick of taking all the blame."

"You took my virginity and ran away." He could hear years of fury in her voice.

"That's true, I was young and stupid and I didn't know what to do with you." He still didn't.

That made her stop moving. He could almost hear her thinking.

"Now, you need to admit that you threw yourself at me and didn't give me many options."

"Oh, so I forced you to have sex with me?"

"No, but you were all innocent and scared. I didn't want to hurt you by turning you away. Plus, I was feeling down and you made me feel better. You need to admit that you put me on the spot, and then got mad when I did exactly what you wanted."

Silence.

"Come on Laura, it's time to let this go. I know I was a moron, but so were you."

"You ran away, you didn't even say thank you."

"I was an idiot."

She was trembling, he wasn't sure if it was the water or the conversation. Suddenly this topic wasn't the great idea he thought it would be. Suddenly, it was serious. He began to panic.

"Was I terrible? Was that it? Were you embarrassed sleeping with me?" Her voice was small.

Damn.

"No. It had nothing to do with you. I freaked. I'd just slept with my sister's best friend. I didn't even know you thought like that about me. It was a screw up from beginning to end."

"So it wasn't me?"

Charlie's shoulders slumped; he turned Laura around so he could look her in the eye. This was his mess and he had to fix it.

"It was me. Sure, it isn't every day a woman comes asking you to sleep with her. I didn't even know you were a virgin until it was too late. I'd like to say knowing would have made me behave better, but it probably wouldn't have. It had nothing to do with you. You were fine."

"Fine?"

Brilliant. That was the wrong word too.

"You know what I mean."

Obviously she didn't.

"Thanks for clearing things up. I feel much better."

She wriggled to get away and he didn't stop her. He didn't know what to say. The fun had been sucked right out of the situation. Charlie watched helplessly as she swam to shore. So much for clearing the air. He was pretty sure he'd just made everything worse.

4

———

Laura had been cycling for three hours and already felt like her backside was on fire. She cycled standing to give her behind a rest only to find that her poor neglected thigh muscles couldn't support her weight. She would have rolled to a halt on the grass verge and given into her misery, but Charlie was right behind her and she definitely didn't want to deal with him. Fine. She was fine in bed. Just what every woman wanted to hear. Okay, so he had been her first time and she didn't know what she was doing, but fine? It explained a lot about why none of her relationships lasted. Obviously she was about as sexy as a pack of paper towels. Fine. Argh.

"Thanks for tonight's Facebook update," he called from behind her.

Against her will, her cheeks burned. She knew he was trying to get her to fight with him again. They got on great when they were fighting. She didn't care. If it wasn't for the article she would dump him and run. She'd had enough of Charlie Lewis to last a lifetime.

"This trip is beginning to have a theme. Pictures of Laura taken from behind."

She bit her lip to stop from answering him. Another Dutch couple cycled past and grinned widely at her; the girl pointed at her bike. At least they didn't call out some supposedly witty comment.

"I hope the modification you made to your bike is worth the humiliation," Charlie said.

"This was the sensible thing to do," Laura told him, astonished at how pompous she sounded even to her own ears.

Sensible. She could sum up her whole existence in that one word. She shifted on her padded seat. The pillow she'd stuffed into her backpack at the last minute had proved a life saver; she'd tied it to her seat for extra cushioning. It helped a lot, but she was seriously considering padding it even further with her fluffy soft sleeping bag. In for a penny, in for a pound.

"Yeah and we know you're all about the sensible."

He was prodding her again. She clenched her jaw and focused on cycling.

"What's the big deal about being sensible?" he called. "There's no fun in it. You need to loosen up. Take some chances, make some mistakes, it's what life is all about."

Anger bubbled through her and out of her mouth before she could stop it.

"I made a mistake once," she told him icily. "A big one."

She took her eyes off of the canal to look over her shoulder at him.

"You're the biggest mistake of my life."

She smiled evilly just before she rode straight into the water.

Charlie was too shocked to laugh. He'd never seen

anything like it. One minute she was giving him her evil teacher stare, the next she was airborne. She flew straight through two bushes and head first into the canal. Without stopping to think he jumped from his bike and scrambled after her. He came to a stop at the edge of the water. Fortunately the canal wasn't that deep and Laura could stand. Her tiny head poked out of the murky depth, her backpack was gone and her bike was sinking.

"Grab the bike," he yelled.

She turned in time to see the handle bars disappear under the water and made a desperate attempt to catch it.

"Help me," she said.

It did cross his mind, but there was too much entertainment value in watching it happen. Plus, what would be the benefit of them both being soaked through? Her face disappeared under the water briefly as she frantically grabbed for the bike. She came up empty handed. Charlie wasn't surprised; he couldn't see it through the black water from where he was standing either. What the heck was in the canal to make the water that colour? Now, that was something to make you worry.

"It's gone."

Laura looked so dejected he almost felt sorry for her.

"Come on." He leaned forward and offered her a hand. "There's nothing we can do about it now."

There could have been a tear running down her cheek, he couldn't tell for sure. Her eyes may have been red from the canal water.

"Take my hand, let's get you out of there and see the damage."

Reluctantly, she put her tiny hand in his and with little effort he pulled her up out of the canal. Her hair was plastered down her back and stuck to her face, her tiny orange vest top showed off every detail of the lime green lace bra beneath it and her denim shorts were so full of water they were falling down. Laura jerked her hand out of his and spun towards the canal.

"What am I supposed to do now?"

Charlie made a non-committal grunt. At least things were back to normal. Fighting he could handle. Heart to heart conversation was a big no no. He'd learnt his lesson. From now on he was only going to argue and tease. Nothing else. Unfortunately she was distracting him from his new resolve. He was inordinately fascinated by the fact she was wearing a bra today. He knew he should have been focused on the task at hand, but he had a really good view of her perfect little breasts through her thin wet clothes and his hands itched to cover them and make them warm.

"How do I cycle without a bike?"

She put her hands on her hips and growled at the water making her nipples strain against the fabric. A small groan escaped him and Laura stilled. Slowly she turned towards him, her huge green eyes wide.

"Seriously?" she demanded.

Charlie shrugged.

"I'm a man."

"You're sick in the head, that's what you are."

He couldn't do anything but shrug again; he wished she would fold her arms over her chest or something because he was seriously losing the battle to reach for her. He cleared his throat noisily and tried to sound like he was in charge.

"Right, first thing we need to do is get you into some dry clothes."

Maybe something like the burkha most women in Afghanistan wore. Then only her eyes would show. He looked into her wide, expressive emerald coloured eyes and swallowed hard. Right now her eyes were signalling that he was losing his mind.

"All my clothes are in there, idiot."

She pointed at the water, just in case there was any confusion.

Charlie pulled his eyes from her long enough to look at his bike. Surely he could find her something. After rummaging around in his pannier, he came out with a pair of swimming shorts and a t-shirt with B B King on it.

"Take this." He thrust it at her before turning away.

"And change here? In the middle of the path, where anyone can see?"

"Sweet cakes, you're not that interesting."

He flushed at the lie.

"Towel," she ordered.

He threw his only towel at her. It was big enough for her to wrap her whole body in. He then watched in fascination as she used it as a changing room and stripped beneath it. It was the sexiest thing he'd ever seen. She showed nothing at all, but the fact she was doing it in full light, outdoors and in front of him blew his imagination wide.

He turned away to study the flat landscape in front of him while he controlled his breathing. What was wrong with him? This was Laura. His arch nemesis. The Iron Maiden. He counted back to the last time he'd had sex and figured that wasn't the problem. He didn't feel desperate. He glanced at her over his shoulder and saw that she was taking her contact lenses out. He kind of missed her old oversized glasses that made her eyes look like an owl. A sexy owl.

"You got a bottle of water?" she said as she pulled the towel away.

She had to hold his shorts up; with the string tied tight they were still in danger of falling down.

"And a belt, maybe?"

He yanked the leather belt from the jeans he was wearing and thrust it at her before rooting around for a bottle of water. He sat on his bike as she cleaned herself up as best she could.

"Well, I can't put these back in my eyes," she said in disgust. "We need to find a chemist so I can get them cleaned up, or an optician and I'll get glasses. Without these I'm blind."

She zipped open the water logged bum bag that had survived her swim and emptied the contents onto the grass. It held her now dead phone, her credit cards, passport and sodden cash. Laura dried everything off, put it back in the bag, along with her contact lenses, and stood in front of him.

"Well, at least there is some small mercy. Without my contacts I can't see you ogling me."

"I can do more than ogle if you like."

Whoa, wait a minute, where did that come from?

Things stilled between them. The air felt charged. Charlie didn't know what had happened. The Iron Maiden was standing in front of him, wet, dirty and drowning in his old clothes and he was coming on to her?

She shook her head then pursed her lips as though deciding on something.

"That's hilarious. I guess you do feel a little guilty about telling me how fine I am in bed, huh? I don't know whether you are trying to make me feel better in your own sick little way, or if you are ironically telling me how unattractive I am. Either way, I'm not interested. I might be the only girl for miles around," she waved around her to illustrate the lack of people in their landscape, "but even I know that isn't excuse enough for you to want me. I know that I come a serious last on your list. And after seeing the women you date, I can only say that knowledge makes me proud."

She bent over and picked up her wet clothes. Charlie bit his lip to stop from telling her that she was wrong. She was wrong, right? There was nothing wrong with her, he could see that, but she wasn't for him. Right? Then why was he suddenly so desperate to make her think otherwise?

"Now what?" she said.

Charlie took a deep breath and focused on the situation in hand. Yeah, now what?

"Well," he said. "You're going to need a new bike and some new kit."

She mumbled something under her breath, it sounded like, no kidding Einstein. He pulled himself up to his full six foot and stared down at her.

"At least this time I can supervise and make sure you don't buy loads of garbage that you don't need."

She clenched her jaw and he felt some of the tension leave him.

"Town is that way." He pointed down the long path in front of him. "Hop on; it looks like I'll be doing all the work."

Her cartoon sized eyes grew wider.

"Hop on?"

He looked towards heaven for some strength in dealing with the most infuriating woman he had ever met.

"You've seen other people pass us doing this. I ride the bike and you perch on the pannier carrier at the back. Hold on tight and you won't fall off."

She looked at him and then at the bike.

"Hold on to you?"

"Get on the bike," he ordered as he climbed on. "I'm

done talking. You've ruined enough of my holiday. Sooner we get to town and get you sorted the better."

Laura wrapped her wet things in his towel and looked for somewhere to put them. With a frustrated growl he pulled a plastic carrier bag out of his pannier and thrust it at her. She filled it and stuffed the whole thing back in his bags. He held the bike steady as she sat on the back-rack, side saddle. He took more than a little joy in the fact she looked terrified.

"Hold on tight," he ordered.

Her arms snaked around his waist. Every movement she made felt uncertain. Good. It was about time she was the one on the back foot. With a push of his pedal, he set them rolling. Laura grasped on tighter. He could feel the heat coming from her against his back. Her tiny hand knotted into his t-shirt at his stomach. Just concentrate on the journey, he told himself. And look on the bright side, tonight instead of a head full of missiles and blood you can think about Laura sailing into the canal. Now that brought a smile to his face.

Laura didn't know what to berate herself about first. The list was too long. Should she choose the fact she just lost hundreds of pounds worth of new gear at the bottom of a Dutch waterway? Or should she go with the fact that there were now two pictures of her bum on the Internet? As the bike jerked over a stone and she pulled herself even closer to Charlie, she squeezed her eyes tight. Nope, the winner in all things humiliating was the fact that she was clinging to The Neanderthal and it was making her heart pound out a salsa rhythm.

She wanted to scream at the frustration of it all. Here she was with a lifetime of experience and knowledge of the man in front of her, a man who frustrated and disappointed her at every turn, and what was she doing? She wasn't thinking about all that, that was for sure. Nope, she was thinking about how he'd looked in the river during his swim. And that led to thinking about how it had felt when he'd trapped her in his arms to talk to her. He'd felt so good. Soft. Strong. Oh, oh. The words from that TV commercial for toilet paper floated into her head. Soft, strong and very, very long. She started to giggle, which made her hold on even tighter. The harder she tried to stop laughing, the more she laughed. It erupted out of her. Charlie, the canal, the whole disastrous camping trip. And now her libido had chosen this moment to wake from hibernation. With Charlie of all people. It was all so very funny.

She felt Charlie let out a heavy sigh.

"Are you losing your mind back there?" His tone was resigned, like he had already decided it was a possibility and that made her giggle all the more. "Because I'm not a psych specialist. You break something I'm your man, but anything to do with your head, we'll need to find you a professional."

Laura rubbed her face on the back of his t-shirt to wipe her eyes and felt him stiffen. Her grin widened. Was it possible that Charlie was reacting to her too?

"Sorry," she said.

"You're making me nervous, short stuff."

She was making him nervous? There were so many possibilities for fun. Laura waited until he was relaxed and focused on his cycling to make her move. She pressed herself into him as she splayed her hand flat across his stomach. Yep, he tensed again. She rubbed his stomach as though she was trying to shift her grip, to get more comfortable. His pace slowed. Laura grinned wickedly. She ran her other hand up to his chest as she pressed her cheek to his back. The bike wobbled. The hand she's placed on his stomach moved lower to grab the waistband of his jeans as an anchor.

"Laura," his deep rumbling voice vibrated through her cheek. "What are you doing?"

"Just trying to get comfortable," she said as innocently as possible.

She rubbed her face on his back as she tightened her grip on his jeans. She couldn't resist pressing a little kiss against his spine. The bike screeched to a halt. Laura let out a yelp as she landed on her back on the grass. She shielded her eyes against the sun as he towered over her.

"I know you're amusing yourself," he said as he folded his arms across his chest, "but it isn't funny."

Laura grinned. It was kind of funny. He scowled and pointed at her.

"Stop trying to turn me on."

She looked down at his jeans.

"Trying?" she said sweetly.

He shifted uncomfortably.

"Any more funny business and you'll be the one doing the cycling. Got it?"

"Aye, aye captain," she saluted before struggling to her feet.

As she climbed back onto the bike she couldn't stop grinning. There was something about Charlie that made her behave like a reckless girl. She'd forgotten how good that felt.

"I HEAR mum jeans are all the rage," Charlie said, imitating Tim Gunn from Project Runway, a programme he insisted Maddie made him watch when he was home on leave. Yeah, right.

Laura wriggled in her seat.

"I'm glad you're amused."

"Hey, you were lucky they let you raid the second hand clothes at the church, otherwise you'd be wearing my t-shirt as a dress."

Lucky. Yep, that was the word. She looked down at her "new" outfit. Her jeans were stone washed, high waisted and straight legged. Exactly the kind of thing Wham! would have worn in the eighties. They were almost up to her bra line. To complete the eighties pop theme she was wearing a faded white t-shirt with a bright pink "relax" printed on it. The whole thing made her regret that her contacts were back in her eyes; it would have been better if her clothing was a blur.

"My stuff will be dry tomorrow," she told him again.

"Oh no, I think you should keep that on. I like it. It's entertaining. Plus, if anybody needs a reminder to relax, there it is."

They were eating in the town's only eetcafe - a cross between a restaurant and a pub. It consisted mainly of one large open room, filled with modern oak furniture. Laura didn't like the old style oak furniture that she'd seen, it was all so solid and heavy looking, but this stuff was different. It was bright and contemporary. It made her relax. The walls were painted a pale lemon and dotted here and there, as though someone had arranged the displays while drunk, were several Delft blue tiles and plates. The overall affect was charming. She understood why it was busy; if she'd lived nearby she would have loved to hang out there. Laura ate breaded chicken with boiled potatoes and spinach, while Charlie ate everything else. She reserved comment because she'd seen how much energy he'd used during the day, most of it just for thinking.

"Seriously," he said. "Wear that tomorrow, it cheers me right up."

Laura narrowed her eyes at him and imagined his head popping like a squished grape.

"You're doing that thing again," he said through a mouthful of chunky chips. "The thing where you imagine evil things and think none of us know."

She grunted. Obviously her face wasn't as deadpan as she thought it was. Charlie chuckled.

"How about I wear this tomorrow if you let me ask you one interview question?"

She tried to smile sweetly, innocently, but even she knew she wasn't pulling it off.

"I don't think so."

"I'll wear any of those ugly clothes in the Church for the day, for one question."

Nothing was worse than the stuff she had on.

"How about naked?" His eyes twinkled.

"Bra-less and any clothes you pick."

He almost choked on his steak.

"It's a deal."

Laura grinned widely. At last she would have something, anything to report to her boss.

"Okay," she said eagerly. "Let me get a pen."

She borrowed paper and a pen from the waitress. When she got back to the wide oak table Charlie had relaxed back into his chair and was sipping a tall thin glass of Leffe, a blond Belgian beer.

"One question," he reminded her.

His face had closed up. Getting her interview was going to be like pulling teeth from a crocodile. She'd thought long and hard about what she might ask, but now that she had a chance she wasn't sure where to start. She didn't want to scare him off for the rest of her interview. In the end she picked a question she thought would be easy to answer.

"So, the little girl you rescued. Did you know her beforehand?"

She held her breath as he studied his beer.

"That's your question?"

She nodded.

"I thought you were going to start somewhere else."

"Quit stalling and answer my question."

His luminous blue eyes looked into hers as his honey coloured hair flopped over onto his forehead. He brushed it away, but he never broke her gaze.

"Yes," he said at last.

"How did you know her?"

"That's two questions. You only get one."

Laura desperately searched around for another bargaining chip.

"I'll go without any underwear tomorrow."

She didn't consider being underwear free a great sacrifice. The only lingerie she had left came from the local supermarket. It scratched and pinched her with every move she made. Charlie's mouth twitched as though he was trying not to smile. Laura felt a pang of insecurity. She looked down at her body. It wasn't exactly Playboy material. Offering to go underwear free probably wasn't much of a bargaining chip.

"Or, I can cook dinner?" she offered instead.

It was as though he could read her mind. Her face flushed under the scrutiny of his gaze.

"No, I think I'll go with the first offer. No underwear for the whole day and I get to pick the clothes."

"Fine."

Was that relief she felt that she wasn't repellent? Laura ignored it and concentrated on the question.

"The little girl?" she prompted then reached for her water to signal it was his turn to talk.

His face closed off and his eyes took on a faraway glaze. His shoulders slumped. Laura held her breath.

"We knew all of them," he said at last, "all the kids who were killed and injured that day. They lived in an orphanage close to the barracks and we would spend time there helping out. I held clinics and some of the guys taught English or played football with them. Stuff like that. The girl in the video is six years old; I'd tried to save her brother a couple months earlier when he'd been hit by sniper fire."

He looked up into her eyes and Laura felt the world shift. She couldn't even describe the things she saw there, but she had never seen them before. This was a new Charlie. Someone with depth she hadn't believed possible.

"There were Taliban guys who would fire randomly trying to pick off the people who fraternised with us. The kids were easy pickings. No matter how many times one of our guys caught a sniper another would pop up in his place. The kids were never safe. Never. Because of us."

Laura couldn't speak. She couldn't even begin to imagine what it had been like.

"I couldn't let the girl die too. Not after losing her brother. That's why I ran back."

"What happened to her?" Laura whispered, afraid to break the spell.

"Another city, another orphanage." He rubbed his hand over his face before his shoulders shook with a heavy sigh.

"Do you keep in touch?"

"That would put her in more danger."

"So, did you..."

He held up a hand to stop her.

"You used up your two questions. I need another beer."

He pushed his chair back and headed for the bar. As she watched his lazy smile for the waitress, Laura had a niggling feeling that there was more to Charlie than met the eye. She was even beginning to suspect that he may have hidden depth. Well hidden. She'd always thought he'd joined the army on a whim, because he was bored. But now she wasn't so sure. In fact there was a lot about him that suddenly didn't make sense. He'd spent ten years studying to be an emergency department doctor, that didn't seem like the actions of a guy who lived by the seat of his pants. Whenever she heard him talk about medicine, he always made a big deal out of how he followed a pretty girl into the study and got stuck. But for ten years? She motioned to him to bring her a white wine. If she was going to entertain thoughts of Charlie having hidden depth then she would need alcohol to do it.

It was almost one a.m. before they were forced to deal with their sleeping arrangements. With Laura's tent at the bottom of a canal, Charlie had to come up with an alternative. One that didn't bear thinking about. And it seemed that Laura agreed. They were both content to while away the hours in the bar rather than to face each other in the dark. He would have loved to have gotten so incredibly drunk that Laura and her attitude didn't bother him. Unfortunately, gone were the days when he could drink all night and cycle all day. So he couldn't take refuge in an alcoholic haze. Instead, much to the amusement of the old guy behind the bar, he ordered a strong coffee. Laura finished making notes on the napkin in front of her before following him to the bar.

"I need your phone," she held out her hand. "Mine went swimming with the fish."

Charlie handed it over. He sat at the bar sipping his coffee while Laura sat in the corner and tapped furiously away on the tiny keyboard that came with his phone. No doubt updating her boss on their mini interview. Now that, he didn't want to think about. It led only to dark places.

"She's a pretty girl," the bar owner said as they both watched her.

Charlie had to think about it. He'd always thought she was sexy in a terrifying I-will-eat-you-after-the-act sort of way, but he'd never really considered her pretty. She absent-mindedly brushed her mane of hair over her shoulder as she worked. Her tiny pink tongue licked her full bottom lip and her cheeks were flushed deep pink from the warmth in the bar. He could just make out the row of freckles across her nose as her long lashes fluttered on her cheeks as she looked down.

"Yeah, she is pretty," he told the guy.

They watched her chew her bottom lip and Charlie felt something tighten in his gut. He wasn't stupid. He knew what it was. He'd felt it before, twelve years earlier. He wanted the Iron Maiden. Fortunately a man can gain a lot of self-control in twelve years and he wasn't going to make that mistake again.

"Girlfriend?" The guy behind the bar put a bowl of nuts in front of Charlie and he helped himself to a handful. The wonderful rich thickness of Dutch coffee warmed him through as he questioned the wisdom of caffeine in the middle of the night. Too late now.

"No," he said casting around for a decent explanation. "She's my sister's best friend."

"Mm." The guy stroked his handle-bar moustache. "Is your sister on holiday with you too?"

"Nope, just us."

"And you are not together?"

"No."

Charlie was fed up with the inquisition. He watched Laura shift in her seat and saw her eyes gleam. She was pleased with herself. Pleased with something she'd written.

"I think you are fooling yourself a little bit." The guy behind the bar laughed.

Charlie spun in his chair to face him.

"Look, we're not together, there is nothing going on. If you want her you can have her. Honest."

"Charming," Laura's voice came over his shoulder.

Charlie winced.

The bartender grinned widely before erupting into a belly laugh.

"Come on Romeo," Laura said drolly, "time for bed."

She handed him his phone and stalked from the bar.

"Oh, you're in trouble now," the bartender said. "You're not going to get any tonight."

Charlie rolled his eyes. It was obviously pointless to explain again.

"This is your big idea?" Laura put her hands on her hips as she glared up at him. "Your great plan for the night?"

Charlie counted to ten before he spoke, but the words were still squeezed between his teeth.

"Believe me when I say that I don't like it any more than you do."

Laura's eye began to twitch. It had been doing that a lot lately. In fact everything about her seemed to be wound up tight as though she was trying desperately to fit herself into a box that was completely the wrong shape. She put her hands on her hips and glared at the tent. His tiny one man tent.

"Why can't we sleep in the church?"

"Melinda said they had rules about that sort of thing."

He was tired of explaining this to her. When did her IQ slip so low that simple concepts escaped her?

"What if one of us slept in there? i.e. me."

"Look, do I have to go over this again?" He took one look at her determined little nose stuck in the air. Obviously he did. "When Melinda let me back into the church to get your clothes for tomorrow she said that it would be wrong to have an unmarried couple sleeping there for the night."

"We wouldn't be sleeping together. Did you tell her that?"

"Yes, believe me; I was clear about our relationship."

"And I can't sleep in there, even if I'm alone?"

She motioned to the old stone building.

"No, you can't. They have rules and they don't know us well enough to believe us when we say it would only be you."

Laura looked so dejected that he tried to cheer her up.

"At least they let us use the bathroom to wash up."

She glared at him. So that didn't work.

"There's no way the two of us will fit into that thing."

She pointed at the tent which seemed to be getting smaller by the second. Sure they would fit, but he didn't want to imagine the positions they would get into to make it happen.

"Aren't they worried about what we would do in a tent that size in their garden?"

She glared up at him as though this was his fault. On

second thoughts there may have been a hint of panic in her eyes.

"Well there is that," he said.

Her eyes went wide and her mouth made a little oh shape. He watched as she looked around the village for another alternative. There were none. He'd looked too. They had to be in the smallest town in Holland, and the only one that never expected any tourists. There weren't any hostels, hotels or guest houses. There wasn't any place else he could buy a tent. He'd even asked the nice Melinda if there was a tent he could borrow and after several phone calls she'd come up empty handed. It was his tiny tent or nothing.

"I hate this," Laura mumbled. "I hate you," she said with more force. "I hate that you are making me do this just to get a story. And I hate my evil boss for blackmailing me into it."

With that she stomped off in the direction of the pub.

"Where are you going?"

And please, if you're getting alcohol, bring me back some.

"To use the toilet."

No luck on the Dutch courage then. The phrase made him chuckle, which made Laura think he was laughing at her and she gave him the evil eye. It was going to be a long, long night.

When Laura returned she was in practical take-charge mode. He'd seen her do this time and time again with her parents when she was growing up. She'd always had this attitude of being stuck with things and having to make the best of it. Now that he thought about it, with her parents that was pretty much what she did have to do.

"Get in," she ordered. "Then I'll squeeze in beside you."

He didn't like her tone.

"I sleep naked," he told her.

Her eyes narrowed.

"Not tonight you don't."

Fine, if she wanted things clinical that's what she would get. He was a doctor. He could do clinical. He smirked in her direction as she turned away when he began to strip, but he kept his boxers on before climbing into his sleeping bag.

"Your turn," he challenged.

Now this was going to be funny. He waited for Laura to strip but all she did was take off her shoes before she started to climb in beside him.

"You're joking, right? You're going to wear everything to bed? At least take off your jeans. They'll scratch the two of us all night long."

He could see her weighing her options.

"If it helps I plan to keep my hands out of the bag."

Reluctantly, she took off her jeans. Charlie looked towards heaven and asked for some patience. With the long t-shirt and underwear she had more clothes on that she'd been wearing for most of the trip. Women. There was no explaining their logic.

With an action that reminded him of ripping off a plaster bandage, she threw back the sleeping bag and slipped in beside him. She lay stiff as a board with her back to him. Charlie shook his head before leaning over her to zip the tent shut. Then he lay back down.

They were both on their right sides facing the tent entrance. He put his arm over her body.

"No way." It sounded like she was shouting she was so close. "Keep your hands to yourself."

He counted to twenty, ten wasn't enough.

"Think about it, sweet cakes, where am I supposed to put my arm?"

She did think.

"Fine, but no touching anywhere."

"Like I want to."

She made a huffing sound.

"Are you going to zip up the bag?" he asked using every tiny bit of patience he had left. Including the extra he got from heaven. She didn't answer.

"If you don't zip up the bag we're both going to be really cold in an hour or two."

"Fine!"

She shuffled around and he felt the bag tighten pulling them closer together. He could feel the length of her down his body and regretted telling her to close the bag; now they would both overheat for sure. Every single nerve ending he had was aware of her. Her hair tickled his jaw making him want to bury his face in it. She smelled of nothing more than cheap soap but it was intoxicating. It was the weirdest experience, lying there in the black darkness in silence trying not to be aware of each other.

"Go to sleep, Charlie," Laura said wearily.

"Yeah," he answered.

At least with Laura at his side sleep was a possibility. He smiled into the darkness as his eyelids grew heavy.

Laura knew the minute Charlie was sound asleep. It didn't take long. A few seconds. She wished she could perform that trick. It always took ages for her to fall asleep; there was too much in her mind to allow it to shut down quickly. Tonight there was more than usual. She wasn't sure if she was relieved or insulted that Charlie had gone to sleep so quickly.

As she listened to Charlie breathing she began to relax a little. The man was like a furnace, so much for being cold in the night. Slowly, and quietly, she slipped the zip of the sleeping bag down a little to get some air in. As she moved away from Charlie his arm tightened its grip on her stomach and pulled her even closer to him. Laura held her breath. He was sound asleep and breathing deeply. It felt so good to be held, she tried to remember that it was Charlie doing the holding, but it didn't seem to matter.

The ground was hard beneath her; as far as she could see the thin yoga mat made absolutely no difference – she could still feel every tiny bump and rock. The little tent made her feel strangely secure. As Charlie grunted and moved in his sleep, he wrapped a leg over her legs. She was effectively pinned down. The hairy skin of his muscled thigh rubbed hers, sending tingles through her. She didn't see the harm in leaning into his embrace; he was asleep after all.

Slowly Laura snuggled back into Charlie. His arm wrapped up around her to find her hand as he pulled her tight. She could feel his heartbeat through her back - slow, solid, and reassuring. He mumbled something in his sleep as he nuzzled into her hair. It felt perfect. Laura couldn't remember ever feeling so secure. Perhaps it was the time of night, or the fact they were both exhausted? Or the atmosphere in the tiny tent? Nothing felt real. It was as though she'd stepped out of her life for a moment and let someone else be the strong one.

As Laura drifted off to sleep, she wished the moment would never end.

5

———

Charlie was dreaming. And it was fabulous. There was a naked woman writhing on top of him. She smelled like vanilla and cheap, sweaty sex - wonderful combination. He wove his fingers into her hair and pulled her towards him. Her nails bit into his shoulders making him want her more. He didn't start with gentle teasing kisses; no he plunged into her mouth, tasting all of her. Oh man, but she was delicious. She was slow to kiss back, but when she did it blew his mind.

Waves of wanting washed over him. He ran his hands down her back to cup her behind. He vaguely wondered why she had so many clothes on. Her rear was small and firm, it fit perfectly into his hands. He held her tightly so that he could position her where he wanted her to be. So she could feel exactly how much he wanted her. A small gasp escaped her and he grunted his satisfaction. That was more like it.

Too many clothes. There were too many clothes. And it was so stinking hot in his head. He ran one hand over her hip to push her t-shirt up, tracing soft skin as he did so. Her kisses grew more desperate as his hand slid round to grasp her breast. Something about it felt familiar. He flicked his thumb over the nipple and the woman gasped as she arched her back. She ground against him, making him pant with need.

He tried to shift into a position to give her more, but there were too many barriers. He had on underwear for a start. That didn't make any sense. He never wore underwear to bed. His feet felt trapped. Was he tied up? He tried to kick loose but it seemed to tangle him more. The air was getting heavy. And although it was dark there was a dim light coming from somewhere. It was hard to pinpoint. Something wasn't right. Shouldn't everything be perfect in a dream? Was this another nightmare?

The woman ran her hands down his chest making him forget about the darkness. Her mouth travelled to his neck, kissing, teasing and he forgot about his trapped feet. She flicked her tongue over his nipple and something tugged at his brain. This was familiar.

He put a hand on each side of her tiny waist to pull her up to him, so that he could taste her again. Her lips were full, and eager, and tasted better than anything he had ever tasted. He wanted her badly. All of her. Deeply. Over and over.

"Charlie," she whispered.

He knew that voice.

Small breasts rubbed against his chest making him desperate to undress her.

"Charlie," she groaned.

What the hell? He jerked her away from him. In the dim light he could make out the sleepy and confused features of Laura Prentice and reality hit him like a brick to the head.

"What the heck?" Laura said mirroring his thoughts. "What do you think you're doing?"

She sat astride him.

"You're the one on top of me," he pointed out.

She scrambled to get off of him, wiping her mouth with the back of her hand. Charlie thought that was a bit much, since she'd been groaning his name not ten seconds earlier.

"What did you do to me?" she hissed. "I told you to keep your hands to yourself."

Charlie pushed up onto his elbows; he felt at a distinct disadvantage lying down while having this conversation.

"Look." It was obvious one of them had to be the voice of reason and from the look of hysteria on her face it would have to be him. "Obviously we were both asleep and things got out of hand."

"In my sleep?!" Her voice was high pitched. "Both of us? What are the chances of that? Are you sure you weren't taking advantage?"

Now that cheesed him off.

"Laura, I woke up with you wiggling your backside on top of me. I was kissing you before I knew who you were. It seems obvious that the small space and the heat made the situation confusing."

"Ha!"

"Fine, don't believe me. The only other explanation is that you were desperate to get your hands on me and jumped me while I was asleep."

"Like that would happen."

"You were kissing me too." He felt the need to point out.

"I was asleep!"

This was beginning to become offensive.

"You were hot for me. Asleep or not."

"That is not true."

Now he was really annoyed.

"You still are," he told her. Even in the dim light of early morning he could make out her flushed cheeks and her heavy breathing.

"Charlie Lewis, you are the last man on earth I would be hot for."

She turned away from him, but Charlie was seriously fed up now. He sat up, grabbed her shoulder and spun her around towards him. In a second his mouth was on hers. She squeaked with shock and tried to pull away, but Charlie held her as he kissed her, making his point. It didn't take long. Laura melted against him, kissing him more passionately than she had before.

Charlie didn't know what happened, but he did know that he wanted her and he wanted her badly. He swung her beneath him, running his hand up the length of her. Laura's fingers worked their way down his back as she kissed him passionately. He had to know. Had to be certain. A kiss to make a point was one thing, but this was another.

"Laura," he croaked. "Do you want this?"

Please say yes, please say yes.

"Yes," she whispered, and then pulled his mouth back to hers; biting his bottom lip to make sure he got the message.

She didn't need to say anything else. In ten seconds he had her t-shirt off and was working on the bra clasp when he heard a voice.

"Good Morning," the voice called. "Wakey, wakey, I have breakfast for you."

They stilled. Entangled in each other's embrace.

"Hello, are you in there?"

"It's Melinda," Charlie whispered.

"Who?" Laura sounded dazed.

"The church lady. The one with the clothes."

Laura let out a groan that was half way between disappointment and frustration. He understood it perfectly.

"We're here. Give us a minute," he called to Melinda.

They scrambled to pull on clothes, no doubt making the tent jerk as they did so. A minute later Charlie unzipped the tent as he wondered how they were going to deal with each other now. Laura didn't look at him, but her cheeks were red.

Melinda cleared her throat. It was obvious that she was pleased they hadn't been allowed to sleep in the church building. Charlie ran a hand through his mussed hair and smiled sheepishly. There was no explanation for this. He felt like a teenager caught making out on his mother's couch.

"I didn't mean to wake you," Melinda stumbled over the word "wake'. "It's just you wanted this bike and I had to drop it off before I went to work."

She smiled apologetically.

"Thank you," he said.

There was an old Dutch bike resting against a tree.

"This is for you too."

Melinda handed him a plastic box and a flask.

"Coffee and sandwiches. Leave the containers in the church when you are finished. I hope you enjoy the rest of your trip in Holland."

Charlie thanked her and waved her off, all the while wondering if Laura was ever going to get out of the tent. His mind was completely blank as to what to say to her. One thing was for sure; they weren't getting back in the tent and carrying on where they left off. At last she emerged. She'd managed to pull her jeans on inside the tent.

"That was a mistake," she said before he could say anything. "Close quarters, lack of sleep, hormones." She counted the reasons off on her fingers. "And it's been a very long time since I slept with anyone."

She looked him in the eye. He'd always liked that about Laura, she was always honest no matter how much it cost her. He always knew where he stood with her.

"You woke up my libido," she said, "sorry about that."

He felt his eyes go wide. She was apologising for trying to have sex with him? What was the appropriate response? Thank you? Anytime? No problem? He had no idea what to say. Thankfully he didn't have to say anything.

"Let's forget all about it. Did Melinda say there was coffee?"

With flushed cheeks, she took the flask from his hand and poured herself a cup.

"Lovely," she said with a sigh. "So what's the plan for today?"

Charlie felt his mouth open and shut like some sort of hooked fish. He was Alice down the friggin" hole. And by the look on Laura's face she was the Hatter. There was nothing to do but join in.

"Well," he said as he pulled out a sandwich, "first there is the little matter of you wearing what I picked out." He looked her in the eye. "Without underwear."

She didn't even blink. If it wasn't for her pink cheeks he would have thought their adventure in the tent had never happened.

"THIS IS OUT OF ORDER," Laura complained again. "This is sleazy, even for you."

"I'm a man," he told her making no effort not to sound smug. "You said no underwear. You said you would wear whatever I wanted you to wear – For. My. Pleasure. It was a deal. You wouldn't shirk on a deal, would you, short stuff. I mean, if you did then I would have to think twice about keeping our other deal, the one where I give you an interview at the end of this trip."

Although he was behind her he could imagine her grinding her teeth into dust. It made him grin. Man, but she wanted this interview badly. It was hard to take anything she said seriously when she was struggling to stay upright on her new bike. Melinda had told him it was a traditional Dutch bike; they called it an Oma Fietsen – granny bike. It was heavy, huge, had no gears or brakes. If Laura wanted to stop she would have to cycle backwards, and from the look of things that wasn't a concept she grasped easily. Add to that the fact her toes couldn't reach the ground and the moment was gold. It didn't even need the clothes he'd picked out for her, that was just icing on the cake.

"This shows everything," she huffed. "I may as well be naked."

"That's your call," he told her, although he had to disagree, it didn't show everything. That was why it was so sexy; it left a lot to the imagination.

"I was very considerate," he told her. "I picked out the biggest item of clothing they had, just so that you wouldn't feel exposed as you rode."

That was enough to make her stop, which she did by slowing and falling off her bike onto the grass. She stood quickly and dusted herself off before confronting him with a scowl, hands on hips. It might even have been scary had it not been for the fact she was standing with the light behind her and he could make out the line of her figure in minute detail. His mouth watered as some part of his brain wondered at the wisdom of playing sexual games with the Iron Maiden.

"It's transparent, moron."

She held out one arm to show him and he grinned appreciatively. It was indeed.

"It's a tent. You're covered from neck, to wrist, to ankle. What's to complain about?"

Her head went almost as orange as the paisley pattern on the sheer fabric.

"It's a 1970's Kaftan and it's supposed to be worn over something." She looked down at her body. "Like underwear."

Charlie got off his bike and sauntered towards her. He rubbed some of the yards of fabric that swallowed her between his fingers.

"If you don't like the consequences, don't make the deals," he said.

His mind was on other things, like what it would feel like to rub his hands all over her. The kaftan looked better every minute.

"When I made the deal, I thought you would put me in a halter and tiny shorts, or a boiler suit, or that wet suit I saw..."

"...there was a wet suit?"

That might have been better. The breeze caught the fabric and flattened it across her chest. He had a sudden urge to see what her nipples tasted like through the cloth. Nope, this was much better than a wet suit.

"But this?" She flapped her arms like a chicken. "At the first gust of wind it's going to blow up and give the world a show."

"We can only hope."

His voice came out more of a growl than he had intended.

One swift kick to the shin and he wasn't feeling so horny anymore.

"Grow up, moron," she told him as she climbed back onto her bike. "You constantly act like you're fifteen. It grates on my nerves."

Charlie didn't care. The sheer fabric pulled taut around her behind as she pedalled in front of him. He could live with being immature any day.

Laura's head hurt. She was dressed in a transparent mu mu, riding a bike built for a giant with The Neanderthal staring at her backside. Oh yeah, her head hurt all right. On top of that she was practising deep denial over what had happened in the early hours of the morning. What had she been thinking? She hadn't been thinking, that was the problem. That was always the problem, there was something about him that sucked out her common sense and made her do rash things. Things she would regret later. She thought she'd learnt from her encounter with him years earlier, but she hadn't. He was everything she wasn't – he oozed sex appeal, he looked like he fell out of a poster for underwear and he was so free and easy with his life. When he wasn't making her act irresponsibly, he was making her feel bad because she didn't! The sooner she was away from him the better.

She cast a nervous glance over her shoulder; he spotted it and winked at her making her wobble on her bike. He had on an old pair of grey shorts and his favourite U2 t-shirt, his toffee coloured hair was dishevelled and he had a day's worth of stubble. He was freaking Adonis. She had no doubt that there were women out there who would worship at the feet of him, if they had a chance. Dangerous. He was dangerous. He was the only person who had ever managed to get her to do something spontaneous, to do something out of her comfort zone. He was the only man who had ever made her lose control. Unfortunately, he was still the only man who could do it. And she didn't need that. Not again. Never again. She needed an interview. That was all she wanted from Charlie Lewis. She peeked over her shoulder again. His smile made her catch her breath and her cheeks flush. She stared back at the road in front of her. Yep, she lied to herself; all she wanted from the Neanderthal was an interview to save her career.

THEY SAT at the water's edge with the canal behind them, looking down from the dyke and over the town. The sun was high in the sky as a ferry passed behind them.

"I like the crooked houses, do you think they worry that they might fall over?" she asked before biting into her apple.

For an impromptu picnic it was pretty good. There was even a box from the local Dutch bakery that was winking at her. She'd promised herself that she wouldn't open it until she'd eaten the healthy stuff first. Well, most of it. The box sparkled in the sun. Well, some of it.

"Holland was reclaimed from the sea," he said. "Most of it would be underwater if it wasn't for the dykes. It takes some serious engineering to build here, the ground is basically sodden." He pointed at the grid of smaller canals running through the town, there seemed to be one at the end of every garden. "That's why there are so many canals, there has to be a way to control the water and get it to the places they need it to be, otherwise there wouldn't be any towns. It's also why the houses are wonky, the foundations are basically in swamp. Engineering stops that from happening now. The Dutch are great at engineering."

She gaped at him.

"How the heck do you know all that?"

One pastry, then she'd have a salad sandwich, seriously who would it hurt? She was doing more exercise than she had ever done in her lifetime. That was using calories right? In fact she was probably in negative energy; she probably needed the cakes just to have energy to function on a basic level. Yep, she needed the cake more than the vitamins.

Charlie pushed the box of cakes towards her.

"Laura, just eat the cake. Watching you think about it is giving me a headache. And for your information, I read. What did you think I did during down time in Afghanistan?"

"Internet porn?"

His lips twitched as she opened the pastry box with a deep sigh. Bliss. There was a small round cake, shaped like a chunky tube with chopped hazelnuts around the outside and cream on top, she took a big bite. Yum, dacquoise, it was a favourite of hers. There was a hint of coffee in the cream. Delicious.

Charlie cleared his throat making her open her eyes. He swallowed hard before reaching for his water bottle.

"Maddie said you had a thing for cake," his voice seemed strained. "She said you bake now."

He was talking about her? Well that was news. She nodded through a mouthful of hazelnut bliss.

"When we were poor students we couldn't afford treats so we got baking books from the library. Maddie was more into the eating than making, but I enjoy it. It's relaxing."

"You don't look like you eat a lot of cake," he said eyeing her figure through the bloody horrible mu mu.

"Is that your way of telling me that I look okay, or that I'm not fat yet?"

He looked briefly confused.

"You have a sexy body, Laura," he said seriously.

Her cheeks burned.

"Don't be stupid, I look like a kid. I can still buy jeans in the children's section of some shops."

"Slender, curved in all the right places, smooth skin. What's not to like?"

Laura didn't know what to say. She felt exposed. From the look on Charlie's face he regretted talking too. His phone rang and he pounced on it with obvious relief. Laura picked up a strawberry tart and took a bite. Sexy? Her? He'd obviously been in an all-male environment far too long. It had messed with his head.

"It's for you," he said as he thrust the phone at her.

She frowned, wiped her fingers on the mu mu and reached for it thinking it was her boss looking for an update. She was the only one Laura had given the number to since her phone drowned.

"Hello, Laura here," she said hesitantly.

"Laura darling, you have been so hard to track down. I had to get your number from Maddie's mother of all people. She said you were on holiday with Charlie. Charlie? I thought she was losing her mind, but here you are answering his phone."

Her heart sank as her shoulders slumped.

"Mother," she said in monotone.

"Well who else would it be?" her mother shrieked in her ear. Her mother never spoke, only shrieked, signalling to everyone within hearing distance that she was "dramatic, darling'.

"Apart from your father and Maddie, who else would call you?"

"No one, I guess. What do you want, Mum?"

"Now what makes you think that I want anything?"

There was a beat of silence. Laura didn't play along. Her mother only ever called if she wanted something and they both knew it. She could almost see her pouting on the other end of the line. Her dyed blond hair styled into the latest fashion, her ample curves poured into something slightly too small and way too sexy. At last her mother caved, as Laura knew she would, and sighed heavily.

"It's your father," she said in that high pitched voice Laura had prayed she wouldn't inherit. "He won't let me into the house. He says he's had enough and that I need to find somewhere else to live."

Laura pinched the bridge of her nose as she squeezed her eyes shut. Here it goes again, she thought. Her role in life, referee for her parents.

"I'm sure it will pass," she said evenly, "it always does."

"Laura." Even her mother's tone pouted. "You make it sound like this happens often. Really, you shouldn't imply such things."

That was a fight she wasn't going to get into.

"Go to one of your friends, it will blow over in a couple of days and he'll come looking for you."

"He threw my clothes onto the lawn."

Well that was new, he hadn't done that before.

"You need to talk to him. He won't take my calls."

"Mum." Laura felt bone weary, years older than the twenty nine she had legal claim to. "This is between you and Dad. You need to sort it out yourselves."

Like that was ever going to happen.

"Please, pretty please," her mother whined. "You know I can't live without him."

It was on the tip of her tongue to tell her mother if that was the case then she should stop sleeping with other men. She'd tried it once when she was a teenager, the tantrum was huge and Laura decided the fallout wasn't worth the effort. She had long ago come to terms with the fact her parents had a highly dysfunctional relationship.

"Mum, I'm in Holland."

"I know, with that idiot boy."

Laura ground her teeth.

"Honestly Laura, if you want a man I can find you someone far better than Charlie Lewis."

"No," Laura snapped. The last thing she wanted was for her mother to set her up with anyone, ever.

She looked over to where Charlie was standing, hands in pockets looking out over the water. He was listening to every word. She didn't know why that should make her feel embarrassed; it wasn't anything the whole street hadn't heard when she was growing up. Still, she turned away from him in a vain attempt at gaining more privacy.

"Really," her mother sounded thrilled with herself, "I know the most delightful young man. Another actor, in the West End."

She made it sound like he was saving the planet.

"No," Laura almost shouted. "I don't want, or need, you to set me up with anyone. Okay?"

There was silence. Laura knew from experience that there was only one way to get her mother to drop the latest whim that popped into her mind: change the topic to her favourite subject – herself.

"Look, I'll call Dad okay. I'll see what I can do, but he probably won't listen to me this time. So don't get your hopes up."

Her mother squealed in her ear.

"Wonderful, darling, I knew I could count on you. You always were so capable at sorting these things out. You are so sensible dear. I'm sure you'll make him see reason."

Her mother hung up without so much as a goodbye or a thank you. Laura closed the phone and stared at her lap. Two deep breaths and she flicked it open to dial her father.

"You don't have to do that you know," Charlie said beside her. He sounded tense.

"No, I don't."

She punched in the number.

"Let them sort out their own mess," he said.

Easier said than done. That would mean dumping a lifetime of training. Hadn't she been born for this task – mediator in the war of the Prentices?

Charlie crouched beside her as the phone rang. He placed a hand on hers, stopping her from taking the phone to her ear.

"Seriously Laura. This isn't your responsibility."

She stared into his deep blue eyes and felt an ache inside.

"Isn't it?" she said.

"Hello, hello, who is this?" her father said from her lap.

"Let it go," Charlie said. "They're adults."

It was very simple for Charlie. But he wasn't the one who had to deal with them.

"They are also my family," Laura said feeling pathetic at the thought. "The only one I have."

He shook his head slightly.

"I'm hanging up," her father threatened.

Laura put the phone to her ear.

"Hi Dad," she said. "Mum called."

Charlie walked away.

6

"We're going on a detour," Charlie announced two days later.

"I wasn't aware we were following a route in the first place."

He grinned down at her, perfect white teeth sparkling in the sun.

"Ye of little faith," he said.

"In you, yeah."

Charlie plopped on the grass beside her. Over the past few days they had relaxed into an easy routine. Cycle all day, set up camp at night, have dinner in a pub, then go to sleep – in separate tents. Something had changed. Charlie wasn't flirting with every woman that crossed his path; instead he was spending time with her. He teased her and talked to her, sometimes she even thought he was flirting with her. It boggled her mind. And, much to her amazement, she was enjoying every minute of it.

"Well." He nudged her with his elbow making her drop the romance novel she was reading. "Aren't you curious, don't you want to know what we're doing?"

"Uh, no."

She grinned at his downcast face, sometimes it was like squishing the exuberance of a toddler on a sugar high.

"Fine." She made a dramatic sigh that her mother would have been proud of. "What are we doing today Charlie?"

"That's more like it."

He raked around in his back pocket and came out with a brochure.

"I'll give you a clue; we're half an hour from Edam."

His sense of fun was contagious and she smiled in spite of herself.

"We're making cheese?"

He rolled his eyes.

"Would I be that obvious?"

"We're not going on a boat are we?" She tried not to sound as panicked as she felt.

"No, no boat."

"Something to do with clogs?"

She was running out of options.

"Hopeless," he said cheerfully. "We're doing a cooking class."

He thrust the leaflet at her.

"We're going to learn to make authentic Dutch apple tart."

Laura was speechless. She stared at the leaflet, which explained in perfect English that the deep appelgebak sold in most cafés was a Dutch staple and to master that was to master the beginnings of Dutch cuisine.

"You like baking?" she said.

"No, stupid, but you do and this looks like fun."

He jumped to his feet as he averted his eyes.

"Don't make a big deal out of it. I need a break from cycling and it was this or clog dancing."

"Good choice," Laura said. "Your dancing is rubbish without wooden shoes. I couldn't risk my toes with you wearing them."

"Exactly."

He bent over and rummaged in his tent allowing Laura time to smile at him without him seeing. It wasn't every day someone thought of her. It might not be a big deal to Charlie, but Laura was touched. And then he blew it.

"If I have to cook all day, can you wear that Kaftan thing again without the underwear?"

She threw the leaflet at his head.

THE COOKING LESSON took place in the kitchen of a farmhouse that just happened to be attached to a microbrewery.

"How self-sacrificing," Laura said as the host offered them a selection of beers to taste.

"I do what I can," Charlie said solemnly as he pounced on the tray.

After a long winded lecture from the owner of the brewery on the different types of beer - which no doubt became more interesting for people the more they sampled, although Laura didn't know about that, she didn't like beer – they were led into a wide farmhouse style kitchen.

There was enough space for eight people, two to a bench. There was one other English couple, two Japanese girls who giggled a lot and an older German couple who corrected everyone around them. Charlie helped himself to a pink frilly pinny and tied it round his waist. Although it brought a smile to Laura's face, the apron had the unnerving effect of making him look more masculine rather than less.

"I wore something like this for a kinky Swedish girl once," he told her out of the side of his mouth.

"Yuk."

Laura elbowed him in the ribs making him yelp.

The woman at the front of the room explained how to make a basic sweet pastry. Charlie looked at the mixing tools as though they'd fallen from a space ship.

"Like this."

Laura showed him what to use. Once he knew what to work with he was quick to learn.

"Don't work with the dough too much, you'll ruin it," she told him. "You want to keep it cold."

He played with the dough as though it was plasticine.

"I like how it feels."

He popped a piece in his mouth.

"I like how it tastes."

Laura gulped.

"I suppose you're going to tell me you like how it smells too."

"Nope," he leaned in towards her. "I can only smell you."

Laura froze as he nuzzled her hair.

"And you smell good."

She looked up at him wide eyed.

"Bet you taste good too," he said.

Her mouth fell open slightly. Was he flirting? Charlie winked. Her world shifted. Yes. He was.

"Good work," the woman said from the other side of their bench.

She was pointing to Laura's beautifully lined deep pie pan.

"You want to put it in the fridge to keep it cold while you work on the apples."

Laura nodded as though that was something she didn't know.

"As for you young man," the woman said to Charlie. "If

you don't stop playing with the dough you won't get any tart."

Charlie looked over the woman's shoulders to Laura and grinned widely.

"I don't know about that," he said.

Laura stuck her face in the fridge to cool down.

"Peel the apples, slice finely and mix with custard powder and sugar," the woman was saying. "Then you can work on the raisins in orange juice..."

"So what's your favourite cake?" Charlie asked Laura. "Chocolate right? Women always go for the chocolate."

She rolled her eyes. He was standing close to her. Bumping into her with every move he made. A stroke here, a hand on the back there. He was deliberately trying to make her hyper aware of him. It made her dizzy.

"It's a genetic thing. There was a woman on base who would go mental for chocolate once a month. We took turns supplying her so that she wouldn't take a knife to anyone's throat while they slept."

He grinned. It took her breath away.

"Chocolate was easy to get in Afghanistan?" Laura said.

"Care packages."

She remembered, she'd helped Maddie on several occasions to send some to Charlie.

"People liked to send food; we always had loads of food kicking around. Sometimes we played poker with boxes of tea and coffee that no one wanted."

Laura marvelled that he was talking so freely about his time away. She filed all the details he was giving to use as colour in her article.

"What was your favourite thing to receive?"

"Maddie always sent comics. They were great. Took my mind off things, but didn't stretch the brain. You could pick them up and put them down a million times and not miss anything. Comics were good."

Laura felt inordinately pleased with herself. The comics had been her idea. Okay, so she'd said it derogatorily, something like – send the Neanderthal some picture books it's about his level – still it counted right?

"Some of the guys liked to read romance novels." He gave her his goofy grin. "If that gets out I'm a dead man."

"Understood."

She found herself grinning back.

"You read that stuff too," he pointed out to her.

"I like to believe it's possible. Passionate love that doesn't mean treating each other like rubbish."

She got the impression she'd said something more than she'd intended because Charlie's face darkened.

"You know what your parents have isn't love right?"

Whoa, heavy topic alert! She arched an eyebrow in an attempt to inject humour.

"And you're the expert?"

"No, just not an idiot. There may be passion, but it isn't love. Mum always said that they thrived on the high drama. She put it down to them being creative. It looks more like selfishness to me."

Laura brushed her hair away from her face and tied it in a band, to give herself something to do. She'd always known her family were a hot conversation topic, but even Maddie had steered clear of telling her what people said about them.

It had been a long time since Laura had felt the need to explain or excuse their behaviour, but it didn't mean she was comfortable talking about it. So she changed the topic.

"So, were you in the same place in Afghanistan or did you move around?"

Charlie studied her as though he could see right through her. For a moment she thought he wouldn't let her off the hook by answering the question.

"I moved around," he said stiffly.

"Your raisins are burning."

She leaned over and switched his hob off. He grabbed her hand and held it. Laura looked up into his eyes and felt the room begin to fade. She held her breath.

"When you love someone you don't sleep around on them, and you definitely don't allow someone you love to do that to you." She tried to pull her hand away, but he held her tightly. "And you never, ever get your kids involved in that sort of sick set up. Don't confuse their games with passion and love. They've got it all wrong. When you want someone you don't go off with someone else."

He was so close she could see his heart beat out a rhythm in the base of his throat. For a split second she entertained the thought of kissing him there. She pulled away instead, forcing an easy smile.

"Aye, aye captain," she said with a salute.

He waited a beat as he studied her, his shoulders relaxed, he was going to let her lighten the moment.

"It's lieutenant to you," he told her as he stirred his raisins.

Laura let out a quiet sigh.

"Well la-di-da, Lieutenant Lewis."

She gave him a little curtsy. Charlie winked at her.

"Don't you forget it."

Laura brushed a stray strand of hair from her cheek, which felt as though it was on fire. Charlie watched her from behind eyelashes most girls would kill for. He reached for a cloth and stepped towards her.

"What is it?" she said, her voice hoarse.

"Apple on your cheek."

He sounded equally strained as he reached up with his cloth to wipe her face. Half way he stopped. He put the cloth on the counter and wiped away the apple with his thumb. Slowly he licked it off his thumb.

"Yum," he said.

And just like the women in some of the sillier romantic stories she read, Laura went weak at the knees.

Charlie stepped closer, making her back into the counter. She could feel the edge of it nip her lower back.

"If we weren't here," he said softly, "I would eat you all up, Laura Prentice."

"What makes you think I would let you?"

He cocked an eyebrow before leaning in to nip a tiny kiss below her earlobe. The world went out of focus as her breath hitched in her throat.

"I think that answers the question," he whispered, his breath on her ear made her shiver. "I think we need to finish what we started that night in the tent. What do you think?"

Laura struggled to find her voice. When she did it was embarrassingly breathless.

"But you call me the Iron Maiden when you think I can't hear."

His smile was slow as his eyes darkened.

"Yeah, it's a mystery to me too."

He brushed his fingers across her bottom lip, making her breath catch, before leaning into her.

"I'm taking a leaf out of your book. I'm laying my cards on the table. I want you."

"Oh," was all Laura could manage to say.

He kissed her neck again before whispering in her ear.

"I want you Laura."

He slid his fingers into her hair at the base of her skull

and gently pulled her towards him. His kiss was slow and easy. It reminded her of the way she ate a cheesecake. Every mouthful a wonder.

"Hey," a loud German voice called out. "This is a kitchen. Take it to the bedroom you two."

Charlie scowled at the man while Laura flushed like a teenager caught necking. The Japanese girls giggled. The woman running the class beamed at them and waved her wooden spoon in their direction.

"Apple tart is known to be the cake of love," she told them proudly.

Laura made some non-committal noise while she busied herself with her ingredients. Charlie gave her a smile that signalled he wasn't through with her. She swallowed hard. She felt like she was in the eye of the storm, first phase over, but the rest of it still to come. As his broad shoulders hunched over the counter she bit her bottom lip to stifle a groan. There was no use pretending otherwise. She wanted him too. Badly. When it came to Charlie Lewis, her body had a will of its own. It always had.

She wasn't sure if he brought out the worst in her, or made her a more interesting person. It didn't really matter. She felt like she was stuck on a roller coaster, she couldn't get off. She looked at Charlie, as scary as it was, she may as well enjoy the ride. They worked in silence, preparing their tarts for the oven, sharing secret smiles and touches like lovers. Anticipating later when they would be alone. It was exquisite torture. As they waited for the oven, sipping thick Dutch coffee, Laura couldn't stand the silence any more.

The sexual tension had her wired ready to snap. She grasped around for something to say. Anything to say.

"So," she said at last, "did you meet William or Harry when you were at Sandhurst?"

Charlie rolled his eyes.

"Women always want to hear about those two."

"Well," she prodded, nudging his big feet off the stool they were resting on.

"Fine." He threw up his hands in surrender. "I did hear a funny story about them from a guy who trained with Harry."

Laura loved the way his eyes sparkled with mischief as he spoke.

"Do tell, I promise you'll still get first billing in my story, but the public do love to hear about Harry. Especially now William is taken."

"I bet they do, but I'd forgotten about the story, so I better wait to share my info until you've written yours. Wouldn't want the Palace on my tail."

"Tease," she said.

"I can be." His eyes darkened.

Laura flushed and turned away from him. She wasn't sure what had shifted or why he was coming on to her. She couldn't think straight from the electricity that crackled between them. From the slow lazy smile he gave her, he knew exactly what he was doing. She was out of her depth.

CHARLIE COULDN'T KEEP his hands off Laura. They were wedged side by side in a booth in the bar, but it still felt too far away. He'd tried for days to keep away from her, to put what had happened in the tent out of his mind. But he couldn't. Not thinking about it made it worse. The only way he was going to get her out of his system was to finish what they started. It was the only thing that made sense.

"Do you want your sandwich?'

Laura smiled before pushing the plate towards him. She

hadn't had much of an appetite anyway. He'd been watching her push the food around for almost an hour.

"Thanks."

As he reached for the food, he pressed closer into her. Her eyes widened. Her cheeks flushed. He felt her hand on his thigh and his pulse quickened. She made tiny circular motions with her thumb and it drove him wild.

"Another drink?" he said.

"Diet Coke," she told him.

Her hand slid to his inner thigh. He briefly wondered if it would be crass to move it to where he really wanted her to touch. Yeah. Probably best to wait. Bummer.

He pushed the plate away, relaxed back into the booth and put an arm around her. She didn't resist when he pulled her tight against him. That was better.

"You're driving me crazy," he told her.

She smiled like she knew it.

"Why don't we get out of here?"

She motioned towards the window.

"It isn't dark yet."

That one sentence took his breath away. He'd been watching too. All his plans for the tent needed darkness. Still, he wasn't sure if they were on the same page.

"We could go to a motel," he said quietly.

Laura looked up at him. A small smile curled her lips.

"I'm kind of attached to the tent."

It didn't answer his question. The band started to play. He ran his fingers up and down Laura's arm making her shiver. A woman came to the table selling tickets for an outdoor gig later in the week. He bought two just to make her go away. Laura moved her hand to his stomach. His muscles tensed. He leaned towards her ear. He had to know.

"Are we on the same page?" he said.

He felt her grin. She moved so that she could talk in his ear instead of shouting over the music.

"Well, I was planning to have sex in the tent. What were you planning?"

His mouth went dry. Before he could say anything else she spoke again.

"What do you say Charlie? Do you want to sleep with me?"

Blood rushed from his head to the more important parts of his body. He wanted to shout: "yes, one hundred percent, yes'. Instead he wove his fingers into her long hair and angled her head so that he could see her face. Slowly, deliberately, he kissed her lips. She melted against him. He could feel her heart beat pounding right through his chest. It took all his self-control to end the kiss. He moved to her ear.

"You know, sweet cakes, just once, I would like to be the one who says those words."

That made her smile.

He pulled her tight against him while they listened to the music. Laura's hand drifted under his shirt to caress his chest and he kept a close eye on the sky outside the window. Crazy woman. He had absolutely no idea what to make of her, but at least, for this night anyway, he knew what to do with her. That made him grin. He kissed her hair.

Laura was in a daze. Her brain had left her body and it was all Charlie's fault. All she could think about was getting her hands on him. They made it back to the campsite in pitch blackness. All around them were the sounds of night, low mumbled conversation, and soft laughter. Charlie held her hand tightly as though he expected her to bolt. She wasn't going to. She didn't want to. Not tonight.

Charlie crawled into her new, and larger, tent. He reached for her to come in after him. Laura did as she was told.

"Okay," Laura said. "We're doing this huh?"

Charlie didn't say anything. Instead he reached for the bottom of her t-shirt and pulled it over her head.

"I guess that's a yes."

He shook his head slightly, before bending over and taking her nipple in his mouth. He sucked her through the lace of her bra as his hands held her waist tightly. Laura swayed as her breath quickened. At last he stopped and sat up to look at her. It took effort to open her eyes, her eyelids were so heavy.

"That's a yes," he said.

And then his mouth was on hers. Laura grabbed at his t-shirt, making him stop kissing her to take it off. She didn't know what to touch first, all of that muscle. She ran her hands wherever she could reach as his tongue stroked her lips.

"Let's get these off," he growled as he tugged at her jeans.

She wriggled to get them off, but there wasn't enough space, they fell over onto one another with Laura's jeans trapped around her knees.

"Wait a minute," Charlie said. "I can get them."

He knelt beside her, grabbed the top of her jeans and pulled. They came off too fast. He lost his balance on the edge of her replacement air bed and fell into the side of the tent. It knocked her bike over and it crashed to the ground. They stilled. Fortunately, no one rushed to see what the racket was.

"Okay," Charlie said at last. "Where were we?"

He lay beside her on the mattress. They wriggled to get into position. It wasn't built for two and as Charlie leaned in to kiss her there was a pop and a hiss. The mattress deflated beneath them. They lay still until they hit the ground.

"We can still do this," he said determinedly.

"Yes. We can," Laura said, although she was beginning to have her doubts.

Charlie ran his hand down the length of her body, leaving a trail of tingling flesh in its wake. That was more like it. Gently he kissed from her shoulder up to her neck. Laura bit her lip as she reached for him.

"Wait," she said. "Do you have condoms handy?"

He stopped dead.

"I meant to buy some," he said dejectedly.

Laura pushed him away from her.

"I don't have any either."

Charlie plopped on the ground beside her. They both stared at the roof of the tent.

"Well this is a disaster," Charlie said at last.

Laura started to giggle. It bubbled out of her until she was clutching her sides from laughing so hard; through it all she could hear Charlie laughing along with her.

When they calmed down he pulled her towards him, wrapped his arm around her and held her tight against his chest.

"Next time better," he said. "Promise."

"Well, it couldn't be worse, moron."

He kissed the top of her head before pulling the sleeping bag over them. Laura smiled contentedly and fell asleep listening to the steady rhythm of his strong heart.

"So, you're never getting married?"

Laura had discovered, much to her disgust, that Dutch people mainly ate sandwiches for breakfast. Fortunately most cafes offered pastries as an alternative. She tucked into a large croissant and waited for the answer.

"I won't say never, but it's not on my list, no."

As usual Charlie was eating enough food for a small army. Plus, he'd made the waitress leave the full coffee pot on the table beside him.

"That's way too much caffeine," Laura told him.

"I need it." He gave her a pointed look. "Someone kept waking me up last night with her wandering hands."

Laura flushed and reminded herself again that the first thing she needed to do was buy condoms. It had been a very long and very frustrating night.

"So," she brought the conversation back to marriage, "why not? Too many women, not enough time?"

She prodded him with her toe under the table. Every movement seemed to take the most amount of effort. She felt like her bones had been removed and replaced with jelly. She needed sleep or sex, probably both, and she needed them fast.

"Marriage just isn't for me."

She scowled at him which made him grin.

"Enough with the interrogation already. I just don't see myself in the suburbs raising kids and worrying about dental bills and football games. It sounds so..."

"...boring?"

"Exactly."

He handed her the Danish pastry on the edge of his plate without her having to ask.

"And?" she prompted.

She might not be the investigative journalist she'd always dreamed of becoming, but she could tell when Charlie was holding back. He got the same constipated look that his sister did.

"Fine." He shrugged like it was no big deal, which meant it was. "When I was in the army I saw the toll it took on the married guys. They were out there every day risking their lives, living half a world away from their families. They missed a lot. They heard about baby steps and first teeth via Skype. And they worried what life would be like for their families if they didn't make it back. I kept thinking about the strain on everyone. I don't know how they did it. I couldn't do it."

She pointed her coffee spoon at him.

"But you don't have to do it. You left the army, remember? So you don't have to leave a wife and kids to go off to war."

"Yeah, but I can't stay at home with them either. I'd drive us all nuts."

"That's true," she conceded. "So why did you leave? You're the poster boy for bravery right now, not to mention easy on the eye. The army must want you back in the worst way."

His face closed off a little.

"It was the right time."

"I don't get it."

She thought he wouldn't answer her, that he would back off completely, instead he gave her a sad lopsided smile.

"I'm a coward, short stuff, I can't hack it."

Laura stilled with the pastry halfway to her mouth. She didn't know what to say. He held her gaze.

"Those kids, remember?"

She nodded; suddenly she didn't have any appetite.

"We put them in danger. We killed them. In that uniform we paint a target on ourselves and the people around us. Those guys," he rubbed a hand over his face, "they know that, but they know how essential it is for them to be there. The good outweighs the bad. They're not just fighting for the rest of us, but because it's right. That's where I fell down. The fact I made everyone into a target outweighed everything else." He paused. "Ergo, no army for me."

"You're not a coward." Laura said, mainly because she didn't know what else to say.

"I joined for the excitement, then it bit me in the backside. Those people actually needed me."

She looked around for the right thing to say. She couldn't see it in the busy square or the town hall that was built in the Middle Ages.

"It's not a bad thing to realise," she said at last.

"Maybe, maybe not. It's kind of counter to my life motto."

"Party hard?"

He laughed and she felt relieved.

"Yeah, but I might go back, just not with the army. I got to know a guy who runs Medicine International; they're like Doctors without Borders. They set up clinics all over the place and they always need people. I might do something with them."

He shrugged like it was nothing. Laura's mouth went dry. He was planning to go back to Afghanistan without the backing of the army? Without guns? And he thought he wasn't brave?

"Don't look at me like that; I'm in it for the rush remember? Boredom equals death. This is not a bid for sainthood."

Laura grinned wryly. He actually looked like he believed himself. And maybe he did mean it. Maybe it was all about the excitement. He was a lot like her best friend in that way. Maddie was all about her latest idea, her next exciting thing and Charlie was born with itchy feet. Something clicked in her head.

"That's why you became a doctor. A profession that would take you anywhere."

She smiled triumphantly.

"Good try, Sherlock, but no that's not why I became a doctor." He bit off half of a giant cheese sandwich while he studied her. She vaguely wondered if she had food in her hair. "Actually, you were the reason I became a doctor."

Wow, she really didn't see that one coming.

"When I was in my last year at school wondering what to do with my life, well, what to study at least, you informed me that I was a complete loser. That I was wasting my brain and talent for dealing with people and that it was my responsibility to get off my backside and make a difference with my life."

Laura honestly couldn't remember ever saying anything to him. It was back in the days when she was struggling with her crush on him. And being Laura her crush didn't mean she got to look at him with rose coloured glasses, nope she saw reality. So she swayed between lusting after him and being repelled by how shallow he was. Now that she thought of it, it was just the kind of thing she would have said to him if she'd had a chance.

Charlie's eyes twinkled at her.

"I do believe your exact words were – use your God given ability or lose it, moron."

She cringed.

"In my defence, I was very young."

"And yet so wise."

"So boring."

"Or sensible."

"I'm beginning to think that sensible is just another word for repressed," she scoffed.

"Well, since you brought it up. I can help with that repression. One night with me and you'll be wondering what the words sensible and self-control actually mean."

He looked so cocky that she was almost sad to burst his bubble.

"You mean like last night?" she said innocently.

He cringed.

"Tonight. You and me. Hotel. Fireworks. I'm going to rock your world."

Laura grinned.

"You sound like a teenager."

"Some." He looked at her pointedly. "Might say that's when I peaked."

7

———

Laura had suddenly discovered a need to shop, which left him to pack up their camp site on his own. Typical. Although he couldn't help grinning, he was pretty sure he'd seen her wander in the direction of the lingerie shop. As he stuffed all of her junk into her backpack a thought struck him - he really hoped she didn't buy condoms. In his experience women did one of two things. They either went for colour, and what man wants a luminous green penis? Or they bought XXL, and that was just wishful thinking.

"Hey man, we meet again."

Charlie stopped packing about a million romance books to find the two young English guys from their first campsite grinning down at him.

"They're not mine," he said, nodding towards the books.

"Whatever you say." One of them winked while the other nodded.

"They're my friend's." He stumbled over the word. He wasn't sure what category Laura fell into. He'd have to make up a new one.

"Where's the air bed girl?" The floppy one asked.

"Shopping."

They seemed disappointed. They shuffled on the spot.

"Can I help you guys with anything?"

"Naw, it's okay."

With that they wandered off leaving Charlie to shake his head. They were probably hoping that Laura would generate some more excitement for them.

He'd started packing again when his phone rang. Seriously. A man could not get a minute's peace.

"Hello," he barked.

"Well hello," a woman's voice drawled. "You must be the hero of the moment. It's an honour to talk to you. We've all enjoyed watching your video on YouTube; you make a person feel very patriotic."

Everything within him stilled. Reporter.

"Who is this?" He kept his voice even.

"Oh, apologies, apologies. This is Claire Douglas, executive editor of Francine."

Charlie vaguely remembered Laura using his phone; she must have given out the number.

"Laura isn't here," he said dryly.

"Well that's fine, we can have a cosy chat instead." She oozed insincerity. "I do hope you are cooperating with our little Laura. We are all so very anxious to get this interview to print. We wouldn't want anything to go wrong. After all, her job does depend on it."

Charlie wondered if there were some women you could hit.

"Her job depends on the interview?"

"She didn't mention it?" The woman laughed like Cruella de Vil. "Let's just say that she is on probation until we have the article in our hands. I'm sure everything will be fine. You are, after all, having a wonderful holiday..." She paused. "...together. Those pictures Laura sent made us all blush. It certainly looked like you two were having fun."

Pictures? What pictures? The woman made him feel dirty and that was saying something.

"What do you want, Claire." He used his most patronising tone, the one he reserved for junior doctors who thought they knew everything straight out of Uni.

"Just wanted to let you know how excited we are to include you in our hunky heroes edition. We're thrilled. Now, can you let Laura know that the website teaser had gone viral? The world is waiting for her exclusive..." There was a pause. "...as am I."

Charlie's mind was reeling.

"In the meantime," Claire continued, "you two be sure to have a good time."

Charlie cut her off mid laugh. She sounded like a hyena after prey. For a second he didn't know what to think or do. He flicked on his phone and Googled Francine. A minute later he was swimming in cold fury. He stormed in the direction of the site office, looking for a computer with a printer.

LAURA WAS EXTREMELY pleased with herself. She had a bag full of sexy new lingerie, a pack of condoms - just to make sure there wasn't another screw up - and a lovely bottle of wine. Now all they needed was a hotel. As she walked into the campsite she wasn't sure what excited her most, the thought of a night naked with Charlie, or the thought of a night in a proper bed. She was grinning when she reached the tents, only to find that Charlie hadn't packed them up.

Typical, he only had one job to do and he got distracted. She pulled back her tent flap to get her bag and stopped dead. Her mattress was covered with printouts, all of them showing pictures of Charlie half naked swimming in the river. She felt the blood drain from her face.

"Sexy eh?" The voice said behind her.

She spun around to find Charlie standing a few feet away. His posture was relaxed, his face was blank, his tone even. He showed nothing. Laura felt sick. She'd only seen him really mad a couple of times in her life and this was how it looked. Her tongue stuck to the roof of her mouth, which made words impossible. Even if she had any words, which she didn't.

"Had a little chat with your boss," he said. "She's pleased with your progress. Especially the sexy pictures that they're all drooling over. So I had a look." He motioned to the tent. "So tell me Laura, do you think they're sexy?"

She swallowed hard.

"It's not what you think, it's only a teaser, get the readers in. The article won't be like this. It will be serious."

"Yeah, I heard how serious. Hunky heroes?"

She felt light headed.

"I wouldn't let them do that to you, I promise. This is nothing." She waved behind her to the tent full of evidence. "I had to do it."

He turned away. Laura reached for him, but it was futile.

"I printed the teaser and comments off for you. Enjoy reading it; it's all you're getting. I'm done."

"No!"

She rushed towards him and grabbed his arm. The look he gave her was contemptuous.

"I need this article. I need this job."

He sneered.

"Well, that's nice. I thought today, tonight was about us. I didn't know you were still on the clock."

She shook her head. It was all too confusing. Her hand dropped from his arm.

"It is about us," she said, but he was walking away.

"You said you wanted me," she whispered as he disappeared from sight.

Laura turned back to the tent. She felt bruised from head to toe. She crawled in amongst the printouts. They were terrible. Everything he didn't want. Everything he hated. And she had done it to him. Headlines screamed at her, Hunky Hero wet for you, Doctor Hottie cools down, Army Doc aims to serve. It was bad. And the blurb? It was nothing like the copy she'd sent. Claire had been at it. Each sentence was full of sexual innuendo. It mentioned his career and his act of bravery, but made it sound cheap. It made him cheap. And out of all of the comments she read there was nothing about Afghanistan, or how serious the situation was over there.

All the while the video had been out there Charlie had managed to duck the press. He knew he was being called Doctor Hottie, he knew where it would lead and he'd side stepped it. And what had she done? She'd brought everything he didn't want right to him.

With tears in her eyes she ripped up the pages. It was a terrible thing to do. She wasn't sure he would ever forgive her, let alone understand.

But, she had to try.

With heavy heart she staggered to the bathrooms to splash water on her face. She couldn't go after Charlie with red eyes. This was hard enough without attracting attention.

Memories of the past couple of days flooded her mind. Charlie holding her through the night, Charlie taking her to cooking class, Charlie kissing her all night long. Charlie. Charlie. Charlie. He had invaded her senses.

She looked at her sorry reflection in the mirror. Although her actions had been clearly wrong, she was more upset about the fact she'd hurt him. Even with her dysfunctional upbringing she knew enough to know that you didn't treat the people you love badly.

Love.

She stared at her reflection.

Oh no.

Wide red rimmed eyes stared back at her.

This was absolutely the wrong thing to think. She didn't love him. She cared about him. She wanted him to be happy. She was upset that she hurt him. She DID NOT LOVE HIM.

Her heart pounded fast, she started to hyperventilate, she bent over and stuck her head between her knees.

No. She was wrong. She was just emotional.

When she'd calmed down she splashed water on her face. Right, obviously she wasn't thinking straight. She was overcome with guilt. The only way forward was to find Charlie, apologise and fix this mess. After all she needed the story. It was all about the job. She'd just lost sight of that for a minute. That was all it was. It couldn't be anything else. She wouldn't let it be anything else. She stared at her reflection with determination.

She did NOT love Charlie Lewis.

Because loving Charlie Lewis was absolutely the worst thing that could happen to her.

With new resolve, she wiped her face and went off in search of the Neanderthal.

8

———

It took Charlie a while to calm down. When he did things became clear. This whole mess was his own fault. He'd lost sight of things. Laura had bullied her way onto the trip to get a story. And that was what she was doing. The whole lust thing was simply a case of too much time together. Because the last person he wanted to do the dirty with was the Iron Maiden. Seriously. No good ever came of that. Nope. This blow up was a good thing, maybe not the part where she turned him into a fantasy object for her sad little readers, but the rest of it. It was good to remember where they stood - which was separately.

He looked around the cafe terrace and smiled. As a free agent he could chat to any of these lovely women. Chat, dance and hopefully get laid. That would help a lot.

"Hello gorgeous," he said to the girl beside him.

She smiled widely.

"Please tell me you're Dutch, because I have had it up to here with English girls." He put his hand above his head.

She laughed.

"You are in luck, I am definitely Dutch."

"Well all right then," he rubbed his hands together. "Let me buy you another drink."

He signalled at a passing waiter.

"What do you do for a living?" he shouted over the noise of the band. He remembered them being a whole lot better the night before when he'd bought the tickets.

"I'm studying to be a dental assistant," the blond told him.

"You don't write?"

She looked confused.

"No."

"And let me ask you this, if you had to choose between your friends and your job, what would it be?"

"Friends?" Now he'd really lost her.

As the waiter arrived with their drinks he put a hand on her lower back and led her over to a table.

"We are going to have a great evening together," he told her. "I'm Charlie, and I'm a doctor."

Her eyes lit up and he felt a pang of guilt. Okay, so he wasn't above using the title for sex, it was when other people did it that it bothered him. He frowned.

"Are you okay?" his new friend asked.

"Yeah, just trying to get a bad taste out of my mouth."

Her eyes sparkled.

"Oh, I can help with that."

She leaned over and gave him a gentle kiss.

"Better?" she said.

"All gone."

They clicked glasses. The evening was looking up.

And then someone tapped him on the shoulder. When he turned his heart sank.

"Hey you," Laura said with a fake smile. "I've been looking everywhere for you."

"Well keep looking. I'm busy."

Her smile tightened. She put her hands on her hips. He wondered if she was trying to look intimidating in a pair of blue jeans and a Minnie Mouse t-shirt.

"Say goodbye to your friend, we need to talk."

"I've said all I'm going to say to you."

"Well you can listen."

"No," he turned his back on her.

Barbie looked confused. He gave her a reassuring smile. Laura walked round to the blond, who was a least a head taller than her. She fiddled with the silver friendship ring Maddie had given her before she stuck out her hand.

"Pleased to meet you," she said. "I see you already met my husband."

The girl's mouth fell open.

"We're not married," Charlie said. He waved a dismissive hand in Laura's direction. "I already told you that I'm a doctor, well this is a psychiatric patient that follows me around. She's delusional."

When the woman looked back at Laura, Laura held up the hand with her ring finger, now complete with ring.

"Five years this week, we're here to celebrate our anniversary. We had a fight and he stormed off. You see, he wanted to bring the twins, but I said we needed time alone. You know how it is."

The woman looked from one to the other, it was clear she didn't know what to think. Charlie made a little circle motion beside his temple to indicate Laura was bonkers. Laura narrowed her eyes.

"Oh dear, he's been using that doctor line again, hasn't he?" She cupped her mouth as though whispering at the girl. "He likes to boost his ego; he's still embarrassed about being a stay at home dad."

She had the blonde's full attention again. She leaned over and patted him on the hand.

"I keep telling you honey, you don't need to feel insecure, you are attractive. I don't value you any less because you don't work. Looking after the kids and making dinner is important stuff."

"I need to go see my friends," the girl told them before making a hurried exit.

"Good idea," Laura said.

Charlie growled at the evil pixie. Once the girl was gone Laura turned to him.

"We can talk here, shouting our business to anyone who can hear or we can go somewhere else. Your choice."

"How about not at all?"

She had that look in her eye that signalled she was about thirty seconds away from causing serious damage.

"Fine." He pointed to the old stone bridge over the canal. "Over there."

They walked in silence across the cobbled street towards the bridge. When they got to the middle of it Charlie leaned against the wall, his back to the canal. Laura stood in front of him, hands on hips, like it made her bigger and more intimidating. Yeah, right.

"I'm not interested in anything you have to say," he told her.

"Fine. You can listen anyway." She stuck her little nose in the air and glared at him from behind huge glasses. "You knew why I came on this trip. I'm here for an interview, for a women's magazine. Just how did you think this would go exactly? Did you expect them to do a detailed report on the war on terror? To print graphs and statistics? Seriously, this is how we hook women in. The story will be light but it will take the topic seriously. It will take you seriously. So how about you get over yourself and grow up?"

The yellow lights glowing along the canal bank made the air around Laura glow, which was slightly disconcerting - she looked like a really grumpy angel.

"Grow up? Really? You're telling me to grow up? Who exactly made you the judge of all things mature? Let's have a look at your life shall we?"

Laura started to say something but he held up a hand, so she stopped, which surprised him.

"One." He ticked the points off on his fingers. "You are being blackmailed into writing a story you don't want to write to keep a job you don't really want. And why? Because you're too much of a coward to take a chance and do something else."

Laura snapped.

"Do something else? Get another job?"

She took a step towards him and poked at his chest.

"You have no idea what you're talking about. You just float around doing what you like, expecting your family to put you up when you need it. Well it doesn't work like that for the rest of us, buster. Some of us have to be responsible."

"Responsible, responsible. That's all I hear. You're a coward. If you wanted to get another job, a better job, you'd get one."

He was pretty sure he could see steam coming out of her ears as the top of her head turned red.

"We're in the middle of a massive recession, moron, jobs aren't lying on the pavement. You don't just pick one up. And what do I have to offer anyway? Eight years writing about vampires. Eight years."

He opened his mouth to take issue with that, but shut it

again when she threw her hands up in the air and stamped one foot.

"I took the first job that was offered. Teen mags. Once you start off in a path you're stuck there. My only option was a related field that was willing to take a chance on me. Women's magazines. That was it. And after three years trying, I got this crappy job. What do you think would have happened if I'd rocked up to the BBC and asked to report on Africa or the Middle East? Or called National Geographic and asked to write about a journey through South America?"

She poked him in the chest again. He got the impression she was trying to do actual damage with her tiny finger.

"You are such a moron. I haven't had a roommate since Maddie got married, but I do have double the rent and no place else to go if I can't pay it. Unlike you, I don't have family to take me in. The last time I was between houses my dad paid for a hotel room for a week for me, he said having me at home disturbed his creative rhythm and he had an exhibition coming up. I couldn't even find my mother to see if she could help, turns out she was shacked up with the very young male lead in her latest play. So if I lose my job what do I do? Can I come stay with you?" She smacked her forehead. "Oh no, I can't because you are house sitting for your sister and then you'll go back to your parent's house while you try to find yourself."

She stepped towards him, her fury gaining momentum with every word that came out of her mouth. Charlie took a step back, only to find the bridge blocking his retreat. He was pretty sure that the guys who disabled bombs might be able to handle her, but he was out of his depth.

"Let me give you some advice. You're thirty five. There is nothing to find. You are a complete person. All you have to do is take stock and move on with your life. In other words, stop acting like a teenager. Be responsible for yourself. Make some decisions and stand by them. That's what I do. That's what I've always had to do. You see, while you have had the luxury of being a teenager for most of your life, I never got the chance to be one at all. In my house I was born the adult. And here I am again. Making the hard choices, dealing with an unreasonable boss who is blackmailing me to get a story I told her I didn't want to do and didn't think I could get anyway. And are you helping? No. You are getting in my way."

She turned away from him. Charlie felt his own anger beginning to build.

"The mess you've made isn't my fault, sweet cakes. You used me to get a story. I told you that I'd talk at the end of the trip but you couldn't wait. So you had to go manipulate things. You knew exactly what you were doing when you asked me to go swimming. You knew what you were doing when you wrote all about the hot doc as a teaser. You used me. So don't go getting all huffy on me now."

"Well you used me too," she spun back at him. "You said you wanted me when all you really wanted was any woman that came along. I was just convenient."

She waved her hand in the direction of the blond she'd scared away. Charlie's eyes narrowed.

"Damn straight I was using you. If I have to suffer your controlling, judgemental behaviour for the duration of my holiday then I figured I may as well make the best of it."

She looked as though she'd been slapped. Anger took over Charlie's words.

"And let me tell you, it wasn't worth it, there are plenty of women who can make me feel a whole lot better than you could."

She reeled backwards.

"Well why don't you go get one?" she said.

"That's exactly what I'm going to do."

He stormed in the direction of the bar.

"Fine!" Laura shouted behind him.

He didn't care. There was no one in the world that could make him as mad as the Iron Maiden could. He'd had enough of her. He was going to find a nice uncomplicated woman and have some fun.

Laura could jump in the canal for all he cared.

LAURA WAS oblivious to the quaint crooked houses that lined the street. The sparkling canal decked out in fairy lights made no impression. She stumbled over centuries old cobble stones, marched over the old wooden bridge and through the gate that told people it was built 1682. She was running on rage.

All she could think of, all she could hear, were his words.

She was boring. She was cowardly. And worst of all, she was convenient.

She kicked a stone sending it flying into the canal. It plopped before disappearing in the blackness.

"Hey," a voice called behind her, "it's the air bed girl."

She ignored it. A second later two guys appeared, one on each side of her.

"Remember us?" the floppy haired one said. "We helped you the night you fell asleep with your bum stuck out the tent."

Laura looked between the two of them, they were young, maybe late teens and they seemed harmless enough.

"I sabotaged your boyfriend's bike," the one on her left said.

"I remember you now."

She kept up her fast pace, propelled by rage.

"Where are you going?" the other one asked.

"Campsite."

"We'll walk with you," they told her.

Laura stopped walking.

"Look boys, I don't need the company. I'm fine."

They shared a look.

"Oh, oh, did you and your boyfriend have a fight?" the floppy haired one said.

The other nodded.

"Yeah we saw him at the tent earlier and he was pretty mad."

Laura glared at the two of them.

"He was mad? He had no right being mad; I'm the one that has to put up with him."

She spun on her heels, the guys marched alongside her. She was fuming.

"He's just like my mother," she told them. They nodded, clueless but attentive. "Every time he gets bored, or things get tough, he goes running off to find another woman. And that's fine when it's just him. But this time I'm here. And we were together. Or at least I thought we were." She looked at the two of them aware that she was rambling and not making any sense.

They didn't seem bothered; in fact they seemed kind of thrilled to be included.

"He shouldn't be running off with other women when he's with you," one of them said.

"Exactly. And what am I supposed to do? Act like my dad, pretend it isn't happening or throw a hissy fit and then expect someone else to sort it out? I'm not that crazy. Charlie said it. I'm the sensible one. I don't lose control."

One of them patted her shoulder reassuringly.

"But I do take chances." Her anger built with each step she took. "I'm here aren't I? Putting up with this rubbish, trying to get a story. I was going to sleep with him. If that isn't losing control then what is?"

"You tell him sister," the floppy guy said.

"And now he's off chasing other women. Sleeping with other women. When he said he wanted me."

She turned to face them at the entrance of the camp. They looked a little stunned.

"He told me himself, he said: when you want someone you don't run off with someone else. So what is that supposed to make me think?"

They looked at each other then shrugged.

"Well?" she demanded.

"That he doesn't want you?" one ventured, looking a little confused.

"Exactly!" They looked pleased that they had the right answer.

She stormed through the gate.

"He is a low life. A scum sucker. A belly crawler."

She confronted her two new friends.

"I tell you one thing. There's no way he's bringing a girl back to his tent."

They nodded like it was the wisest thing she's said. Laura's eye began to twitch furiously. She pressed a finger to stop it and the other one started.

"She makes me crazy," Charlie told the girl in front of him. She patted his hand as she sipped a drink that was multi coloured and had an umbrella. "Not just today. Oh no. This has been going on as long as I've known her. Today was just special."

The cafe bar was packed with people in their twenties; he felt a little old for the crowd, but the woman sitting with him was nice. What was her name again? He wasn't sure.

"She's seriously judgemental. It's all - what are you doing with your life? You're wasting your talent. You're so immature, Charlie. I'm immature? She's the one that won't quit a job she hates and do something with her life."

"Maybe she is a little scared?" the brunette offered.

Charlie blinked. For a minute he'd forgotten she was there.

"Cowardly. Too scared to do something that isn't planned in detail."

The brunette smiled.

"You know, maybe you balance each other out. You can take all the chances and she can keep your feet on the ground. A good team, no?"

Charlie held up his hands.

"No. No. No. It's nothing like that."

She smiled pleasantly as the waitress stopped to take their order. Charlie bought another round, something multi-coloured for her and coffee for him.

"See, the thing that gets to me most," he told his new friend, "is that this whole responsibility thing isn't even her. It's conditioning. Her parents are nuts and she's been the sane one all her life. Who knows what her real personality would be like if she just loosened up a bit."

The girl smiled sagely.

"I'm not even mad that she used me to get pictures for her boss. I'm mad because she won't stand up to the witch in the first place."

His coffee was thick and delicious.

The wind went out of him. He looked the girl in the eye.

"I worry about her," he said. "She's wound up so tight, who knows what happens when she eventually blows. Seriously, her eyes twitch, she grinds her teeth and I swear I've seen her bite her tongue. One of these days she's going to go boom."

"Perhaps you should not push her then, if you are worried?"

Charlie took a second to look at the girl.

"Are you a shrink?" he said.

"Hairdresser."

"Ah, that explains it."

He signalled for the bill.

"I need to go check on her," he said apologetically.

"I understand," the brunette smiled.

She was really a pretty girl in her pink mini dress and platform heels. Any other day he would have loved spending time with her. But Laura was ruining his love life too. He couldn't think straight when she was driving him so nuts.

"Thanks for listening," he said as he left money for the bill.

She shrugged like it was nothing.

"I need to go," he pointed to the door. "The woman needs constant supervision."

The brunette finger waved good bye as Charlie stepped out into the warm night air.

LAURA WAS ON A MISSION. He may have blackmailed her into the trip from hell. He may have teased her to the point where she humiliated herself enough to sleep with him. He may even be stringing her along with the promise of an interview. Oh yeah, he may get away with a lot of things. But he wasn't going to have sex with some girl he picked up in the tent next to hers.

"Listen lady," one of the English guys said. "Why don't you come sit with us, we can have a drink, chat a little. Wait until your boyfriend gets back."

"He's not my boyfriend," she said with a snarl.

"No, right, absolutely." They shared a look that telegraphed she was a few sandwiches short of a picnic. "Still, how about that drink?"

She ignored them. She was fed up being pushed around. She'd reached her limit. She didn't give a flying fig if Charlie slept his way around the whole of Holland; she just wanted him to wait until she was far, far away from him to do it. In the meantime she would make it as hard for him as possible. She had a plan.

"Either of you carrying cooking oil?" she said.

They shared a look before shaking their heads.

"There will be some in the kitchen." One of them pointed to the small building by the entrance.

"Matches?" Laura asked.

"Are you cooking again?"

They shared another gleeful grin. She was about to be camp entertainment all over again.

"Well?" she prompted.

The floppy one rummaged around in his backpack.

"Here." He thrust a box at her. "If you need help with the stove let us know. Your boyfriend, I mean the guy you're with, wasn't too pleased we didn't help out last time."

Laura smiled. She could feel how cold and menacing it was and from the look on their faces they could see it too.

"I won't need any help," she said evenly. "This, I can do all on my own."

Then she walked calmly, and purposely, towards the kitchen.

CHARLIE SAW the flashing lights before he saw anything else and picked up his speed. Years of dealing with trauma at home, and abroad, made him run to the centre of the commotion, to the centre of the campsite. Someone might need a doctor.

Instead he found a couple of cops, a fire crew packing up their gear and a black scorched patch of ground where his tent had once been. No sign of Laura.

"What happened?" He grabbed a cop. "Was anyone hurt?"

"I'm sure someone else will tell you, sir," the guy said before turning back to his notepad.

Charlie ran his hands through his hair.

"That was my tent," he said.

Now that got their attention.

"The woman -" He almost choked on the words. "My girlfriend, is she okay?"

"She's fine; we've taken her to the hospital." One eyebrow flicked upwards. "Apparently it was an accident."

Charlie had dealt with enough cops to see clearly that accident was the last thing he thought this was.

"Unless you have something to add, we're finished here."

He waited, almost hoping that Charlie was going to tell him it was an attempt on his life.

"No, nothing. I wasn't even here."

They seemed to want something more.

"She is very accident prone."

The guy flicked his notebook shut, adjusted his sidearm and stared at Charlie for a minute before deciding that there was nothing he could do. He turned away. The air gushed out of Charlie. She was at the hospital. He was about to ask how bad Laura's injuries were when two guys popped up beside him. The two English guys from earlier.

"As we told the nice officer," the floppy haired one said with a false smile, "we saw the whole thing and it was a complete accident. We also told him that we saw something similar almost happen in the last campsite."

His voice was deliberately loud and he had one eye on the cop. The cop shook his head and sauntered off. Charlie let himself be led away by the boys. Once they were out of earshot, they became hyper.

"We couldn't stop her," the other one said.

"We tried," the floppy one said.

"She was determined."

Charlie took a deep breath, let it out slowly, folded his arms over his chest and looked at the two of them.

"First things first, is she badly hurt?"

They shook their heads in unison.

"Burns on her hands; she freaked when the tent went up and tried to put the fire out."

"And her hair." The floppy one looked at his friend for confirmation. "She burnt her hair. We told her she didn't need cooking oil, these things," he motioned to a tent nearby, "will go up easy if you just hold a match to them."

"Highly flammable," the other one nodded. "Whoosh!"

He motioned the way the fire had gone with his hands.

"Cooking oil?" Charlie shook his head to clear it. This wasn't making sense. "She was cooking?"

They shared a look; the floppy one shook his head.

"Uh, no. She went to the kitchen to get some to pour over your tent. Then she set it on fire."

"I gave her the matches." The other boy seemed earnest. "I wouldn't have if I had known what she planned."

"Let me get this straight." Charlie looked between them. "She set the tent on fire on purpose?"

They nodded. He rubbed his face.

"Any idea why?"

The non-floppy one shuffled his feet.

"She said you were with another woman."

Aw, hell. His arms fell to his side.

"And then when the blaze got so big so fast and caught the tree above it, she went bonkers. She poured her water bottle on it, then started hitting it with a towel."

"That's when she burned her hands."

"And she kept shouting."

"Yeah, it was totally mad."

"Over and over again, the same thing."

Charlie held a hand up to stop them.

"What was she shouting?" he asked with the last of his patience.

"I am not my father."

They both shrugged. Charlie closed his eyes briefly. He knew exactly what that meant. Laura had gone to the one place she was terrified of going. She'd snapped. He'd broken her and it had only taken just over a week.

"I need to go see her," he told them.

"Yeah." The floppy one nodded. "And you might want to apologise for the other girl. Chicks don't like that."

He gritted his teeth. Advice from teenagers. As he turned away one of them grabbed his arm.

"Which campsite are you going to after this?" they wanted to know. "We don't want to miss what happens next."

Charlie looked towards heaven before turning his back on them and heading in the direction of the local hospital.

He found Laura sitting on the bed in a cubicle in the emergency department. Relief overwhelmed him, making him pause before he let her know he was there. Her hair was singed, her hands were bandaged and she was wearing an old pair of blue scrubs. Her shoulders were slumped in a way he'd never seen before; everything about her screamed that she was defeated. Broken. Charlie felt sick to his stomach. He had caused this. With a deep breath he pulled back the curtain. Her head snapped towards him and she flinched. Something inside of him died a little.

"Well this is a helluva way to get your interview." It was hard work to keep his tone light and a smile on his face.

Wide red rimmed eyes peered up at him.

"I suppose you'll want the pity vote now, well you can forget about that, you still need to keep your end of the deal. A whole holiday, you can't even get out of it by setting fire to my tent."

One heavy teardrop slid down her cheek.

"Aw honey," he said.

He stepped towards her and wrapped his arms tight around her. Laura buried her face in his old t-shirt and sobbed. Her whole body shuddered with them. Charlie rubbed her back and muttered soothing things. He wasn't even sure what he was saying. At last Laura pulled away, wiped her nose on the bottom of his t-shirt, and then looked up at him.

"This is all your fault, moron," she told him, then hiccupped.

Charlie grinned wide with relief before wrapping his arms around her again. Things were going to be okay.

9

———

"You look cute," Charlie told her.

Laura gave him a look that she hoped would kill. She'd told the moron to bring her some clothes and instead of raiding her tent, he'd gone shopping. Unfortunately she was going to wear his idea of appropriate clothing out of the hospital. She looked down at herself and grimaced.

"I always said you should come with a warning." Charlie was clearly amused.

Above the pink hot pants he thought were shorts, she wore a t-shirt with the slogan Lizzie Borden Lives. On the back it said - Watch your back.

She growled in Charlie's direction. He grinned as he pointed to his t-shirt it said, I married an axe murderer.

"See. Matching set."

"Oh how the simple minded are easily amused," she told him.

Unfortunately there was nothing she could do about it. It was wear these stupid clothes or leave the hospital naked. She pursed her lips before pulling her hair back into a tight ponytail. She winced from the pain in her hands, and told herself to get over it. It was her own stupid fault and the burns weren't that bad. She would be fine in a few days.

"Here, let me." Charlie took the hairbrush and the hair band from her hands.

She sat on the chair to let him work.

"I'm not sure this is such a great idea," she said. "I remember what you did to Maddie's Barbies."

He chuckled.

"Ah, the military haircut. Works well on both sexes."

In a surprisingly short time he had her hair in a ponytail. She studied her reflection. It wouldn't win any awards, but her hair wouldn't drive her crazy all day either.

She forced a smile for the mirror, took a deep breath, closed her eyes and silently reminded herself that everything would be fine.

"Okay, let's get out of here."

Laura was more than ready. She knew she had spent the night in the hospital because Charlie had thrown his weight around. Her injuries were minor at best. She scanned the pastel coloured room. There were no belongings to gather, paperwork had been signed, bandages changed. There was nothing left to do except leave. She looked at Charlie. Well, one more thing. She took a deep breath.

"I need to explain about last night."

Instantly his face took on the look all men got when a woman suggested they talk – panic, fear and a huge dose of "oh no'. He held up his hands to ward her off.

"It's fine, we all go mental now and then."

That was the problem. She took a step towards him.

"I don't," she said.

She actually saw him gulp as he tried to calculate how far he was from the door.

"Seriously, it's fine. So you set fire to my tent. It happens all the time."

Laura wasn't going to be swayed by his charm.

"I don't lose control. Think about it. You've known me most of my life. How often have I done anything spur of the moment? Anything that you would consider normal and the rest of the world would consider irrational?"

She could actually see the wheels turn behind his eyes and knew the moment he came to the same conclusion she had reached.

"Not often," he said tightly.

She took another step towards him.

"You only came up with a handful of things didn't you?"

He looked away as he plopped onto the bed beside her chair.

"And they all involved you. Didn't they?"

She placed a hand on his denim clad knee.

"Charlie, we have to face facts. You are a bad influence on me."

His eyes snapped up to hers.

"I thought for years that you just irritated me," she said, "but it's more than that. You bring out the worst in me."

"Now wait a minute."

He sat up straight. Laura held up a hand to stop his words.

"It's fine, you can't help it. We're like oil and water. No, more like electricity and water. We get together and things go bang."

"We only went bang once, if you don't count the times in the tent when we nearly went bang."

She rolled her eyes.

"I'm talking about my mental state." There was no easy way to say this. "Look, when this trip is over I think it's best if we keep away from each other. Arguing over the years took energy, but at least I managed to stay myself. Becoming friendly, like this, it makes me insane. I'm not explaining it very well."

"You think I make you lose control?" Charlie didn't look too sure.

"Exactly. You bring out the worst in me. All the elements of my personality that I get from my parents bubble to the surface. It's not really me; it's their influence on me. When you're not around I can be myself."

She hoped he understood.

"So," he said slowly. "You're a better person when I'm not around and you don't want to be friends because I make you act like your parents?"

Laura sighed with relief. She gave him a "well-done-idiot" smile.

"That's exactly it." She patted his hand. "I'm glad you understand."

Charlie pushed himself up from the bed and headed for the door.

"I understand all right," he said slowly. "Apparently I'm the only man alive who can make you lose control."

He grinned widely.

"Now, see that sounds like a challenge to me. Right now I'm wondering how out of control I can make you."

Laura swallowed hard.

"Come on, short stuff, let's get out of here."

Laura followed him into the hallway, wondering where their conversation had taken a wrong turn, because she was pretty sure he was on a different page from her. Again.

Charlie wasn't taking any chances. So far Laura had

ridden into a canal and set fire to his tent. He needed to man-up, take control, or he wouldn't make it through the rest of his holiday alive. There was only one thing for it.

"A tandem?" Laura folded her arms over Lizzie Borden's face and stared at him open mouthed.

"I traded our bikes."

He was actually kind of proud of his ingenuity. This way she wouldn't cycle so slowly that old people passed them. She couldn't fall in the canal, not with him doing the steering. And he could keep a close eye on her, just in case she decided that his influence made her itch to do something rash again. Honestly! He made a choking sound at the thought of it.

"Are you okay?" she said suspiciously.

"Super."

"I don't want to share a bike with you. I seriously don't want you staring at my bum that closely for the rest of the trip."

"You," he left the "stupid" unsaid, "will be in back."

"Oh."

She stared at the bike again. He'd already strapped their luggage onto the back of it, which was considerably lighter since he'd lost most of his during her arson attack.

She crossed her arms over her chest and turned to face him.

"I really don't think I can face camping anymore, Charlie," she said.

He almost laughed. Like he was ever going to take her camping again. He'd never sleep. He'd spend his whole night worrying that his tent was going to go whoosh around him. And yes, he'd mainly brought her along so that he would have something else to think about at night, but he sure as hell didn't mean that.

"We're staying in hotels."

She grinned.

"You're paying."

Her face fell, her shoulders slumped and then she suddenly brightened.

"I have an expense account," she said proudly.

"Now why didn't you mention that earlier?"

He checked the dressings on her hands, feeling queasy at the sight of her red broken flesh, which didn't make any sense. He'd dressed millions of burn wounds over the years. Images of Laura coming to her senses and fighting the blaze popped into his mind. She must have been terrified.

Her huge green eyes watched his every move and he had a sudden urge to kiss her. Before he could stop himself he did exactly that. She tasted of vanilla and smelled faintly of smoke. An interesting combination.

"What was that for?" she said.

"Just testing that control threshold of yours. Trying to gauge what the minimum contact would be to set you off. Obviously it will take more than a kiss."

She made some sort of disgusted grunting noise, which made him laugh. If she thought he was going to take anything she said seriously, then she had lost her mind after all.

"Ready?" He steadied the bike.

Laura mumbled something behind him and he took that as a yes. A second later they were away.

"I like this bike," Laura said behind him.

He grinned and bit back telling her that he obviously was the smarter of the two of them.

"And I like this view," she said with a sigh.

Charlie looked over at the old stone windmill with the water behind it. It was picturesque.

"Yeah, it's pretty spectacular," he said as he powered on.

He thought he heard her giggle.

Now why the heck hadn't Laura thought of a tandem bike? It was fantastic. She perched her feet on the bar thing in front of her and watched as the pedals miraculously went round and round all by themselves. Wonderful. Add to that, she had a view to die for – Charlie's bite-able backside and powerhouse thighs. Oh and that strong back leading up to those broad, broad shoulders. Delicious.

She let out a deep contented sigh as she turned her face towards the sun. She'd done the right thing telling him that they couldn't spend any time together after the trip, she was sure of it. There was no way on earth she could live out a repeat of her parent's lives and if cutting Charlie out of hers meant it wouldn't happen, then it was worth the effort. Although, it wasn't as easy as she thought it would be. One kiss and all she could think about was getting her hands on him. She bit her bottom lip as she watched the muscles in his thighs flex. The sight turned her brain to mush. Pathetic.

He had turned out to be quite good company and all things considered, even with the arson and the river stunt, it was one of the best holidays she had ever had. And it was getting better every minute. Now she didn't have to exert herself and tonight she would get to sleep in a proper bed. Hoorah!

His grey t-shirt became damp with sweat, which made it hug his back all the more. The sight was doing something to her brain. Suddenly her idea to cut all ties didn't seem like such a good one after all. Still, they had four days left in Holland, would it matter if she lost her mind a little while they were there?

He pulled a water bottle from the holder in front of him, sat up straight and glugged at it. Her mouth went dry. Her fingers actually tingled at the thought of touching him. Laura tried to think straight. She couldn't. Before she could stop them words formed in her mind and popped right out of her mouth.

"Charlie," she said. "If you still want to have sex with me, that would be okay."

The bike swerved into the opposite lane causing a kid to brake hard. He shouted something in Dutch that sounded rude. There was silence.

"Charlie," she poked him in the back and was momentarily distracted by how solid he felt. "Are you listening? Do you still want to sleep with me?"

The bike screeched to a halt. Charlie twisted in his seat to look at her.

"Are you losing your mind again?" he said. "Is this what you were talking about earlier? The way you go nuts in my presence?"

"No, I just thought that since we have four days left we could have sex. If you want to, that is."

With a heavy sigh, he climbed from the bike, but kept a grip on it so that she could stay seated. He rubbed a hand over his face, stared at her as though she'd just landed on the planet then shook his head slightly.

"So, let me see if I understand you fully," he said. "You don't want me in your life because you lose control, but you don't mind losing control a little before we go back home."

"Exactly."

He looked up at the sky for what seemed to be the longest time.

"Well?" She prodded him with the toe of her trainer.

"Just once, I would like to be the one who initiates sex between us. Just once I'd like it to happen normally and not in the same way people schedule a work meeting. There is nothing sexy or romantic about being propositioned out of the blue. I know you think there is, but there isn't."

"You want me to be more romantic?"

He growled deeply. In one step he was in front of her, his hand cradled the back of her head. He mumbled something under his breath and then his lips were on hers. This wasn't the friendly peck from earlier; this was a full blown exploration that took her breath away. Laura's head exploded. She grabbed onto the front of his t-shirt and wrapped her fingers in tight. His lips pounded hers, over and over until she relaxed into him and her mouth fell open. Oh, his tongue was so sweet; he lazily traced it around her mouth, making her think of all the things that tongue could do to her. He nipped her bottom lip with his teeth, ran his tongue over the spot he'd bitten then stepped away from her. Laura had to actually think about letting go of him; her fingers weren't willing to do it on their own.

Charlie climbed back onto the bike.

"Wait," she grabbed his t-shirt and pulled him back towards her. "You never answered the question."

"Seriously? Why don't you think about it while we ride?"

With that he pushed the bike back onto the cycle path and powered away. Laura put her fingers to her swollen lips. She hadn't wanted the kiss to stop, instead she'd wanted to swivel in her seat and wrap her legs around him. Oh. What an idiot. She smiled slowly at his broad back.

Although they laughed and joked all the way into the hotel room, Laura was strangely nervous. This was what she wanted, she was sure, but it felt huge. She spied on Charlie out of the corner of her eye as he put the bags beside the dresser. Her stomach lurched.

"I'm going to have a shower," she told him.

He smiled at her.

"I'll order food. It's been a long time since lunch."

Did he know she was nervous? It didn't matter, she ran for the bathroom. Once inside she held on tight to the sink while she looked herself in the eye. It's only Charlie, she told herself. You've done this before. Heck, you would have done it on this trip if things had gone as planned. Get a grip. She took two deep breaths and headed for the shower.

Once she was finished, she wrapped a towel around herself and stepped into the room. She stopped dead. The curtains were drawn; there were candles on most of the surfaces and food set up on the tiny table. Chinese take away and a bottle of wine. Charlie switched off the TV to smile at her.

"This is," she stumbled over her words, "this is pretty."

"Thought I'd educate you in the art of romance," he told her.

"I better get dressed then."

"Oh no, you have more than enough clothes on."

He grabbed her hand and led her to the table. Laura kept a tight grip on the towel and wished she was dressed.

"You're going to like this food, I had some already." When he saw her face he shrugged. "What? You were in there a long time. Anyway, it's more Indonesian than Chinese. Tasty."

Laura smiled at him as he put some on her plate. It could have been hay for all she cared, her appetite had left her the minute she stepped into the room.

"Wine?"

He poured her some and she had a tiny sip. They sat facing each other in awkward silence before Charlie sighed, shook his head and pulled his chair towards her.

"What's up, short stuff, don't you want to be seduced?"

She was seriously beginning to wonder if he could read her mind.

"You're making me nervous. I don't like being nervous. I like to know where I stand."

"Control," he mumbled. "Fine," he said louder, "what do you want to do?"

"Why don't we just have sex and eat later?"

His look was full of pity tinged with amusement.

"I have never met a girl like you, sweet cakes, you're one of a kind."

Laura wasn't sure if that was a compliment or not so she kept to the main subject.

"I'm all ready," she told him. "I bought condoms."

He groaned.

"Green?"

"No," she scoffed. "Seriously, what woman wants to look at a green penis?"

"Well that's a relief."

"Yep, they're purple and ribbed for my pleasure."

Charlie threw back his head and roared with laughter. Laura wasn't sure what to do. At last he wiped his eyes.

"Come here," he said and pulled at her towel.

Laura held it tight as she let him pull her to stand between his knees.

"What am I going to do with you?" he said as he rested his forehead on her chest.

Laura ran her fingers through his hair. She wasn't sure how to answer that question. Charlie looked up at her, his eyes pooled dark. She felt his look through to her toes.

"Just so you know," he said as he tugged at her towel. "I'm not wearing purple."

The towel came loose and fell in a puddle at her feet. For

one brief second Laura felt exposed and self-conscious, then Charlie gently kissed her in the soft space between her breasts and her fears evaporated. Slowly, tenderly, he kissed his way up her neck to her lips as his fingers traced circles in the small of her back.

"Is this what you want?" he whispered against her lips.

"Yes." Her reply was little more than a breath.

He wrapped his arms tight around her and stood, lifting her as he did so. Slowly, he lowered her onto the bed.

"Beautiful," he said hoarsely as he looked his fill.

"Charlie?" Laura said as her cheeks flushed.

"Mm?"

"Take off your clothes. Now."

His eyes snapped to hers and they sparkled with amusement.

"Yes ma'am," he said and did as he was told.

Now it was Laura's turn to be mesmerised. Soft skin over taut muscle. She would never be able to look enough. She reached for him. There would be time for looking later. Right now, she wanted to let her fingers memorise him.

Charlie crawled onto the bed; he put a hand on the pillow beside her head.

"Hold on tight Laura, it's going to be a bumpy ride."

His mouth was on hers before she could hear her laughter.

LAURA FELL BACK into the soft pillows with the sheets twisted around her body. Her breath was laboured, her skin tingled from top to toe and she knew her cheeks were flushed. Charlie landed beside her, threw a heavy arm over her body and propped himself up on his other elbow.

"See that wasn't so bad," he said teasingly. "You managed to lose control and nothing burned down."

If she'd had any energy left, she would have hit him. Instead she looked up into his amazingly handsome face and wondered what had hit her. She lifted a leaden arm to pat his cheek. Stubble nipped at her sensitive skin.

"That wasn't bad," she told him.

"Wasn't bad? I was there. You lost it big time."

"It was definitely better than the last time."

She thought she saw him flinch slightly at the memory and she hoped she was better than the last time too.

"You do know you are the only girl I've ever run out on like that," he said earnestly.

"Well, that makes me feel a whole lot better."

"You freaked me out. I never thought of you like that, then there you were saying take me. It's every guy's fantasy."

"So you didn't say no."

He smiled that self-depreciating way that made women lose their morals.

"If it's any consolation, I may not have thought of you like that before that day in the shed, but I have thought about you often since."

Her ears perked up.

"Yeah? Like when?"

She stretched out towards him, moving her body so that his hand caught her breast. For a minute she forgot about the question as he traced his finger around her nipple.

"Well." When he spoke his voice was deeper. "There was Maddie's wedding. You looked hot in your bridesmaid's dress. I entertained some thoughts that night."

Her body moved of its own freewill pressing up into his touch. Little bubbles floated inside her head and her eyelids suddenly felt a lot heavier. She was finding it hard to concentrate as his hand roamed from her breast up and down the length of her body.

"What kind of thoughts?" she managed to say.

His touch came in waves, feather soft, then hard and determined. She began to float away.

"Well, I can tell you," his voice was hoarse, "or I can show you."

She couldn't speak. Instead she reached for him, looking deep into eyes that were suddenly black, before she pulled him to her.

"You know Laura," he whispered against her mouth. "I think you've been so self-contained for so long that you don't know what losing control really is. I don't think we've even scratched the surface."

His hand slid under her to flatten against the small of her back, wedging her against him. She should have felt threatened by his size and strength, instead she felt secure and strangely liberated. Was this freedom? Could she let go and really be herself? Did she even know who that person was?

"You're thinking again, we can't have that."

His mouth dipped to her breast and her mind went completely blank as sensation after sensation assaulted her.

"So incredibly sensitive," he murmured against her skin. "This is kind of like a controlled environment right?"

She knew he was talking but his words didn't make sense, she willed his mouth to move back to her skin.

"I say we experiment," he said. "Let's see just how far we can take this loss of control of yours."

He perched on strong muscled arms above her.

"Do you trust me?" he said.

Laura's heart actually strained within her.

"Yes," she said. "Yes."

A slow smile curled out from the corners of his lips.

"Then you ain't seen nothing yet."

And then he was kissing her, touching her, tasting her. She bit into his thick shoulder as he nipped her ear. The feel of him. All that softness and strength, it drove her crazy. She was driving fast in a car with the top down. She was jumping from a cliff into icy waters. She was sailing through the air with no idea where she would land. And all the while she held on to Charlie. He was the source of her adventures and the strength that kept her safe.

"JUST BECAUSE YOU let loose now and then, live a little, doesn't mean that you're deranged like your old folks."

"I set fire to your tent," she said wryly and held her hands up, burnt palms towards him to make her point.

It was the wee small hours of the morning and they were eating cold Indonesian food straight from the boxes, while propped up in bed.

"That's what I mean. If you allowed yourself to lose control every now and then, you wouldn't go so mental when you did let loose. You need to let that wildness out in more controlled circumstances, in ways that will only benefit you."

He was doing his best to look innocent but was pretty sure from the amusement in her face that he wasn't pulling it off.

"And I suppose you know the exact way I should go about ending this repressed life I lead?" she said with mock solemnity.

"Absolutely."

He swept the empty containers onto the floor.

"I know exactly what you should do."

She started to giggle.

"You can stop that for a start. Admit that Charlie knows best." He leaned towards her and heard her breath leave her. "Trust me Laura, I'm a doctor."

She was laughing heartily when his lips covered hers.

She smelled of roses and maybe vanilla. And she tasted like cake. The best cake he'd ever had. She groaned as she rubbed against him. Charlie angled his head to get better access to her mouth. No matter how deep he kissed her, he never quite managed to get to the spot he wanted. There was something about her that was out of reach. It was driving him crazy. Laura Prentice was driving him crazy.

He broke the kiss and held himself above her. Man, but she was beautiful. Her whole heart was in her eyes, her cheeks were flushed the deepest pink and he could see her pulse beat a salsa rhythm in the base of her neck. His lips found the pulse beating in her neck and he sucked on it. Nope, the thing he was looking for wasn't there either. He'd have to search all of her. Because one way or another he was going to find the thing about Laura that was driving him nuts. In the back of his mind he wondered who exactly was losing control. And then he thought nothing at all. All he could feel, all he could taste, and all he wanted was all of Laura.

As THE SUN sneaked through the curtains Laura snuggled in deeper to Charlie's embrace. She wasn't an idiot. She also wasn't very good at fooling herself. She was head over heels in love with the man. And it would end badly. There was a pain in her chest as the truth settled there. She shook her thoughts free from it. She would deal with truth and the reality it brought later. Right now she had Holland, freedom and Charlie.

His breathing was heavy and steady against her back. The man was like a furnace, the heat coming from him made the room stuffy, but she didn't want to move. She didn't want to ruin the moment. They had two more days together and she didn't want to forget even a moment. Even in his sleep his hand roamed her body. Her eyes drifted shut. She felt contented. She felt like she belonged. It was a bittersweet realisation.

Charlie's phone started to buzz beside her head on the night stand. She reached for it.

"Leave it," he growled into her hair.

Laura smiled at him before looking at the phone. Her heart sank. There was no leaving this. She struggled out of Charlie's grip so that she could sit on the edge of the bed.

"No," he groaned. "Put it in the bin. I never wanted it anyway."

She wrapped the sheet tight around her as though it offered some sort of protection against the conversation ahead. She glanced at the man sprawled in the bed beside her. What she really needed was protection for her heart.

"Hello," she said into the phone.

"Idiot," Charlie mumbled against the pillow.

"Well hello to you too." The sharp voice of her boss was like a spike in her ear. Laura winced. "I hope I'm not interrupting anything."

From the sleazy tone of her voice that was exactly what she was hoping; otherwise why call this early in the morning.

"What can I do for you Claire?" Laura asked.

She felt Charlie stir on the bed behind her.

"Well, for starters, how about you get me my interview?"

Laura rubbed the bridge of her nose.

"I'm working on it," she said, aware of how that sounded to Charlie's ears.

"Well tick tock. The deadline is today. Story or job. The choice is yours."

Laura sat up straight.

"You said until the end of the holiday."

"Deadlines change. Things happen. I need it by the end of today."

Deadlines didn't change. The woman was simply exerting her ability to make Laura jump through hoops. She ground her teeth, but stopped when she felt a hand rubbing her back. The tension eased slightly.

"I'll do what I can," she said into the phone.

"No," Claire's voice was sharp, "you do what you have to do. Get my story."

There was a pause.

"It had better be a good one, Laura. I have high expectations and even higher standards."

The line went dead. Laura listened to silence for a minute while Charlie stroked her back.

"It's over, isn't it, short stuff?"

She nodded. The words were stuck in her throat. Yeah, it was over. She'd taken a holiday from herself and now she needed to get back to reality.

"Come here," he said as he tugged at her sheet.

She looked over her shoulder and her heart actually ached. It was written in his face. He wanted to comfort her; he wanted to make everything better. No one in her life ever wanted to do that for her. And she couldn't take what he offered. She blinked back tears. How could she have ever thought that this man was still the irresponsible boy she once knew? His face saddened when he realised she wasn't coming. Laura stood up to increase the distance between them.

"I need the interview, Charlie."

She felt pathetic asking. She knew that if he was in her position he wouldn't do it. He'd quit the job and take his chances. Unfortunately she wasn't him.

His smile was gentle.

"It's okay, I know. Why don't you get dressed, I'll get breakfast and we'll deal with it?"

Relief and shame in equal measure rushed through her. Deep down Laura knew he would keep his end of the bargain. Beneath it all he was honourable. Probably more so than she'd realised over the years.

She nodded and headed for the bathroom without looking at him again.

"WHAT DO YOU WANT TO KNOW?" Charlie said after he had polished off both of their McDonald breakfasts. Laura's appetite was gone. She wasn't sure it was ever coming back.

"You don't have to do this if you don't want to, I won't hold you to our deal," she told him.

He gave her a sad little smile.

"No. I have to." He took a deep breath, settled back in his chair and gave her his full attention. "So what do you want to know?"

Laura shifted in her seat; she arranged her notepad on the table in front of her for the millionth time. Everything about this felt wrong. Everything.

"Tell me about that day," she said at last, "if you remember."

He snorted and shook his head slightly.

"I don't need to remember, I relive it every night. Well,"

he shrugged as though it was nothing, "at least I did until our holiday. I've been able to sleep just fine these past two weeks."

His blue eyes pinned her down.

"Thanks for that."

Laura didn't know what to say. She hadn't known how traumatised he'd been. He was thanking her for stopping the dreams? An ache like nothing she'd ever felt before started in her chest. As he looked away it began to spread throughout her body. It took a minute to realise what it was. Her heart was breaking.

"It was an ordinary day," he began. "We were on rotated duty and I was working that day. Some of the guys were volunteering at the orphanage. There was a football game. Kids were laughing."

His eyes took on a faraway look.

"I was worried about a couple of the kids, they had infections and I wanted to check up on them, but I was needed with the patrol. If they'd let me go to check, I would be dead."

Nausea assaulted her. Her pen stilled. She didn't need to write this down; she would remember every terrible word.

"Jones, good guy from Sussex, said his gut was off. It was midday, we'd just eaten, I thought he meant he was sick. He looked at me kind of funny and said no. We were walking down the main street when we saw a glint coming from a rooftop. Anywhere else it would be a reflection in glass, nothing to worry about. Over there it was enough for a call to go up and we scrambled. We thought it was a sniper. We took cover against walls and behind vehicles."

His eyes gave nothing away. Laura desperately wanted to touch him, to soothe him, but they were past that now.

"That's what they wanted. They wanted us against the

orphanage walls; probably they wanted us all to run for cover into the building. About ten seconds later, it felt longer, the first blast hit. The wall behind Jones crumbled trapping him in the rubble. There was screaming and panic. I tried to get to him, to see what I could do. I was running towards him when the second blast hit. My ears were ringing; I couldn't hear what was being called. My radio was static."

His face paled, he wasn't with her now, he was back in the desert. His whole body was tense; sweat broke out on his forehead. If this was what it was like for him to talk about it during daylight, Laura could only imagine what his nights were like.

"Jones was beyond my help," he said coldly. Laura's hand flew to her mouth. His friend dead.

"A shot rang out. Sniper. A woman in the yard of the orphanage went down. I ran towards her. It was chaos all around me. I couldn't stop the blood. She wrapped her fingers in my uniform and repeated the same word over and over as she died. I found out later it meant "your guilt" – she was blaming us. Me."

Laura's cheek was wet. She rubbed at it to find she was crying.

"That's when I saw her, the little girl. She was standing in the middle of the compound. Just standing there. Dirty, terrified, completely unable to move. People were shouting. I couldn't hear anything through the chaos. I thought it was a call to retreat, to get out of there. I wasn't sure. Honestly, I didn't care. There was a kid standing, waiting to die. I threw off some of my gear and ran. Straight at her. The house to our left blew up. Gunfire kicked up the dirt around us. I honestly didn't think about any of that. I just grabbed her and ran."

He seemed a little bemused when he looked at her.

"I've never ran as fast as that, short stuff."

"Gunfire will do that to you."

Her lame attempt at humour fell flat, hampered by the fact she was crying.

"Back up came. We retreated. The little girl was wounded, gunshot to her lower abdomen. We took her back to base and I worked on her. She was pretty serious, it was touch and go. But we saved her. Afterwards I found out what had happened. Taliban members had infiltrated the orphanage months, maybe even years earlier. They were waiting for us to relax and we did. They had the whole place rigged; half of it didn't go off. Our guys took out that sniper, but they're like weeds, always another. I got reprimanded. Disobeying an order. I really can't say for sure I heard the order anyway."

He looked her in the eye. A very different Charlie to the one she knew. There was nothing carefree about this one.

"I would do it again."

She held her breath. He was terrifying. Strength oozed from him, backed up by absolute conviction. She swallowed hard, her throat was dry.

"We lost three men that day. Eight children and four Afghan adults. Jones" parents asked me to speak at his funeral. I did the best I could, but I don't think it was enough. Now that guy, he was a real hero. All I did was pick up a kid and be unlucky enough to get filmed doing it. Jones knew about the attack. He was well trained; a complete expert and he had instincts that would blow your mind. He'll be missed."

She supposed the implication was that he wouldn't be missed. She kept her mouth shut.

"I don't know what else to tell you, Laura. Do you have enough for your story?"

She nodded. She couldn't trust herself to speak. It was humiliating to put him through this just to entertain the readers of a woman's magazine. She wasn't going to ask for more. For a minute they sat in silence. Everything that was said and unsaid became a wall between them.

"I didn't know about the nightmares."

She wanted to say she was sorry, but it didn't feel enough somehow.

"Don't sweat it. You scared them away for me." He gave her the lopsided grin that made her want to taste him. Instead she was left with an empty echoing pain. "You sure make life interesting."

That was one way to put it.

"I need to file my story."

She felt foolish telling him.

"Deadline looming. Rent due."

"Yeah." She stood, pulling her oversized bag over her head so it sat diagonally on her body. "I think it's best if I catch a train to Amsterdam and fly home."

"Probably right."

Words ran through her mind. Would he be okay? Would he sleep without her?

"It's been a blast," was what she settled for.

Charlie grinned.

"Literally."

Laura flushed red.

"So, uh, I guess I'll be seeing you."

"Sure." He stood in front of her. "We both know Maddie."

The message was clear. The only way they would meet

would be accidentally through his sister. If it was what she wanted then why did it hurt so much?

"Good. Okay. Well thanks again for the interview and the trip. Hope you figure it out. Life I mean, and what to do with it."

"Enjoy the new job."

They stared at each other awkwardly. Laura turned away first. She pulled open the door, smiled goodbye and stepped out into the hallway. And then she was gone. Tears stung her eyes as she plodded down the steps. Had she hoped he would stop her? Did she want him to change completely and offer to compromise his life to be with her? Did she mean anything at all to him?

Tiny little sobs squeezed themselves out of her mouth as she marched to the train station. Even though she kept checking over her shoulder, Charlie was nowhere in sight.

CHARLIE LOOKED around the hotel room, which suddenly felt shabby and cold. He slumped down onto the edge of the bed. It was time to put Laura out of his mind and get on with things. It was time to make some decisions about his life. He could float around London for the foreseeable future or he could choose a direction. Maybe it was time to become a little more responsible. He rubbed a hand down his face and let out a frustrated breath. As usual Laura had been right about him too. He had found himself. He knew what he was. Now he had to decide what to do about it. That was what adults did right, took stock, did what was right, not just what they felt?

He looked at the doorway which had swallowed Laura. That's what she'd done. She'd been mature, responsible. Right? He squared his shoulders. It was time to grow up.

He picked up his phone, scrolled through his contact numbers and dialled one in the UK. As it rang he wandered to the window. Laura was nowhere to be seen. His chest felt tighter. He felt cheated. His holiday still had two more days on the clock and yet she was gone. How was he going to sleep now?

"Mark Chambers," the voice in his ear said.

"Mark, it's Charlie. Are you still looking for an on-call doctor?"

"Are you kidding me?" He could imagine the guy, huge as he was, bouncing in his seat. It made him smile. "You'd be helping us out of a bind. Are we talking permanent or short term?"

Charlie watched people wander down the brick inlaid street in front of him. Folk cycled past, bikes laden with shopping. Over the road, the café overflowed out onto the broad pavement. The tables were full of people, even though it wasn't even lunch time yet.

"Charlie, you there?"

"Yeah." He took a deep breath. "I'm thinking permanent. Well, as permanent as anything is these days."

There was a whoop. He held the phone away from his ear.

"That's the best news I've had all day."

"Yeah, that would mean more if I didn't know it was mid-morning in England."

Mark ignored him.

"I'll draw up a contract. It will be good to have you on long term. You know how much we need you. And don't worry, if you freak out at the permanence, you can always quit."

He could hear the grin in Mark's voice and it made him

smile wryly. It appeared even folk he didn't know that well had him summed up.

"I'm in Holland right now. I'll be home tomorrow and I'll pop into the office then. But I want to start straight away, what have you got for me?"

He heard paper rustling.

"We have a desperate situation in Bolivia; the doctor we hired broke his leg and won't get there for another six weeks, at least."

"Bolivia it is."

"This is fantastic man." Mark's enthusiasm was contagious, Charlie felt his mood lighten. "You'll be making a huge difference. These people really need a doctor. You won't regret this."

They said their goodbyes and hung up. Charlie hoped Mark was right, he hoped he wouldn't regret working with Medicine International. They were a great charity, did a lot of good work around the globe, but it was a huge commitment and it worried him. After all his regrets were beginning to stack up and there were only so many a man could take. He counted them off in his head, first there was Jones and the fact he couldn't save him. He looked down the street. Second there was Laura and the fact he hadn't stopped her.

He let the curtain drop. Yeah, he regretted that. Even though he still had no idea what he would have done with her. He looked around the empty room. It wasn't the same without her. After he threw his meagre belongings into a bag he headed for the tandem. Once he'd traded it in for a better bike he planned to cycle as fast as he could back to his car. Maybe then he wouldn't have a head full of regret.

The door slammed hard behind him.

10

Laura hesitated outside Claire's office. She held the flash drive so tightly that it bit into her still raw skin, but she couldn't seem to loosen her grip on it. Maggie, Claire's assistant, smiled at her sympathetically. It didn't help; it only made the butterflies in her stomach turn into full-fledged bird. She swallowed hard.

"Do you want to sit down and have a glass of water first?" Maggie whispered.

Laura shook her head and tried to smile. No. She needed to get this over with. It was just that her feet weren't working properly. She seemed to be stuck to the spot.

"I need a minute," she whispered back.

Maggie nodded. The sympathy on her face almost made Laura start to cry again and she couldn't do that anymore. The bags under her eyes were so big that even make-up couldn't camouflage them and she was back to wearing her huge black rimmed glasses because she couldn't keep her contacts in for very long.

Deep breath. She stared at the door as the flash drive containing Charlie's story felt heavy in her hand. She had no idea why she didn't just email it in, but she couldn't. Even the thought of it had made her ill. So here she was, staring down the witch's door and wondering what to do next.

"You'll get used to her," Maggie whispered. "We all do eventually. You learn pretty fast around here that life is a lot more pleasant if you give in to her demands early on. Less stress."

Yeah, and Maggie looked less stressed. With her wide eyes and grey skin she looked every bit a terrified mouse.

"It's a good place to work. People are queuing up to work here. We should be grateful."

The woman sounded as though she was trying to convince herself.

"I'm okay," Laura said, although no one had asked her.

She took a deep, shaky breath and stepped towards the door. She knocked boldly.

"Come in," the ice queen called.

Maggie gave her a thumbs up gesture and then Laura was inside the room.

"Why on earth didn't you send the thing to me?" Claire scolded. Her lips pursed making the tiny lines around her mouth, that screamed she used to be a smoker, all the more pronounced. "This story was supposed to be here last night. Are you trying to make us miss a deadline? I had to get Patty to write a backup story in case you screwed up. At least we can use it next month. Come on then." She held out her hand. "Hand it over. Let's see what masterpiece has turned you into a snivelling wreck?"

Laura hesitated.

"Charlie was wondering what else would be in the issue along with this, he asked me to tell him how we were playing the story?"

She held her breath waiting for the answer.

"What and you can't hand it over until I tell you?"

Claire's blood red fingernails tapped the desktop.

"Fine," she sighed at last. "We've got some great photos of the event, a couple of your boy looking like an underwear model and we're running it in our hot to trot hero issue. Jane came up with a fireman who strips in his spare time, but was awarded community hero of the month last June and there is a vet who rescued a koala during an Australian fire, while he was on holiday there. He came in for a photo shoot. Happy now?"

Hot to trot? No, she wasn't happy.

"This," Laura motioned to the flash drive she seemed to have a death grip on, "is quite a serious piece. I'm not sure it fits."

Claire's eyes narrowed as the temperature in the room fell.

"I'll be the judge of that."

"Men died, a friend of Charlie's amongst them. I don't think he would be too pleased with us taking the hunky hero angle. Don't you think it trivialises the story?"

Claire stood on her twenty inch heels. She managed to glide around the desk to face Laura.

"I think it will sell magazines." Her tone was as icy as the atmosphere. "That is what I do. So hand over the story Laura. That is, after all, why you went to Holland in the first place. To get the story." She paused in front of Laura. "And to save your job."

Laura licked her dry lips. Charlie would be devastated. A story like this trivialised him and turned him into a pin-up boy. She remembered his reaction to the website teaser. This would cause way more damage. She suspected that under other circumstances he would have welcomed a spread on his looks, but not in this one. This meant too much to him.

This had changed him. A stark realisation hit her. If she published this story, in this magazine, he would be disappointed in her. The world shifted on its axis. She'd spent most of her life disappointed in him, she wasn't sure if she could cope with a reversal.

"Laura, this is no time for second guessing. You said yourself; you are like a dysfunctional family. Does it really matter what the slant is? The story will get out. Your friend will be centre stage and the army will get some good publicity."

And Jones would get lost in the side bars on which hero had the best bachelor appeal. Her grip on the flash drive tightened. She took a deep breath.

"I can't do it."

The words surprised her more than Claire.

"I'm sorry; I don't think I heard you properly. Are you refusing to give me my story? The one I commissioned. The one I paid for?"

Laura stuffed her sore hand, and the drive, into her jeans pocket and held it tight.

"I'm sorry. I can't do that to Charlie and to the men who died. This story deserves respect. They deserve respect."

For a second she thought Claire might actually slap her and she took a step backwards. Instead the witch folded her arms across her designer grey suit and gave Laura a withering look.

"Think about this carefully, Laura. This isn't only a decision about a story. It's a decision about your life. You must ask yourself, are you being sensible? After all, it's only a story. Next week we will all be interested in something else. Do you really want to throw away your career over something like this?"

Laura felt a rush of adrenalin flow through her; it

brought a wave of courage, of certainty. She began to smile. For the first time in her life she wasn't being sensible. She had no idea what she would do next or how she could survive this decision. Her life would be in tatters. It was terrifying. She pulled herself up to her full five foot two and looked Claire in the eye.

"This is the right thing to do," she told her and was proud that her voice didn't waver.

"Oh my hairy aunt." Claire looked towards the ceiling, because it couldn't have been anywhere else. Laura had no doubt that Claire had absolutely no awareness of heaven. "You stupid child. You're in love with the man. You're making serious decisions with your heart. Don't be a fool. Men come and go, careers last a lifetime. You only have yourself to depend on. Don't throw that away over a man."

Laura smiled as her words came back at her through Claire's mouth.

"This isn't over a man. It's the right thing to do. And if that means I don't have a job..." She shrugged like it didn't matter, a gesture Charlie had perfected. She grinned wider. He was such a bad influence on her. "Then I guess I don't have a job," she said.

The witch pointed a long manicured talon at her.

"No, sweetie, you don't have a career. By this time tomorrow there won't be a women's magazine in Europe that will employ you. You can kiss goodbye to teen mags too, I plan to spread the word there as well."

Laura felt nauseous.

"You have to do what you feel is right," she told her now ex-boss. "That's all each of us can do."

With that she turned and let herself out of the room, leaving the rest of the staff to deal with a furious Claire.

Maggie was whiter than chalk.

"What are you going to do now?" she said with a trembling voice.

Laura gave her an equally unsteady smile.

"I have no idea."

She waved goodbye to Maggie, and to her life, before heading to her desk to clean it out. As she held her head high she wondered how long she could live on principles alone, because that was all she had left.

"BREAK TIME?"

Charlie looked up from his cup of weak coffee to see the clinic manager enter the room. He was exhausted. He'd seen more patients in one shift in a jungle clinic in Bolivia than he'd seen in a week in a busy emergency department in Central London. Word had gotten out that there was a doctor in town and the people flooded in.

"Ten minutes. What I really need is a decent night's sleep."

"Yeah, me too." He gave Charlie a meaningful look before he dumped his sandwiches on the table beside him.

"Yeah, sorry about that." Charlie eyed the food and his stomach rumbled. "I'll find somewhere else to sleep as soon as I get a minute to do it."

"Who is Laura anyway?" his roommate asked, as he slid half his sandwich in Charlie's direction. "You were screaming her name most of last night. And not in a good way."

Charlie scoffed the food in a couple of bites. He knew about the screaming. The dreams were getting worse. Now Laura was in Afghanistan too and every night he had to save her. He always woke before he could manage it.

"I'll find another bunk as soon as the clinic closes,"

Charlie said wearily. He'd sleep in the supply cupboard if he had to.

"Whatever." Jacques waved the offer away.

An African born Parisian, he was currently managing the clinic for Medicine International. The guy was a veteran, ten years with the organisation and this was his third posting. He was a wanderer, a lot like Charlie, his job was to start projects, get them up and running and move to the next. Charlie's job was to go where they needed a doctor short term and fill in until the permanent person turned up.

"So what is the problem?" the Frenchman said. "Did this Laura break your heart?"

Charlie grinned in spite of the effort it took to stay upright. Even though he was desperate for sleep, he was too wound up to actually fall asleep – and wasn't that a kicker?

"I know all about heartbreak. I have caused many," Jacques said. "Ask me anything. French men are experts with women."

He looked so smug that it made Charlie laugh.

"If you are such an expert why are you single?"

"That is why I'm an expert my friend. I have experienced many women and I can share that experience with you." He tapped his temple. "Extensive knowledge."

Charlie rolled his eyes. Yeah, right.

"Well?" Jacques prompted.

"It's complicated," Charlie said. "Anyway, she's half way round the world doing her thing. So it doesn't matter. We're not going to see each other again."

No, because she might lose control, he scoffed to himself. Like that made any sense.

"Ah, you are in love with her?"

"No," Charlie held up his hands. "No, no, no. I'm just worried about her and we have some unfinished business."

Like the fact he could never quite find the thing about her that drove him nuts.

Jacques raised an eloquent eyebrow.

"Seriously." Charlie felt he had to explain. "I'm not a relationship type guy. I'm like you - too many women, not enough time. I mean what am I supposed to do, change my life, give up on who I am to work in the suburbs for her? Because she's never going to do anything spontaneous or anything that involves risk. You don't know her, she's stubborn, she'll carry on making stupid choices and living half a life all because it's the sensible thing to do. She should have sensible tattooed on her backside, it's her life motto."

He glared at Jacques.

"I'm not going to spend my days in some repetitive job so that she'll have someone to make sure she doesn't die of boredom, or make one sensible decision too many so that her head explodes."

Jacques smiled smugly. Charlie didn't like it one bit.

"Yes, that is a problem," the Frenchman said. "I can see why it is keeping us up at night."

Charlie was pretty sure that he was missing something. He just wasn't sure what.

"I can't fix her life for her. She needs to do that," he told his friend.

"Absolutely."

"She isn't my problem."

"I can see that."

"It would take a whole medical team to sort out what's in her head."

"I agree. Too much of a challenge for one man. I can see how that would lead to a very boring life."

Charlie narrowed his eyes. He was being mocked. He changed the subject.

"I heard shouting earlier, what was that about?"

Jacques grinned with mischief.

"Big Mike, somebody insulted his plane and he pushed them in the water."

Charlie grinned back. Big Mike was a jungle legend. He flew a rust bucket and took it very seriously.

"You don't want to mess with Big Mike," he said.

"No, you would have to be very foolish indeed."

Jacques patted him on the shoulder before he went back to work. Charlie looked out of the glassless window over the fields to the rain forest beyond. He couldn't help but think that there was more he could have done about Laura. Maybe when his six weeks were up he'd drop in on her and make sure she was okay. If it wasn't against her stupid rules. He smiled. Who knew, maybe the simple act of turning up would be enough to make her lose control again. Now that alone would make it worth the trip.

LAURA TUGGED at her stiff black skirt and wondered again why she bothered wearing it. No one else in her new workplace was dressed formally. With a silent sigh, she acknowledged exactly how low she'd sunk – she'd worn the suit so that she would feel she was in control, even though it was pathetically obvious that she wasn't. As the phone beside her rang again, she reminded herself that she was lucky to have a job, that it wasn't a bad job and that it gave her the time and space she needed to look for a better one. All good. Right? So why did she feel like she was dying inside every time she put pen to paper? Because she was pathetic, that's why. With a frown she squared her shoulders and she picked up the call.

"Trash or Treasure," she said in as cheery a voice as she

could manage. "The free paper that helps you find a home for your unwanted goods. How can I help you?"

She listened dutifully as the person on the other end of the line described the ad they wanted her to write, all the while wondering why they didn't go online and fill out the form. Her temple began to throb as she reminded herself that computer illiterate people were the reason she had a take-home pay. Okay, a minimum wage take-home pay, but it was money, right? Her jaw hurt from constant teeth grinding and the twitch in her left eye had become a fully-fledged random spasm down the side of her face.

But. It. Was. All. Okay.

Her elbow hit the wall of her cubicle for the millionth time that morning as she reached for a pen that worked. Over the top of the partition wall she could see her twelve year old boss point to the clock and glare at her. Apparently she didn't work fast enough; the last moron who held her job could deal with twice the number of calls in the same amount of time. She narrowed her eyes and imagined that his head blew clear off his shoulders. His face went pale and he scurried away.

Laura turned her attention back to the caller instead of the clock. All the clock did was remind her that there was still four long hours left until she could go home.

As the pain in her head thumped louder, she wondered if it was a good idea to take aspirin and antacids at the same time. Surely they cancelled each other out in her stomach?

The caller sounded impatient in her ear and she realised that she'd tuned the man out. She gave him her full attention.

"No." She rubbed the bridge of her nose. "We don't charge more because it's a large item you're selling. We charge by the size of the ad, not the size of the bed."

Then she reached for the pills.

Laura's land line rang at the same time as her microwave meal pinged it was ready. She took the meal, along with a can of Diet Coke, and plopped it all on the tiny dining room table. At least there was space on the table to plop it; when Maddie had lived with her the table had been used for storing clutter.

"What is it?" she said by way of hello.

"What the hell are you doing with your life?" her best friend said in her ear.

Tears sprang to Laura's eyes. She hadn't realised how much she'd missed Maddie until she heard her voice.

"Well hello to you too," she said.

"I just read your email. I can't believe you didn't submit your interview with Charlie, he wouldn't care. It would take a bomb to get his attention. That was silly."

"No, it was right, he does care. He's really upset about the whole thing and he didn't want it to be trivialised."

"Come on Laura, we're talking about Charlie. He quit the army because he was bored. Heck, he's already off somewhere else chasing the next thrill."

Laura shook her head.

"You've got it all wrong. He isn't like that. I thought he was, but he isn't. I guess we all change."

Well, all of them except her. She never changed. There was silence.

"What happened between you two?" Maddie's tone was suddenly serious.

Tears pooled in Laura's eyes.

"I fell in love," she said pathetically.

"I'm going to kill him."

"It's not his fault."

"It is. I told him not to hurt you again. I told him that he pushes you too much. I warned him and as soon as I get home I'm going to kill him."

Laura took the phone with her into the bathroom while she blew her nose on some toilet paper.

"He says I need to take more risks. That I'm too uptight," she said. The tears wouldn't stop.

Maddie cursed her brother before answering.

"Of course he would say that, he rarely thinks anything through and is convinced it's a great way to live. You do take risks, you just think about them first. Look at you now; you quit your job, that's a risk. You went on holiday with Charlie, that was risk. Cut yourself some slack. When it's important you can take chances with the best of them. Don't let him get to you."

Laura stopped crying. Maddie was right. She'd been measuring herself against Charlie. That was like a mouse measuring itself against a lion. The comparison was laughable. So she wasn't a daredevil, she still took chances. Lots of them. She looked around herself. She did it all the time and nothing life threatening happened. She started to smile.

"Don't worry honey. I'll deal with Charlie," Maddie threatened.

Adrenalin coursed through Laura. She didn't want Maddie to deal with Charlie. No. She had a better idea.

"No, don't do that. I'll deal with him. Where did you say he was, exactly?"

She reached for a pen as a plan formed in her mind. She hung up and returned to her now cold meal. Excitement grew while she ate. Could she do it? The phone rang again, as she was finishing a meal that tasted like plastic and cardboard.

"Your father said you're back from your trip with that idiot boy. Didn't it even occur to you to tell me?" Her mother's voice was like a pin to her bubble of excitement.

"Hi Mum, good to hear from you too."

"Honestly," her mother said, ignoring her as usual, "it would only have taken one more phone call. You know what your father is like when he's painting towards an exhibition. It may have been months before he told me where you were."

If he remembered at all.

"I'm sorry," Laura said automatically even though she had called her mother. As usual it had made little impact.

"That's fine. Remember next time. Now how are things at your new job? I've always loved Francine, maybe you could get them to write something on my new play? You never could write anything for the children's magazine, but now you have an audience that would appreciate knowing about me."

Laura gritted her teeth. Guess the fact she had changed job hadn't sunk in either.

"I'm sure they'd love you," she said vaguely. There was no point going over it again.

"Now, about my play. Rehearsals are finished and opening night is Thursday, I thought you might like to come. Your father is too busy, but I can save a seat for you, if you're free. It's a wonderful show and the leading man is so talented. You'd enjoy it."

Laura heard the real message in the words. Come see me perform and tell me how wonderful I am and while you're at it you can meet my latest toy boy. You'll find him dreamy too and will think I'm so super lucky. Her brain began to pound. There was no point saying no. She'd learnt a long time ago that it was actually better to take the ticket and not turn up, rather than deal with her mother's huff on the phone. She'd managed to avoid three out of the last four plays by using this tactic and her mother hadn't even noticed. On opening night there were enough people fawning over her for her not to miss her only daughter.

This time would be different.

"That would be lovely." Laura began to grin as she spoke. "But I can't make it." She took a deep breath. "I'm going out of the country."

"What?" At last something that got her mother's attention.

"Yes," Laura said with glee. "I won't be here Thursday, but I'm sure you'll be wonderful as usual."

"But where are you going? You never miss my opening nights."

Laura rolled her eyes and wondered how she could ever have thought that she was in danger of becoming like her parents.

"I'm going to Bolivia," she said. Her heart raced at the thought.

There was a lot of bluster coming down the line. It felt so wonderful to hear it that she almost giggled.

"Why are you going to Bolivia? What is in that third world country that's more interesting than my play?" Trust dear old Mum to make it all about her.

Laura grinned so wide that her cheeks hurt.

"Charlie is in Bolivia," she said.

There was a shriek.

"Yes, Mum," Laura said, "I'm chasing after the idiot boy."

With that she hung up.

She was halfway through her happy dance when a thought struck her - what if the idiot boy wasn't pleased to see her?

Laura swallowed hard. It didn't matter. One way or another she was taking this chance.

For the first time in her life she hadn't planned things out, she didn't know where things were going, and it was terrifying.

She caught sight of her manic grin in the bedroom mirror while she started to pack.

11

———

Charlie heard the commotion before he saw it.

"What's going on?" he asked his Bolivian nurse.

She grinned up at him. Everybody in this country was as short as Laura. He felt like a giant.

"Some tourista upset Big Mike," she said.

Charlie grinned back at her before returning to his paperwork. As entertaining as Big Mike was, there would be another tourist to upset him soon enough. Right now, Charlie had a tonne of paperwork to get through before the clinic opened again. He eyed the clock; better get a move on.

"Hey Charlie," Jacques shouted. "You've got to come see this. I've never seen anything like it before. Big Mike is seriously upset."

"I'm busy," he called back.

His colleague appeared beside him; Charlie felt a hand on his shoulder.

"No, my friend, you need to come now. This has something to do with you."

Charlie was curious, but the paperwork was calling.

Jacques took the pen from his hand and pushed him towards the door.

Outside there was quite a crowd. They parted before him, like the red sea for Moses. Now, he was on high alert. Was this a practical joke? Some sort of hazing for the new guy? Fine, he'd play along. He walked to the high bamboo fence at the edge of the compound and that's when he heard it. An angry English accent that was eerily familiar.

Laura? Blood pumped fast through his veins. It couldn't be. He pushed past an overgrown bush that got in the way of the gate to the compound and stopped dead. There was Big Mike, the man mountain. He was standing with his back to Charlie with his arms folded. Behind the big man Charlie could see arms and legs waving in mid-air. Very familiar arms and legs.

"What's going on?" he said.

At the sound of his voice there was silence. Big Mike stepped aside and pointed at the arms and legs.

"Does this belong to you?"

Laura was hanging from the top of the bamboo fence. Mike had picked her up and hitched her there by the back of her t-shirt. From her position high on the fence, she was face to face with Big Mike. A fact neither of them appeared to be thrilled at.

Charlie shut his eyes tight, then opened them. Nope, it wasn't a dream. She was there. He wanted to run at her and scoop her into his arms. But she was hanging on the fence.

"Charlie." Big Mike was losing his patience. "Does this belong to you?"

"Hey, imbecile," Laura shouted at Big Mike, "slave trading is over. I don't belong to anyone. Now let me down."

The crowd gasped with glee that someone dared take on the giant. Charlie wasn't surprised. He looked at Laura's bright pink cheeks, her freckled nose and that pouting mouth, which was so naughty in his dreams.

"Yep, unfortunately, she belongs to me."

Against his better judgement his chest rose with pride at the thought.

"Hi, Laura." He waved up at her. "Did you get lost on the way to the office?"

Laura peered down at him as he stepped in front of her.

"I came to see you, numb nuts, now make the moron put me down. I'm going to kick his backside all the way to Brazil."

There was hysterical laughter behind him. It was like a fly had dared take on a lion. He had to admire her guts, or stupidity.

"That's my girl," he told Big Mike, who wasn't amused. "What did she do anyway?"

Laura was affronted, her little arms and legs waved in protest.

"What makes you think it was me? Is he the one hanging on the fence? No. Are you listening, moron?" he shouted at Big Mike. "You can't treat people like this. Just who do you think you are?"

There was more laughter. Mike growled deep in his wide, wide chest before turning to Charlie.

"She mocked my baby," he rumbled.

Laura rolled her wide emerald eyes.

"Your flying rust bucket? I had to tie the door shut with string. Seriously. You shouldn't be taking people up in it. It's dangerous. You -" She pointed at Mike. "- are irresponsible."

There was more growling.

"Then she bullied me into driving her all the way into town," Mike said.

That brought some amazed gasps. Mostly people were

wondering how Laura could have bullied anyone, let alone Big Mike.

"And, to top it off," the man glared at Charlie, "she said I have a personality problem."

Charlie's lip twitched as he tried to take the big man's complaints seriously. People behind him were falling over laughing, but Charlie was too close to Mike to lose control.

"That's terrible," he said as calmly and as soothingly as possible.

"Terrible?" Laura gaped at Charlie and Mike. "If he doesn't have a personality problem then why am I hanging on a fence?" She turned back to Mike. "Normal people don't do this sort of thing."

Mike took a step towards Laura. Charlie panicked and stepped between them.

"Are you saying I'm abnormal?" Mike's deep voice asked Laura.

Anyone else would have heard the warning in the tone. Not the Iron Maiden.

"I'm beginning to think you are seriously stupid as well," she told Big Mike.

"That's it," Mike said to Charlie, "get out of the way. I'm throwing her in the river."

"Just try it, buster. As soon as I'm free you're dead meat."

Charlie held up his hands to stop Mike, while wondering how Laura planned to make good on her threats.

"We need to calm down," he told them. "By we I mean you two," he added, just in case there was any confusion.

"I am calm," Laura shouted as she tried to kick him out of the way.

"Yeah," he told her. "I can see that."

Mike grunted.

"Look," he told Big Mike, "she came to see me. She's my

problem. Why don't you let me sort it? That way no one has to go in the river."

Laura was shouting abuse behind him, but he ignored her.

"I don't know," Big Mike said. "She's really annoyed me." He looked Charlie up and down. "And I'm not sure you can handle her, Doc."

Charlie wasn't either.

"I'll be fine," he said.

"Let me down," shouted Laura.

"Okay," said Mike reluctantly. "What do you want me to do? Do you want her down?"

He didn't seem too pleased with the idea.

"Not yet," Charlie said as he turned to Laura. "We've got some stuff to talk about first and it's better with her up there."

Now that really made her mad.

Charlie grinned. Even in the chaos that Laura generated wherever she went, he still felt more relaxed than he had in weeks.

Laura was beyond angry. She was volcano mad. If someone didn't let her down from the fence soon she was going to... Going to what? She was stuck. The wind left her sails. She looked down at Charlie grinning up at her; he was enjoying every minute of this. It wasn't the wonderful reunion she'd planned in her head. Nope, it was about as far from it as she could get. So much for taking a chance. She took one and look where it got her. She was a freak show for the afternoon session at a jungle clinic. She glared at Big Mike. He glared back. I'll get you later, she promised herself.

"Charlie," she said, disgusted that she was left to appeal to his good sense. Not that she'd ever seen any in him. "You need to let me down. This isn't comfortable."

He leered up at her.

"Yeah, but it's a pretty cool view."

Laura counted to ten under her breath.

"I am seriously beginning to wonder why I came to see you," she told him.

He folded his arms over his blue t-shirt. His face had a few days of stubble on it and from the look of the dark circles under his eyes he'd been getting about as much sleep as she'd been getting.

"Let's talk about that," he said. "Why did you come see me? I thought I was a bad influence on you. That I made you do crazy things. That you lost control around me."

Her eyes widened as the crowd was quiet. No one wanted to miss a word.

"Seriously?" she said. "You want to do this here with everyone listening?"

He looked behind him and shrugged.

"I thought you wanted sensible, boring and safe," he continued.

Laura scowled down at him.

"Let me down and we'll talk."

"You're kidding right. I like having the advantage. You might decide you don't like the conversation and run away again."

"Let. Me. Down."

He waved her words away.

"So why are you here, Laura? Do you need another interview?"

"I didn't need the first one Neanderthal."

Something shifted within him.

"What?"

"Don't you talk to your sister?"

"Not recently, no."

Laura huffed towards the sky.

"I didn't hand in the interview. I quit my job."

Something began to rumble through Charlie's body. He looked up at her.

"You what?"

She flapped her arms in exasperation.

"Quit the job. Left the country. Came to find you," she looked at him pointedly. "Took a chance. And I have to tell you Charlie; right now I'm pretty much regretting it."

Charlie spun away from Laura to rub a hand over his face; he was surprised to find that his palms were sweaty. The crowd grinned at him. He suddenly felt more than a little confused. He looked back at Laura. This wasn't making any sense. But one thing he knew. He was glad she was there.

"So, I'll ask again," he said, his stomach clenched; he thought he knew the answer. "Why are you here?"

Laura took a deep breath. Looked him straight in the eye and told him the truth, as he knew she would. That was the thing about Laura, she had courage. She would always tell you honestly what she wanted. He thought he saw her lips tremble before she spoke.

"I'm here because I love you."

The crowd gasped. Charlie felt sick.

"I am in love with you, Charlie Lewis," she said.

Charlie felt light headed and bent over to restore the flow of blood.

"Great," Laura said. "Someone get the idiot a glass of water. I think he's going to vomit."

CHARLIE WASN'T PROUD. He was sitting in the dirt hyperventilating looking up at the woman who said she loved him.

And she wasn't happy. If looks could kill he would be squashed like a bug.

"Love?" he said.

"Man up," Big Mike told him. "You're embarrassing yourself."

No kidding. Now if only the world would stop moving so he could stand again.

"Typical," Laura said. "You tell me to let loose and live a little, so I pack up and come to visit you and this is how it goes. I can take rejection. I can even take making a fool of myself in front of a crowd. What I can't take is staying where I'm not wanted. Let me down Big Mike. I'm going home."

"Wait a minute," Charlie told her. "I didn't say I didn't want you. I just need a minute to think."

"Mike," she demanded. "Let me down and take me back to the air strip."

Mike toed him with his massive flip flop covered foot.

"What do you want me to do?"

Charlie didn't know. His head was spinning. Love? Heck, he'd only come to terms with liking the woman. Love?

"What did you think would happen when you came here?" he asked her.

"I didn't think. That's what you do to me. You make me nuts. One tiny affair and I threw away the life I worked hard for and jumped on a plane into the jungle. I keep trying to tell you this. You make me nuts."

"Charlie?" Big Mike nudged him again. "Do you want me to take her to the airport?"

No. He didn't, but he wasn't sure what else to do. He wasn't ready for love. For commitment. For security in suburbia. And then something occurred to him. He wasn't in suburbia. Laura wasn't asking him to give up his life to be with her. No. She had done that for him.

He stood up to tell her that he wanted her to stay. He planned to say that they could have some fun together and see where it led. When he opened his mouth to speak he looked up at the Iron Maiden. That's when he saw it. One tiny tear running silently down her pale pink cheek.

For a moment everything stopped.

And then, when it started again, it was different. The panic he had felt earlier was gone. The fear had evaporated. He knew, without a doubt, that for this woman he would do anything. He would give Laura Prentice anything she wanted, no questions asked.

"No," he told Mike, "you can't take her to the airport and you can't unhook her. I need her exactly where she is."

"Charlie?" There was a pleading element to her voice. He knew instinctively that it was taking all her energy to keep it together.

"So what do you want to do with her?" Mike asked, clearly exasperated.

"I'm going to marry her," Charlie said.

And the crowd went wild.

"Have you completely lost your mind?" Laura demanded.

Her armpits were beginning to hurt where her t-shirt bunched up and held her captive against the fence. She was hot. She was hungry. She was tired. And now, apparently, she had to deal with mass insanity. As she watched, people rushed forward to pump Charlie's hand and congratulate him. It didn't seem to bother anyone that his so called fiancé was hanging from a fence.

"Big Mike," Laura hissed at the giant. "I take it back. When you're surrounded by this lot you look positively sane. So please, unhook me and get me out of here."

His mouth twitched and she thought the man may actually smile for a minute.

"He can't do that," Charlie called to her over the crowd, "we're getting married. I sent for the local minister."

Breathe, Laura told herself, breathe.

"Charlie, I need to talk to you now," she took a deep breath and screamed, "alone!"

That got everyone's attention.

"People," said some French guy, "why don't we give the happy couple a little space?"

She was grateful when he managed to herd them into the building. Charlie smiled up at her; he seemed really quite pleased with himself. Laura counted to ten and tried to calm her breathing so that she sounded sane when she spoke.

"Charlie, I don't want to marry you."

"Rubbish. Of course you do."

She wanted to kick the fence behind her as hard as she could. Instead she used the same voice she would use to take a pair of scissors away from a toddler.

"No, I don't," she said. "I want to go home. I want to be back in London, alone, forever."

Charlie sauntered towards her. He ran his hand up her calf, she kicked him away.

"I can't sleep without you," he said.

And just like that, a brick fell out of the wall she had built.

"I think about you all the time."

Another brick toppled from her defence.

"I was so worried about you that I planned to come find you in London as soon as my six weeks here were up."

Crash went the top of the wall. His beautiful eyes looked up into hers.

"You need to marry me."

There was a hole in her wall so big now that a tank could have driven through it.

"Why?" she whispered.

"Because you love me."

"I can get over that," she told him.

He nuzzled the bare skin of her belly making her blood pump faster.

"Well how about because I love you?"

What was left of her wall began to sway.

"Do you?"

He looked her in the eye.

"Yes, I do."

The wall crashed down around her. She was defenceless against him.

"How do you know for sure? A minute ago you almost fainted when I said it."

He arched an eyebrow.

"I didn't almost faint."

"Whatever. How do you know for sure?"

He settled his hands on her waist as he looked up into her eyes.

"You scare the life out of me," he said at last. "You make me a better man, even though most of the time I don't want to be one. You take away my nightmares. You give me something to worry about and think about besides myself. I thought I wanted to fix your life, but I was trying to fix mine. I need you with me. And if getting married will make that happen then that's okay with me. Anything you want is okay with me. Because all I want is you."

A tear slid down her face as she stared into the core of him.

"Do you believe me?" he asked. His voice was hoarse.

Laura nodded.

"Great," he grinned, "so we're getting married?"

"It seems a rush, why hurry things, why not hang out for a while first? I mean we need to think things through. It would be rash to rush into this. Weddings need planning."

Her mind ran so fast her words couldn't keep up with it.

Charlie kissed her belly.

"That's exactly why we need to do it now. We wait any longer and your planning and control issues might screw the whole thing up. Nope, we do this now."

"Or what?" He couldn't make her marry him.

"There is no or what. We're getting married now, whether you like it or not."

"You can't make me get married."

"You haven't met the local vicar yet."

With that he wandered off.

"Where are you going?" Laura demanded. "You can't leave me here."

Five minutes later she had Big Mike for company. They glared at each other.

"I'm so going to kill you when I get down," she told him.

"Bring it on, tiny sister."

They waited in silence. At last Mike looked at her.

"Do you really want to marry the Doc?" he said. "Because if you don't, if this isn't for real, I'll let you go."

Laura looked out towards the rain forest and blinked. Never in her life had she imagined this scenario.

"Crazy lady?" Big Mike said.

"Yeah," Laura sighed heavily. "I do want to marry the idiot."

"Well all right, we have a party."

Yeah, Laura thought wryly, one where the bride is

immobilised and gets married wearing shorts and a t-shirt which is up around her neck.

Super-duper.

IT DIDN'T TAKE LONG to spot that the vicar was a lush. By the looks of him he'd been drinking for days. He wore a Hawaiian shirt, cargo pants and a pair of blue deck shoes. Apart from the beard and something that looked like bird poop stuck in his hair, he looked like he was in the middle of a beach party.

"Do you, English doctor take the flying lady to be your husband?" he said between hiccups.

The French guy mumbled in his ear.

"I mean wife."

"I do," said Charlie loudly, setting off another round of cheering.

Laura actually felt a warmth buzz through her body at the words. He did. Charlie blew her a kiss.

"Do you lady on a fence; take the doc to be your awful wedded husband."

"You're kidding?" Laura asked Charlie. "This is how you want to do it. With a drunken preacher and your fiancé stuck to a fence?"

"Answer the man Laura, the sooner you do, the sooner you'll have your feet on the ground."

She pursed her lips. This was insane.

"Come on honey." Charlie grinned, he was loving every minute. "You know you want to. I'll make it up to you later. I promise."

"How?" Her eyes narrowed.

He shrugged.

"I'll do anything you want."

"Anything?"

"Cross my heart. Now answer the man before he falls into a coma."

She stared at Charlie. Looked at the group of strangers. She was a million miles away from her life and had turned into someone she didn't even recognise.

"I do, I do, I do, I do," started a chant in the crowd.

As it got louder Laura found herself struggling not to laugh.

"Fine," she shouted at last. "I'll marry the Neanderthal."

"That's good enough for me," said the vicar. "Consider yourself hitched."

The crowd cheered as they threw brightly coloured petals at her.

"Can I please get down now?" she pleaded to anyone who would listen.

Apart from anything else she had been hanging around for hours and really needed to visit the toilet.

"Big Mike," Charlie shouted above the crowd. "Please put my wife on the ground."

Big Mike reached up, grabbed her under the arms and unhooked her. As soon as she was on the ground she kicked him as hard as she could in the shin. It barely registered with him.

"That's for starters," she promised.

Charlie stepped towards her, his arms open wide.

"Wife, you may kiss your husband."

Laura punched Charlie in the stomach making him double over. The crowd were silent, jaws hanging open.

"That's how we celebrate in England," she told them. "Now the drinks are on Charlie."

There was a whoop as they all ran in the direction of

town and the only place within miles that sold anything to drink.

"That was a bit low," Charlie said when he stood up.

"You made me really angry," she told him.

"I also made you my wife."

He took a step towards her with the goofiest grin on his face.

"Only until I find out how legal this whole thing is," she said.

"Okay, then we better not waste a minute of married life."

In a flash she was in his arms.

"I do love you, Mrs Lewis," he said before he kissed her.

His touch made a milkshake of her insides.

"I love you too," she told him when she came up for air. "Although I'm seriously disappointed in myself because of it."

"I can live with that," Charlie told her as he dragged her off in the direction of his bunk house.

Laura's smile was so wide it made her cheeks ache. She hoped it would never stop.

EPILOGUE

"Do you have any idea where my wife is?"

Charlie paced the tiny office that belonged to the medical centre manager. Jacques was out of town and his assistant wasn't being helpful.

"She said there was a group of children in the hills that she needed to interview."

Charlie gritted his teeth. A habit he'd picked up from Laura.

"And when will she be back?"

The woman shrugged.

"When the plane gets back."

With a disgusted ha, he picked up the car capsule with his daughter strapped in it and stomped out of the office. Typical. She would wait until he was holding the baby, literally, before she went running off after a story.

He could hear the noisy engines of the small plane in the distance. It was time to settle this once and for all. He strapped the baby into the jeep and gunned down the dirt road towards the air field. The jungle humidity was getting to him today and he hoped the rainy season would arrive soon. He checked the sky but there was no sign of a single cloud. He could however see the plane.

He arrived at the air strip just as the plane landed. Laura waved enthusiastically as she climbed out of the tiny aircraft and Charlie tried not to let his sense of relief at seeing her ruin the fact he was mad.

"Honey." She trotted over to him, went up on tiptoes and planted a full kiss on his lips.

So he kissed her back. Men can compartmentalise when they're mad. Laura skipped round to the baby.

"Ruby darling," she cooed and cuddled their daughter.

His heart softened at the way her face glowed when she was around their baby. She glanced his way out of the corner of her eye. He was being played. Again. He folded his arms across his chest and stood up tall. At least she could never win on the height thing.

"I thought we agreed you weren't going to go into the jungle alone anymore. Especially not to chase stories."

She tried to look apologetic, but she couldn't quite pull it off.

"And you." Charlie turned on Big Mike. "I thought we agreed that you weren't going to enable her anymore?"

Big Mike held up his hands in surrender.

"She threatened me," he said.

Charlie rolled his eyes; the two of them were as bad as each other. He was beginning to think he was the only sensible person in Bolivia. Ever since she'd wrangled a spot reporting for the BBC, he hadn't been able to stop her chasing anything. The first whiff of a story and she was gone. But things were different now. They had Ruby.

He watched as Laura cuddled Ruby to her chest and chatted to her. It made him want to puff out his chest and shout to the world that this was his family. His woman.

"I won't do it again," Laura said when she noticed him watching. "Honest. This was too good an opportunity to pass up."

"She was safe with me," said the man mountain, which was probably true. But still, they had a family to think about now. She couldn't do every crazy thing that came into her head. They had responsibilities.

She walked around the car to lean against his chest; instinctively he put an arm around her. When had things changed so much, when had he become the responsible one?

"Seriously, Laura. It's too dangerous."

She looked up at him with those wide green eyes that always undid him.

"I know. It won't happen again."

He pulled them tight to him. It won't happen again. Yeah, right. He seriously considered taking the office job that they kept offering him in London. If this was what it was like now what would it be like when they had two kids, or more? He should never have encouraged her to loosen up in the first place, once she got a taste for the wild side she'd never looked back. He felt Laura smile against his chest. No doubt she was planning her next trip into the Amazon. He'd created a monster. All he wanted her to do was lead a full life, not become a dare devil.

As he looked down at his wife and child he realised for the first time that he'd actually succeeded. She was living a full life. And it was all thanks to him.

Of course, she probably thought that she'd made him a better man too.

There was just no winning with her.

WANT MORE?

Continue on to read an excerpt from *Lingerie Wars*, the first in my contemporary romance series set in the Scottish Highlands.

LINGERIE WARS

CHAPTER 1

Lake Benson's midlife crisis lasted exactly twenty-four hours. In that time he quit his career with the army and bought a lingerie shop. All things considered, he was glad the crisis hadn't lasted longer.

"I told you," whined his little sister. "I can do this myself. I have a business plan. You're only interfering because you're bored and don't know what to do with yourself."

"That's not the point," Lake told her as he looked up at the sign on the front of the shop. "The point is, you obviously need my help. You're haemorrhaging money. My money."

He hadn't even set foot inside the shop and already he could see a problem.

"That"—he pointed at the sign—"has to go."

Rainne twisted a strand of her long hair, a dead giveaway that he wasn't getting the whole story.

"I can't get rid of the sign," she said at last. "It's part of the town's heritage."

Lake folded his arms tight across his chest. Heritage his hairy backside.

"You also didn't tell me how isolated this place is," he said.

"It's busy during the tourist season—you know, summer."

For Scotland that was about two weeks in August.

"And you neglected to mention that we have competition."

He cocked his head towards the lingerie shop, which sat opposite them on the high street. Unlike the shop that had eaten all of his money, the one over the road actually looked like people would buy lingerie in it.

"Ah, yeah," his sister said as she toed the pavement with her pink Doc Marten boot. "But Kirsty's shop has a different clientele than ours."

"One that buys underwear?"

She missed the sarcasm.

"Uh, no, she sells sexier stuff—you know, for occasions. We sell everyday wear. Think utilitarian."

He was about to tell his sister that she was talking rubbish when the shop door flew open and a tiny cube of a woman hobbled out. Lake guessed her age to be close to two hundred.

"You," she said as she pointed at him. "What are you and why are you here?"

Rainne shrank beside him. Her face shot past pink and straight to purple. Here it comes, thought Lake, the catch. Every time he got involved with his family there was a catch.

"I'm Lake Benson," he told the Hobbit. "I own this business."

The woman's eyes narrowed under eyebrows that were hairier than her head.

"Rainne girl," she said, but she kept her eyes on Lake. "I thought I sold my business to you."

His sister shuffled on the spot, making all the tiny bells sewn into the bottom of her tie-dye skirt jingle.

"Ah, well," she said. "My brother here, he's, um, like my silent partner."

"I've been watching," the woman said. "He's doing an awful lot of talking for a man who's supposed to be silent."

Before Rainne could answer, the woman jabbed her finger in Lake's belly. She seemed surprised when it bounced back off him.

"What do you know about underwear, boy?" she demanded.

Lake stared at the woman calmly. He'd been face to face with drug lords and terrorists. There was no way a little Scottish woman could intimidate him. Amuse him, maybe—if the bulk of his savings weren't tied up in the joke.

"I know how to unhook a bra in two seconds flat," he said.

"If I was sixty years younger, boy, that might impress me. Right now, I'm just wondering why you're blocking the customers from getting into my shop."

Lake took a slow look around him. He saw a cobbled road, a row of crooked old houses that had been white-washed and turned into shops and a loch at the bottom of the street. He didn't see any people. Let alone hoards queuing up to buy underwear.

"Yeah, I can see how I'm getting in the way," he drawled.

Rainne started to inch away from him. He got the distinct impression that she was on the verge of running. Lake reached out, grabbed her vintage velvet jacket and hauled her back to stand beside him.

"Leave me alone," she grumbled. "I'm not five."

"What do you mean your shop?" he asked the Hobbit.

The old woman pulled herself up to her full height, which must have been all of four foot six.

"Betty McCloud. I started this shop in 1964."

"And I bought the business six months ago."

"It's still my shop, son." The woman tried to fold her arms over her ample belly as she glared at him.

If he were prone to dramatic gestures, he'd have rolled his eyes. Instead he kept his face as expressionless as usual.

"Rainne, want to explain this to me?"

His sister looked like she'd rather eat dirt. Lake didn't care. He'd driven up the length of England, through Scotland and into the Highlands. He was tired. He was hungry. And he was wondering what insanity had made him think managing a shop would be good for Rainne. Most of all, he'd run out of patience.

"Rainne," was all he said.

"Okay, okay." She held up her hands in surrender. "In the contract I signed, there were some unusual clauses." She cleared her throat as Lake's heart sank. "The business is ours to do what we want with, but Betty here stays—think of her as an underwear mascot."

He looked at Betty, who gave him a toothless grin. In her ankle-length tartan tent, cable knit jumper and hairnet, she oozed sex appeal.

His sister took a deep breath.

"And the sign stays too," she said.

They all looked at the sign. There was silence.

"I hand-painted that sign myself," Betty said proudly.

"It could be worse," Rainne mumbled.

Lake almost let his shoulders slump.

"So, let me get this right," he said at last. "I bought a lingerie shop in a town in the middle of nowhere. I have my very own underwear mascot. The main competition is the shop facing us, which actually appears to have customers. And to top it all off, the first business I've ever owned is called Betty's Knicker Emporium."

Betty grinned with pride as Rainne tried to appear invisible.

"I need a beer," Lake told them and headed towards the local pub.

"THERE'S trouble brewing over the road," Magenta said by way of hello.

It took Kirsty a minute to focus on her employee. Her brain was still frozen from studying her bank account details.

"Trouble?" she asked.

"Big brother has ridden in to sort things out. Betty looks like she wants to set fire to a village in retaliation and Rainne looks like she'd rather be anywhere else than sunny Invertary." Magenta studied the sky through the shop front window as she shrugged out of her black leather coat. "Okay, maybe not sunny, but she still looks like she wants to run."

Kirsty snapped the laptop shut, aware that the same grim set of numbers would be there to greet her when she opened it again.

"Poor Rainne, I should have made more of an effort to help her out."

"You've been up to your eyeballs keeping this place afloat."

"You're not wrong there," Kirsty said on a sigh. "But still, I did tell her we could coordinate window displays and advertise together. We just never seemed to get round to it. I hope her brother didn't give her a hard time. Did it look like he was mad?"

"I didn't see him. I saw the aftermath. So I'm guessing he was mad. Wouldn't you be if your life savings bought Betty's Knicker Emporium?"

"I'd be happy just to have access to my savings, so I could waste it on whatever I chose to."

Magenta winced.

"Sorry, that was insensitive."

Kirsty waved her words away with a flick of her hand. It was old news. Literally. She had the newspaper headlines to prove it. She went to join Magenta at the window. Sure enough, there was Rainne, looking like she'd been exiled from a hippy commune and didn't know what to do with herself. Her shoulders drooped, her eyes were dark and her skin almost as pale as Magenta's—and that was saying a lot considering Magenta's white goth makeup.

"I'll go talk to her," Kirsty said.

"Why bother?" Magenta said. "All she's going to do is whine and whimper. Look at her. I can't understand how she stays upright when she doesn't have a backbone."

"Magenta!" Kirsty said, giving her young friend a look heavy with meaning. "That's harsh. She's struggling. Running a business is hard enough without having to deal with Betty too."

Kirsty's heart broke for Rainne; she looked every bit as lost as Kirsty felt. Magenta frowned.

"It's eat or be eaten out there," she told Kirsty. "And that girl has "tasty snack" tattooed to her forehead."

"Remind me to tell the town council never to let you volunteer for the Samaritan help line. I can hear you now: "Stop whinging about your life, suck it up and get on with things.""

Magenta gave Kirsty a rare grin. Kirsty couldn't help

smiling back as she went out to talk to Rainne. She felt the crunch of autumn leaves underfoot as she trotted across the road towards Betty's place. The old underwear shop had been an Invertary institution as long as she could remember. She'd been dragged there as a child to get her first bra, and later she'd suffered the humiliation of being present while her mother bought a girdle. She smiled at the memory. The only problem with Betty's Knicker Emporium was that it was about four hundred years out of date. Well, that and Betty. Betty was a big problem.

"You okay?" she asked Rainne.

"Great. Fabulous. Wonderful," Rainne said flatly.

"Tell the truth, girl," Betty said as she elbowed Rainne in the side.

Rainne was too polite, or too scared, to tell the old woman off. Kirsty wasn't—it was one of the perks of being a local.

"Cut it out, Betty," she told her. "Or I'll tell the vicar that you're bullying again."

Betty scowled but didn't protest.

"What's going on?" Kirsty asked Rainne. "Is your brother shutting you down?"

"Ha!" Betty said. "He can try."

They ignored her. Rainne hung her head and looked dejected.

"Really, he can do whatever he likes—it's his money. I shouldn't have borrowed it. I don't know anything about running a business. I don't know what I was thinking."

Kirsty couldn't have agreed more, but didn't think it was the time to tell her.

"You have some good ideas," she said to be encouraging.

"Yes," Rainne sighed sadly, "only I can't implement them."

The two women stared at Betty.

"What?" Betty demanded. "I have veto. It's in the contract."

"That was some contract you had drawn up," Kirsty told her.

"You're not wrong." Betty grinned. "I never thought anyone would sign it."

"There's a neon sign above my head with the word idiot and an arrow pointing at me, isn't there?"

"No, of course not," Kirsty said while Betty nodded.

"This is your last warning," Kirsty told Betty.

"You're no fun at all," the old woman said.

"So I've been told."

Betty stalked back into the shop in a huff.

"I don't know how you do that," Rainne said as they watched the shop door slam. "I can't seem to stand up to her at all."

"Don't be fooled by the old lady exterior, inside she's tough as nails and will walk all over you. I'm used to her, she's got a good heart and she can be really funny, but you need to stay on top of it or else you become her lap dog."

"Woof," said Rainne.

Kirsty put an arm around Rainne's shoulder and squeezed.

"Oh, honey," she said. "Look, why don't you bring your business plan over later and I'll help you with it? Maybe we can put together some sort of advertising campaign for Christmas? Something that will benefit both our shops— like a lingerie party, or something. Two heads are better than one, don't you think?"

"I do, actually," said the deep voice behind her.

Kirsty jumped as the man stepped into view. There were men, and then there was this man. He was the kind of man that made the rest of the male population seem feminine. It was everything about him—his broad shoulders, his square jaw, the tiny dimple in his left cheek, the intense look in his blue eyes. Everything screamed man with a capital M.

"I do think two heads are better than one," he told her in an English accent that broadcast his south coast roots. "But I think the other head should be mine and not the competition's."

She reeled backwards, dropping her arm from Rainne's shoulders.

"Competition?"

He arched one eyebrow. It was the only expression he made. The rest of him—his face, his posture—seemed relaxed. Yet somehow he managed to radiate irritation.

"You do own the shop over the road, right?"

Kirsty nodded dumbly. Without thinking about it, her arms wrapped around her high-necked lambswool sweater and she hugged herself as she spoke.

"I might own the only other lingerie shop in town, but I'm trying to help here. That's how we do things in Invertary."

"If that's the case, then where have you been for the past six months while my sister's been throwing my money down the drain?"

He folded his arms over his wide chest, making the denim jacket strain across his shoulders. Her heart beat faster. Her mouth opened to defend herself, then snapped shut when she thought better of it.

"The same could be said about you," she said instead. "At least the help I'm offering is backed by expertise. What exactly do you know about the underwear business?"

He took a step towards her. Kirsty took a tiny step backwards. He noticed, and his eyes crinkled slightly at the corners.

"I know that women buy the stuff for men, and I'm a man. That gives me the advantage. They'll be queuing up to get my advice."

Rainne jerked to attention.

"You're staying?" she squeaked. "You plan to run the business."

"You got a problem with that, little sister?" he asked, but his eyes never left Kirsty.

"You know what I think?" Kirsty said, saving Rainne from having to answer.

"I'm not sure I care what you think, but go ahead anyway."

Kirsty hands fell to her side and balled into fists. It had been a long time since she'd felt the urge to thump someone.

"I think you're in over your head," she said. "You obviously don't have a clue about running a shop or selling lingerie, and you've just insulted the only expert in town who was willing to help you."

His lips twitched slightly, giving the impression that he was going to smile, but nothing happened. His face was still impassive.

"Do you know what I think?" he said. "I think you're scared of a little competition."

Kirsty barked out a laugh that surprised her more than him.

"You're not competition. This"—she pointed to Betty's handmade sign—"is not competition. There's no way you could be a threat to me, or to my business."

"We'll see. Prepare to shut up shop."

Kirsty pursed her lips as she felt her cheeks burn.

"That is incredibly arrogant of you," she said.

"Or honest. It's obvious there's only room in this town for one lingerie shop. I'd rather it was mine."

"If you think I'm going to let you run me out of town then you're deluded. This is my home. You're the foreigner here."

He rocked back on his heels as he thrust his hands into the pockets of his jeans. Although there was nothing in his manner to give him away, she got the distinct impression he was enjoying himself.

"Ah, that old chestnut. We hate the English. The English are the root of all our problems. Blah, blah. You guys need to get over yourselves. You lost. We won. We own you now. There's no point being bitter."

Kirsty reeled before blustering nonsense.

"That's right. The English are here to stay."

"That's it," she said at last. "You've crossed the line." She turned to Rainne with a tight smile. "I'm sorry, honey, but I can't help you now. You're stuck with him." She hooked her thumb towards the brother. "You have no idea how much I feel for you."

"I get that a lot," Rainne mumbled.

"As for you," she told the English imbecile, "bring it on. You don't stand a chance."

"So, last shop standing?"

"It'll be mine."

"I like a healthy imagination in a woman."

"You're going to regret annoying me this much."

At last he grinned. Kirsty felt her world shift as something unseen pulled her towards him.

"It's on, then?" he said with delight.

"It's on." She stepped back, feeling slightly disorientated.

"Great." He nodded. "War. This I do know."

"Ah, but you don't know lingerie war," Kirsty said. "Sit back and watch, soldier boy. You're about to have your backside handed to you."

With that she turned on the low heels of her tan leather boots and stalked back across the street.

"So," Magenta said once Kirsty had slammed the door shut. "It didn't go well, huh?"

Kirsty eyed her sole employee grimly.

"That man is insufferable. He has no idea how to relate to people and he sure as heck doesn't know how to run a shop." She let out a breath she hadn't even been aware she was holding. "He wants to close me down. Can you believe it? He's rude. He's ignorant and he's off his head."

Magenta blinked hard before she gave a wicked little smile.

"Been a long time since I saw you this wound up," she said.

Kirsty felt the wind go out of her. It had been years since she'd felt wound up about anything. That sort of passion belonged in her old life. She worried her bottom lip for a moment as she felt the will to fight drain out of her.

"You okay?" Magenta asked.

"Fine," Kirsty said. "I just have to figure out how I'm going to stop Betty's Knicker Emporium stealing what little business we do get."

Magenta's smile took on a pitying turn. Kirsty looked away from her.

"I'll be in my office," she told her. "Working on a marketing plan."

With that, she fled.

ABOUT THE AUTHOR

I'm a Scot, living in New Zealand and married to a Dutch man. I write contemporary romance with a humorous bent – this is mainly due to the fact I have an odd sense of humour and can't keep it out of anything I do! If I wasn't a writer, I'd like to be Buffy the Vampire Slayer, or Indiana Jones. Unfortunately, both these roles have already been filled. Which may be a good thing as I have no fighting skills, wouldn't know a precious relic if it hit me in the face and have an aversion to blood. When I'm not living in my head, I'm a mother to two kids, one pet sheep, one dog, two cats, three alpacas and an escape artist chicken.